THE BLUEGRASS FILES: TWISTED DREAMS

THE SECOND IN A SERIES OF MYSTERIES
SOLVED BY THE AGENTS OF BLUEGRASS
CONFIDENTIAL INVESTIGATIONS

F J MESSINA

Enjoy!

F J Messina

The Bluegrass Files:
Twisted Dreams

The Second in a Series of Mysteries
Solved by the Agents of
Bluegrass Confidential Investigations

f. j. Messina

© 2016/2017 Blair/Brooke Publishing

ISBN: 978-0-9998533-3-7 (Soft Cover)

PCN: pbi1503

❀ Created with Vellum

ACKNOWLEDGMENTS

For those of you who read my first novel, *The Bluegrass Files Series: Down the Rabbit Hole*, it comes as no surprise that this book is set in my well-loved home, Lexington, Kentucky. It is great fun to write stories set in places I know so well and, as I've been told so many times, great fun for readers who are familiar with this lovely city to see some of their favorite places come to life on these pages.

All this familiarity, however, creates a problem. No mystery novel is worth its salt without a few dastardly individuals doing things that go well beyond being untoward. We need villains and heroes and crimes. Thus, the question arises, "How do we set murders and mayhem and misdeeds in our own cities and towns without casting aspersions on the real and mostly wonderful people and institutions that reside there?" My best effort at absolving all of those people and institutions from any unfortunate association with the evil-doing in this work is to direct readers to the admonition on the copyright page, pointing out that this is a work of fiction. In other words, *I'm just making this stuff up!* On the other hand, some of Lexingtonian's favorite places are mentioned by name, but you'll probably notice, only in the most positive of lights.

Now, as to the people who have helped me bring this story to life, my gratitude goes out to a group of special people—special in the help they gave me, special in who they are. I thank my sister (and partner in crime), Judy Thompson, for reading this work while in progress. So many twists and turns in this plot were held up to the "believability test" by her keen mind. Some made the cut and some didn't.

Then there is my daughter, Jennifer Al-Rikabi, who can spot an extra space or a missing quotation mark with the best of them. More importantly, it was her input that kept Sonia working at the highest possible level in her quest to be a true professional private investigator.

It is my daughter, Kristin Morford, who took on the responsibility of being my feminist filter. It is not easy for a man, especially an older man, to be in touch with the ever-evolving views of our society on women and their emerging empowerment. On more than one occasion my own understanding of those issues was enhanced by our discussion of what it was that Sonia and her partner, Jet, might say, or think, or feel. I am grateful that both Kristin and Jennifer helped me to avoid writing things that women might find demeaning or insulting, or even just unbelievable.

Thanks also go out to Marcos Valdes for his help with authentic Mexican dialects, Rick Fern, for insights into the ever-fascinating world of accounting, and George McCormick for his willingness to read the manuscript several times over, looking for problems in text and thought.

Finally, as always, I thank my wife, Denise. Without her patience and support, this book and the ones that surround it in the series could and would never have been written. When I write about a man truly loving and cherishing a woman, I write what I feel about her.

Readers: Please note that this is a slightly revised version of the text first published in 2018.

1

"They should call me Lucky," she whispered out loud as she drove her car through the early morning darkness and onto the property. Her eyes followed the beams from the vehicle's headlights as it moved along the winding driveway.

She smiled and nodded as she thought about her life. Lucky. I'm lucky to be doing what I love, working with these majestic beings. Lucky to be working on a farm that's so beautiful I can see its wonder all around me, even before the sun really comes up. Lucky to be helping these animals, and those I'll never even have the chance to see. Life is good; I'm blessed. And soon, soon things will be even better. Soon this will have all been worth it.

First to arrive, as usual, she pulled her car into the same spot she used every day, just next to the old east barn, a building constructed sometime in the late 1800s. She stepped out into the brisk morning, a quick chill running through her body.

The sound of her car had brought the giants inside the barn to life. Her heart lifted as she heard the rumble of their voices and the sound of their thousand-pound bodies moving on the old wooden floor. She loved these animals. And though her employment had more to do with breeding and development, she cherished the depth of the relationship she engendered with them by being the first face they saw each morning, the one who fed them and welcomed them to a new day.

She didn't want to pull open the large sliding door the horses would use later in the day, so she stepped through the human-sized door and turned on one bare-bulb light, creating a dim, almost surreal, atmosphere in the barn. Heads bobbed and hooves clumped, stretching long, powerful muscles. The sweet smell of hay, straw, and grains filled her senses. Her already-muddied boots moved quietly over the well-worn floors of the barn. Big, brown eyes stared at her, while snorts and the occasional whinny welcomed her into this special domain.

She headed for the large bin in which breakfast was held, a blend of oats and other grains. A strange sensation crept up her spine. She turned her head to peer into the dim recesses of the building. Pausing, she saw nothing. She went back to her task. But as she scooped out the first bucket-full of grain, the sensation returned, this time verified by the shifting and nervous responses of the animals. She spun completely around. He was right there.

"Oh, you scared me. What are you doing here?" It was almost a whisper. A deeper, much darker chill ran through her body.

His voice was smooth, almost soothing. "Oh, my dear. Now, you didn't think our last conversation was going to be the end of it all, did you?"

She took a small step backward. "Wait, wait. We can talk about it. We can—"

He stepped into the space she had vacated. "No, child. I'm afraid the time for talking is over."

She just barely saw it coming out of the corner of her eye. Her head was wracked by the sudden blow from his large hand. It would have sent her reeling to the ground if he had not caught her himself. He pushed her backward into one of the stalls; he struck her again. This time the back of his hand sent her down into the straw that covered the wooden floor.

He was on top of her almost immediately, the weight of his body sitting squarely on her tiny hips, pinning her to the ground. His powerful hands wrapped around her sleek, thin neck.

"Believe me, child. This was never what I wanted. I never planned it this way. But now, this is where we are and this is what we must do."

She struggled, kicking her mud-covered boots, trying to get even a tiny bit of that cold morning air to descend into her lungs. His now-monstrous hands, hands she used to admire, were crushing her windpipe. His eyes bore into hers. She could just barely hear what he was saying as her mind and body screamed out for oxygen, struggled against the pain. A few phrases came to her, "long trip . . . your own car . . . before they find you." Darkness began to creep into her mind. She struggled even harder. Her body relaxed. Blackness came.

2

At ten o'clock on Monday morning, the mood in the offices of Bluegrass Confidential Investigations was somewhat festive. The recently-installed television in the waiting area was rarely on; this morning, however, things were different. This morning the two young women who ran the firm had a special interest in a local morning show interview taped the day before. Jet leaned against the molding in the doorway to her office, her arms crossed. "Well, look at that. We're TV stars."

Sonia took a seat on the brown leather couch in front of the television. She smiled. "I'm not sure the word 'stars' actually fits, but it is kind of exciting to watch, isn't it?"

"Sho 'nuff is," Jet replied, slipping ever-so-briefly into one of her many accents.

A quiet sense of pride filled Sonia's heart as she watched the images of the three PIs being interviewed. Sitting on wooden chairs with dark red cushions, they were all facing Mark Sullivan, the young, attractive male host with the blonde hair and the quasi-beard. It being March, both women were wearing heavy sweaters, Sonia green, Jet white. Both had on dress pants. The man was wearing a navy V-neck sweater over a white shirt and snug-fitting jeans.

"I'm here with Sonia Vitale, Joyce Ellen Thomas, and Brad Dunham," Mark had started as he sat on his matching wooden chair, a small jungle of artificial plants behind and beside him.

"Jet," Joyce Ellen had corrected. "Everyone just calls me Jet. Apparently, I was a bit of track star at Woodford County High." She'd smiled. "And Sonia's name is pronounced Vi-tah-lay, with an accent on the 'tah' and a long 'a' sound at the end."

Mark had turned, speaking directly to the camera, reading from the prompter. "Over the last few weeks, these three local private investigators combined the resources of their two firms. Together, they discovered illegal activities that were taking place right here in Lexington and beyond." He'd turned to Sonia. "Now, Sonia, is this the kind of work you usually do at Bluegrass Confidential Investigations?"

Not used to being on television, even local television, Sonia's voice had sounded a bit tenuous. "Well, we generally have more of a local focus at BCI. You know, helping people find missing loved ones, checking up on missing things. Personal matters."

"I understand." He'd turned to Jet. "So, Joyce," he'd lifted his hand, "excuse me, Jet. This must have been exciting work for you all."

Sonia had been a bit surprised when Jet had come off cool and collected. "Really, I have to say that it was mostly Sonia and Brad that did all the heavy lifting. They followed some of those folks right down I-75 into Tennessee; they followed others all the way to Memphis." She had grinned. "And things got a little dicey after that."

"That's true, isn't it Brad?" Mark had turned slightly in his chair.

Given Brad's experience as an investigator with the Naval Criminal Investigative Service, NCIS, it had been no surprise to Sonia that Brad had seemed even more at home on set than Jet, although much less enamored of the attention. "Well, I can't deny that things got a little dangerous for a while. And I do have to thank my good friend from the DEA, Special Agent Roberto Alvarez, for saving our bacon on the way back from Memphis."

Mark Sullivan had looked down and checked his notes. "Now, Sonia, am I correct in saying that it was your interest in the John Abbott Hensley affair that got you involved in all of this?"

A quick image of Dahlia Farm and a man dressed in a madras shirt had flashed through Sonia's mind. "That's true, Mark. And at this point, I think we all have a better idea of what was going on there."

Sitting on the couch in the BCI offices, Sonia's eyes drifted from the screen. She remembered well how she had felt at the beginning of the Hensley case—committed to doing the right thing but fearful that the whole situation might be beyond her. She didn't feel that way anymore. She'd seen the case to its completion. She'd stared death in the face—three times. She was no longer the same person.

Her attention returning to the television, Sonia watched as Mark had continued. "Now ladies, your offices are right here in town, correct? Right on East Main, over Magee's bakery?"

"Well, yes they are," Jet had answered, flipping her perpetual blonde ponytail. She smiled. "Bad for the diet but great for the soul."

"And Brad, your office is right across the street?"

"That's correct." Brad had answered evenly, with no emphasis. "In the white house, right next door to the school district's Central Office."

"And I assume the name Semper Fi Investigations implies that you're a former marine?"

The mention of his time in the Marine Corps had brought Brad's bright blue eyes to life. "Yes, sir. That it does."

"So, Brad, how is it that you all started to work together?"

Brad had looked quickly at Sonia, then back to the host. "Really, Mark, it's a long story."

SONIA AND JET watched the television as the interview went on for a few more minutes, Sonia looking carefully at their images on the screen. In all modesty, she had to admit that all three of them, the women in their thirties, Brad in his early forties, looked pretty darn good. Sonia's trim, smallish body, dark hair, and dark eyes created a pleasant counterpoint to Jet's taller, leaner body, her blonde hair highlighting an attractive, blue-eyed face. For Sonia, however, it was the image of Brad that drew her attention. His large body and rugged countenance were set off by blue eyes brighter than Jet's.

After the interview ended, Jet turned and stepped into her office. She took a seat at her large wooden desk. It was at least fifty years old and had a lot of "character."

Sonia turned the television off and followed, sitting in the red padded chair opposite Jet's desk. She tried her best to come off as modest. "I thought that all went very nicely."

"Yeah, it did. I'm just glad that you and Brad are getting the credit you all deserve for solving the Hensley thing, and for setting Robbie Alvarez up to take down the others."

"Uh-huh." A hint of pride slid quietly across Sonia's face. Her eyes opened wide. "Not that you didn't play your part as well."

"Come on now, Sonia," Jet rocked back in her chair, her accent creeping southward. "You know that ol' Jet, here, was just along for the ride. It was you and Brad that treed those guys, and it was you alone who figured out what happened to Hensley." She paused and picked up a paper coffee cup, one look at its contents apparently discouraging her from taking a sip. "Speaking of Brad, how's all that going?"

"What do you mean?"

Jet looked at Sonia over invisible glasses.

"Oh. Well," Sonia shrugged her shoulders gently, "great, I guess." Her voice was less than firm. "I mean, ever since we wrapped that other thing up, I've seen him almost every night."

"Hmmm, shackin' up with Semper Fi? Got a toothbrush over there yet?"

Sonia squirmed, rolling her eyes.

"Good for you. You take your time." Jet reached out and pushed some folders around through the clutter on her desk, apparently looking for a particular document. "I've got to say it. I'm glad all this attention has our phone ringing off the hook. We certainly have more cases now than we've ever had." She stopped and looked directly at Sonia. "Speaking of that, now that you and Brad are a 'thing,' how is that going to work?"

"What do you mean?"

"Business-wise." Jet tapped the folders in her hand into a neater rectangle then seemed at a loss as to where to put them. "I mean, I'm assuming we're still going to be BCI, just the way it's always been."

Sonia ran her fingers through her hair. "Sure. I guess so. Brad and I haven't really discussed it."

Jet sat up taller in her chair. "Listen, honey. I know it's only been a little while, and you and Brad are just getting used to," her fingers created quotation marks in the air, " 'being together.' But you'd better get that part of your relationship squared away. The last thing you need is to make some assumptions and then have everything blow up in your face."

Sonia knew there was work waiting for her on her own, much more organized desk. She stood up to leave. As she did, she glanced out the window at the white house across the street from the BCI offices. In it, Sonia assumed, Brad Dunham was sitting at his desk working on one of his Semper Fi cases. She straightened the close-fitting red sweater she was wearing—a color that suited her well. "We'll be alright. The business thing can't be that much of a problem." Her voice sounded just a tick less than convincing.

Sonia began walking out of Jet's office then turned. "I've got to get started on the pile of stuff on my desk. Want to go downstairs for lunch sometime around noon?"

Jet shook her head. "I'm afraid I'll be leaving before then to meet some guy at Bronson/Brownlee. We'll be talking about the possibility of us doing some work out there." "Bronson/Brownlee. That's a big plumbing company here in town, isn't it?"

"Yup. Can't imagine that's going to be all that exciting," Jet shrugged. "But work is work. I'll see you after I get back."

"Okay." As she walked from Jet's office to her own, Sonia wondered if the transition from being business competitors to being a couple—if that's what they were—was going to be more difficult for her and Brad than she had imagined.

3

The BCI offices occupied the entire second-story space of a two-story building constructed in the 1950s. A locally owned bakery, Magee's, filled the first floor and was the most likely place to find Sonia and Jet, other than their offices. Unfortunately, the only access to those offices was a long, two-story flight of wooden stairs with no turn-around landing.

The atmosphere above Magee's was quite pleasant, with wood flooring, exposed brick walls, and ceiling beams. Unfortunately, being a semi-finished attic, the slightly adequate heating and cooling system left a lot to be desired. Cheap rent and the smell of Magee's baked goods floating through the vents were its only redeeming qualities—other than a great location. It sat right on East Main Street.

The front half of their space had been turned into two offices with wood and glass walls, each with a window that looked out onto East Main. Sparsely decorated—old desks, comfortable desk chairs, simple padded chairs for clients—each office subtly featured a picture of Sonia and Jet at a shooting range. The message to clients was obvious. The back half of the space had been set aside as a waiting area.

It was almost ten-forty-five when Sonia took a seat at her own wooden desk, smaller and a bit more modern than Jet's. She, too, used an old armoire to create some sort of closet space in her office. Just before eleven, her phone sang out its silly version of *The Star-Spangled Banner*, a point of frustration for her at times, since it was Jet who had changed the ringtone on Sonia's phone. Recently, however, Sonia had come to enjoy the subtle reminder of her relationship with her partner. Looking at the phone, she knew it was Brad calling. "This is Sonia Vitale, famous TV detective. How can I help you?" There was a smile on her face.

"Wow. This must be my lucky day. How's it going, babe?"

Sonia loved the sound of his voice. "Better, now that you've called. What's up?"

"Well, I've been at my desk since seven o'clock this morning and I'm thinking it's time for a little break. I saw the light on in your office. Want to come downstairs for a cup of coffee?"

Just thinking that he'd looked out of his own office window and across the street to hers, Sonia could feel her heart warm. "Strangely enough, I had to skip my normal coffee run in order to catch the TV interview this morning. Just give me a minute to finish this one task and I'll be right down."

"Yes, ma'am. See you in a minute." She loved the sound of his smile.

Sonia dropped one last piece of information into a file and stood to leave. As she did, she looked up and saw a man standing at the very back of the waiting area. Wearing plain, loose-fitting jeans, he had on a T-shirt bearing some sort of logo and held a faded, red ball cap in his hand. He was not tall; surrounded by the bare brick walls, he seemed even smaller. "Can I help you?"

The man walked to the door of her office. When he spoke, it didn't surprise Sonia that she heard the rhythms and accents of a man whose native tongue was Spanish. "Are you Ms. Vitale?"

"I am. How can I help you?"

He spoke quickly, with great intensity. "My daughter. My

daughter is missing. One night she was right here, with me at the restaurant. The next day she was gone. I don't know where she's gone, why she's gone. I need your help. Can you help me?"

Sonia's heart flipped at the thought of a missing daughter, any missing daughter. She sat back down. "Please, come in sir. Have a seat. Just give me a moment, would you?" She pulled out her phone and sent Brad a text. NEW CLIENT. WON'T BE THERE TIL 11:15 OR LATER. CAN U WAIT?

Sonia put the phone down on her desk. "Now, sir. Can we start from the beginning? Your name is?" She reached for a pen and pad.

As he answered, Sonia took in his plain clothing and simple manner. "My name is Francisco Castillo, but everyone calls me Paco. My daughter's name is Mariana, and she's missing now more than two weeks. I'm very, very worried."

"And what makes you think your daughter is actually missing? I assume you've tried to contact her?"

The man clasped his hands, rubbing them together. "Oh yes. I've called over and over. She doesn't answer. She doesn't call back." He sighed.

"And you've gone to her home?"

"Of course, Ms. Vitale, of course. She was not there. Nothing looks strange in her apartment." He shrugged sheepishly. "I have a key."

"And her car?"

"No," he shook his head again. "Not there. It's gone, just like her."

"And have you been to the police, Mr. Castillo?"

"Paco. You can call me Paco. Yes, of course I went to the police. And they said they are searching, but they haven't found anything. Not her. Not her car. Nothing."

"And how old is Mariana?" Sonia was working hard at staying relaxed, exuding a professional calm that would help this new client tell his story accurately.

He looked up. "Twenty-six. She just turned twenty-six. His eyes brightened just a bit. She's very beautiful and a nice girl."

Sonia wrote as she spoke. "So, she's twenty-six and missing. Is she married?" She looked up. Paco Castillo just shook his head.

"Do you think there's any chance she's just decided to go somewhere? Gone off with some friends, or to meet someone?"

"That's what the police asked, too, but no, I don't think so."

"You know, Mr. Castillo," Sonia tried to ask her next question as gently as possible, "a lot of women meet men on the internet these days. Any chance she's been in contact with someone and has just, I don't know, set up an opportunity to meet them in person?"

"You don't understand, that's not the kind of girl she is. She's very reliable, and smart, too. She went to that school just north of Midway."

"Midway University?"

"No, that one is *in* Midway. The other one, Mayweather College. It's more out in the country." There was pride in his voice. "She studied the horses."

"You mean she was in their equine research program?" Sonia had stopped writing.

"*Sí.* Yes."

Sonia knew both schools were well known for equine studies. "Well, that's a very prestigious program." She smiled broadly. "You're right. She must be smart. And is she still in school?" She made another note on her pad.

"No." He reached for his wallet. It was fat and well-worn, over-flowing. "She graduated three years ago. See? Here." He held out a worn photograph, his somewhat delicate hand shaking subtly. "It's a picture of the whole family at the ceremony. We were all very proud."

Sonia could see the depth of his pride as it radiated across the man's face. Before she could respond, however, her phone cooed like a pigeon. "I'm so sorry. Give me just a second Mr. Castillo, would you?" She looked at the text. BE WAITING, COFFEE IN HAND, CROISSANT ON PLATE.

Sonia smiled and turned back to the man, his eyes looking down at the floor, clearly not wanting to intrude. "So, what does Mariana do now? Is she working with horses?"

Again, his face lit up. "Oh yes, she works at Downstream Farm out on Ironworks Pike."

Sonia smiled. "How nice. What does she do out there?"

The man shrugged again. "I don't really know. Helping to breed horses better or something like that." He wagged his finger. "She's no stable hand. She knows a lot about the horses. She does important work."

Sonia nodded. "And everything is going well for her out there?"

"*Sí. Sí.* They like her very much." He was almost smiling. "And she is so happy. She tells me how lucky she feels. Lucky to have gotten such a good job and still be close to her family."

"And you, Mr. Castillo—"

"Paco."

"Yes, Paco. Where do your work?"

"I work at Papi's." He gently pinched a tiny section of his black T-shirt and stretched it, showing off the logo on its front. "It's a Mexican restaurant here in town, on Euclid avenue, right above Charlie Brown's."

"Oh. I think my partner eats lunch there sometimes." Sonia could hear, in her memory, Jet regaling her with stories of sumptuous Mexican meals she had eaten there, usually with an ample supply of margaritas to wash them down. "And you said she was at the restaurant with you the other night?"

"Yes. Yes." He became more animated. "I am a server there and she said she was stopping by to see me, just to say hello."

"And was that unusual?"

"No. She did that every once in a while." His energy didn't lessen. "We don't get to see each other a lot. She works early in the day. I work at night. So, it's nice when she stops in to see me there. Of course, sometimes she sees her mother and me at home. But, you know, the people who work with the horses, they don't have a very regular life."

Sonia thought about her first year out of college. She had lived at home with her folks. It wasn't the best, but she had fond memories of being surrounded by her family. She leaned forward on her desk. "Mr. Castillo, you say that the police are investigating her disappearance. Do you think they're doing everything they can?"

His eyebrows rose and he leaned forward, putting his hands on Sonia's desk. It was as if he was going to say something—something angry. Then he collapsed back into the chair, his energy slipping away. "I guess . . . but they are busy with many other things. After the first few days, it felt like they were just moving on to something else." His energy, his voice, rose again as he sat up taller. "Still. She is a good girl. She wouldn't just disappear. She wouldn't do that to her mother. I told them that. I did." His frustration hung in the air. Finally, his eyes fell to his lap. "Maybe they are just waiting for something to happen. Then they'll look hard again."

Sonia paused for a moment, knowing there were clear limits to what the police could do in the case of an adult who might be missing. Still, she could sense the pain in Francisco Castillo's heart. She sighed. "And what makes you think that I, uh, we can help?"

The man brightened, looking directly into Sonia's eyes. The shift in his energy was palpable. "You are the ladies that were on TV this morning, right?" He smiled. "You went after those other people and you found out about the man who died. I think you must be very special."

Sonia was flattered that he had seen her and Jet on TV. Still . . . . . "Mr. Castillo, it's just that I don't know that we can do anything the police can't do."

"*Por favor*, please. I don't know who else to turn to. And my Mariana, she's out there somewhere. I know she is." His eyes became red and watery. "Who would hurt a beautiful young woman like her?"

Sonia brushed a wisp of hair out of her face as she thought. "Tell me again, Mr. Castillo—

"Paco."

"Yes, Paco. What is it that you think the police haven't done?"

Paco Castillo looked at her blankly. "I don't know, Ms. Vitale. I only know that when I talk to them all they say is, 'Be patient, Mr. Castillo. We're doing everything we can. Something will turn up.' There must be something, something else you can do."

Sonia sat silently, taking a long, hard look at the broken man. "Okay . . . Paco. Let me talk to my partner and see what she thinks."

"The lady, Jet?" His voice had perked up.

Sonia smiled. "Yes, the lady, Jet. Let's see if she thinks we can be of assistance. Here, write your phone number down on this notepad and I'll call you later this afternoon." She pushed the pad across her desk. "And just know that I really want to help. I can't imagine how difficult this must be for you." She smiled. "Just let me talk to Jet. We'll put our heads together and try to come up with a plan that can help us find your daughter for you."

Sonia watched as Mr. Castillo stood up and walked out of her office, bowing slightly as he said goodbye. She had thought of him as smallish when she had first seen him. Now she believed some of that impression came from the great weight he was carrying. She hoped that one way or the other she and Jet would soon be doing everything they could to help this father find his missing daughter. They just had to.

4

After Mr. Castillo left, Sonia sighed, stood up, and walked through the empty waiting area. Pulling on her cloche hat for one last wearing before the weather became too warm, she pushed the ancient exterior door open and stepped onto a small landing. She looked straight down the old wooden stairs that went directly to street level. It was those steps, plus the steps to her apartment over a garage on Central Avenue, that sometimes drove her crazy. However, on a bright sunny day, and going down instead of up, the stairs didn't seem much of a burden to her at that moment. Shortly, she was at the bottom of those steps and turning into one of the three places in town in which she felt most at home—Magee's Bakery.

Magee's had been around since 1956. It was an inviting environment, with brick interior walls, high raw-wood ceilings, a beautiful stained-glass sign, and one of the most engaging, full-wall murals Sonia had ever seen. More importantly, the room was filled with wonderful aromas, hot coffee, warm pastries, and friends.

Most mornings, before going up to her office, Sonia would stop in Magee's. She was almost always greeted from behind the counter by Hildy, an older woman in her eighties who had worked there for years. "Almond croissant and a small coffee?" Hildy would ask. "As usual," Sonia would reply and her day would be off to a pleasant start.

There was no need for that this morning, however, since she knew Brad Dunham had already gotten her coffee and a croissant and was waiting with those treats at a corner table near the front windows. Sonia thought back to how, just weeks ago, Brad had been an almost mythical figure to her—former Marine, proprietor of Semper Fi Investigations. She remembered having had no desire whatsoever to be in contact with "Mr. Hotstuff." She remembered as well, however, that when she'd come to believe that the death of a local horse farm owner had not been what it seemed, he had been willing to help, willing to "do the right thing." During the course of those investigations, she'd learned that he was not only a former marine but that he had been assigned to NCIS for many years.

Sonia smiled as she walked to the table at which Brad was seated, khaki pants and a white polo shirt giving him a crisp professional look—professional, but relaxed. His closely cropped brown hair fit the image, while his rugged face and bright blue eyes set him apart. She sat down. "What, no croissant for you, Captain Dunham?"

"Sorry, Ma'am. You know how we PI's have to keep ourselves in tip-top shape."

Sonia tore off a tiny piece of her croissant and brought it to her mouth. "Oh, and that's why you're plying me with hot coffee and a warm pastry? So I can stay in tip-top shape?" She popped the morsel into her mouth and grinned.

"Listen, sweet thing." His smile was warm and inviting, "There's nothing that can interfere with your staying beautiful, especially when you're out there pounding out three-mile runs all the time. And," he turned both of his hands upward, "should there be just the tiniest bit of slippage in that regard, I'm sure we can find some other physical activity that could work off any excess calories."

Sonia liked the way Brad played. "Very clever. But I'm afraid I'm not really in the mood right now." Her countenance had changed.

"Why, babe? Something wrong?" His face and voice reflected her shifting tone.

Sonia stirred her coffee then took a careful sip. "It's that new client who came in unexpectedly this morning. The one that made me late getting down here."

"What about him?" Brad's voice was protective, almost accusatorial.

Sonia shook off his concerns with her hand. "It's his daughter. She's twenty-six years old and missing." She took another sip. "It seems she graduated from that equine research program at Mayweather University, just north of Midway. Now she works at Downstream Farm. She's been gone over two weeks and the whole family is going out of their minds."

Brad swallowed a sip of his coffee as well. "He's been to the police, I assume."

"Yes, of course. But you know how it is. Once they've gone through the usual procedures to find a missing person . . . ." She raised her shoulders in a tiny shrug.

"Yeah." Brad swirled the coffee in his cup. "They ask around, go to her apartment, the last place she was seen. They put out a bolo alert, you know, 'be on the lookout.' After that, they just have to watch the electronic notifications to see if anything comes across the wires about the missing person being involved in an activity that caught somebody's attention."

Sonia nodded, her voice soft. "Right."

"Look," Brad shrugged, "it would be different if she were a suspect in a crime." He put down his cup, his energy level rising slightly. "Then they'd be looking at credit card usage and all those kinds of things. But in a case like this, they've got to start from the premise that the girl had every right to just get up and go." He raised an eyebrow before he spoke again. "And she's an adult. They're actually constrained by a lot of privacy issues."

Sonia took a small bite of her pastry, then a sip of her coffee. "I know that. I could have told him so. But he, the dad, wants us to find her. He's convinced that something bad has happened to her, but it's obvious that he's also convinced that she's out there somewhere."

Brad looked at Sonia with his bright blue eyes. They seemed just a little cold. "I don't know. We're so busy. We've got two different clients who need help with research on legal cases. That work pays big. And I just got a call from an old client up east. I may have to go do some work for him. All that's going to keep us busy, really busy."

"Us?" Sonia squinted. "Were you thinking we would work those cases together?"

"Of course." Brad gave her his best smile. "Didn't I say the other day that I'd have to hire you and your technology skills to work with me at Semper Fi?"

Sonia's face didn't respond in kind. "Well, in passing you did. I didn't think you were serious."

"Of course I was serious." There was a bit of surprise in his voice. "We're together now, aren't we? We're a couple, right?"

The coffee cup in Sonia's hand began to shake, almost imperceptibly. "Yes, yes. Of course we're a couple." She took a tiny breath. That's a new word—couple.

"Well then, it seems logical that you'd come work for me at some point, doesn't it?" He sounded a bit like a salesman closing the deal before the customer could think it through.

"*For* you? As an *employee*?" Sonia could feel the muscles in her jaw tightening.

"Well, you don't have to think of it that way. We'll work together." Brad waved his hand. "The employee thing, that's just a technicality."

Sonia's right foot started tapping. "Well, as an *employee*, don't I get to know how much I'm going to get paid? What kind of benefits I'll get?"

"What's going on?" Brad seemed honestly confused. "I thought you'd want to come work with me. You just said it yourself, we're a couple—we're together."

Sonia's mind was spinning. She would have loved having a conversation about their moving forward, becoming a real couple. But not this way. Not while they were negotiating about work. "Yes, we're together," she said, her voice terse. "But that doesn't mean I give up being who I am, does it? Jet and I have put a lot of time and money and effort into building BCI; we've got more clients than we know what to do with. And you think that without even asking me you can just assume that I would walk away from that—walk away from my best friend?" Her voice was rising, and the shaking of her hand was no longer imperceptible.

"I never said that. I just . . . ." Brad simply stopped. The silence at the table was palpable.

Brad turned his head to the left and looked out the large picture window. He spoke as if the person he was conversing with was on the other side. "So how do you see this going?"

Sonia took a very deliberate sip from her cup. "Well, honestly, I don't think I've thought this through much more than you have. It's just been so nice lately, you know, being together. I just hadn't thought much about a business relationship." She moved closer to him. "And of course, I always want to help you in any way I can. But I can't stop being me. I've learned so much professionally. And I know I could be that working with you," she shook her head, "but it's not the same."

Brad remained silent while Sonia paused, getting her thoughts together. She took a quick breath. "And then there's Jet. She took me into her vision, the agency, as a full partner. We've worked so many cases together. And now we've got so many more, more than she could handle alone. Do I walk out on her?

Do I just say, 'Hey it was great while I waited for something better to come along, but now I'm with Brad, so I'm out of here? Good luck?' " She paused again. Her tempo increased. "Come to think of it, if I come and work for you, doesn't that put me in direct competition with Jet? Doesn't it?"

Now it was Brad's turn to think for a moment. He looked down into his cup as he swirled the coffee in it round and round. Finally, he took a deep breath. "Let me ask you a question."

"Okay." Sonia knit her brows. Where's he going with this? Her foot started tapping again.

He looked up. "These new jobs you're getting. What kind of work is it?"

"Well," she sat a bit taller, "mostly the same stuff we've always done, cheating lovers, missing kids like Mariana."

Brad moved forward cautiously. "And you know what kind of work Semper Fi focuses on, right?"

"Yeah, mostly corporate work." She watched him carefully. Where is he going with this?

"That's right." He sounded stronger, more confident. "All the other stuff, that's more of a hindrance to me than anything else. It takes me away from the larger accounts."

"I can see that." Sonia felt like she was holding her breath as she waited. In fact, for a few moments, she was.

Brad leaned in, his bright, blue eyes looking directly into Sonia's. "How about this. You stay at BCI. You do the work you guys have always done. Something comes across your desk that seems, well, maybe a little more heavy-duty, you send the account to me. On the other hand, I keep doing corporate stuff, but I give up doing anything else." He raised his eyebrows. "Someone comes to me with a job that's right up your alley, I send them to you. How does that sound?"

Sonia was a little taken aback. Hearing Brad imply that only he could deal with larger clients, corporate clients, "heavy-duty stuff," put a knot in her stomach. Hadn't she worked shoulder to shoulder with him bringing down that last group of dangerous, very dangerous, people? Still, she knew in her heart that he had a lot more experience than she and Jet had, not to mention a veritable armory of sophisticated equipment. Her lip curled a bit as she spoke. "So, we never work together again?"

"No, that's not it at all." Brad, the salesman, was full throttle and talking fast. "You and I may be working in different firms, but we're still us; we're still a couple. If I need computer help or just an extra pair of hands or two, you guys come and help me. Maybe on some kind of contract—just for business sake. Then, if you guys need help from me, some equipment or, God forbid, some muscle, then I come and help you. Isn't that what a couple would do, no matter what the business relationship?"

Sonia looked down and thought for a good solid minute, Brad waiting—staring at the top of her head. Reluctantly accepting the current reality of their different situations, and eager to allow room for their relationship to grow, she spoke, slowly. "Actually, that sounds like it might just work." Her voice was soft, tentative. She looked up at him. "That might just be okay." A vision of Jet's sardonic smile crept across Sonia's mind. "But I've got to run it past Jet. I think she's been ahead of us in thinking about the ramifications of you and I being . . . together. And I think she's a little nervous. Let me see what she thinks. It's got to be okay with her, too."

The discussion seemed to end there. Sonia's level of frustration ebbed slowly. At the same time, she realized that this was the first uncomfortable conversation they'd had since they'd become . . . whatever they'd been lately. She took in a deep breath. *I guess that's what being together . . . a couple . . . in a real situation . . . in the real world, is like. Not always peaches and cream.*

Sonia and Brad spoke for a few more minutes, mostly about what they might do that evening and on the upcoming weekend. Soon, however, she felt the need to get away, the intensity of the previous discussion still jangling her nerves. She stood. "I've got to get back to work. Thanks for the coffee. I'll see you tonight, okay?"

"Okay, babe. I'll see you tonight." He rose to give her a quick kiss. It was nice but less than comfortable. She rose, walked out the door, turned the corner, and looked up those steps. Her mind was spinning. The conversation with Brad had been difficult. She wasn't a hundred percent sure how she felt about the new arrangement, nor if Jet would be on board with it. And what was worse, a worried father had come to ask her help in finding his daughter—and no one had the slightest idea of what had happened to her.

5

S onia was sitting at her desk when she heard the ancient door to the BCI offices open and saw Jet walk in. "Two o'clock," Sonia said loudly enough for Jet to hear while she was still in the waiting area. "That must have been some meeting."

Jet spoke as she walked toward Sonia's office, her high heels clicking and reverberating off the empty brick walls. "Yeah, well, I just had a *fascinating* meeting with Steven Brownlee. You can't imagine how wonderful it was to be given the complete, and I mean the *com-pl-ete* tour of the Bronson/Brownlee plumbing universe. There were butterfly valves and CL flange reducers, drainage pumps and sump basins." She gave Sonia a snarky smile. "Hell, I even saw box after box of ballcock valves, whatever the hell they are."

"Pretty sexy, huh?" Sonia's smile was mischievous.

Jet brushed invisible dust off her clothing and hands. "Oh yes, Steven Brownlee about swept me off my feet. Never mind the fact that he's almost eighty years old."

"Good." Sonia smiled benevolently. "I'm glad to see you getting a little romance in your life. Any chance you two might . . . you know . . . ?"

"Yeah right. God knows what condition his plunger is in."

Sonia let out a hearty laugh. Then she asked, "So how can we be of assistance to Misters Bronson and Brownlee?"

Jet shook her head. "Oh, there isn't a Mr. Bronson, not anymore. He's been dead for thirty years or more. It's just out of respect for his old friend that Brownlee keeps the two names on the firm. He said, 'That's the way it started and that's the way it'll end.' "

Sonia nodded. That's the way it should be. "So?"

"So, Mr. Brownlee, given his age, has had to bring in new folks to actually run most of the operation. Last year he brought in a bright computer guy, just graduated from Transy two years ago. The guy's brought the whole thing into the twenty-first century. Ordering, inventory, billing, etc. They all go through his computer program now."

Sonia leaned back in her swivel chair, a mechanical pencil eraser touching her lips. "And, what's the problem?"

Jet took a seat in the red padded chair opposite Sonia's desk, one that matched the chair opposite her own. "Well, as you can imagine, Mr. Brownlee is old school." She rolled her eyes and smiled. "Pretty pencil-and-paper, you know what I mean?" She shrugged. "Listen, he still knows everything under the sun about plumbing supplies, it's just that he can't keep up with the financial information anymore—the way it's all laid out in spreadsheets and the like." She closed one eye and raised the other eyebrow. "And he's starting to get pretty suspicious that there are some shenanigans going on there."

Sonia sat forward in her chair, her forearms leaning against her desk. "So, this guy graduates from Transylvania University with a computer science degree. Then he finds himself a great business being run by a true old-timer and uses a lot of techno smoke and mirrors to rob the old guy blind. Is that it?"

Jet twisted her lips. "That's what Brownlee's afraid of."

Sonia rocked back in her chair again, resting both her elbows on its worn wooden arms. "And are we going to help?"

"I'd sure like to. Mr. Brownlee seems like a sweet old guy. Aaand," she winked, "he's more than willing to pay top dollar to protect his business."

"So, what's the problem?"

Jet adjusted herself in her chair. "The problem, sweetheart, is that we need two things to figure out what the hell is going on down there. First, we need someone who is computer savvy, and it just so happens that one of us is the geekology queen of East Main. Second, we need someone who understands accounting. And," she looked at Sonia over the glasses she wasn't wearing, "neither one of us knows grits from gravy when it comes to accounting. I just don't know that we can do the old guy justice on this one."

Sonia started tapping her pencil against the edge of her desk. "Now, wait a minute. You said the old guy didn't mind spending money on saving the business, right?"

"Right."

The tapping stopped. "Then what we've got to do is bring in someone who does know about accounting, a forensic accountant, or something like that."

Jet thought for a moment then reached into her purse and started searching on her phone. "Okay. There are two firms in Lexington that offer forensic accounting services. One is up near Hamburg Pavilion, the other down on Harrodsburg Road."

"Alright, then, why don't you give them a call and see how much it costs to get one of their folks to come work with us? We'll just take our regular fee from Brownlee and tack on the cost of the forensic accountant." Sonia picked up a small pile of papers on her desk, tapped them into a perfect rectangle, and slipped them into a blue file folder. "I think he'll understand that it's going to take a team to find out what's going on out there."

Jet picked up her purse; she stood and turned to leave the office. "Yes, your highness."

Sonia sat up in her chair. "Listen before you go, we need to talk about something."

Jet turned back toward Sonia but remained standing.

"No, you'd better sit back down."

"Oh, my, my, my," said Jet, slipping into one of her infamous southern accents. "This doesn't sound good."

"Actually, I think you're going to be okay with this."

Jet took a seat but kept her purse in her lap. "Okay. Go ahead. Spill it."

"Right." Sonia took a quick breath. "So, I had two very interesting conversations today. First, just after you left, a client came in. His name is Francisco Castillo, but everyone calls him Paco. His daughter has been missing for two weeks and he wants us to find her."

"Two weeks? That's pretty quick. What about the police?"

Sonia ran her fingers through her hair. "Well, he said they were cooperative, but there was just so much they could do in a missing persons case. It's not like they've got any reason to believe she was the victim of a crime. I'm sure part of their thinking is that she's just up and left."

Jet rubbed her nose with her index finger. "How old is she?"

"Twenty-six."

Jet put her purse on the floor next to her chair. "Yeah. Young woman—just old enough to go off without telling anyone—maybe just to meet some guy she's met on the internet."

Sonia nodded. "Right. That's what I said to Mr. Castillo." She leaned forward onto her desk again. "But he says she's not that kind of girl." She went on to fill Jet in on the few other details she had about Mariana Castillo.

Jet bent down and picked up her purse. "Look, honey. I don't mean to sound callous, but this could be one tough gig. Searching for someone who may have just run off, someone who may not want to be found? Sounds like we could spend a hell of a long time on this one. Does it look like Mr. Castillo has the financial resources to pay for all of that time?"

Sonia thought back to the image of the smallish man standing at the back of the room—the way he was dressed, the way he moved. She knew the answer. "Honestly, probably not. But you should have seen him, Jet." Her voice became plaintive. "The way he was suffering. And just imagine his wife and the rest of the family."

"Sonia," Jet gave her a firm look, "you've got to remember we're not a non-profit." Jet stopped and sighed. "Or maybe we are." Then she regained her momentum. "But we're not supposed to be. We need to get paid for our time or we won't be able to pay for our own needs."

Sonia looked at Jet. She didn't say anything. She just kept looking straight into Jet's eyes. The seconds passed. Jet didn't say anything either, but her lips slowly twisted, as if in resignation. Finally, Sonia realized the implication of Jet's silence. "Great, but put your purse back down. There's more."

"Boy, Sonia Vitale," Jet let out a big sigh, "you've sure got a way of piling things on, don't you?"

Sonia remained sitting forward, her forearms leaning on her desk. "Again, I think you're going to be okay with this." She paused for a moment, tightening and relaxing her fingers. "Now, after I spoke to Mr. Castillo, I went downstairs to have coffee with Brad. I told him about the case and he said the weirdest thing." Sonia rolled her eyes. "Okay, maybe not so weird."

"What did he say?" Jet's voice had a bit of an edge to it.

Sonia took a quick breath. "So, he tells me he doesn't think we have time to take on Mr. Castillo because of all of *his* other cases." She leaned back in her chair, motioning with her hands. "And I say, 'We?' And then he tells me he thinks I'm going to be an employee of Semper Fi from now on."

"Well, son-of-a-bitch." There was no pleasant southern accent attached to those words.

"Yeah, I know, right?"

"And what did you say to him?" Jet seemed ready to pounce.

Sonia went on to tell Jet about the entire conversation between her and Brad, not leaving anything out. She asked Jet if she was okay with the arrangement Brad had proposed.

Jet sat quietly for a while. Then she said, "Honestly, I think that's the best solution. Let him take his fancy-dancey corporate work and we'll just stay here and keep helping real people, people who are getting screwed by someone else . . . or missing someone they love."

Sonia remembered how BCI had gotten started. Jet had caught her husband and the hot young secretary he worked with in *flagrante delicto*. That experience was the driving force behind Jet's desire to start BCI, and it was no surprise that she was content to keep that kind of work as the main focus of the firm.

Sitting back, as if to indicate the conversation was over, Sonia said, "Good. I'm glad you're okay with that. I think it's the best way to move forward, too."

Jet stood up once again. "Can I go now? I still haven't had a chance to eat lunch."

"Are you going to eat downstairs?"

"Yeah, I'm starving and I just want to get something as quickly as possible."

Sonia stood as well. "Come on. I'll join you. I haven't eaten lunch yet either. But tomorrow I want to go to Papi's for lunch."

There was surprise in Jet's voice. "I love that place. But why do you want to go there?"

"That's where Paco Castillo works. And that's where he was the last time he saw Mariana. I'd like to get the lay of the land."

"Sounds good to me," said Jet. "Papi's for lunch tomorrow, one of Magee's turkey sandwiches for lunch today. We're on a roll. Get it? On a roll?"

Sonia grimaced.

As the two women walked out into the warm sunlight and down the steps to Magee's, Sonia felt a sense of relief. Jet was going to work with her on the Castillo case. Another paying job had come their way. And most of all, she had a sense that business arrangements were going to work out just fine for her and Brad. In the back of her mind, however, she kept wondering how in the world they were going to find an attractive twenty-six-year-old who had simply disappeared.

6

A t eight o'clock on Tuesday morning, earlier than she liked to be at work, Sonia found herself leaving her apartment, driving through town, and heading up Newtown Pike toward Ironworks Pike—horse farm country. In truth, the whole city was surrounded by horse farms of one type or another, but she was heading for Downstream Farm, one of the truly significant farms in the horse breeding business.

Downstream Farm sits on a 180-acre parcel of prime horse-breeding property. Sonia's initial access to the farm was on a winding, tree-covered road. The idyllic setting included a log cabin which she guessed might have been built in the seventeen-hundreds. Still driving, a passing glance through one of its windows told her the interior of the cabin had recently been refurbished and fitted to a more modern purpose, perhaps as the farm's office. She passed one fenced paddock after another, maybe ten in all. There were several barns, each of which seemed recently modernized, yet in a style that was in keeping with the farm's long and illustrious history.

Eventually, Sonia found herself in front of the largest barn, the one she assumed was the center of the operation. Stepping out of her car, she immediately noticed a tall, sunbaked man approaching her.

"Hi." He touched the rim of his dark blue baseball cap. "James Racine." The rugged-looking man with young Robert Redford looks extended his hand. "You must be Ms. Vitale."

Sonia smiled and nodded. "Yes. Thanks so much for letting me come out here today." She took in the man—scuffed-up, real-life working western boots, tight-fitting jeans, a light blue oxford shirt with the farm's logo embroidered over the pocket, and a warm, easy smile.

Sonia had already explained the reason for her visit in an earlier phone call and was glad when she found Racine cooperative and comfortable answering all of her questions. Unfortunately, as Racine walked her around the most central part of the farm, he was unable to give her much in the way of significant new information about Mariana's whereabouts.

As they turned the corner of the main barn, Sonia saw a large man with bushy, red hair, much in need of a haircut, forty or forty-five years old. He was wearing what every worker wore on horse farms that time of year, a long-sleeved T-shirt, jeans, and work boots. She nudged Racine. "Who's that?"

"Oh, that's Limey. He says he comes from some kind of royal bloodline back in England, but that's probably a bunch of bull."

"Big man."

"Yeah, he's big alright. He's got to be close to six-seven." Racine clapped some dust and dirt off his hands. "Sometimes, when we need something done that would usually require a small forklift, we just call for Limey. Look at the size of those hands. I swear he can pick up a bale of hay in each hand and toss them onto a truck without even breaking a sweat."

Sonia tried to imagine what it would be like to have that man angry with you. "Scary."

"Limey? No. He's a gentle soul. I've never seen him get into a dust-up with any other guy. In fact, I think it's the women that get most of his attention."

Sonia looked up at Racine, squinting into the sun behind him, shading her eyes with her hand. "Does he give them problems?"

Racine smiled. They started walking again. "No, no. He's no stalker or anything. It's just that sometimes I see him watch a woman walk by; his attention to his task most definitely flags. It's like he hits the PAUSE button for a moment. But then he's right back to work."

Sonia tried to absorb the man—his size, his presence. "So, did you ever see him talking to Mariana?"

"Of course." Racine put his hand on Sonia's shoulder, gently moving her in a new direction. "First, they both work here. She was all the time asking him to do this or that for one of the horses. Second, they're friends. I've seen them sitting outside at lunchtime just talking, shooting the breeze, laughing. They're both quiet people, nice people." He looked down at her and smiled. "Now, they were no kind of couple. He's too old for her and she's, well, too good looking for him. But they made a nice pair . . . as friends."

Sonia and Racine walked along the center aisle of the barn, past empty stalls, the smell and essence of the great animals surrounding them nonetheless. They stepped out again into the bright chill. Sonia stopped and looked around the farm. "So, what exactly were Mariana's responsibilities on the farm?"

Racine's smile was warm, and tiny lines crinkled around his eyes. "I'm telling you one thing. We're very lucky to have the right ownership on this farm." He began walking again. "You see, most farms wouldn't invest the money necessary to keep someone with Mariana's background on the payroll. But George Masson, he's the owner here, he has a real sense of the value of someone who understands the true science of breeding . . . not just the history of husbandry in the development of great Thoroughbreds, but the actual science, on a molecular level." He nodded to one of the farm hands as she walked by leading a beautiful mare. "And that's not all. Mariana's scientific background is incredibly useful in improving our disease prevention protocols." He took a deep breath. "And the whole industry has had some challenges in that area lately."

Sonia stopped their progress once again. "So, having someone like her on staff is actually kind of unusual?"

Racine grinned. "Yup. I've got to hand it to Masson. He's kind of on the cutting edge of trying to take breeding to a whole new level."

The conversation fell into a lull as they began walking yet again. Eventually, Sonia posed a few more questions about the folks Mariana worked with, if Racine thought she might have a reason to leave town, or if he could think of anyone who might want to harm her. None of Racine's answers gave Sonia much more to go on. She thanked him for his time, headed for her car, then drove slowly off the property. It was a pleasant day for early spring but there was a darkness to the image Sonia brought with her—the image of the large, powerful man they had left on the other side of the barn.

7

J ust before one o'clock Tuesday afternoon, Sonia and Jet met in the parking lot outside of Magee's. They got into Jet's Camry, turned right out of the parking lot, and made another quick right, heading down Ashland Ave. They turned left onto Euclid and were lucky enough to catch a metered parking spot right in front of Papi's.

Together, they stepped through the door and up the stairs to Papi's Mexican restaurant. It was everything Sonia had imagined. Directly in front of her, she saw a short bar with stools and a few tall bar tables. To their left was the cozy main room. From where they stood, Sonia could just barely make out the party room at the back of the restaurant.

Sonia watched as Jet was greeted by the hostess, clearly someone who recognized her as a regular. *"Buenos días,"* Jet started, very upbeat.

"Buenos días," the hostess replied.

"Cómo estás?" A bit of pride flashed across Jet's face.

"Bien, gracias. Dos?" the hostess asked, clearly aware of Jet's desire to use as much of her limited Spanish as possible—and lifting two fingers just in case.

"*Sí, dos.*"

Sonia enjoyed watching Jet strut her Spanish stuff, what little of it there was, but she was more interested in learning something else. As the hostess led the way and Jet followed, Sonia tapped Jet on the shoulder. "Ask her if Paco Castillo is working today."

Jet asked, in English, and when the hostess replied that he was, Sonia told the hostess she hoped they could be seated in his section.

It was only a matter of moments before Paco Castillo showed up at their table. "Ms. Sonia, how nice to see you. And this must be Ms. Jet. Can I get you something to drink?"

Jet smiled in acknowledgement. "Nice to meet you. *Dos margaritas, por favor.*"

While they waited for their drinks to come, Sonia asked Jet, "So, what's good for lunch?""Everything," she said enthusiastically. "This is my favorite Mexican restaurant." Jet smiled and turned her attention to the menu.

Sonia's eyes roamed the room—white walls, dark ceiling beams, colorful tables and chairs, festive lights hung throughout the room, beautiful framed pictures on the wall. Before she knew it, Paco was back with their margaritas, extra-large glasses rimmed with coarse salt. "And what can I get for you to eat today?"

Without even asking Sonia, Jet jumped in. "*Dos chimichangas, con carne, a la carta por favor.*" She turned to Sonia. "Beef chimichangas à la carte."

Paco smiled directly at Jet. "*Bien. En seguida*, right away." He turned and was gone.

Jet took a long sip of her drink. "So, tell me about your morning."

Sonia told Jet about her time at Downstream Farm, how beautiful it was and yet how frustrating. "It's like she just vanished into thin air. Everybody seemed to like her—a lot. She was great with the horses and really knew what she was doing. But no one had any idea about what might have happened to her." Sonia took a sip of her drink, the salt and the tartness drawing her lips inward. "What about you? How did your meeting go this morning? Who was it with again?"

Jet shook her head slowly back and forth. *"Bur-nett Saun-ders."* She'd said the name one syllable at a time and with a certain amount of disdain. "I called both of those accounting firms yesterday and asked them about using one of their folks to do some forensic accounting for us. The first firm I called said they didn't work that way, but the second one said they'd be glad to send someone over this morning to discuss the project. Having met the guy, I think they were just trying to get him out of the office."

Sonia smiled, intrigued. "Why? Is there something wrong with him?"

Jet snorted. "Nothing a time machine couldn't help."

Sonia took another sip. Damn these are good. "What do you mean?"

Jet squeezed her shoulders together, making herself strangely thinner. "Tall, lanky." She released her shoulders. "Wearing a suit two sizes too big, one that his father must have bought in the 1950s. Honest to God, he was wearing a bowtie."

"No." Sonia's eyebrows were raised.

"Honest to God." Jet tugged at the ends of an invisible accessory. "Bowtie. And not one of those smaller ones the cool guys wear today. It was huge. Everything but the plastic pen protector." She rubbed her chin. "Although he might have had that hidden in his suit jacket."

Sonia took her next sip, a long one. "An older man?"

"No. He's our age. Well, maybe more like Brad's. But maybe not even forty."

Sonia smiled. "Now you've got me imagining all kinds of things."

Jet sat back in her chair. "I don't blame you. But honestly, if you just looked at the guy, the man inside the ridiculous suit, he really wasn't bad looking. In fact," she seemed to come to a new realization, "he was kind of good looking—nice smile, attractive hazel eyes." She took a tiny sip of her drink. "It's just . . . it's just almost impossible to look past the other stuff."

Sonia leaned in to take yet another sip of her margarita and realized it was almost gone. She sneaked a quick peek at Jet's, only to find that Jet had barely made a dent in hers. *Man, I've got to slow down.* "So, besides being funny looking, what's this Bernard like?"

"No, Burnett." Jet scrunched her face. "Burnett Saunders. I could swear he comes from old Lexington money, like he lives in one of those huge houses on Richmond Road, with the big lawns and the stone fronts. And stiff? He's stiff as a dog's tail." Jet leaned in and took another quick sip of her margarita. "Probably smart as a whip though. I'm guessing if you put him on the trail of a financial impropriety, he could sniff it out quicker than a hound dog following one of those portable barbeque smokers they pull around."

Sonia rolled her eyes, and before she could continue the conversation, Paco arrived with the meals. He laid them in front of the women and asked, *"Algo más?* Anything else?"

"Uno más margarita," Jet was quick to say, nodding her head toward Sonia. "I'm driving."

"Otra margarita más, verdad," Paco corrected gently, then he smiled and walked quickly away.

Sonia took a quick silent breath. *This is not going to end well.* "So, do you think this is our guy?"

Jet poked her straw around in her drink. "Oh yeah, this is our guy. Or would be if I didn't have a reputation to uphold."

"Why? Sounds like he'll do exactly what we need him to do."

"That's not what I mean." Jet stroked her long blonde pony-tail, pulling it down over her right shoulder. "What I'm trying to say is that I can't be seen having meetings with a guy straight out of the 1950s. Hell, people will think it's something right out of the *X-files*." She wiggled quotation marks in the air with her fingers. "Beautiful woman from new millennium has lunch with 1950's accountant, bears child seventy-five years old."

Sonia's smile was getting broader and broader. Her eyes were slightly watery. "Oh, so you're thinking of sleeping with this guy?" Sonia seemed unaware of the very slight slurring of her words and the fact that the volume of her voice had slipped up a notch.

The second drink arrived just as Jet was explaining further how she had a reputation in town. She would probably never be asked out by another normal human being if she was seen in public with Burnett Saunders.

"And when was the last time you were asked out by a normal human being?" Sonia was surprised to find she had apparently lost any ability to filter her thoughts before they came stumbling out of her mouth.

"Well, there was Robbie Alvarez, wasn't there?"

"Ohhh. Now that you mention it, you never gave me the full, I mean *complete*, rundown on what happened with you and him."

"And I'm not going to." Jet's tone was quick and sharp. She softened and smiled demurely. "Some things a lady just doesn't share."

"Yeah, right." Sonia wondered if someone had turned up the heat in the room.

Sonia and Jet began eating, and by the time Paco returned with the check, Sonia and Jet had finished off two chimichangas, along with three margaritas, and were thoroughly enjoying themselves. Before they left, however, Sonia was able to pull herself together enough to tell Paco that they were working hard on his case and doing their very best to locate his daughter as quickly as possible.

"In fact," Sonia said, trying to act as professional as she could, "I was out at Downstream Farm this morning asking lots of questions, just trying to get a feel for how things were going for her out there. I don't know that I learned anything that will help me find her, but you'll be glad to know that everyone out there liked her. They're all praying that she's okay."

Paco Castillo stood at the table, between both women. He looked back and forth from one to the other. "Thank you so, so much, Ms. Sonia, Ms. Jet. We, the whole family, we're so grateful. Please, let me know if there is anything I can do to help—anything."

Sonia reached out and took his hand. "Actually, I'd appreciate it if you would stop by and bring me a photograph of Mariana. I just feel like it might help us, I don't know, get more in touch with her." She had spoken to Paco earlier on the phone, filling out a demographic intake form with Mariana's address, phone number, type of car, list of friends, and so forth. Still, she felt the need to become more aware of Mariana the person.

Paco's hand swept around the room. "Everyone here knows her. You could talk to anyone. Wait," He shook his finger. "Gabriela. You should talk to Gabriela."

"And who's that?" asked Jet.

"Gabriela is Mariana's cousin. They're *muy unidas*, very close."

Sonia had her phone out and was putting the girl's name in her notes. "And how old is this cousin?"

"A little older than Mariana. Twenty-eight or twenty-nine, I think. But still, they're very close. You should talk to her."

"She's not here now, is she?" asked Jet, putting aside the light spirit of the lunch and getting down to business.

"No, but she works here on the weekends. I could get you her phone number. You can call her."

Sonia stood up, ready to go. "You do that Paco. You get us her number and we'll be sure to get in touch with her as soon as possible."

"*Gracias, gracias*, thank you." In a moment, he was off to another table.

Sonia stood. Jet stood as well, looking down at the check. "Sonia, what about this check?"

"Hey, it's your favorite lunch spot. This one's on you." Her smile made obvious the pleasure she derived from having such a dear and close friend—one you could stick with the check. She was glad, as well, that the business arrangement she had worked out with Brad was not going to put that in jeopardy. That thought, however, led her to wonder what kind of jeopardy Mariana Castillo was in at that very moment.

8

Around ten the next morning, Sonia entered the BCI offices, croissant and coffee in hand. She could see that Jet was already at her desk. "Morning sunshine."

"And a hearty good morning to you, Ms. Vitale. How they hangin'?"

Sonia shook her head broadly. "They're hangin' just fine. Have you been able to reach that Gabriela yet?" She walked into Jet's office and took a seat in the red chair.

Jet leaned back in her swivel chair, stretching her arms above her head. "No. I've been sitting at this desk since eight o'clock this morning. I've tried several times, but no luck. I've left several messages, but . . . ." She shrugged. "What's that you've got in your hand?"

"Exactly what do you think I have? Ten o'clock. Stopped in Magee's. Saw Hildy. Walked out with an edible object and a cup of hot liquid. Any other questions? Or was that just a sly way of saying you'd like half of my morning treat?"

"Ah, my precious," said Jet in a distorted voice. "She sees the evil in our question. We must better hide our intentions next time."

Sonia was surprised by the tone of voice. She knew it was supposed to be one of the characters from those "Ring" movies, though she couldn't name him. "Okay, whatever-your-name-is. I give up. You are most certainly welcome to share my morning treasure. Would you like me to go downstairs and get you a fresh cup of coffee?"

"No," Jet scrunched her face, "we have our own vessel filled with hot, steaming brew."

Sonia pushed a wisp of hair out of her face with the back of her hand. Damn, she's got that voice down. Scary. She tore the croissant in two and laid half of it on a clean piece of paper sitting on the edge of Jet's desk. Hoping the slimy evil creature was no longer inhabiting her dearest friend, she asked, "What or who got you in here so early today?"

"Before I answer that," Jet picked up a manila envelope, "here, this is for you."

Sonia took the envelope. She opened it and pulled out a five by ten photograph of an attractive, dark-haired, dark-eyed, young woman. Sonia looked at Jet, "Mariana Castillo?"

"Yeah. Her father dropped it by early this morning." Her voice was subdued.

A darkness slid over Sonia as she ran her fingertips gently across the image. Where are you, young lady? What has happened to you? She put the photo down.

Jet took a bite of the croissant and flicked some of the flaky crust off her fingertips. "By the way, have we gotten any information on Mariana's car?"

Sonia twisted her lips in frustration. "Not a thing."

"Too bad Detective Sergeant Adams left town after the Hensley case got wrapped up. I'll bet he would have been willing to do some digging for us, maybe have somebody looking for it out of state or something."

Sonia chuckled. "Listen. I'm pretty certain I know a former Marine who still has NCIS connections that can find out that kind of information for us. I might just have to spend an evening with him soon. You know, just to worm some information out of him." A warm smile of anticipation slid across her face.

Jet returned her knowing smile then shifted gears. "Now, as for who got me in here so early. Who else? That damn Burnett Saunders. Son-of-a-bitch called my cell at six-thirty this morning. Said he would have called when he got to work at six, but he didn't want to disturb me too early." She popped another small piece of croissant into her mouth.

"Yikes."

"Yikes, is right. I barely knew who I was talking to, or should I say, to whom I was speaking, for the first five minutes."

Sonia carefully removed the lid from her coffee. "And what did ol' Burnett want at six thirty in the morning."

"He was just ready to get started on the Brownlee case. I had to tell him I hadn't even gotten a confirmation from Brownlee indicating that it was okay to bring on a forensic accountant."

Sonia took an almost non-existent sip from her extremely hot coffee. "How'd he react?"

"Silent. Just silent. I'm telling you, this guy is as stiff as a board."

Sonia waved her hand. "Don't worry about it. I'm sure that Brownlee understands we need the accounting help. Mr. Saunders will get his permission to move forward in a day or so."

Jet picked up her University of Kentucky coffee cup, one with a bold, blue UK image. Looking into it, she found nothing but a quarter inch of brown liquid. Her lips pouted in response before she continued. "And that wasn't the only weird thing. You should've heard him when I said that you would be the one who would be working with him. Hell, it was the first time I got a rise out of him about anything."

Sonia blew on her coffee, trying to cool it. "What do you mean?"

Jet reached down and plucked her battered, old, red thermos

off the floor. "I told him, since this was both an accounting issue and a technology thing, he would mostly be working with you." She poured some warm coffee into her cup. "You're our technology person, and you and he would take apart the computer files to see if the young hotshot, a guy named Michael Oakley, is screwing Brownlee."

"And?" Sonia was only mildly interested.

Jet took a quick sip and her voice perked up. "And he starts coming up with one cockamamie excuse after the other as to why he has to work with both of us."

"Like?"

"Oh, I don't know." Jet looked at Sonia with disbelief on her face. "Like three is a prime number, and when people work in groups of three they solve problems better." She ran her ponytail through her hands. "It's all a bunch of crap."

Sonia decided her coffee was still too hot and put it down. "So, what did you say?" Jet put her elbows on her desk and interlocked her fingers. "Look, I think we need this guy. As strange as he is, I bet he's a real whiz at this stuff. So," she shrugged, "I just told him we'd all work together as much as he'd like, as long as I wasn't needed somewhere else." Her hands opened up. "Heck, it probably is true that three brains are better than two, especially if one of them keeps running off at lunchtime and getting wasted on margaritas." A mischievous smile crept across Jet's face.

"Whoa." Sonia's hand went up. "Wait a minute. That was *your* doing. I never ordered that second margarita. Hell, I never ordered the first one."

Jet's eyes rose to the ceiling. "Funny how it's always somebody else's fault." She shook her head broadly. "How sad, how sad."

Sonia raised her hand again then gave it a twist. It was a move she'd seen her Italian uncle use when he was upset. It wasn't meant to be a compliment. Just then, Sonia heard the exterior door to the BCI offices open. She turned and looked back over her shoulder.

Along with a beam of sunshine, a youngish woman in jeans and a bright pink spring jacket entered the space. She was thin and wore the kind of running shoes you don't really run in. Brown-eyed, with a long face, her blonde hair looked tired, as did she. She carried a mother-sized purse, large enough to carry a juice box and a zip-lock bag of Cheerios without a bit of trouble. Inside the jacket, she wore a thin, white top. She stood at the back of the room looking lost and fragile—weary. Sonia turned further in her chair. That's how so many people look when they enter our office, either lost and fragile—or pissed as hell.

"Can we help you?" Jet called out, rising to her feet, still standing behind her desk.

"Is this the office of Bluegrass Private Investigations?"

"Close enough," said Jet. "Come in."

The woman walked across the waiting room and stepped into Jet's office.

Sonia stood and extended her hand. "Hi. I'm Sonia Vitale."

Jet followed suit. "And everyone calls me Jet."

The woman looked around the room, clearly uncomfortable. Her voice was tentative. "Hi. My name is Mandy Petropoulos. I need to speak to someone. It's about my husband."

"I'll bet it is." The look on Jet's face was one of muted disgust.

Sonia gave Jet a quick look, then turned back to Mandy. "Is he okay?"

"I guess you'd have to ask him that."

Sonia figured that Mandy must have been quite attractive just a few years ago and could still be if she weren't so exhausted. Exhausted and sad. Neither Jet nor Sonia said anything.

Mandy seemed to brace herself. "You see. I think he's cheating on me."

"Now," Jet's eyes lit up, "that's right up our alley, sweetheart."

Almost immediately, Sonia picked up her coffee and took Mandy by the elbow. "Yes, we do that kind of thing, but I'm afraid that Jet, here, has to make some phone calls about another case. Why don't you come into my office so we can talk?"

As Sonia led Mandy to her office, she looked back over her shoulder and saw frustration on Jet's face. She'd learned, however, that it was often better for her to get the details about a cheating husband. Jet, she knew, could get personally involved so quickly that sometimes the clients got the wrong impression—the impression that the fine ladies of BCI were more interested in assassinating a cheating spouse than simply proving that they had strayed.

Sonia sat at her desk and directed Mandy to the seat in front of it. She watched Mandy's eyes search the tiny room, eventually falling on the pictures of Sonia and Jet at the firing range.

"You ladies, you're serious about your work, aren't you?"

Sonia smiled. "No need to worry. We rarely go beyond taking a picture or two in this kind of work. Now, tell me what's going on."

Mandy leaned forward, clutching her purse on her lap as she started. "Well, my real name, my maiden name, is Hamilton. I'm Mandy Hamilton Petropoulos."

"So, you married a Greek guy?"

"Right, Nick Petropoulos. His real name is Nicos, but everyone calls him Nick."

Sonia leaned back in her chair. "I grew up Italian myself." She smiled. "So, tell me about your husband."

Mandy took a short breath. "Well, his father, Vasilios Petropoulos, owns a roller-skating rink. Not Champs, the other one, The Wildcat Roller-Skating Emporium, out on North Broadway."

Sonia had never been to The Wildcat, as the kids referred to it, but over the course of the past two years, private investigation work had led her through almost every part of town. "And how long have you been married?"

Mandy absentmindedly rolled her wedding ring back and forth on her finger. "Six years. We've been married six years."

"Kids?"

Mandy looked up. "Two. Two boys. Five and three." A weak smile crossed her face.

Sonia's face reflected the small smile. "You started your family right away?"

Mandy's eyes dropped once again. "Yeah, I guess."

Sonia worked hard to keep her voice level. "And your husband, what does he do?"

Mandy looked up. "That's the thing. Two years ago, Nick's father retired to Florida. He left Nick in charge of the skating rink. Of course, he works mostly at night."

Sonia took a sip of her now somewhat-drinkable coffee. "And you? Do you work?"

"I do. I started out at UK studying accounting. I dropped out of school to marry Nick when I found out I was . . ." she took a quick breath, "I was pregnant. But I know enough to handle the books at the rink. I do the accounting, order the soft drinks and popcorn, all the concession stuff. Sometimes I work the birthday parties and things like that."

"And you and Nick are on opposite shifts?"

"Yes."

Sonia leaned forward in her chair. "That's tough, isn't it? Not seeing each other much?" She felt like she was already getting a pretty good idea of what was going on.

"Yeah, I guess. It's just that Nick says that's how it has to be for now. The business isn't doing well enough for me to stay home, or for him to hire someone to run the place at night."

"So, Nick stays home with the little one during the day while the other boy is at school?" Sonia's voice reflected her growing sense that she could probably fill in all the blanks.

"Yeah, until about four. Then I come home and he goes off to the rink."

"It doesn't seem like that leaves a lot of time for him to get involved with someone else. Is it someone at work?"

Mandy's eyes roamed around the room, looking for a place to land. "Well, kind of."

Sonia started to take another sip, then paused. She waited for Mandy to continue.

"You see, there's this sorority, at the university, and they're having this semester-long fund-raising event every Tuesday night. It's for a good cause, something about kids with a certain kind of cancer." Mandy almost huffed. "Lately, it seems like when he comes home from work every Tuesday night all he wants to do is go to sleep."

The words struck Sonia as both expected and surprising. "Well, it's late, isn't it? He works late hours, doesn't he?"

Mandy squirmed in her chair—just barely, but Sonia noticed it. "You don't know Nick."

"What does that mean?"

"Well," Mandy leaned closer to Sonia, as if being close would make her explanation more credible. "I think Nick always thought being a man meant certain things. His father was a real ladies man, a womanizer actually. And Nick thought it was his destiny to be just like that. He's got a voracious appetite." She lightened up a bit. "And I don't just mean for baklava. Every night." She shook her head. "Just every night. Honestly, it's exhausting."

Sonia leaned away again and began tapping on the arms of her chair with her fingertips. "Whoa."

"Yeah, whoa." Mandy's eyes dropped to her purse. "But now it's not every night." Sonia sensed a trace of anger in Mandy's voice. "It's every night except Tuesdays. Now, on Tuesdays," Mandy's voice became more sarcastic, "it's, 'I don't know honey, I'm beat. I'll take care of you tomorrow, okay?' " She shook her head. "Honestly, I'm glad for the break."

Sonia paused, wondering what that must be like, to feel that way about your husband. She plowed on. "But you're wondering why, after all these years, Tuesday's are a no-go, right?"

Mandy sat up straighter in her chair. "Actually, it's not so much that I'm wondering. More like I want to prove it. I don't think there's any question that he's getting it on with one of those sorority girls—maybe more than one."

Sonia sat up taller as well, matching Mandy's posture. "Well, I hate to say it, but that's something we do all the time; we prove that someone is cheating. What else can you tell us?"

"Not much I'm afraid." She was more businesslike. "All I know is that it's every Tuesday, like clockwork, and that it's never happened before in six years of marriage."

Sonia and Mandy finished their conversation, coming to terms on a fee and a timeline for finishing the case. A few minutes later, Sonia watched as Mandy stood and walked out of the BCI offices, her running shoes creating not a sound, her face casting a sad and silent smile in Jet's direction.

As soon as Mandy was gone, Jet walked into Sonia's office, apparently eager to find out about another slimebag husband. "Well?"

"Well," Sonia said, unenthusiastically, "looks like we've got ourselves another case."

9

After their unexpected visit from Mandy Petropoulos, Sonia and Jet each worked in their own offices for about an hour. Jet was squaring away arrangements with Steven Brownlee as regarded bringing on Burnett Saunders to do forensic accounting work with them. Sonia was trying, via numerous social media sites, to find out everything she could about Mariana Castillo.

A little before twelve, Sonia knocked on the window to Jet's office and spoke to her through the glass. "C'mon. We've got a one o'clock appointment out at Mayweather, and we need to get some lunch first."

Jet stood and walked out of her office, toward Sonia's. "Hey, I think they've cooked up some new kind of sandwich downstairs, a Philly cheesesteak or something. Want to get one before we go?"

Sonia nodded. "Sure." They walked out of the BCI offices, down the steps, and into Magee's.

Magee's was pretty full, a good-sized lunch crowd lining up for the combination of breakfast and lunch meals that were available until the place closed at two each afternoon. Sonia didn't mind waiting; this place was a second home to her. She spent her time looking around at the people and at the delicious pastries that were on display.

After they'd ordered, Jet asked, "So, what did you find out about Mariana?"

"Not a whole lot." Her eyes had locked on a cherry-cheese Danish, though she knew she wouldn't get it. "I looked on every site I could, but there are two problems." She turned to Jet. "First, Mariana is a rather private person. There's a very limited amount of her life that's available to the public via social media. Second, she's one hard-working young lady. Seems to me all the girl has time for is work. I've only been able to identify two current friends and neither one could tell me anything useful. In fact, they say she barely has time for them. I saw a few postings about her being at work by five-thirty in the morning or working twelve-hour days. It doesn't appear that she has a lot of energy left for her social life. I did notice, though, that she was involved in some sort of project that she hoped continued to go 'so well.' "

"What kind of project?"

"I don't know." Sonia shrugged. "She didn't say. I don't know if that's because it's particularly private or just because that's who she is."

It only took a few minutes for the girls to finish their Philly cheesesteak lunches, sitting across from each other at one of the long, high tables that had recently been added to Magee's interior. Neither did they have time to linger over the cold drinks they had gotten. By twelve-thirty-five, they had gotten into Sonia's red Subaru, turned left out of the parking lot, and headed all the way through town on Main Street. They passed the old Lexington Cemetery, final resting place of the famous statesman, Henry Clay, and left town behind.

As they drove through the rolling hills of Central Kentucky, toward the small hamlet of Midway, Jet kept her eyes focused straight ahead. "So how are things with you and Brad?"

A satisfied smile crossed Sonia's face and she glanced

momentarily at Jet. "Great. He and I get together most nights. We eat dinner, maybe watch a movie or something. A couple of times we've just taken long walks through my neighborhood. It's nice."

Jet turned. "Sonia, I'm not asking what y'all do together. I want to know. How are things going with Brad? C'mon. Spill."

Sonia was quiet for a moment. Then she spoke softly, carefully, her eyes on the road. "Well, they're okay."

"But?" Jet's eyebrows reached for her hairline.

Sonia let out a small sigh. "I don't know. I just can't tell how serious he is about things. He just seems content to be where we are right now."

Jet huffed. "Really? After that big display he made the other night, when all the shooting stopped, holding you and giving you a big Rhett Butler kiss right in front of God and everybody?" She glanced over at Sonia. "Look, I know you all haven't been together for a long time. But geez, the time you've been together has been intense, really intense. Hasn't it?"

Sonia's head bobbed. "You can say that again." Her voice began to rise. "The night on that side street in Rocky Top. The car chase on the way back from Memphis. The gunfight. The night in the autopsy room." She brushed a wisp of hair from her face. "Dang. We've lived a lifetime in the last few weeks. And I know he feels that, too."

Jet stroked her long blonde ponytail with both hands, pulling it over her shoulder and tipping her head down to the right for a moment. "And after all that he doesn't want to talk about the future? What's that all about?"

Sonia paused a moment before speaking. "Well, don't forget. He's had some tough things happen to him in the past." She checked her mirrors. "I know it must be hard for him to actually commit to a future with someone."

The car was silent as the miles and minutes ticked by. As they were approaching Midway, the farm fields and the six-foot-tall rolls of freshly cut hay giving way to the beginnings of the town,

Jet finally spoke. "Now, you listen. You've been hurt, too. That bastard, John Eckel, left you standing at the altar. But you're ready to move on. Don't you let Brad keep you from moving on to better things."

Sonia let out a deep sigh. "Yeah." A moment later, Sonia sat up taller in her seat. "Is this it? Is this where we turn?"

Jet pointed. "Yup. Up that road, right there."

Sonia followed the signs to Mayweather College, just outside of the town proper, and found a parking spot in the lot next to the Equine Sciences building. "This is it." She looked around, taking in the view of the campus. It was a beautiful, quaint, old school. Not a large university campus, a small college.

Jet asked, "So who are we meeting with?"

Sonia pulled her phone out of her purse and checked her notes. "Professor Spencer Andersen. He's the head of the Equine Studies department." She slipped her phone back into her purse. "It's a big deal program and he's the big deal guy. Their equine research major is highly respected. And who do you think is the leading researcher in that department?"

Jet was still taking in the campus. "I'm guessing it's Professor Andersen."

"And you would be correct."

They stepped out of Sonia's car and into the early spring sunshine. They walked toward a large, old, red brick building. Classic lettering on its edifice indicated it was the home of the equine program. Sonia pulled the heavy, white, eight-foot wooden door open and they stepped inside. The halls were empty at the moment, the students and faculty most likely in classes. On the half-brick, half-plaster walls hung large, glassed and framed photographs. Almost every one of the photographs contained an image of a beautiful horse, though many of them also featured images of students working with those horses or in labs.

Sonia shivered slightly. "Feels like the AC is on; it's cold in here."

"And the temperature matches the atmosphere." Jet's shoulders lifted toward her ears. "So why, again, are we meeting with this professor?"

"Really, I don't know a lot about this whole deal," Sonia said as she sought the correct office. "But I spoke to Paco Castillo again last night and he said that Mariana was all about working with the guy, like it was some kind of honor. So, I looked him up this morning, and I've got to say his credentials are pretty impressive."

They walked through the silent halls and down a broad set of stairs before they found the professor's office. Just as Sonia was about to knock, she paused.

Jet chuckled. "Go on girl. He's not *that* big of a deal. Hell, for all you know, he's in there playing video games."

Sonia gave Jet a quick look. "I doubt it." She knocked firmly.

10

"Come in." The voice was higher than Sonia had expected.

Sonia stepped in first; Jet was right behind her. Sitting at the desk directly in front of them, his back to them, the man's silver hair was sparse, longish and combed straight back. Sonia took in the white office. Bookcases filled with journals lined the walls. Boxes cluttered the tiled floor near the door. The paint on the dampish walls had peeled around the window frame.

The professor spoke without looking up from his work. "Can I help you?"

"Yes. Hi. I'm Sonia Vitale. We talked on the phone earlier today?" Her voice was strong and clear.

There was a momentary pause as the professor appeared to finish typing a thought on his computer. He spun around in his wheeled, swivel chair. A rather large man, he was wearing a wrinkled lab coat over a blue-checked shirt and khaki pants that could best be described as frumpy. His eyes were alert, his smile almost jovial. "Oh yes, I remember. The private investigators. Welcome."

He stood and shook Sonia's hand. His grip struck her as a bit limp or weak. A moment later, his gaze moved beyond Sonia. "And who is this lovely lady?"

"Jet, everyone just calls me Jet."

"Jet it is." The professor turned back to Sonia, giving her a crooked smile. "And you've come to talk to me about Mariana Castillo, correct?"

"Yes," said Sonia. "She's been missing for over two weeks. Were you aware of that?" Her voice had just the slightest touch of interrogation in it.

The professor motioned almost awkwardly for Sonia and Jet to each take a seat in one of the two wooden chairs across from his desk. He seemed to take no notice of, or at least no offense to, Sonia's tone. His own voice saddened. "Yes, I'm afraid I am. I didn't hear about it until late last week. I'm not in regular contact with Mariana, but I heard one of the other students mention it. Honestly, I don't know how she knew. It's been several years since Mariana graduated and moved on. So sad. Any idea where she is?"

"I'm afraid not." Sonia was trying to get a measure of the man as she continued with her questions. "Did you know that she was working on a horse farm here in Lexington?"

"Oh, my, yes." He sat and his smile warmed again. "I got her that job at Downstream farm. She was a bright, bright student. I wanted her to wind up in a great situation."

Sonia smiled too, trying to warm up the conversation. "I was out there yesterday talking to folks. They appeared to be very pleased with her work, and everyone seemed to really care for her."

"Not surprising." He gave them a knowing nod, though his eyes saddened again. "Bright, dedicated. A lovely girl as well. Is she married?" Sonia sensed some pride, or was it affection, in his response. She replied, "No."

"Strange." His gaze moved to Jet and back to Sonia. "Very

attractive girl. I would have thought someone would've scooped her up as soon as she got out of school."

Sonia wondered why the conversation had moved in that direction.

Jet spoke up. "So, we understand that Mariana was part of a special research project while she was here. Is that correct?"

The professor's face brightened. "My, my, yes." He rubbed his hands together. "She and several other students worked with me on a cutting-edge research project." He looked directly at Jet and smiled, his eyebrows dancing. "It was fascinating stuff."

Sonia slipped to the front edge of her chair, "What kind of research?"

Andersen opened his hands in a "what-can-I-say" gesture. "Well, there are proprietary concerns, but let's just say we were working on different ways of understanding equine disease at the cellular level." He shifted into professorial mode. "You see, contagious diseases can be devastating to the horse industry. That's especially true for sporting horses, both Thoroughbreds, the horses most people think of as racehorses, and Standardbreds, the horses that are used in harness racing.

"I don't know if you recall, but there was an outbreak of a contagious disease called nocardioform placentities here in Kentucky in 2011. It caused spontaneous abortions in pregnant mares. There was a loss of hundreds of foals due to be born that year. Since stallion owners typically collect fees only on a 'live foal' basis, or when the foal stands and nurses, millions of dollars were lost in stud fees. Every part of the industry was impacted. It was tragic. And what's really terrible is that there was another spike in the disease just last year.

"Up 'til now, much of the focus has been on diagnosis and cure of those contagious diseases. But to work on prevention, you've got to look at diseases at the cellular level. That's what we've been working on here for several years now."

Sonia and Jet sat silently, not knowing what to say.

The professor seemed to relax. "Now getting back to Mariana, why have you come to see me?" He turned rather suddenly and took a sip from a water glass filled with a thick green liquid.

Sonia assumed it was some sort of health drink. She answered. "You see, we've been asked by Mariana's family to try to locate her. We've spent the better part of two days researching Mariana's presence on social media as well as interviewing her family and friends and the folks she worked with. So far, we haven't turned up any new or relevant information. It seemed like the next logical step was to try to find out a little bit about her college connections." Andersen shrugged and gave them a little-boy smile. "As I said earlier, I can't really say much about the work we were doing. Again, proprietary information and all." He seemed almost sad about it.

Sonia ran her fingers through her hair, her foot tapping discretely. "Well, what can you tell us about her time here with you."

"Oh, dear me, Ms. Vitale," he shook his head, embarrassed. "I'm afraid you've got this all wrong. Mariana was not *with* me." He raised his shoulders sheepishly, "She was just a student in the research program and one of almost a dozen students who participated in the project at one level or another."

Sonia still wasn't satisfied. "And what about Mariana in particular. What about *her* level of involvement?"

The professor paused, his hands steepled in front of his mouth. "Well, she, along with several others, did spend quite a bit of her extra time here in the lab. They were all quite dedicated to the work we were doing."

Jet leaned forward, interjecting herself into the questioning again. "Anyone special she worked with on a regular basis? Did she have friends here?"

The professor reached into the printer on his desk and pulled out a clean piece of white paper. "I guess I could jot down a few names of students who worked on the project at the same time she did."

"Yes, that would be very helpful." Sonia glanced at Jet, looking for a cue as to any other questions she should ask. Not getting a response, she said, "Well, if you can think of anything else that might be of help . . . ."

Sonia and Jet stood to take their leave. The professor handed Jet his list of Mariana's friends, a hint of pleading in his voice. "Please let me know if you find that young lady. I'd love to be able to let anyone who remembers her know that she is," his voice trailed off, "okay."

Sonia placed a business card on his desk. "Thank you very much for your time, Professor. If you do think of something, you can reach Jet or me at one of these numbers." With that, they left the professor's office.

SONIA WAS BACK behind the wheel of her car before she spoke again. "So, what do you think?" She hadn't started the car.

"Of Professor Andersen?"

"Yeah."

"I don't know. Obviously a very bright guy. Doing important work. But," she snorted, "a bit of a wuss. Wouldn't you say?"

The rolling of her eyes was Sonia's only response. A moment later she glanced at Jet's hands, "you've got that list of her friends he gave you?"

Jet opened the folded paper. "Yup."

"How many names?"

"One, two, three, four, five, six, seven. Hmm. For a guy who doesn't pay much attention to his student's personal life, he was able to list seven students who worked with Mariana. Five girls, two boys."

Sonia nodded and started the car. "He did seem to care about her, though. Don't you think?"

"I guess." Jet glanced out the passenger-side window. "So how do you think we should proceed?"

Sonia put the car in gear and took off. "I think we make some phone calls. We track down each of those students. Let's see if they know anything."

"Right," Jet nodded. "And that would be a lot easier if we could get their phone numbers from the school's registrar, but that's not going to happen."

"Privacy, girl, privacy. But, thank goodness, we live in the twenty-first century. They're all up there somewhere on social media, and most of them are so careless with their private information we'll be able to locate them within a couple of minutes." Sonia checked her mirror. "Don't you worry. We'll find them. Believe me, we'll find them."

11

S onia and Jet had spent all day Thursday working on several of the other cases they had taken on since their success with the John Abbott Hensley affair. They were the kinds of cases that were becoming routine for Bluegrass Confidential Investigations. One was a cheating husband who worked the overnight shift at a large manufacturing plant just outside of town. While his wife worked during the day, he would share his "leisure time" with the attractive young woman who lived next door. Another case had to do with shoplifters who kept stealing makeup from a local drug store and avoiding detection. Jet had pretty much figured out that it was a group of young girls who were managing to get away with the stuff; she just had to catch them in the act.

At eight o'clock that evening, Sonia and Jet met in Magee's parking lot. Mr. Brownlee had agreed to take on the extra expense of using a forensic accountant, and it was time for them to gather some raw data from which they could determine if Michael Oakley was, in fact, mishandling the Bronson/Brownlee finances. They had already discussed the fact that if they used the direct approach, simply asking Oakley for his files, he might be able to cover his tracks. They were convinced this case would demand a more covert operation.

It was a short trip to the warehouse of Bronson/Brownlee, one block down Main, turn right on Walton. Jet pulled her car into the parking lot and the girls got out, Sonia carrying her laptop. It was after-hours, so the facility looked dark and deserted. Just as the girls were wondering how they were going to get inside, Brownlee appeared at the front door. "Welcome to my world." The near-octogenarian's green eyes were shining through his metal-framed glasses almost as much as his bald head shone in the overhead light. His brown corduroy pants and red-plaid flannel shirt hung loosely on his five-foot-ten-inch frame.

Sonia smiled as she noted his emphasis on the words "*my world.*" She had been told by Jet that he was still leading the company. Nonetheless, she was still taken by his spry, almost childlike manner. She could tell she was going to like this man.

Brownlee led the girls down the corridor to the offices of Michael Oakley, Technology Director. "It's locked," he said. "But don't worry," he winked at them with a leprechaun-like grin, "it's still my company, and I've got the key to every room, closet, and cabinet in this entire place."

Sonia had been surprised at the sheer size of the facility and was a bit shocked when she saw the number of keys on the old man's ring. She grinned silently. Almost eighty-years-old and he doesn't want to give up control. Good for him.

Brownlee led them into Oakley's office. Sonia immediately noticed that there was a continuous security feed from several cameras being displayed on monitors that were hung high on the walls. She hoped she wouldn't see anyone else appear on any of those cameras.

It wasn't hard to find the computer the Technology Director worked on. Sonia could tell it was the latest iteration of one of the high-end business machines, and it was surrounded by all kinds of monitors and peripheral equipment.

Sonia stepped over to the computer and switched it on. A few moments later she was looking at a screen indicating that the machine was, of course, password protected. Not a problem.

Ever since getting involved with Brad Dunham and his former colleagues at NCIS, Sonia had spent what little spare time she had learning computer tricks—tricks she'd never imagined learning when she was a computer science major at The Ohio State University. It was an outstanding program, but it spent its time teaching students to do things that were legal. What a shame. Now, Sonia had a few new tricks up her sleeve, and she had no compunction about using them—for the right purposes.

Earlier that day, Sonia had obtained a sophisticated program for unlocking computer passwords and copied the program onto her flash drive. She inserted the drive into Oakley's computer. Within a few minutes, she was looking at a screen which told her that she was about to change the password, "oldfool666," and asking if she wanted to continue. Sonia looked furtively at Jet, indicating that Jet should check out the current password; she was hoping Brownlee hadn't noticed it.

Writing down the password, Sonia wiped the program from the computer and ejected the flash drive. She knew she needed to eliminate any chance that Oakley would know that the computer had been hacked. She restarted the computer, used its password, and was in.

Jet put her hand on Sonia's shoulder and squeezed. "Lordy, Lordy, girl. You've become one hot computer hackin' momma. Yes, you have."

Sonia turned briefly and smiled at her. "Thanks. Now, let's see what we've got here."

It didn't take Sonia long to find the company's financial records and download them to a different, large-capacity flash drive. "That's it. Let's get out of here."

Jet made certain that everything on the desk was exactly the way they had found it and checked the security monitors several times. Steven Brownlee led them out of the room and locked the door behind them.

As they were leaving, Brownlee spoke. "Thank you. Thank you so much." The sincerity of his words was unmistakable. "I've got to tell you that I just don't have a good feeling about this. I don't want to accuse the young man unfairly. I've just got to know for sure that he's not ripping me off."

Sonia hesitated before answering; the "oldfool" at the beginning of Oakley's password had already convinced her that sweet Mr. Brownlee was going to be disappointed by the results of their investigation.

Jet stepped in. "Don't worry Mr. Brownlee. You give us a day or two and, with the help of Mr. Saunders, we'll be able to tell you exactly what's going on."

Sonia's and Jet's eyes met. Sonia could feel a heaviness in her own heart, but what she thought she read in Jet's eyes was pure anger.

12

Having a pretty good idea of what to expect, both Sonia and Jet had gotten to the BCI offices a little early on Friday. Precisely at ten o'clock, just as they had assumed, Burnett Saunders walked through the door and into their waiting area. Earlier, Sonia had gone downstairs and gotten some pastries and coffee while Jet had set up a large, white, plastic folding table; it provided enough space for the three of them to sit and work together.

"Greetings, Mr. Saunders," Jet said. "Come. Let me introduce you to my partner, Sonia Vitale."

Saunders bowed ever so slightly at the waist. "Yes, pleased to meet you, Ms. Vitale."

Sonia found him to be exactly what she had imagined, based on Jet's earlier descriptions. Tall, with neatly combed hair, round wireless glasses, and a face that was anything but unattractive, he stood near the door, ram-rod straight. It was hard for her to picture what his body was like since it was lost in the gray, pinstriped suit that was clearly too large for him. As Jet had said earlier, his clothing seemed to have been transported to this time directly from the 1950s. Sonia chuckled softly. *Maybe she's right.*

Maybe his dad bought that suit in the 50's and passed it on to his son. And that bowtie? Sonia directed Saunders to a seat at the table. "Welcome, Burnett. It's very nice to meet you. Is it alright if I call you Burnett?"

"Certainly, Mr. Saunders will do."

Sonia was perplexed.

They all sat down at the makeshift work table. Jet and Sonia began nibbling at their treats, while Saunders eschewed both the coffee and the pastries stating, "Never eat unless you're hungry." He straightened his already straight bowtie. "So, you've gotten hold of the financial files from Bronson/Brownlee?"

"Actually, we got them last night." Jet gave Sonia a little smile. "You can thank Sonia for that. They're all here on this flash drive."

"You're certain there are no viruses on your device?" Saunders' hands went absently to his bowtie. "I would not appreciate introducing a virus onto my laptop, now would I?"

Sonia was jarred a bit by his unusual verbal style. "No, the drive's clean, and I've taken the precaution of running a new virus scan on it since I downloaded the files last night. We should all be okay on that count."

"Very well." Saunders slid his hands along the outside, then inside, of his thighs, smoothing his pants. "Let's proceed to download those files onto my laptop. I'll be taking them with me to work on back at my office. I work best in my own space."

"Do you get out of your office much?" Jet asked with just a touch of sarcasm, one that Sonia picked up on immediately.

"Not often." Now it was Saunders who had a somewhat perplexed look on his face. "Although it appears that lately, my colleagues seem more and more interested in sending me out to do on-site work. I'm not sure I understand that. I do my best work in my own space."

Jet threw a look at Sonia.

Sonia had to look down in order to keep Saunders from

seeing her swallow a laugh. She quickly regained her self-control. "Well, Mr. Saunders, Jet says that you're quite the forensic accountant. Are you confident that you can tell whether or not Michael Oakley is mishandling funds at the company?"

"Oh yes, Ms. Vitale. Accounting is a science, you know, not just a discipline. Many people think of it only as a discipline; they think it's just a compilation of procedures that lead to an accurate rendering of financial truths. But they're wrong."

Sonia and Jet looked at each other, expecting that Saunders would go on. He didn't.

Finally, Jet spoke. "Wrong in what way?"

Saunders seemed taken aback by the question. "Wrong that it's just a discipline."

Again, the girls were stumped, wondering what he was talking about. Then it was Sonia's turn. "Can you tell us more?"

Burnett Saunders made two short tugs on the lapels of his jacket and straightened his already straight bowtie again. "Accounting can be so much more than a discipline. It's a science. We use the science of physics to explain how things work in the world. We use the science of mathematics to explain sophisticated relationships of shape and space and time. In the same way, we can use the science of forensic accounting to understand and explain the intricacies of human behavior as it relates to the acquisition and expenditure of financial resources. Trust me, ladies, if you want to understand, truly understand, the darkness that abides in the human soul, spend some time looking at the financial activities of humans through the microscope of forensic accounting. You'll not be pleased with what you find."

Saunders continued. "You know, the early development of accounting systems can be traced back as far as ancient cities in Mesopotamia between 450 and 500 BC. And—"

"Yes, yes," Jet shot a quick look at Sonia. "we're sure that's all true. Now about this particular case. How difficult do you think it will be to discover if Oakley has been sticking it to the old man?"

Saunders looked at the flash drive in his hand as if he could see the data stored inside. "Not difficult at all."

Sonia leaned back in her chair. "That's good to hear. How would you like to proceed?"

Saunders opened the laptop he'd brought with him. "I'll simply download those files to my computer right now and then take them back to my office. I do my best work in my own space. Then I'll be back to you on Tuesday with my report."

Jet leaned forward. "No chance it might be before that?"

Saunders inserted the flash drive and touched a few keys on his computer. "It's Friday. I do not work on the weekends. On the weekends, I do other things. I will finish my investigation on Monday and tell you the results on Tuesday."

Sonia was curious. "What if you're done early on Monday?" She wasn't that concerned about the results coming on Monday or Tuesday, but she was fascinated by Saunders' insistence that he would not deliver his results until Tuesday.

Saunders took a deep breath and let it out slowly. "Never promise more than you can deliver. I may or may not be done early on Monday, but I am confident that I can give you my results by Tuesday."

Sonia was really curious now. "But, if you are done early on Monday?"

"I will deliver my results on Tuesday." He pulled the flash drive out of his computer and handed it back to Sonia.

Sonia and Jet shared a strange look with each other. Burnett Saunders, on the other hand, was totally at peace with the discussion.

"Okay, then," said Sonia. "I'm sure you'll be running another virus check when you get back to your office."

"Yes, I do my best work in my own space."

Sonia nodded. "I'm sure." Glancing at the exterior door, Sonia continued. "Jet will walk you out, and we'll look forward to hearing from you soon."

"On Tuesday." Saunders stood, tugging on his lapels and adjusting his tie. "You'll hear from me on Tuesday."

"I'm certain of it." Sonia smiled. "Jet, would you like to show Mr. Saunders out?"

The look on Jet's face made it clear that she had no idea as to why she had to, "show Mr. Saunders out," of such a small room, but she did it anyway.

When Saunders had stepped through the doorway, Jet turned and asked, "What the hell was that all about? Show Saunders out?"

A big smile crossed Sonia's face. "You didn't see it?"

"Didn't see what?"

"Saunders. While he was pontificating about forensic science and the darkness of the human soul, you didn't notice that he never took his eyes off you?"

Jet shrugged. "He was talking to both of us."

"The words may have been relevant to both of us," Sonia's eyes were lit up with mischief, "but he was talking to you."

"Get out of here. You're crazy." Jet looked like she'd just sucked on a lemon.

Sonia was clearly enjoying this. "Oh no, oh no. *Lui ti ama.*"

"What? Don't you sneak that Italian stuff in on me. What the hell did you just say?"

"*Lui ti ama.* He loves you. He's got it bad for you. *Male, male, male*, Bad, bad, bad."

"Mr. Bowtie?"

Sonia started laughing. "Oh yes. Mr. Bowtie's got it bad for you. C'mon Jet, can't you just hear it now," her voice dropped low, " 'And now, for the very first time, let's welcome Mr. Burnett and Mrs. Jet Saunders.' "

Jet took the last remaining morsel of a delicious Magee's pecan Danish and threw it at her best friend. "Take it back. You take it back."

Then Sonia started to sing in the voice little children use. "Mr. Bowtie's got it for Je-et, Mr. Bowtie's got it for Je-et."

Jet plopped down in her chair and raised the top of her arm to her forehead. She spoke in an accent covered in white gravy. "Never, never before has the honor of this maiden been so besmirched by the likes of this dastardly wench. How is it that my reputation has been so completely defiled? How shall I ever hold my head up high as I walk through the hallowed halls of high society?"

Soon, they were both laughing so hard they could barely control themselves. Tears ran down Sonia's face. She stood and started for the door. "C'mon. Let's go downstairs. I think we both need some fresh coffee and some fresh air."

Jet got up to follow. Her accent remained deeply southern. "The time has come to face my great embarrassment. Lead on, fair maiden, and stand by me as I suffer the slings and arrows of outrageous fortune."

The laughter of the past few moments and the sunshine that landed on her as she stepped out of the offices felt wonderful to Sonia. However, as she continued down the stairs to Magee's, her spirits sank a little as well. She couldn't help but feel just a tiny bit guilty laughing and having fun with her best friend while Mariana Castillo was . . . was what?

13

Sonia's good mood had returned by the end of her workday. She had left the office around five and made the short walk down Ashland Avenue, onto Central Avenue, and up the stairs to her apartment. She was waiting for Brad to pick her up and take her to dinner. She didn't know where he was taking her . . . and he didn't know the surprise she had for him.

Punctually at six o'clock, Brad pulled up in front of her apartment in his brand-new Corvette. Sonia could just barely see the car, which was mostly hidden from her view by the house and large pin oak tree in front of her apartment. Almost skipping down the steps in jeans, a red top, and a light jacket that was white, Sonia was at the car by the time Brad had gotten out.

Brad made a "what gives?" gesture. "Why are you down here? I'm supposed to come and knock on your door. Don't you know I have a reputation as a gentleman I'm trying desperately to uphold?"

Sonia smiled broadly. "And I've got a desperate need to be swept off my feet. Who's need do you want to satisfy first?"

Kentucky blue polo.

"Fine with me, babe." He turned to the 'Vette. "So, what do you think? Pretty nice, huh?"

"Very nice."

"Good thing I had the other one insured as a business vehicle. Otherwise, I wouldn't have been able to replace it."

"Absolutely." She remembered that car—remembered the danger, the fear, the damage.

Sonia slid into the car, loving the smell of the beautiful leather, running her fingers over the silky seats and burled wood interior. "So, where are you taking me?"

Brad gave her a quick smile. "Well, I know you like to eat at Saul Good, the one downtown, across from the Opera House."

"That I do." She gave him a pleasant smile.

"I thought you might like to go there. Or we can go to a real manly-man place like Logan's and get us a great steak." He suddenly sounded like a character in one of those movies set in the hollers of Eastern Kentucky. "Maybe we could eat it good and bloody, and burp and fart while we throw peanuts at each other and drink beer."

Sonia smiled and spoke with a girlish huff. "No, Saul Good will do nicely."

It was a short trip to the restaurant and they had gotten there early enough to avoid much of a wait. The multi-level room had a cozy feel to it, a bar against the side wall and windows that looked out onto North Broadway. Sonia ordered her favorite, the Szechwan Steak Sandwich with sesame-ginger dressed spinach. Brad got his steak, a nice ten-ounce sirloin.

After a pleasant and delicious dinner, Brad asked, "Would you like to just take a walk around downtown? It's a nice evening."

Sonia stared where she loved to stare, into Brad's bright blue eyes. "That sounds great."

They walked toward the fountains of Triangle Park, right in front of the famous college basketball venue, Rupp Arena, where the storied University of Kentucky basketball team plays. Sonia looked up at Brad and said, "I've got something to tell you." She was feeling nervous.

Brad didn't seem to notice. "I've got to tell you something, too."

Sonia smiled. "Let me go first."

"Okay."

Sonia dove in. "We've been invited somewhere," she hurried on, "somewhere I hope you'd like to go."

Brad looked at her, his brow furrowed. "And where is that?"

Sonia looked straight ahead while they walked as if trying to soften her next statement. "Home. Home to my folk's place in Cincinnati." She turned back to Brad with a tentative smile. "They'd like to meet you."

There was a slight pause as Brad looked away unconsciously then turned back to her. "Great. That sounds great. When are we going to do that?"

Sonia stopped walking, turning toward him. "Well, that's the thing." She took a short breath and spoke quickly. "My cousin is getting married in California in two weeks. Her parents are throwing an informal party for her this weekend. They'd love for us to come up tomorrow. It'd be a great chance for you to meet the whole family and for them to meet you." She reached out and put her hand on Brad's forearm. "What do you think?"

Brad was silent. He looked off into the distance then turned his face to hers. "Listen, babe. That sounds great."

The tone of his voice told Sonia that what was about to follow was going to disappoint her. She pursed her lips.

"It's just that there's the thing that I had to tell you." He turned his body toward her. "You see, I just got a second call from that former client up east. He's having problems, and he needs me on the first plane tomorrow morning. I leave at 6:00 AM and I'll be gone for at least a week."

Sonia's heart skipped a beat. "Really? You have to leave tomorrow? Saturday?"

"Yeah, tomorrow. He says he needs me up there right away."

"Where? Where do you have to go?"

"Massachusetts. Boston."

Sonia turned her head and looked away. "Oh."

"Listen, babe." Her hand was still on his forearm; he laid his hand over hers. "I'm so sorry. I would love to go meet your family. But this is a big client and I really have to do what he asks. We can go up some other time. Sometime soon. I'd love to meet your parents."

Sonia spoke very slowly and softly, still avoiding his face. "And what kind of trouble is he in?"

"Honestly," Brad raised his shoulders, "I don't know. He said he would tell me all about it when I got there. I'm just going to have to trust that there's something I can do to help this guy."

"I see." She released his forearm, turned and started walking again. Brad stepped quickly to keep up.

They were both silent as they walked through the park, crossed Main Street and went up one more block. Right across the street was a Roman Catholic church. It being Friday evening in the spring, it wasn't surprising that they saw a group of young men and women standing outside the church, clearly part of a wedding party that would be using the church the next day.

Somehow, seeing the wedding party standing on the steps of the church, joyful and excited, Sonia was quietly rattled. It wasn't long before memories stirred in her mind and tears started to form in her eyes. Try as she might, Sonia wasn't able to stop one or two from running down her face.

Brad noticed. He stopped her and turned her toward him. "Babe. What's wrong? What's the matter?"

"Nothing. It's nothing. I guess the wind is just making my eyes water. That's all."

"I don't think so." He gently brushed a tear from her cheek

with his thumb. "Tell me, babe. Is it because I have to go up north?"

"No. That's fine." Sonia brushed that wisp of hair out of her face. "I understand. It was last minute after all. I can't expect you to just drop everything and change your plans for me." She stood still, looking at him. *Why? Why can't I be more honest with him? Why am I holding back what I really want to say?*

"Babe, this is business. I told you. I'd love to go meet your folks." He was holding her hands now. "And I would gladly drop everything and change my plans if I could. But this is work. I just have to go help this guy."

"I understand. I really do." There was silence between them for a few moments, then Sonia slipped her hands out of his. "Maybe we can just go home now. Would that be alright with you? I'm kind of tired, and I know you have to get up early in the morning if you're going to make that flight at six in the morning."

"Are you sure?" Brad put his hands on her shoulders. "At least let me come in for a little while and just be with you."

"No. You need your time to get ready for your trip." She forced a smile to appear on her face. "Just take me home and drop me off. We can talk on the phone tomorrow if you'd like."

They were both silent again as they walked back to Brad's car. When they got to her place, she leaned over and gave Brad a kiss. It was nice, but the passion that usually accompanied their kissing was definitely missing. As she walked up the stairs to her apartment, Sonia knew that Brad would be wondering why she'd had such a dramatic response to his being unable to join her on the trip to her parents. She shook her head. *He must think I'm crazy. I get it. He has to work. But seeing that wedding party standing on the steps of the church . . . . Is there a bride who's going to be standing at the front of that church tomorrow wondering why the man she's about to give her life to hasn't shown up? Will she cry into her father's chest, with her knees shaking, unable to breathe? Will her whole world come tumbling* down around her? Will she feel betrayed? Will she feel worthless? Will she feel like I felt when John Eckel left me at the altar?

By then Sonia was in her apartment, lying on her bed, still dressed in all her clothing, including her light spring jacket. The tears had been squelched. The pain had not.

14

S onia awakened on Saturday, the taste of disappointment still in her mouth. She sat at her tiny kitchen table drinking coffee and thinking. It's okay. It's work. I get that. Still, if he'd just pushed the flight back a few hours I could have dropped him off at the airport in Cincinnati and he would have at least been able to meet my family. I would have been glad to go pick him up when he got back.

She sighed, trying to accept the situation but unable to separate the current episode from past disappointments. She stood up, pushing back her chair. "That's just how it goes. I'll just get myself up there and enjoy my family without him. I don't need him for that."

Around one o'clock, Sonia got herself together and drove north on I-75, to Cincinnati. When she arrived at her parent's home, a small, two-story brick building almost identical to the ones on its left and right, thoughts of Brad not being with her were supplanted by a warm sense of being home. She parked on the street and walked up the few concrete steps to the front porch. In no time, it was hugs, kisses and smiles. Sonia enjoyed it all, even bending down to kiss her elderly Italian great-aunt, who stood only four-foot, ten inches tall. Her perfume smelled like something from Walgreens and her breath smelled heavily of garlic.

When they all sat down to an early dinner, Sonia was surprised at how much the meal she was about to eat was lifting her spirits. It was the classic Italian meal she'd enjoyed so many Sundays on visits to her grandmother's home. It started with antipasto, the appetizers before the *pasto*, before the meal. There were olives, anchovies, sliced sausage, peppers, artichoke hearts; it was the real deal. Then came the lasagna, which for most Americans would have been the main dish. But not at this meal. After the pasta dish came the chicken with cooked carrots. The meal ended with cold cheeses, fruit and, finally, Italian pastries. Throughout the dinner, the room was filled with laughter and rendition after rendition of "*salute*" and "*alla famiglia,*" as everyone drank ample amounts of wine and teased each other about who would be the first one asleep in an armchair after the meal.

The evening was warm, and after dinner, Sonia wandered back out onto the front porch and sat in the swinging love seat. It wasn't long before she was joined by her sister, Teresa, who sat on the love seat with her. Her two brothers, Tony, who sat in a wicker chair, and Jimmy, who perched half-on, half-off the porch railing, were there as well.

Teresa was younger than Sonia, twenty-two. Everyone called her Tee. At five-feet eight, her dark-eyed Italian looks and shapely body were even more striking than Sonia's. Whereas Sonia used a small arsenal of styling products to keep her hair professional-looking, Tee's hair was wild and flowing, often hanging in her face in the style of some pouty rock star. She wore a flouncy bohemian top, dyed with a strange mix of dark reds and bright greens that somehow worked well together. Along with her very short suede skirt and "too-early-for-the-season" sandals, her look boldly communicated her artsy view of life and the world.

Tony was the oldest of the Vitale kids at thirty-four and Jimmy the baby of the family at twenty. They were both dark-haired, good-looking men, and clearly brothers. Tony carried himself like the man he was—tall, muscular, with a constant five o'clock shadow on his broad face. His smile came quickly, though it was always restrained, under control.

Jimmy seemed more like a boy in a man's body. Also tall, his white, sleeveless T-shirt revealed his thin, angular frame. More attractive than his older brother, with Sonia's dark chocolate eyes and a warm smile, his boyish look couldn't hide the fact that his slender body was taut, powerful. Sonia had long thought that the young women in their neighborhood considered him quite the "Italian Stallion."

Tee started. "We're so sorry that Brad wasn't able to join us today. It would have been great to meet him."

"Yeah. Like I said, he was called away at the last minute." Sonia's smile was tight.

Jimmy gave her a teasing grin. "You sure he just didn't want to come and spend time with a bunch of wine-swilling Eye-talians?"

"No, no. He's not like that." Sonia felt her spine stiffen. "He's a great guy. He really did want to come. I just popped it on him at the last minute, and at the same time he was being asked to go help a client in Boston."

Tony, the only one still drinking wine, finished his glass. He spoke, holding the empty glass up to the fading sunlight. "Boston? Now there's a great city for Italians. Go up to the north end on Wednesdays and everybody's eating the same thing for dinner."

Tee gave him a strange look. "What do you mean?" She was twirling her hair around her finger in front of her cheek.

"Wednesday, in Boston. It's Prince Spaghetti Day. Been that way for years. Radio, billboards, the TV ad with the kid running home for dinner because it's Wednesday. Got to be close to fifty years of that. In Boston, Wednesday is Prince Spaghetti Day."

Tee shrugged her shoulders. "Oh." She turned back to Sonia. "Does he go up there often?"

Although Sonia knew that going away to help clients had been, and always would be, part of Brad's professional life, she was still struggling with the fact that he hadn't been able to make an exception to see her family. "No. Not to Boston. But he does know people all over the country, and I guess it's not unusual for him to get a call to go almost anywhere to work."

Jimmy spun around, sitting squarely on the railing, his feet easily touching the porch's weathered wooden floor. "Must be cool, flying all over the country doing private investigation stuff. Stuff like you do, right, Sonia?"

"Oh yeah," Sonia smirked, "I'm a real hot shot, driving around in Brad's new Corvette."Jimmy's expression lit up. "He drives a 'Vette? New?"

"Uh huh."

"Cool. What'd he drive before he got the 'Vette?"

"A different 'Vette." Sonia's voice lacked the enthusiasm she knew Jimmy was expecting, but she enjoyed stringing her baby brother along.

Jimmy's voice, on the other hand, matched the expression on his face. "So, why'd he get a new one? Did he wear the other one out?"

"In a manner of speaking. I guess you could say he drove it 'til he couldn't drive it anymore." Visions of that car, torn to pieces by bullets, slipped through her mind.

Tony and Tee had remained silent through the brief interchange, but Sonia could sense that Tee wanted to say something. She adjusted herself on the swing. "Why don't you two big, handsome Italian men go and see if our father is making some espresso for us. Give your sisters a little alone time."

The brothers stood. "Come on, Jimmy." Tony gently slapped his brother's arm with the back of his hand. "I can tell when we've been given our walking papers. Let's go see what Pop has cooking. You ladies enjoy the warm breeze."

After the brothers left, Sonia said, "Go ahead, ask."

Tee gave her a "What, me?" look. "Ask what?"

"Whatever it is that you've been wanting to ask all day. I could see it in your face every time we had a half-a-second alone together."

Tee was quiet for a moment. Finally, she began. "I was just wondering about you and Brad. You seemed so excited about the idea of him coming, and then he couldn't make it." She squinted. "Or did he choose not to make it?" Her expression was filled with genuine concern. "What's going on? Is everything okay with you guys?"

"Sure, sure. Things are fine. They're great, really."

Tee turned and looked directly at Sonia. "Not according to what I'm seeing. Come on, Sonia. I'm your sister. Talk to me."

"Look, honey." Sonia took a long breath then tried to sound upbeat. "Things really are great between us. We're happy. We've even worked out a good plan for being kind of partners in our work while still keeping our own businesses. It's just that this was a special opportunity for him to meet everyone and I'm disappointed that it didn't work out."

"For real. You really are okay?" Her fingers were twirling in her hair again.

"*Tutto sta bene.* Everything's fine." Sonia needed to change the subject. "What about you? What's going on in your life?"

"Well, the semester is ending. Soon I'll be a college graduate just like my older brother and sister." Tee absently watched a car full of young men drive past their house, loud music thumping from the car's stereo. "Now, if only there was something a studio art major could do for a living. That would be nice, wouldn't it?"

Sonia took her hand. "Honey, you're so good. Your paintings, your sculpture. Surely you should be able to sell your work."

"Yeah." Tee slipped her hand free and pushed her hair back

gently, looking at the empty street. "Once in a while. But I've got to find a way to make some steady money. The only thing I'm doing now that brings in any kind of regular money is singing with Ralphie and the guys. And that's just weekend gigs." Her hand went back to her hair.

Sonia tried to sound encouraging. "What's the name of your group again?"

"The Displaced Souls." She chuckled. "It's kind of a retro sixties name. But then again," she shrugged, "that's pretty much what we play, retro sixties. You know, Stones, Animals, Joplin." She gave Sonia a quick look. "Janis, not Scott."

Sonia took Tee's hand again and squeezed. "Don't worry, honey, it'll all work out. You'll find your way. You're beautiful and talented. Something'll come along. Trust me, I wish I had your talents, your gifts. You're going to be just fine." She let go of Tee's hand and tapped her gently on her bare knee. "Now let's go and see if the men in this family have figured out how to make us a decent cup of espresso."

15

———

Sonia had stayed in Cincinnati through Monday morning. On her way back to Lexington, she'd received a text from Jet. It had the phone numbers Jet had been able to find for several of the students Professor Andersen had identified as friends of Mariana. As she drove, Sonia had made a few calls. They'd all remembered Mariana and spoke kindly of her. None of them, however, had any idea of where she might be.

Punctually at 10:00 on Tuesday morning, the door to the BCI offices opened and Burnett Saunders walked in. It being a rainy day, and he being him, they were not surprised that he was wearing a slightly oversized suit meticulously protected by his oversized umbrella.

Sonia and Jet were both sitting in folding chairs next to the temporary work table they'd set up again in the waiting area of their offices. Coffee and pastries sat at the end of the table. Though she wasn't quite sure why, Sonia stood as he entered.

Jet stood as well and was the first to speak. "Good morning Mr. Saunders. How are you today?"

"I'm fine, and please feel free to refer to me as Burnett."

Sonia's eyes darted quickly to Jet and back. Strange, last week it was, "Mr. Saunders will do."

Jet motioned to a chair across from where she and Sonia were seated. "Have a seat. Can I get you some coffee or something to eat?"

"No, thank you. Never eat unless you're hungry."

Sonia barely suppressed a smile. "Oh, yes. I remember now. Well then, can we get started? We've been eagerly awaiting Tuesday morning and your report."

"Certainly, certainly." He took a seat. "Now then." His hand went absently to his bowtie. "I downloaded your information to my computer and worked on it at my office."

"I know," Jet said. "You do your best work in your own space."

Sonia shot her a stern, "Don't tease the poor guy," look. Jet just smiled.

"It really didn't take me long to discover what young Mr. Oakley was doing at Mr. Brownlee's firm. It's really quite distasteful . . . and, I might add, quite dishonest. I'm really not surprised, because—"

"Yes," Jet interrupted, "the darkness of the human soul and so on."

"Yes, yes, precisely."

Sonia leaned closer to him. "Can you tell us exactly what he's doing?"

Burnett Saunders sat back in his chair, tugged on his jacket lapels with both hands, and once again straightened his bowtie. "Well, certainly. But first, you need to be fully informed as to exactly how the purchasing process must proceed in an effectively run organization."

Jet's words suddenly had a strong hint of a southern accent. "Well, inform away, professor." Once again, Sonia shot Jet a disapproving look; this time, however, she was having trouble not giggling herself.

"Of course." He tugged on his lapels. "Now, in an effectively run organization, the purchasing process must proceed as follows. First, someone in authority makes a request that a certain item or items be purchased, either for use or for resale. The request must be in writing. Then, someone with higher authority must sign off on that request by creating a PO, or purchase order. That PO, or purchase order, must then be signed by someone with ultimate purchasing authority before copies are filed and that document is sent to a vendor."

He barely took a breath before continuing. "Now, upon the vendor's delivery of the item or items deemed appropriate for purchase, there must be a receipt of delivery form filled out. Some people refer to that as a ROD form. I, however, do not, since that terminology is not currently accepted by the Financial Accounting Standards Board, the organization officially recognized by the Securities and Exchange Commission as the governing body for the accounting profession."

This time it was Jet who shot Sonia a not-so-subtle look of disbelief.

Saunders was oblivious. "Nonetheless, when the item or items are delivered, someone must sign off on the appropriate form to indicate that the item or items have been received. The next step in the process occurs when that form is given to someone with the authority to pay outstanding debits, sometimes a treasurer, or even a bursar. That person is then responsible to check incoming invoices against the forms indicating receipt of delivery. At that point, the organization knows, or should know, that the item or items in question have been received and that the invoice requesting payment for such items is, in fact, valid."

Sonia began gently biting her own tongue. It was the only way she could keep from breaking out in laughter as she watched Burnett Saunders reveling in his own knowledge of the intricacies of an appropriate purchasing process at an effectively run organization.

He took a moment to straighten his tie. "Now, the next step in the process occurs when the person with the authority to pay incoming invoices has duly checked both the purchase order and the receipt of delivery, reconciling them with the incoming invoice, and generated a check to the vendor that proffered said invoice. Oftentimes, the process ends when the person with the highest financial authority, perhaps the CEO or CFO, then examines all the documents involved in the process and signs off on the payment. He or she usually, then, allows an underling to actually send said payment to the vendor who proffered the invoice for the item or items that were delivered to the organization, in response to the purchase order generated by the organization, in order to fulfill the request made by someone in the organization for the item or items, so that they might be used or resold."

Sonia and Jet were silent.

After a moment or two, Burnett Saunders cleared his throat. "Are there any questions?"

Jet's voice reflected her frustration. "So, what in blue blazes is Michael Oakley up to?"

Sonia shot Jet yet another look, then turned to Saunders and spoke gently. "What she means is that we still don't understand how Oakley is ripping off Mr. Brownlee."

Saunders seemed nonplussed. "I thought I made that perfectly clear. You see, somewhere in the process, Mr. Oakley has used digital subterfuge to undermine the integrity of the process."

Sonia was hoping for more, but Saunders stopped there. "Well, how do we find out exactly how he's doing that?"

"Oh, I already know that." Saunders' hands had slipped, palm to palm, between his knees, the apt student having convincingly solved the problem posed by the instructor.

Jet caught Sonia's eye and was subtly shaking her head.

Sonia continued, "Well, Burnett, uh, Mr. Saunders, could you tell us how he's doing that?"

"Oh, it's simple." Burnett's hands slipped upward, finding a place on the table as he leaned in toward the girls, conspiratorially. "You see, one of the vendors, The Bluegrass Sump Pump Company, is no longer in business. Yet, somehow, it continues to send invoices to Bronson/Brownlee. Those invoices are still being paid."

Jet perked up. "Wait a minute. You mean they're paying for things they're not receiving?"

Saunders sat back, tall in his chair. "That is correct."

Jet was fully engaged. "I thought you said that with those elaborate processes in place there were all kinds of checks and balances about paying for things."

Now it was Burnett Saunders whose energy level was rising. "In an effectively run organization, I said. In an effectively run organization. In many organizations, not every step is taken seriously, though, given the natural state of the human heart, one really can't see why anyone would fail to follow the proper procedures laid out by the—"

"Yes, yes," Sonia interrupted. "But exactly how is Oakley doing," she lifted her hands in frustration, "whatever it is that he's doing?"

"Electronically."

Jet's head dropped to her chest and rocked back and forth. Then she looked up and gave Burnett a patient smile. "Please explain."

"You see, it appears Mr. Oakley has taken advantage both of some deficits in the purchasing processes used by Bronson/Brownlee and his ability to electronically steal Mr. Brownlee's signature."

Jet sat up taller in her chair. "Now we're getting somewhere. Tell us more."

"You see," Saunders' eyes bounced back and forth between Sonia and Jet, "the Bronson/Brownlee purchasing process is not one hundred percent in accordance with proper procedures for verifying the receipt of certain items, particularly when it comes to vendors with whom it has a long-standing relationship, as in the case of The Bluegrass Sump Pump Company. Therefore, with The Bluegrass Sump Pump Company going out of business and having digitally stolen Steven Brownlee's signature to create invalid purchase orders, it wasn't difficult for Oakley to create bogus invoices and approve their payment, again, using the electronically stolen signature. Mr. Brownlee is no longer heavily involved in the whole process. Therefore, if he happened to come across some paperwork with the vendor name of The Bluegrass Sump Pump Company, it wouldn't be surprising at all that he might not have any idea the company no longer even exists."

It was Sonia's turn to speak. "So . . . putting it simply, Oakley is creating false purchase orders to back up bogus invoices from a company that no longer exists. What then?"

"Oh, it's dreadfully simple from there, Ms. Vitale." His voice became very matter-of-fact. "He simply creates an account to which he transfers the payment, and, of course, it's an account to which he has personal access."

Jet thumped the plastic table with her fist. "So, the damn bastard pays a bogus invoice to an account he owns, then he walks away with the money, free as a jaybird pluckin' a piece of straw out of the hand of a scarecrow. Well, I'll be damned."

Sonia shook her head and chuckled at Jet's allusion.

"Yes, Ms. ah . . . Jet."

Jet looked at Saunders over her nonexistent glasses. "And you can prove that this varmint has been rapin' and pillagin' the poor old man with your forensic accounting wizardry?"

"Well, yes." Saunders touched his bowtie and sighed. "And no."

Sonia squinted. "Yes and no?"

Saunders clasped his hands and rested them on the table. "Yes, I can use the records you gave me to prove that someone has been producing false invoices and payments." He let out a short breath. "It will be more difficult to prove that it was Mr. Oakley's doing."

Jet was still animated. "I thought you said that he was sending money to an account that he had access to."

"Well . . . yes, but." His hands went back to his lapels, this time actually hanging on them for a moment as he spoke. "You see, he may have used a false identity to create his access to the account." Saunders paused, then a hint of a sly smile crept across his face as he leaned in over the table. "Now don't tell anyone that I used a little skullduggery and the repayment of a long-overdue personal favor to determine this, but it appears that within three days of each payment to the phony account, someone, Mr. Oakley I presume, empties the account."

Sonia leaned back in her chair. "So that would make it difficult to prove it's Oakley, right?"

"I'm afraid you're correct." Saunders crossed his arms and leaned back, sighing.

Sonia picked up her coffee and swirled it as she pondered the situation. Then she took another tack. "Well, at least we can get it to stop, right? We just ask you to write us a report, Mr. Saunders, and we help Steven Brownlee take it to the police."

Jet slammed her fist on the plastic table, sending Sonia and Saunders rocking backward. "No way, sister." Her blue eyes wide open, she bore down on Sonia. "We're not letting that piece of crap rip off Mr. Brownlee. We're going to prove that it's Oakley, and we're going to get Brownlee his money back." She turned and looked across the table. "Right Burnett?"

Saunders seemed taken aback by Jet's directness. "Well . . . ah, Jet. I'm not sure how we could do that. With him emptying the account in three days and possibly using a false identity, I'm not sure how we prove it's him."

Sonia joined in. "Yeah, and let's not forget that he's a computer whiz. As soon as anything goes sideways, he'll be in there covering his tracks electronically."

Jet stood up, almost knocking her folding chair over backward. "Listen. We may be done for now, but we're not moving forward until we can find a way to catch this bastard and get the old man's money back for him. Come on Burnett, let me show you out."

Sonia retired to her office and took a seat at her desk. After showing Burnett Saunders out, Jet joined her, standing in the doorway.

"What was that?" Sonia asked.

Jet cocked her head. "What was what?"

There was a sing-song lilt to Sonia's voice. "Come on, Burnett. Let me show you out."

"I don't know." Jet stepped into Sonia's office. "It just seemed like the right thing to do."

"Oh really?"

"Really."

"You would have done that for any other client?"

Jet shrugged and busied herself getting situated in the chair opposite Sonia's desk. "I guess. What's your point?"

"My point is that I've never seen you do that before." Sonia's eyebrows went up, her chocolate brown eyes smiling. "Except when I made you do it last week."

Jet squirmed around in the chair as if getting comfortable for a long session. "So?"

"So, I did it because I thought it was funny that Burnett Saunders seemed so attracted to you."

"And?"

"Aaand . . ." Sonia's smile was coy. "Now I think that perhaps *you* might be attracted to *him*."

"Get off it." Jet seemed suddenly concerned with the condition of her fingernail polish. "That stiff piece of railing? What could a woman find attractive about him?"

Sonia's shoulders lifted. "I don't know. What if he lost the oversized suit and the giant bowtie? Would he seem like a different guy?"

Jet leaned in and got a mischievous look on her face. "What he if lost the suit and was standing there in nothing but his Calvin Klein low-rise skivvies? What would *you* say then?"

"Are you kidding me?" Now it was Sonia who was off-balance.

"Oh, honey chile." The voice was pure southern belle. "Don't you know that they always say the clothes make the man. Well, sometimes, now mind you, just sometimes, the clothes don't make the man until he takes 'em off."

Sonia sat there wide-eyed. Finally, she brushed that wisp of hair out of her face. "Oh brother. Is it time for lunch yet?"

"Not yet. We just ate those pastries." Jet licked her lips. "But I do know one thing."

"What's that?" Sonia rocked back.

Jet stood, ran her long, blonde ponytail through each of her hands and looked off at the ceiling. "I do believe I am slowly, ever so slowly, developing an unusual appetite."

16

FOUR WEEKS EARLIER

B efore she even looked up at her kitchen clock, she knew it was time to leave for work. Putting her mostly empty coffee cup into the sink, she rinsed it quickly then popped it into the dishwasher. She didn't give it another thought at the moment, but she was pleased that the apartment she lived in offered not only the normal amenities—stove, refrigerator, dishwasher—but an extra bonus: a personal washer/dryer set-up. Along with her small but nice apartment, she was able to afford an almost-new car. She made a pretty darn good salary—and a little more.

Grabbing her coat, her purse, and a battered thermos, she scooted out of her apartment, down one flight of steps, and out into the brisk morning air. Given the time of year, she wasn't at all surprised that she would be driving to work in total darkness.

Stepping off the curb and into the apartment complex parking lot, she noticed another early morning riser—another person who most likely had to be at work much earlier than they would have liked. Though they had obviously gotten into their car before she even stepped out of her building, she surmised they weren't actually late for work. Their car was running, lights on, but stationary. She gave them only a fleeting thought as she walked along a five-foot-tall, brick retaining wall. It separated the twenty-foot lawn at the back of the apartments from the parking lot surface. With the wall to her left and the parked cars a street-width away to her right, she began the rather distant walk down the long line of cars to her own vehicle.

She heard an engine rev up and sensed her compatriot's car was moving. It struck her as strange when a quick glance told her that the car had passed the only exit to the road that ran by the complex—driving beyond the left-hand turn and continuing forward toward her. She wouldn't have given it much thought, but the car was already moving quickly—then faster still. She turned. Looking directly into the blinding headlights, she realized the fool was too close to the wall. If he didn't move to the right the idiot might hit her.

An instant later she understood. This was no fool, this was no miscalculation; the son-of-a-bitch was heading right toward her. She turned. She glanced to her left. It was another thirty or forty yards before the retaining wall would end. She'd have to cross the aisle to where the cars were—cross right in front of him.

Dropping her purse, the thermos, her keys, she ran. She ran as fast as she could. She bolted for the line of cars. A scream welled up in her throat but never made it out of her mouth. The closer she got to the cars, the farther to the right he moved. The lights blinded her; the screaming of the now-speeding car's engine roared in her ears, her mind. Her eyes wide, her body contracted into a ball of energy, she saw an opening. A few more steps and she would be able to leap between two dark and silent vehicles. She took a deep breath; she stretched . . . THUMP.

Her mind was filled with images, sensations, thoughts as she tumbled through the air, bouncing off the hood of the car. It seemed long moments before the hard, cold, asphalt came up to meet her body with another thump—a different kind of thump.

Her mind raced, knowing she should feel pain—trying to find it somewhere in her nervous system. No pain . . . No sounds . . .

No feeling. She tried frantically to unscramble her thoughts. Could it be that I'm not hurt? Did this even really happen? Am I dreaming?

She tried to reach out and touch the ground—touch anything. Nothing. No movement. No sensation. Finally, something registered. The sound of a car—softer. Softer because the car was leaving? No. Everything is softer, darker. The sound of her own breathing—softer—no—gone.

17

THE PRESENT

After their meeting with Burnett Saunders, Jet worked on trying to find phone numbers or email addresses for more of Mariana's friends. Meanwhile, Sonia continued to call the few numbers she'd gotten from Jet. In each case, she tiptoed around questions concerning Mariana and her relationships, finally asking each of them frank questions about Mariana's current location. As she worked, Sonia's eyes kept drifting to the photograph of Mariana that she had put in a simple black frame and set on her desk. Sometimes she shuddered as she thought about all the things that might happen to a young woman.

Just after one o'clock, Jet knocked on Sonia's window. "Time for lunch. Where do you want to go?"

Sonia thought for a moment. "Papi's."

"Again?"

"Yes. Again."

"Okay, but you'd better not get drunk this time." Jet tossed the line at her while she slipped on her light blue spring jacket.

"I did *not* get drunk." Sonia grabbed her jacket and her purse as well. "And any light-headedness I suffered was entirely your fault."

They walked down the stairs in the rain and got into Jet's car. Sonia shivered. "Nasty day."

Jet started the Camry and looked each way before turning right onto East Main. "Yup. April can come back and bite you on the butt, can't it."

Sonia didn't reply. Eventually, however, she did ask, "So, are you ever going to tell me how we're planning on getting shots of Nick Petropoulos messing around on his wife?"

"That I am my dear. Right now." A knowing smile crossed Jet's face. "It involves getting some exercise."

"What does that mean? Getting some exercise."

Jet continued to smile and turned the car down Ashland Ave. "Did you know that roller-skating is recognized as a complete aerobic workout that involves all of the body's muscles, especially the heart. In fact, one hour of roller-skating burns between 300 and 600 calories."

"Well, you don't say." Sonia's voice was light but filled with a touch of apprehension. "And how do you know all this information about roller-skating?"

"There's this new thing." Jet's voice was totally snarky. "It's called the internet."

Sonia watched as they passed the beautiful old homes she saw daily but never tired of. "And are you implying that you're planning on going roller-skating soon."

"No, no, no." Jet shook her head broadly. Then she turned to Sonia. "I'm implying that *we're* going roller-skating soon."

"And would that be at The Wildcat Roller-Skating Emporium?" Sonia's voice was rising.

"Uh huh."

Sonia turned to Jet. "And would we be doing that tonight, because we're interested in supporting a certain sorority's fundraiser for kids with a particular kind of cancer?"

"You've got it." A big smile crossed Jet's face. "Tonight, at eight o'clock, you and I will be going to The Wildcat. We won't actually have to roller-skate. We'll just stand around with the rest of the 'watchers' who'll be there. I'm guessing it won't be too hard to get a shot of some young slut sneaking off with Nick-the-Dick to get a little extra aerobic exercise of a different nature."

Sonia took a deep breath. "Well, I'm certainly glad that's your plan."

"And why's that?" Jet pulled into a parking space around the corner from Papi's.

"Actually, I never learned how to roller-skate. No skiing, no skateboarding, none of that stuff. I run. I run and I keep my feet right there on terra firma. No wheels or slippery sticks between me and mother earth."

Jet whipped her head to her right. "Seriously? You never learned to roller-skate? It's easy. How could you not know how to roller-skate?"

"Hey." Sonia's voice was suddenly defensive. "If you live in an old neighborhood where the sidewalks are all uneven and the streets are full of cars, and you don't grow up near a rink, somehow roller-skating just seems to slip on by."

"Well, don't you worry." Jet's demeanor had become motherly. "I'm sure you can be a good 'watcher' even if you can't skate."

Sonia nodded, glad she had made her point. "Yes, I'm quite certain I can."

"Well, here we are, sweets. The site of your drunken debauchery at our last lunch."

"Cut it out." Sonia slapped Jet gently on her arm. "I was just a bit lightheaded. And it was your doing all along. I didn't order those margaritas."

"Okay, okay." Jet slipped out of her car and spoke to Sonia over its roof. "But let's hope you can handle your booze better today." She headed for Papi's in the light rain.

"One. Just one." Sonia spoke as she tried to catch up to Jet. "And, it's fine with me if we just drink water."

Jet opened the door and led Sonia up the stairs and into the restaurant. "*Buenos dias,*" she said to the hostess.

"*Buenos días. Como estás?*" came the reply. She was a sturdy woman, dark-haired, dark-eyed, wearing jeans and a white top that failed to cover her broad shoulders. She was helpful but slow to smile.

Sonia stepped slightly in front of Jet. "Can we be seated with Paco today?"

Somehow the request had managed to bring out the woman's smile, one that was actually quite warm. "*Claro.* Right this way." She led them quickly to a colorful table in the far corner of the restaurant, Paco's section for the day.

As Sonia and Jet waited for Paco to come to their table, Jet asked, "So why did you want to come here again so soon? Just to see Paco?"

"Yeah." Sonia reached out to the salsa bowl that sat on the table and dipped a warm chip into it. She held the chip in her hand while she answered. "It's killing me that we're not making any progress on this case. I just want to assure him that we're working as hard as we can, trying to find her. And I want to see if there is anyone else we should be talking to, people we should be asking questions." She popped the chip into her mouth, whole.

Paco walked up to the table, standing between them. "*Buenos días* ladies. How are you today?"

Jet gave him a big smile. "*Bien, gracias, bien. Y tú?*"

"*Bien, bien, bien.*" He was all smiles as well. "And you Ms. Sonia. You are well?"

"Yes Paco, very well. How are you holding up?"

Paco's professional demeanor slipped away, replaced by a hint of deep sadness. "It is difficult," he sighed. "We pray every night. I come to work and try to do a good job, but my heart is so heavy. And Lily, my wife. She is broken."

Jet took his hand gently. "We understand, really we do. And we're trying everything we can think of."

Sonia touched his other hand. "We've been out to Downstream Farm and spoken to the people she worked with. We've spoken to her professor from Mayweather. We've called a number of her friends already. No one has been much help. And even though we're licensed PIs, we're not able to see her phone records. But just know that we're not going to give up. We're not. In fact, I was wondering if there was anyone here today we should speak to."

Paco thought for a moment. "*Sí*. Yes. I told you I would get you in touch with Mariana's cousin, Gabriela. Tomás called in sick today; Gabriela is covering his shift. That's her, over there, in the red shirt."

Sonia and Jet both turned and saw a beautiful woman, probably just shy of thirty years old. Her Mexican heritage was obvious, though she seemed unusually tall by those standards. Thin, shapely body, thick long black hair, long dangling earrings, jeans that hugged, really hugged her body, and shoes with heels not normally worn by servers in a restaurant; she appeared more like a flamenco dancer than a woman serving lunch in a small Mexican eatery. The looks men gave her as she walked by them completed the illusion.

Sonia turned back to Paco and saw the look of a proud uncle in his eyes. "Any chance we could get a moment to talk to her today?"

"Oh, yes. When you finish your lunch, I will tell her to come talk to you. I'll cover her tables for her if I need to."

Sonia and Jet ordered enchiladas and margaritas. They talked about a number of cases while they ate, including the fact that Jet had, thus far, been frustrated in her attempts to catch the group of young girls who were stealing the high-end make-up from BCI's drugstore client. When they were finished, they asked Paco to send Gabriela over so they could talk.

The black-haired woman seemed to glide across the red tile floor, her hips swinging back and forth. "You are the women who are trying to find my cousin?" Her voice was soft but dark and powerful. "Have you made any progress?"

Sonia pushed her margarita glass to the side. "Well, not as much as we'd like. We were hoping that you could help. Is there anything that you can tell us? Anything at all?"

Gabriela seemed to hesitate, her eyes scanning the room.

Jet sat up a little taller. "Gabriela?"

"Listen," Gabriela spoke almost without moving her lips, "I don't know if this means anything, and I don't want to get Mariana in trouble, but she came in here the night before she disappeared."

Sonia sat up taller as well. "Yes. Her father told us that. Did something unusual happen while she was here?"

Gabriela continued to look around the room as she spoke, softly, darkly. She began clicking her ballpoint pen, in and out, in and out. "No. Nothing happened. But I know Mariana. I've known her since she was a little girl. We're *muy unidas*. I could tell that she was nervous, nervous about something. I asked her if she was okay, and she said she was. But I knew that wasn't the truth. Something was bothering her."

Jet pressed. "Do you know what it was?"

"No. Like I said, I asked her if she was okay, but she said everything was fine."

Sonia pressed. "Can you think of anything or anybody that she might be worried about. Was she dating anyone?"

Gabriela stopped clicking her pen then answered. "No, not really."

Sonia and Jet exchanged a look. Then Sonia spoke. "What does that mean?"

Gabriela touched her fingertip to her lips. "Well, sometimes she would go out with this boy named Santiago. He's from our *barrio*, our neighborhood; they go to the same church. But I don't think it was anything special for her."

Sonia let out a sigh. "Anyone else that she just spent time with?"

"I don't think so. She worked so many hours at that farm. Actually, now that I think about it," Gabriela pursed her red lips, "sometimes she would go after work for a drink with another man. I think he was older than her. I don't know his name, but she told me once that he was from England and he was some kind of royal man."

Sonia almost popped out of her seat. "Limey? Was his name Limey?"

Gabriela shrugged her shoulders quickly. "I don't know. Maybe. If she told me his name, I don't remember. She said he was different but nice."

Jet's eyes told Sonia that they were thinking the same thing. Sonia had told Jet about Limey, the big strong man from England, the one who could toss bales of hay around. Now, it seemed, there might be more to the relationship between Limey and Mariana than Sonia had learned about on her trip to Downstream Farm. Sonia brushed a wisp of hair out of her face. Her toe started tapping. "Did she ever say anything else about him? Anything at all?"

"No. It was no big deal to her." Gabriela's voice got even darker. "Listen, though, before you leave. I want you to know that I want to help you find my cousin; I want to find the person who did something to her. If anyone has hurt her, I will . . . well, I will make them sorry."

Jet stood up. "We'll take all the help we can get, but why this sudden interest? Why haven't you come to us before?"

"No," Gabriela almost shouted in a whisper. Her eyes bore into Jet's. "This is no sudden interest. This is my cousin, who I love. I have not been thinking of other things. It's you."

Sonia stood as well, her chair scraping noisily on the tile floor. "What do you mean, it's us?"

Gabriela leaned hard toward Sonia. "It's you that I didn't

know if I could trust. I had no idea that my uncle would go to you for help, and I didn't know if I could trust you to find her." Jet inserted herself between the two women. "And?"

"And now," Gabriela reined her energy in just a bit, "now that I've met you, I think maybe you care. I think maybe you might be able to find her, to save her."

Sonia smiled at Gabriela, trying to dissipate the growing tension. "We need everyone's help."

"No, you don't get it." Gabriela's dark voice was brimming with emotion. "You think that something happened to her, you think that maybe someone has hurt her. I can tell. I can see it in your eyes. But if that's true, it could be someone from our barrio. It could be one of *us* who has hurt her. And you don't know our world, the insides of the Hispanic community, the culture, the rules, the way things are done. If she's been taken by someone like that, you'll never find her, not without help from me."

Sonia looked at Jet. They were both silent.

"Now. You go." Gabriela pointed at Sonia, her voice soft but deeply intense. "You look where you think to look, where you think she might be. But me, I'll be looking for her right here, right in the world that she comes from." She turned and walked away without the slightest goodbye, leaving Sonia and Jet speechless for the moment.

Sonia and Jet remained silent as they walked back to Jet's car in the rain, Sonia stopping suddenly as a sporty black convertible turned the corner hard, splashing rainwater on her already damp jeans. "Nice!" she shouted at the car and driver. "Real nice!" She was tempted to flip him the bird. Eventually slipping into the car, Sonia finally spoke. "Wow. That's some woman."

Jet turned toward Sonia and smiled, "My kind of woman. That's a woman who'll kick ass, Mexican style, if she needs to."

"Yeah, and I'm afraid she's absolutely right." Sonia looked out the passenger window and into the rain that was now pouring down. "We're looking into her farm connections. We're looking into her school connections. We're looking at all the friends we can find. But the Hispanic community. I mean, sure, they've come here and assimilated, become part of our world. But that doesn't mean they don't still have their own culture, their own way of doing things, good and bad. If some person from that barrio has hurt her or taken her, we're really going to need help trying to find her. Don't you think?"

Jet started the car and pulled out into traffic. "I'll tell you what I think. I think that Gabriela is one hot jalapeño of a woman, and if Mariana needs that kind of help it ain't coming from us, it's coming from her hell-bent-for-revenge cousin."

Sonia let out a big sigh. "I agree."

Jet kept her eyes on the road. "C'mon. Let's be smart. We look where we know how to look. Gabriela looks where she knows how to look. And let's just hope that one of us finds her before it's too late."

The clatter of the pouring rain on the roof of Jet's Camry and the slapping of the windshield wipers all but drowned out Sonia's voice as she whispered, "Amen."

18

J et pulled up in front of Sonia's apartment on Central
Avenue around eight o'clock that evening. She honked the
Camry's horn several times. As Sonia slid into the car, she
could see that they were both dressed appropriately for an
evening at The Wildcat. Under her white denim jacket, Sonia had
on snug jeans and a dark red and white striped top. Jet wore even
tighter jeans and a bright blue top that brought out her sparkling
eyes. Though the evening was cool, she had no jacket on at all.

Sonia pulled the car door closed. "Well, are you ready for
this?"

The southern belle spoke. "Little Miss Sonia, have you ever
known this poor li'l country girl to not be ready for anythin'?"

Sonia let out a sigh. *I should never have asked.* "So, what's the
plan again?"

Jet pulled the car away from the curb and they headed off to
the land of skates, cokes, and pre- and post-pubescent boys and
girls. "Here's the deal. We go into The Wildcat and stand around
with all the other parents who are watching." Jet slowed the
Camry to a stop at a traffic light and turned to Sonia. "After a
while, we just move around until we think we've got a view of

Nick-the-Dick and his little sorority honey. I'm sure they're not doing it out on the skating floor, so when they slip into some back room or something, we just nonchalantly happen to stumble in a few minutes later and catch them in the act. You get a few images on that phone of yours and we skedaddle."

Sonia spoke with her eyes forward. "Question."

The light changed and Jet hit the gas. "Yeah."

"How many minutes do we wait before we go in?"

Jet turned and looked at Sonia. "What's your point?"

"Well, given that Nick is the kind of guy who expects his wife to 'put out' every single night, I'm guessing he's not," Sonia began singing softly, "a 'lover with a slow hand.' "

Jet gave Sonia a snarky smile. "Agreed."

"So," Sonia turned forward again, "if we slip in too early, they may not be, how should I put it, completely engaged yet. On the other hand, if we wait too long, we may just walk in to find zippers zippin' and buttons buttonin' and we may have missed the whole thing."

Jet checked her rearview mirror. "I guess it just depends."

"On what?"

"On how hot the young sorority philanthropist is."

Sonia paused for a moment. "Agreed."

It only took about twenty minutes for Jet to drive from Sonia's apartment to the skating rink. As they walked up to the ticket booth at the front of the building, Jet put her hand on Sonia's arm. "Now just look like you're here to watch your kid skate."

"What kid?" Sonia was already feeling that they were both inappropriately dressed to play the part of "roller-skating moms."

Jet stopped and looked around. "Right. Okay then, let's just bunch up close to those kids. The girl in the booth will think we're with them."

Sonia laughed. "And expect us to pay for them? Guess you don't have a lot of experience with this mother thing."

Jet's head spun around. She didn't say anything, but Sonia could see hurt in her eyes. Sonia winced. Damn it. She'd wanted kids with that piece of crap husband who wound up cheating on her, and now I've just dredged all of that up for her. Damn it. "Sorry." The words fell softly out of her mouth.

A moment passed. Jet shook it off. "No. You're right. Don't worry about it. I'll just mumble something about our kids already being inside."

After paying the price of admission, the girls walked into the dark, blaring-music-filled cavern known as The Wildcat. Kids whizzed by on skates, laughing and chasing each other, paying absolutely no heed to the long list of "Rules for Safe and Courteous Behavior at The Wildcat Roller-Skating Emporium" that were posted in huge letters on the wall.

Sonia cupped one hand around her mouth and stood on her tip-toes. "What a zoo."

"You're feeling blue?"

"No, I said . . . ." Sonia realized Jet was just pulling her leg.

Looking around, Sonia realized the set-up at The Wildcat was not what she had expected. There was a big sign directing patrons to move forward in one of two directions. To the left was a little bleacher section, like at a high school baseball field, where parents could sit and watch the kids skate. The path to the skate rental room and the actual skating rink was on the right. Over that pathway was a bright yellow iridescent sign. "EVERYONE MUST WEAR SKATES!"

Jet pulled Sonia to the left. "Come on. We sit here and watch."

"Oh yeah, we'll watch alright." Sonia almost had to shout. "But unfortunately, we'll be watching, hoping some father's little girl sneaks off to do the wild thing with that bastard. What a great and high-minded life we live."

"Just the way it is, girl. Just the way it is." Jet motioned to the concession stand. "You want some popcorn or something?"

Sonia stood on her toes again and spoke into Jet's ear. "Something, but more like a Maker's and coke than some cheap popcorn."

Jet's southern ancestry popped up. "Hoo-wee, girl. Let's not start fussin' now. I've taken you out on a school night, haven't I. No need to be choosy about what kind of snack you get, now is there?"

"No, Mom. I'll just sit here quietly and watch." Sonia had spoken at a normal volume. A moment later she realized Jet had never heard her.

It didn't take long for the girls to figure out that there was a flaw in their plan. Although the view of the skating area from the bleachers was almost complete, there were definitely some places in the hall that were out of their line of sight. Unfortunately, having leaned over a railing and taken a peek, Sonia could tell that the offices in which Nick might soon be holding court were tucked away in a corner, out of sight.

"Well, Ms. Jet." She said over the blaring music. "Looks like we're going to have to amend your plan somehow. We're not going to be able to see if anyone sneaks into Nick's office while we're sitting on these bleachers."

"I can see that." Even at that volume, Jet's voice indicated she was just a bit testy. It didn't take long, however, for her to come up with another plan. She stood up. "Okay then. We're just going to have to get some skates and get out there on the floor, where we can see what the heck is going on."

Sonia started shaking her head. "Oh no. No, no, no. I've already told you. I don't know how to roller-skate, and I don't have any intention of learning now."

Jet looked down at Sonia then leaned over and spoke directly into her ear. "Listen up Vitale. If we're going to catch this slime-ball cheating on that poor little over-worked, over- . . . whatevered woman, you're going to have to put on your big girl panties and get out there and skate." Jet grabbed Sonia's arm. "Now get your ass off that bench and let's go get us some skates." She started walking toward the skate rental area.

Sonia followed reluctantly. Damn. What the hell am I doing? I'll bet I'm going to wind up with a broken phone . . . and probably a broken bone to boot.

Jet was already quite a few steps ahead. She glanced over her shoulder and gave Sonia a look.

Sonia hustled. "I'm coming. I'm coming."

It wasn't long before both Sonia and Jet were out on the skating floor. Sonia was surprised to see that Jet not only had no trouble whatsoever skating, but that she could actually spin and skate backward—all the stuff an athletically gifted kid picks up without much effort. Conversely, to say that Sonia was even skating was quite a stretch. It was more like she was walking with high-topped roller-skates on. Clump, clump, clump. She wobbled forward while Jet circled around her, amazed. When Sonia finally started to roll just a bit, her arms shot out and swung around, as if she were balancing on some tiny tightrope at the very top of a huge circus tent. Just as she got barely enough stability to be able to look at Jet, she saw Jet bent over, grabbing the part of her body that would indicate she was about to pee her pants.

"I'll get you for this, Jet. I promise. I'll get you for this."

"C'mon." Jet waved her hand. "Let's get rolling. And keep your eyes open for the Nickster and the young thing he hopes to matriculate this evening."

Sonia was rolling, marginally, wobbling the whole time. "You watch for him your damn self. I'm just trying to—" With a whooshing sound, Sonia's feet launched into the air. The event was followed by the solid thumping sound of her butt hitting the ground.

Gulping for breaths, in between huge bouts of laughter, Jet

said, "C'mon honey. Let's get you off the floor and back on your wheels."

"Oh please." Sonia rubbed her bottom. "Please do. I can't wait to do that again."

Eventually, with Jet pulling her by the arm, Sonia completed her first loop around the floor. It had taken about twelve minutes. Settling into the routine of pushing one leg in front of the other, and still occasionally walking rather than rolling, Sonia started to smile and enjoy herself . . . just a little bit.

Jet had switched her attention from helping Sonia to checking out the manager's office. "Now there's something I didn't expect to see."

Sonia was bent forward in a strange position that somehow was keeping her from falling again. "What's that?"

"One of the bouncers, well I guess they call them something else here, is standing right in front of the office. Bright orange shirt, totally buff." Jet held her hand at the side of her mouth, speaking surreptitiously as if anyone more than two feet away from her could hear what she was saying. "He's probably supposed to be skating around keeping an eye on things. Instead, he's standing there surrounded by some admiring young college girls who probably have as much interest in skating as you do."

Sonia was now standing ram-rod straight, arms out to her sides. "Right."

"Also, I just watched a redhead with a body that looks like it came out of a Barbie display being led into the office by none other than Nick-the-Dick himself. No little flower, either. Tall, long hair, strong and athletic looking. I'll bet she can hold her own for a college girl." Jet tugged on her ponytail. "With a sign above the door that says, 'No Admittance,' and Burly-Bouncer-Boy stationed in front of the door, I'm not thinking that we're going to be able to go busting into the office to catch the dynamic duo saving the world. Know what I mean?"

Sonia couldn't answer. She was on the floor with her legs spread, rubbing her butt and laughing.

Jet looked down at Sonia. "Goodness girl, are we going to have to get you training wheels, or what?" Jet reached down and pulled Sonia up. Approximately thirty minutes later, she pulled Sonia over to the side of the rink. "Well, that does it."

"For skating? Are we done skating?" Sonia's voice was full of expectation as she hung over the railing.

"Yes, honey." Jet sighed. "We're done."

"Why?"

Jet wiggled her thumb in the direction of the offices. "Because Nick and his protégé have completed her educational activities for the evening."

Sonia looked in that direction. "Already?"

"Yup. Already. And thanks to Burly-Bouncer-Boy, we have apparently missed our opportunity." She paused. "Well, at least we've learned some things."

Though standing still at the edge of the rink, Sonia's feet somehow managed to move, each in a different direction, creating a split that would have made any Russian gymnast proud. Fortunately, Jet reached out and caught Sonia just before her butt and the floor had another meeting of the minds.

Sonia finally got herself stable again, "And what did we learn?"

"Two things. First, we're going to have to assume that on Tuesday nights, Burly-Bouncer-Boy will continue to block our access to the office unless we come up with a distraction."

Sonia held on tight to the railing. "And, two?"

"We've got ourselves no more than twenty-five or thirty minutes after the red-headed pecker girl enters the office to get in and get our shots." She grinned. Now let's go home."

19

Wednesday morning, Sonia's phone woke her from a deep sleep. "Hello." She squinted, trying to see the clock.

"Good morning, Sunshine." The voice was upbeat.

"What's so darn good about it. And what time is it, anyway?"

"It's seven o'clock in the morning, sweetheart. Time to rise and shine."

"Wait a minute. Who is this?"

"What do you mean, 'who is this?' It's your bosom buddy, your partner, your BFF. It's the woman all of Kentucky lovingly refers to as Jet."

"No. Can't be." Sonia's head flopped back down on her pillow. "Jet would never call me at seven in the morning, not after punishing my body with physical abuse the night before."

"Oh yes, kiddo, it's me." Sonia could tell that Jet was enjoying this. *"And you can thank Burnett Saunders for this early morning reveille."*

"Burnett Saunders? What's he got to do with it?" Sonia was struggling to keep her eyes open.

"Well, it seems Burnett has come up with a plan to catch Michael

Oakley in the ac of stealing from old man Brownlee, and he couldn't wait past six-thirty to call me and tell me all about it."

"What'd he say?" Sonia sat up in bed and stretched as she brushed that wisp of hair out of her face.

"Oh no." Sonia could almost hear a chuckle in Jet's voice. *"I wouldn't let him just tell me over the phone, by myself. I figured that if I was going to get dragged out of bed at six-thirty in the morning, the least I could do is drag you with me. Just be glad I had the decency to let you sleep until seven."*

Sonia stifled a yawn. "Great." Her voice slid downward. "After our debacle last night, I got home just in time to get a call from Brad. We were on the phone for almost an hour. I don't even know when I got to sleep."

"Everything okay with him? He making any progress on the case?"

"Oh yeah." Sonia swung her legs out of the bed, stood, and stretched as she spoke. "Seems like it's just something about his former client getting caught cheating and thinking that his wife's doing the same thing. Now he's got Brad up there trying to get proof against the wife so the client doesn't lose everything in the divorce. Brad hates it, but he really can't say no." *"And you and Brad? Everything's okay there?"*

"Absolutely." Sonia was aware of the smile creeping across her face. "Honestly, it was great to hear his voice. And I could tell he didn't want to get off the phone either."

"Okay then, sleepy head. I told Burnett to meet us at the office and that we'd be there by seven-thirty."

"No, I'm a wreck." Sonia glanced at her phone. "Call him back and make it eight o'clock. Also, tell him to meet us at Magee's. I've got to get something into my stomach." *"Okay. See you at eight. Now get a move on it."* Jet hung up.

Fifty minutes later, Sonia left her apartment, walked up Ashland Ave, turned left onto East Main, and walked into Magee's just a minute or two before eight. Jet and Burnett were sitting at one of the larger tables in the center of the room. Before she caught their attention, Sonia was taken with the realization that clothing aside, and with a warm smile on his face, Burnett was really quite attractive. She also sensed that below that awful suit there might be a pretty darn appealing male body. "You guys just get here?"

Burnett stood up politely. "No, Ms. Vitale. We've been here since seven-thirty. Sorry you couldn't join us sooner."

Sonia could see a sheepish look on her partner's face. Jet had also let her long blonde hair out of its perpetual ponytail; it was hanging down in front of her shoulders. "Seven thirty, huh? Well, I got here as soon as I could." She turned to Burnett. "I'm certain that Jet has kept you entertained." Sonia was quite certain that Jet could perceive the sarcasm in her voice even if Burnett missed it.

Jet put her coffee cup down on the table. "Business. Just talking business. Glad you're here. Can I get you something?"

"No, thanks." Sonia looked up at the counter. "I'm sure that as soon as Hildy saw me walk in the door she got started with my croissant and coffee. I'll be back in a sec. You two finish whatever it is you were doing before I got here." She surreptitiously gave Jet a look.

A few minutes later, Sonia sat down at the table and started pulling apart her warm, delicious, almond croissant. "You have something to share with us, Burnett?" Sonia knew full well that Burnett had asked her to call him Mr. Saunders. She smiled to herself. *I guess if it's good enough for Jet to call him Burnett, it'll do for me as well.*

Burnett sat up in his chair and went through his normal routine; he tugged on both lapels of his jacket and straightened his already straight tie. "That I do, ladies." A smile crossed his face. "And I must admit this has been great fun for me. You know, normally I just look at financial records. I try to put together, from those records, an accurate account of what has already happened." He leaned forward, his voice conspiratorial. "But now, you're asking me to assist you in *making* something happen, and in tracking it as it occurs. Fascinating fun. Truly, a real hoot for a forensic accountant."

Jet gently placed her hand on Burnett's forearm and gave him the full southern belle treatment. "Well now, professor. Why don't you just start considering yourself one of us? Would you like to be part of Bluegrass Confidential Investigations, just for a little while? I'm certain all the ladies would find you ever so dashing if you did."

Sonia was pretty certain she saw Burnett blush. "Yes, Burnett. Why don't you just consider yourself one of us, a real private investigator." She shot a quick look at Jet then turned back to the forensic accountant. "Now, what is it that you're going to make happen?"

Burnett looked back and forth between Jet and Sonia, but his eyes rested on Jet. "Well, before I tell you what I'm thinking, I have to ask for your utmost confidentiality." He snuck a surreptitious look around the bakery. "You see, what I'm planning on doing, in fact, what I've already done, is, well . . . ." His eyes widened. No words came out.

"Well, professor," cooed Jet, "you can be certain that we'll never tell a soul."

Sonia could have sworn she saw Jet batting her eyelashes.

"Okay then. I began . . ." Burnett Saunders stopped and looked around the room again. "Ladies, would you mind if we moved to that table in the back corner?"

Jet and Sonia looked toward the back of the room and then at each other. A silent message passed between them. Sonia stood up, grabbing her coffee and pastry. "Anything you'd like, Professor." The trio moved to a much more private table near the back of the room.

Burnett began again, very softly. "As I was saying. I've been thinking about how we can trap Michael Oakley in the act of embezzling funds from our client, Mr. Brownlee. What I've done, something I'm certain is not an activity sanctioned by—"

Once again, Jet touched Burnett's forearm. "Yes, Burnett. We understand. Go on."

"Well, what I've done is that I recreated an electronic copy of one of the invoices that Mr. Oakley is using in his illegal activity." He was beaming.

Jet and Sonia were somewhat confused. Finally, Sonia asked, "And that helps us how?"

"Don't you understand?" Burnett looked at Jet, then Sonia, then back again to Jet. "We can now submit one of those invoices to Bronson/Brownlee ourselves."

Jet reached out her hand, this time leaving it on Burnett's forearm. "I'm afraid you need to tell us more, Burnett."

His eyes glanced down at Jet's hand on his arm and lingered. Then he looked up at her. "You see, when Mr. Oakley sees that invoice come across his desk, one of two things will occur to him. First, since we'll make the invoice for the same amount as the last one he posted, he may just think he had forgotten to pay it; he'll go ahead and do so. Or, second, he may realize that someone is on to him, and that will put him in a difficult position."

Sonia reached out and put her hand on Burnett's other forearm, then smiled at Jet. Jet's actions had not gone unnoticed. "Tell us how that helps us, Burnett." Sonia's tone of voice had gotten breathy by the end of her question.

Burnett was a little flummoxed, but he dove into his explanation. "Now then, I've already told you that three days after each transaction, Mr. Oakley empties the account to which he has sent the illicit funds. That makes it very difficult for us to prove that he is the one performing the illegal transfer, particularly if the name he uses to access the account is fraudulent. However, and I learned this on television, if Ms. Vitale can plant one of those computer bugs on Mr. Oakley's computer, the kind that records and transmits any keystrokes made on the machine, we'll be able to demonstrate that he is the one making the illegal transfer."

Jet removed her hand and leaned back in her chair. "Cool."

"Understand," Burnett shook his head seriously, "that won't be enough to prove that he was aware that it was a fraudulent invoice, though it certainly would put him in a precarious position. However, if we are lucky, and if Mr. Oakley is as brash as we believe, he might well sit at that very same computer and orchestrate the transfer of those funds out of that account and into an account in his own name. If so, we will have him dead to rights."

Sonia sat back in her chair as well, nodding, then smiled at Jet.

Jet sat up again and leaned in. She put both of her hands back on Burnett's forearm, giving Sonia a look as she did. "Oh, Burnett. That's so elegant. It's incredible. You . . . you really know your way around accounting, don't you?"

"Well, I was first in my class at the university when I did my M.B.A. work." He was, once again, beaming.

Sonia took a sip of coffee and put a final morsel of pastry in her mouth. Go get him, girl. Lay it on as thick as you can. But you're going to hear about it from me when we get back to the office. She sat up as well. "So, you need me to get back into Oakley's computer and put a keystroke recording program on it? Is that correct?"

Burnett leaned in and whispered so softly his words were almost silent. "Yes. And as soon as you do, you'll have to use the form I created and send in the bogus invoice." He looked around the room surreptitiously yet again. "Can you do that?"

It was Sonia's turn to lean forward and whisper, though not as silently as Burnett had. "There was a time when I couldn't and wouldn't." She, too, looked around the room surreptitiously, but for her, it was an act. "But now that I've immersed myself in the darkness of the human soul, you know, only for altruistic purposes, I'm ready and able to do so."

Burnett's face all but glowed. "Excellent."

Sonia broke the mood and spoke in a normal voice. "Now if you don't mind, I've got to pull Ms. Jet away from all of this. We've got to talk about some work we need to do as regards something that may have happened out at Downstream Farm."

Jet shot Sonia a quick, somewhat dirty look. Sonia just smiled back at her, a big smile. They were both surprised by what Burnett said next.

20

"Downstream Farm?" Burnett smiled. "Oh, they're quite the topic of conversation this spring."

Sonia cocked her head. "They are?"

"Oh yes." His hands made a tiny movement toward his tie then stopped. "They've got a three-year-old who has been performing, how would you put it, out of his class, all spring. He's won several races. Strangely, his name is Frailing, which apparently, is some form of playing the banjo. He's owned by some famous musician who plays bluegrass music."

Jet took the last bite of her cinnamon roll. "What do you mean, 'out of his class?' "

This time, Burnett completed his standard lapel and bowtie routine. "As I'm sure you are well aware, the entire sport of horse racing is based on the notion of breeding strength, speed, and endurance into a horse. Although there are outliers, most racehorses can be expected to perform in relative accordance with the bloodlines from which they were bred. Frailing comes from good, but not great, stock, and was expected to do well, but not exceptionally well. The breeders and owners, of course, are hoping for that outlier, that horse that outperforms its breeding. In fact, there are three horses that are doing so this year, in quite impressive fashion, two colts and a filly."

Sonia had been pulling together her empty cup and plate. She stopped. "And one of those is from Downstream Farm?"

"Yes, Frailing. In fact, he'll be running in the Bluegrass Stakes this Saturday at Keeneland Racetrack."

Sonia looked at Burnett. "How do you know so much about what's been going on in the world of horse racing? You a big betting man?"

Burnett smiled. "Oh, goodness no. A forensic accountant would never dabble in something so unscientific and unpredictable as betting on horse racing. No, it's my interest in the relationship between expected results and actual results that excites me. Each year I follow horse racing results from all around the country. Then I build a mathematical model of predicted results and compare them to actual results. The mathematical permutations are fascinating. I would never actually bet on a horse."

Jet snorted quietly again. "Me either. Why waste my time? I just send them a check. It's easier and faster than going to the track and losing the money."

"Yeah right," laughed Sonia, "you're out there every chance you get. In fact, why don't we go there this Saturday and watch Frailing run? It'd be fun watching one of the Downstream Farm horses, wouldn't it?"

Jet gave Sonia a sly smile. "Well, it would be great fun if *Burnett* would join us and explain everything that's going on." She turned to him, "Burnett, you'd come with us, wouldn't you? You know, just to explain things to us."

Sonia rolled her eyes. Nicely played girl. Got to give you that one. Nicely played.

Burnett had his biggest smile of the day plastered on his face. "Oh, I almost never actually go to the races, but that sounds like it would be great fun. I believe I could do that. You know, I don't work on weekends. On weekends I do other things."

Sonia stood up. "Okay, it's really time we get going. I'll check in with Steven Brownlee and we'll make arrangements for another foray into the offices of Michael Oakley." Then she gave Jet another sly look. "Jet, would you mind making the arrangements with Burnett as to our trip to Keeneland this Saturday?"

Jet didn't answer.

"Good. Then let's go. We've got other work to do." She reached out to touch Burnett's arm one last time. She looked at him with a certain softness in her eyes and voice. "Have a good day, Burnett. I look forward to seeing you Saturday."

Sonia started walking away and didn't turn around as she spoke. "C'mon Jet. Time to go." She smiled to herself. Oh, Jet, my dearest friend, this is going to be such fun. I'm going to make you pay for every single bat of those beautiful eyelashes of yours and every time you put your hands ever so caringly on the forearms of Burnett Saunders.

Jet spoke as they climbed the stairs. "What was that all about?"

Sonia turned around with an innocent look. "What was what all about?"

"All those snarky remarks, and, 'Jet, would you mind making arrangements with Burnett for Saturday?' "

"I'm afraid I don't have the slightest idea what you're talking about." Sonia could barely contain her smile as they walked into the BCI waiting area and she continued into her office.

Jet followed, stepping through the doorway. "Yeah, yeah. Right. And then putting your hands on Burnett's arms and asking," her voice shifted into that of a pouty seductress in a cheap movie, " 'Tell us how that helps us.' "

Sonia spun around, her eyes and mouth wide open. "Oh, that's rich. *I'm* the one who was playing up to Burnett?" It was Sonia's turn to sound like she was asking the star football player to join them at the Friday night bonfire. " 'It would be so much more fun if *Bur-nett* would come with us and explain what was going on.' " Her voice shifted. "Hell, you've all but got a brass plate on the back of one of the seats at Keeneland. You certainly don't need Burnett to explain anything to you about going to the races."

Jet relented and gave Sonia a wink. "Hey, a girl can have a little fun, can't she? What's the harm? And besides, he really is a nice guy."

Sonia took a seat at her desk. "Nice and stiff is how I believe you described him last week."

Jet stopped and leaned against the door jamb. "Well . . . yeah, he's a little formal, but there's something a little sexy about him, too, don't you think?"

Sonia did agree. She leaned back in her chair, stretching her arms over her head as she spoke. "Okay. I'm not sure about that. But where are you going with this, anyway? Are you really interested in him? You know, as a . . . uh . . . I don't know, a romantic interest?" Sonia watched as Jet stood straighter and looked off into the distance. *Here it comes. I'm about to hear from the southern belle.*

"Oh, my, my, my. Can a honeysuckle plant be blamed if hummingbirds are drawn to its natural fragrance? Can the little bee resist the temptation to fly from blossom to blossom, pollinating all those beautiful flowers?" She turned her eyes back toward Sonia and dropped her accent. "Let's just say that Burnett Saunders and I have a natural disposition for being drawn together . . . even if he doesn't know it yet."

Sonia just shook her head and smiled. "Well, just be careful with him, please. I'm guessing he hasn't had a lot of experience with women, and I'd hate to see him get his feelings hurt while you're just buzzing around him like one of those bees. Now let's get to work."

Jet came into Sonia's office and plopped down in the red chair opposite Sonia's desk. "Okay. What is it that you want to work on?"

"Well, first, I just can't get what Gabriela said about Limey out of my head. Maybe there was a lot more going on between him and Mariana than anyone realized. I just feel like we've got to get out there and see if we can get a better handle on Mr. . . . Limey, whatever his real name is."

Jet pulled her silky blonde hair back into its perpetual pony-tail and deftly whipped an elastic around it. "Okay. What else?"

"Well, while I call James out at Downstream and make an appointment for us to go out there again, I think you need to keep poking around with her old friends. Someone, somewhere, must have some idea where she might have gone, assuming she had any choice in the matter."

Jet shook her head. "Look, I'll do it. I'll do it because I know this is how PIs find things that others can't, sheer diligence. But I've got to tell you, I don't have much hope. I've called and spoken to everyone on that list, everyone except that one girl who's gone on some wilderness trip out west. So far, nothing."

"I know, Jet." Sonia struggled to shake off the heaviness in her heart. "You've done a great job. But we've just got to keep trying. She can't have just disappeared from the face of the earth. She can't just be gone."

Jet stood up and started to walk out of Sonia's office. When she was halfway through the doorway, she stopped and turned around. "Sonia, sweetheart. It may be time that you start to enter-tain that exact thought."

Sonia knitted her eyebrows. "What thought?"

Softly, Jet said, "That she might be just that . . . gone."

21

On Wednesday afternoon, Sonia had been able to contact James Racine and make arrangements to visit Downstream Farm again. By ten o'clock Thursday morning, Sonia was standing outside of Magee's, two coffees in hand, waiting for Jet. The air was clear but noticeably crisp. Jet pulled into the parking lot in her Camry and motioned for Sonia to hop in.

Sonia slid into the front seat. "Good morning."

"Morning." Jet backed out of the parking space then eased into traffic, headed west toward the center of town. "So, you managed to get Racine to allow us onto the farm?"

"Yup." Sonia took in the sights as they drove along East Main, a special warmth touching her heart as they passed Thoroughbred Park, with its lifelike statues of horses and jockeys all but flying toward a nonexistent finish line. "They're busy, with the Bluegrass Stakes coming up, but he made an exception for us."

Sonia wasn't much in the mood to be chatty that morning. She watched the streets go by. Dang, Mariana would have been so excited today, preparing one of the horses on her own farm for the Bluegrass Stakes. Big deal race. Frailing doing so well. Maybe a step closer to the Kentucky Derby. And instead . . . . Sonia tried not to finish the thought.

It was almost ten-thirty when Jet turned the Camry into the long driveway leading onto the farm. There were not a lot of extra people on hand for the long day of preparations, but those who were certainly seemed busy.

Jet pulled into the small parking area by the main house and she and Sonia stepped out of the car. Sonia stood tall, taking in the entire scene. As she had on her first visit to the farm, she couldn't help but wonder if the folks who worked there became numb to its beauty, to the splendor of fabulous animals living and being cared for in this idyllic setting.

Sonia nudged Jet. "There's Racine, over there by the smaller barn. We should say hello."

"Agreed."

They walked toward the entrance to the smaller barn and waited patiently as Racine finished a conversation with three men. Finally, he turned to them. "Ladies. Good morning."

"Morning," the girls replied almost simultaneously.

"Thank you for letting us come this morning, James. This is my partner, Jet."

"Jet?"

Jet reached out to shake his hand. "It's a long story. Believe me, everyone just calls me Jet."

Racine, dressed almost the same way he had been on Sonia's first visit—boots, jeans, light blue shirt—turned to the three men and nodded. "These ladies are here trying to help locate Mariana Castillo." He shifted his attention to the tallest of the three. "She's a member of our staff who is missing, and about whom we're all very concerned." All three men nodded solemnly. He turned back to Sonia and Jet and smiled. "And let me introduce these three scoundrels."

His attention went first to the oldest-looking man, a man in his late sixties, early seventies. "This is George Masson. His family has owned Downstream Farm for almost a hundred years."

Masson looked like money—gray-haired but still quite trim and with a bright smile. He shook hands with Sonia then Jet. He was dressed in the manner one might expect of a farm owner—khaki slacks, embroidered belt, a white shirt with the Downstream Farm logo. Even his "field boots" were clearly expensive. "Very nice to meet you, ladies. We're so grateful for your help. You know, everyone around here liked and respected Mariana." He nodded gently. "She's a wonderful young lady, great with the horses, great with people. We miss her."

After an awkward pause, Racine continued. "And this is Jackson Paine. I assume you know of his reputation as one of the finest bluegrass banjo players of his generation."

"Of course," Sonia lied.

The tall, very thin, man with the flowing jet-black hair that should have been gray, given his seventy-something years, smiled. He was pure country in his attire, but "successful country" for sure. From his fancy cowboy boots, to his designer jeans, to his blue western shirt with its gingham yoke, the look was that of a simple country boy—a simple country boy who got his clothing straight from one of the more expensive men's shops in Nashville. He shook Sonia's hand quickly but lingered as he took Jet's. He made such intense eye contact with Jet that Sonia could sense her discomfort. "Ladies. Y'all are a beautiful addition to a beautiful morning."

Racine jumped in, apparently aware that Paine was used to dealing with adoring fans, particularly those of the female persuasion. "Jackson is Frailing's owner."

Paine puffed up even more. "Bought him for a song. And now, look. Gonna win the Bluegrass Stakes and be on his way to the Derby." Everyone nodded politely.

Racine turned to the last man, the shortest of the trio. "And this is Gilberto Ramirez. He's Frailing's trainer."

The slight, dark-haired, dark-eyed man in his late forties smiled and reached out his hand to Sonia. "Good morning." This was clearly a man who actually worked with horses. Simple blue jeans, plain working boots, and a dark-red shirt. Only his ball cap bearing Frailing's name gave any indication of his connection to the animal and the role this man played in bringing racehorses to the winner's circle.

Jet lit up. *"Buenos días."*

Gilberto smiled back. *"Buenos días."* He shook her hand as well. *"Como estás?"*

"Bien, gracias, y tú?"

Gilberto's smile turned just a bit sly. *"Qué tan bueno es tú español?"*

Sonia watched as Jet stood in embarrassed silence, clearly unable to answer the question. Even Sonia could tell it had something to do with Jet's ability to speak Spanish.

Gilberto helped Jet out saying simply, "It's nice to meet you."

Racine put his hand on Gilberto's shoulder. "Gilberto's horses have won every major race in Mexico. And now that he's come to the States to work, he's well on his way to doing great things here as well."

Jackson Paine pointed over his shoulder with his thumb and nodded. "Starting with Frailing." He was still puffed up. Most likely, Sonia guessed, his perpetual state of being. "You know, I was gonna name him G-String, after the top string on the banjo. Wanna know why?" He didn't wait for an answer. " 'Cause he's gonna be nothin' but the top of the heap." He gave his head a quick shake. "But that darn Jockey Club's got to approve the name of every racehorse that's part of the industry, and they wouldn't go with G-String." He rolled his eyes. "They said it had 'sexual implications.' " He took a moment to snort and spit. "Screw 'em, I say. Don't matter. I named him Frailing instead, after the first style of banjo playing ever done here in the good ol' U.S. of A." He swelled his chest as if making an important point.

"Came over from Africa with the first banjos." He leaned back and pointed at the girls, breaking into an even bigger smile. "And you watch, he'll darn well be first himself. First at the Derby that is. You just watch." The smile was broad and somewhat contagious, though Sonia figured that behind all the bravado was a man who was actually out of his league, a man who knew very little about horses—except that owning a winning one might get him even more opportunities with attractive young women.

Sonia sensed it might be useful to meet all these men, but the one she really wanted to get close to was nowhere in sight. "James, I guess everyone is really busy today?"

"Oh yeah." He let his eye scan the farm quickly. "Lots to do. We've got to get ready to move Frailing over to Keeneland this afternoon. It's a short trip, but that doesn't mean we don't have to use all the precautions we normally do when putting a valuable racehorse in a van and transporting him. We do it the same way we would if we were shipping him to any other venue."

"So where is Frailing?" Sonia leaned to her left with the expectation that she might be able to see him in the main barn. "I don't remember seeing him the other day."

"No, ma'am. Frailing's not here." Racine smiled. "This is a breeding farm. He's been out at Running Creek farm. It's a training facility. We'll be picking him up today and bringing him over to Keeneland."

"And everyone's involved?" Sonia scanned the immediate surroundings as well. "All the folks that normally work with him, like Limey, say?"

Racine nodded. "Sure, yeah. Everyone on the farm is focused on this, Limey included. Of course, we still have to take care of all the other horses."

Sonia looked at Jet, then back to Racine. "Well, we should be getting out of your hair. If you don't mind, we're just going to walk around and get a sense of things. You don't mind if we ask some folks some questions . . . if we keep it short?"

"No." Racine looked around again, clearly intent on making certain everyone was as focused as he was. "Go right ahead. Just remember, their minds are really somewhere else today."

As Sonia and Jet walked away from the trio of men, Jet gently put her hand on Sonia's shoulder. "Nicely done. So, I assume we're off to find Limey?"

"You've got it. Let's try the big barn."

The girls walked over and through the bigger barn, noting these horses had accommodations that were nicer than many people's homes. Limey was nowhere in sight. They eventually found him behind that barn, bathing and brushing one of the other horses, a beautiful grey animal with a black mane and tail and a white blaze on its face. There was another man with him, talking to Limey while the big man worked on the horse.

Sonia led the way over to them. "Wow. That's quite an animal."

Limey gave her a broad smile. "Surely she is ma'am. Surely she is." There was a clear touch of English heritage in his speech, though more cockney than Kensington Palace. "Name's Pawtucket, like the city in Rhode Island. Stands sixteen hands tall, every bit of it pure muscle. She won her share of races, too. Now she's one of our most important brood mares."

Having grown up in the city, Sonia was not exactly used to horses. She was anxious about being around such a powerful animal, but she tried to put her fears aside. "Can I pet her?"

Limey chuckled. "She's a bit sloppy now, ma'am, but just come at her nice and slow.

"By the way, my name's Sonia. And yours is?" She very tentatively scratched the horse's face. She was being careful to avoid any part of Pawtucket that might bite her.

"Limey, ma'am. They just call me Limey."

Jet stepped forward. "Sounds like me. They just call me Jet."

Limey turned to Jet. "Now that's an unusual one, isn't it? I'm sure from my accent you can tell why they call me Limey. But Jet, what's that about?"

"Oh, it's a long story." Jet reached out and let Pawtucket's nose nuzzle her hand as she got a good sense of Jet's intentions. Jet's moves were much more confident than Sonia's. "So how long have you been in the states?"

He bent over, picked up a hose, and began gently rinsing the horse. "Came over when I was a young man. Had a run in with some folks who were uncomfortable with me because of my family background." He gave her a sly smile. "Bit of a royal, you know."

Jet stepped a little closer to Limey. "Sounds fascinating. I'd like to hear more about that sometime."

22

S onia had given Pawtucket what she felt was enough attention to sell the notion that she was truly interested in the horse. She stepped back and turned to the other man. "And who are you, sir?"

Limey answered first. "Oh, that's Ron Harris." He directed a snarky smile toward his friend. "Wouldn't know the front end of a horse from its rear. All he knows about is money."

Ron Harris, a smaller, blonde-haired man in his early forties, was dressed more in business casual clothing than farm attire—nice slacks, button-down shirt, loafers. "I'm sorry for the rude interruption. My good friend, Limey, here, doesn't seem to have the appropriate appreciation for the people who make this whole horse racing thing work, thereby giving him and others like him gainful employment."

Sonia tried to take in the man's essence. "And what exactly is it that you do?"

"I'm a broker." Harris held his head just a little higher. "Actually, the proper term is bloodstock agent. We appraise animals, analyze bloodlines, sometimes bid on horses for our clients, or even broker deals between owners."

Sonia smiled at Limey. "So, he really does know the front end of a horse from its rear, now doesn't he, Limey?"

Limey feigned being insulted. "If you've never bathed them, brushed them, fed them, and mucked out their stalls, you don't really know them. That's what I think." He turned and gave Jet a big wink as he began brushing the magnificent animal.

Sonia pressed a little. "And why are you here on such a busy day, Mr. Harris?"

Harris gave a quick wave of his hand. "Oh, you can call me Ron." He ran his fingers through his short, blond hair. "I've got a special interest in Frailing. I'm the one who helped Mr. Paine purchase the horse after it was bred right here on the farm."

Jet didn't hesitate. "And if Frailing wins on Saturday, does that mean a pay-off for you?"

Ron chuckled. "I wish. No, I get paid commissions on deals I negotiate, but none of the spoils if I help someone come up with the buy of a lifetime."

Jet passed a look at Sonia, and Sonia got the message. She gave Harris an engaging smile. "I'd like to know more about that, Ron. Would you mind walking with me as I look around? Maybe you could explain some things to me."

Ron Harris lit right up, clearly pleased by Sonia's attention. "Certainly. Lead on. What would you like to know?"

Sonia gave Jet a knowing look and took off in the direction of one of the smaller barns. It wasn't that she was so interested in hearing what Ron Harris had to say. What interested her most was what Jet would get out of Limey if left alone with him.

Less than thirty minutes later, Sonia and Ron Harris finished the loop from the bigger barn to the little ones and back. Along the way, Ron had explained how the whole horse business worked, who made deals with whom, who bought or sold horses or breeding rights, and so on.

As they approached the back of the bigger barn, Sonia saw Jet sitting alone on a bale of hay. "Thanks for all the information,

Ron. Just fun to know." She shook his hand briefly. "Nice to meet you. Good luck at the races Saturday." As she walked away, she could feel his eyes follow her, a sensation that was not new to her.

It took Sonia less than a minute to make her way over to Jet, taking in the beauty of the farm as she went. "Ready to go?"

Jet stood up. "Absolutely." They began strolling back to Jet's car.

Sonia spoke in a hushed voice, her eyes forward. "Well, what did you find out?"

"Not much." Jet put a piece of hay she had plucked out of the bale into her mouth and chewed on it between words. "I was able to get him to talk about Mariana, after, that is, I squelched his attempts to hit on me. Seems he really did like her. Says he considered her," she made quotation marks in the air, "a friend. "

Sonia turned more directly to her. They stopped walking. "Anything else? Anything important?"

"Nothing's for certain, but he really did seem upset about something when Mariana came up." They started walking again. "Of course, he could just be good at hiding things, but there was this one thing he said."

"Yeah?"

Jet brushed some errant hay off her jeans. "He said that in the last few months she seemed more and more distracted, that she had less and less time to spend with him." She made the quotation marks again, " 'Just as a friend,' he was quick to point out."

"And how did you read that?"

"I don't know," Jet tossed the piece of straw to the ground. "but I do have to say it kind of creeped me out. It was almost like he felt she owed him something, you know, like spending time with him, and she wasn't keeping up her part of the bargain."

Sonia ran her fingers through her hair. "Weird."

"Weird."

By then they had reached Jet's car and were slipping into their seats, each one taking a final look at the beauty that surrounded them. Jet fired up the Camry and started down the drive, heading for their offices. Things were silent in the car for the next few moments.

Eventually, Sonia spoke. "So, you got the feeling that Limey was ticked off at her for pulling away from their friendship?"

Jet glanced over at Sonia, then back to the road. "Pulling away, not having time, something. Something about what she was doing was bothering him, making him feel cheated."

Sonia shook her head. "Wow, I sure wish we knew more about what that meant."

23

J ust after seven-thirty that evening, the girls met back in Jet's
office. It was April, but the evenings were still cool, almost
cold. Sonia zipped up her spring jacket. "Ready to go?"

Jet did the same. "You know me. I'm always ready to roll."

"Okay then. I told Steven Brownlee we'd meet him outside his
place at eight. It sure is nice to know we don't have to worry about
breaking into the place . . . or Oakley's office either."

"Oh." Jet put her wallet and keys in her jacket pocket, leaving
her purse on the floor next to her desk just as Sonia had. "So, now
we're glad we don't have to bother to break into some building?
And me with black clothing and a ski mask in the back of my
car."

Sonia just chuckled. They moved through the waiting area
and down the steps. As they turned the corner and walked
toward her car, Sonia noticed a figure standing near the back
corner of the optometrist's building on the other side of the
parking lot. She peered through the darkness. Tall. A man she
assumed. Strange. Within moments, they had reached Sonia's
Subaru. Sonia looked back. He was gone. She dismissed the
thought, slipped in, and buckled up.

Jet looked over her shoulder as Sonia backed out of the parking space. "Lead on Captain. We've got work to do tonight, and you're the one that's up at bat."

It was a short drive to the offices of Bronson/Brownlee and they could see Steven Brownlee's car in the parking lot as they turned in. As soon as they pulled up next to him, Brownlee got out of his car to greet them. The girls slipped out as well.

As they walked to the building, Brownlee pulled his huge ring of keys out of his pocket. "Thanks so much for doing this tonight, ladies. I know that I had my suspicions, but when Burnett said that Michael is cheating me, I just found it hard to believe." He put his hand on the door, holding the proper key just inches away from its destination. "I mean, why would a young man with a bright future have to do something like that? I gave him a good job and a good salary. Couldn't he have been patient enough to work his way up like we all do?"

Jet put her hand on Brownlee's shoulder, in an almost manly fashion. "Just the way it is nowadays. Some young folks think that anyone older than thirty is too dumb to figure out what they're up to. And they think that if you can't catch them at it, they have every right to do it. But don't worry, Steven. We've already caught him at it, and soon we'll be proving it as well."

Brownlee slid the key into the door and spoke, shaking his head slowly. "I know. It's just sad, isn't it?" He opened the door and went in quickly. He headed to an electronic touchpad on the far in order to get to the alarm before it went off.

Sonia and Jet followed Brownlee into the building, then down the hall to Michael Oakley's office. Brownlee opened the office door and waved the girls in. "There you go. It's all yours." He followed them into the room.

As they walked into Oakley's office, Sonia got a spooky feeling. Everything looked almost exactly as it had the last time they had been there—the desk absolutely clear of clutter, the twenty-four-hour security feed from several cameras rolling on the monitor overhead, the only sound in the room the hum of the heating system. It struck her that it was always weird to be in someone else's space when they didn't know about it.

Sonia sat down at Oakley's desk and turned on his computer. She used the password to get in. As she did, it was the "old fool" part that really galled her.

As soon as the computer was fully running, Sonia stuck her flash drive into the appropriate port and began downloading a keystroke program that hides in the computer's operating system and intercepts keystrokes. The program had software that enabled Sonia to login to Oakley's machine via the internet. With that access, she and Burnett could look directly into data logs stored on Oakley's machine and have Burnett could interpret the financial implications of that activity. And, if Oakley used his office computer to transfer money out of that account to his own, Burnett would be able to see that as well. They would have him for sure.

It was a large program, and Sonia knew it would take several minutes to load. As they waited for the program to infiltrate Oakley's computer, Sonia and Jet spoke softly, surreptitiously, while Brownlee waited patiently. A moment later, Sonia saw a strange look on Jet's face. "What? What is it?"

Jet pointed at a security monitor. "We've got trouble. Someone's coming in the front door. That's the front door, right, Steven?"

Brownlee looked up. "Yes, and darn it, that's Michael Oakley. He's coming right here. I've got to stop him."

As Brownlee scooted out the door and closed it, Jet stepped quickly to the light switch and turned it off. It was just a moment later that they heard Brownlee in the hall, his voice loud and friendly. "Michael, what are you doing here so late?"

Sonia could sense that Oakley was still coming right toward them as she heard his voice grow louder. "Mr. Brownlee. I could ask you the same question."

"Shithook," Jet whispered softly.

"Oh, you know." The tone of Brownlee's voice was almost lilting. "Now that my wife is gone, sometimes it gets lonely at home at night. Some nights I just like to come in and walk around the place." Sonia could hear him fiddle with the large ring of keys in his hand. "Kind of makes me feel close to ol' Bronson, too. I'd bet he'd be surprised we're still at it."

Sonia and Jet exchanged a look. Then Jet whispered, "Good job, Steven. You're spinnin' a good yarn there, buddy."

Sonia moved in closer to Jet. She was staring at the monitor, trying to get a real sense of Michael Oakley, the man. From what she could see on the screen, he was a slight man with darkish hair and a somewhat odd-looking goatee. Though he was dressed in jeans and a sports jacket over a tie-less oxford shirt, there were clear indications that a premature middle-aged spread was taking hold of the young man's midriff. She whispered, "Do you think he'll buy it?"

Jet started to answer. "I don't . . . oh shit. The computer."

"What?"

"The computer. The glow from the computer. He'll see it under the door."

Sonia turned toward the computer, still whispering. "I can't stop it. I don't think there's a separate switch for the monitor, and I can't stop the program in mid-stream."

Jet pulled off her jacket. "Quick. Give me your coat. Quick. Quick."

Sonia watched as Jet slid both jackets under the edge of the office door.

Jet stood up, relieved. "That should do it." But almost immediately Sonia saw the look of panic return to Jet's face; she knew why. They could hear Oakley continuing to make his way toward his office, Brownlee apparently walking with him.

"I know Mr. Brownlee, but this will just take a minute. I've just got to get this one item paid so that when they open their account tomorrow the money will be there."

It was at that moment that it struck Sonia. Oakley's door. It was unlocked. She lunged for the door, grabbed the deadbolt lever and then froze. Gently, as quietly as she could, she slowly, slowly, slowly slid the deadbolt, waiting for the soft but tell-tale click that finally came. She stood there motionlessly.

Sonia's mind was scrambling. What if he comes in. Should we hide? Where would we hide? We can't hide. The coats. Grab the coats. No, they need to stay there. C'mon program, load, load.

Brownlee's voice came to them through the door. "Now Michael, I insist." The voices stopped coming closer. "I've given my whole life to this business. Been here every day for years, and too many nights. You know, I heard this thing once. When you ask a man at the end of his life, what is it that he wished he'd done more of? Do you know what the answer is? Well, I can tell you one thing, it's never, 'I wish I spent more time at work and away from my family and friends.' Now you go home, Michael. You go home and do whatever it is that makes you happy. That money will be in their account when it gets there. We're paying our bills. They can wait one more day if need be. Now go on, get out of here. Go have a life."

Sonia and Jet waited breathlessly for Oakley's response. Finally, the words came. "Okay, Mr. Brownlee. Thanks. Maybe I'll go have that beer with my friends. You have a good night."

"You as well, son."

Sonia turned to Jet, still whispering. "Holy crap. That was close. Thank God he never opened that door."

Just then, they heard Oakley's voice coming to them from farther away, down the hall. "Just one question, Mr. Brownlee. Whose car is that next to yours in the parking lot?"

Jet whispered. "Damn it."

Sonia held her breath while silence filled the hall outside Oakley's office.

Brownlee spoke. "You know, Michael. I was wondering the same thing. It was here when I got here tonight, so I parked right next to it. I swear I don't recognize it. Do you?"

Sonia heard no response. Is he just shaking his head? Is he coming back? What do we do if he comes back?

Finally, Oakley spoke. "You haven't seen anything on the security feed, have you? Maybe we should go look at that."

Brownlee was quick to respond. "No. No. I've already checked that. It was the first thing I did when I got in the building. It's fine. No one else is here. I'm sure of it."

Oakley pressed. "Are you positive? We could go look at the recording of the last few hours."

There was another moment of silence, the girls' ears straining to hear. "No, I'm sure. I'll tell you what. If we find something amiss in the morning, we'll check the recording then. For now, why don't we both just go home."

"Okay. But I want to walk with you to the cars. I wouldn't want someone to be hanging around the building, waiting for an opportunity to sneak in, or worse, to do something to you."

Jet gave Sonia a look. "Dirtbag."

Brownlee was silent for a moment. Then he spoke, more loudly than before. "Sure. Okay. That makes sense. Let's you and I go right now. I'll reset the alarm on the way out."

Jet and Sonia stood there in breathless silence, listening for footsteps either coming closer or fading away. After more than a minute, Jet looked at Sonia. "I guess they're both gone."

"Wow. That was close." Sonia glanced at the computer. "Okay, the program's loaded." She ejected the thumb drive and shut down the computer. "Let's get out of here."

Jet looked at her and started to quietly laugh. "You want to get out of here now?"

Sonia looked at her, her brow furrowed. "Yeah. Right now." Her voice was more than emphatic. "C'mon. I've had enough of this place for one night. Let's go."

"And exactly how are we going get out of here with the alarm on?"

Sonia froze. She turned to Jet. "We're trapped in here?"

"Not sure my friend. But it looks like we may be spending the night sitting in this very office. You didn't by any chance bring a flask of something smooth and warm, did you?"

Sonia let out a huge sigh and plopped back down into Michael Oakley's chair.

onia and Jet spent the better part of two hours waiting in Michael Oakley's office, afraid there might be motion detectors in the hallways and hoping that Steven Brownlee would come to rescue them. Sonia asked Jet to call Brownlee on his phone, but it turned out that Jet didn't have his cell number, she had only spoken to him on his office phone. Finally, a little after eleven o'clock, they noticed some movement on the security camera monitor. It was Brownlee.

Jet slipped on her jacket. "It's about damn time."

Sonia did the same. "Look, at least he's here."

Brownlee finally turned the key, opened the outer door, and walked into the building. It took him another minute or so to turn the alarm off and get back to Oakley's office. "Sorry ladies. I had to be absolutely certain that Michael wasn't sitting somewhere watching, waiting to see if I came back. After two hours, I thought the coast was probably clear."

Sonia walked up to him and gave him a smile and a little hug, patting him on his back. "At least you came back for us. We were afraid we were going to spend the whole night here."

Jet put her hand on his shoulder. "Just glad you came back.

Now don't forget to go back there and lock Oakley's door before you leave. And you'd better wipe that security tape as well. I'm afraid we're all over it. We'll meet you at the cars." At eleven-twenty-five, both cars left the parking lot and the night finally came to an end.

~

Just after four o'clock Friday afternoon, Sonia walked into the BCI offices looking somewhat glum.

Jet looked up from her desk and spoke loudly enough to be heard in the waiting area. "Well, look what the cat drug in. Hard day today, lady?"

Sonia trudged across the visitor's area and into Jet's office. She stood in the doorway. "Not terrible, but not great."

"What's going on?"

"I spent the afternoon trying to close the case of the cheating husband who works at night then goes next door in the afternoon to mess around with his young, attractive neighbor."

Jet looked up from her computer. "You get some shots?"

"Oh, Mr. Afternoon Delight did get together with his happy, home-making hussy, but I got nothing that was really worth using." As she took a seat in the red, padded chair, Sonia's eyes scanned the rubble on Jet's desk, hoping there was a cup of something from which she could sneak a sip. She saw nothing. "So, did you accomplish anything today? Is that why you're in such a good mood?"

Jet leaned further back, stretching her arms above her head and then relaxing them. "As a matter of fact, I did. Listen up. I think you'll like this."

Sonia sat up taller. She was hoping that what Jet had to share would make up for the frustration of the morning and, more importantly, for the lack of progress they'd made so far on Mariana's case.

Jet pointed to a yellow pad on which she had a list of names, mostly crossed off. "You know that girl I told you about, she was on some wilderness adventure out west and I couldn't reach her?"

"I remember."

"Well, she's back and I reached her this afternoon."

Sonia yawned. She was interested, but it had already been a long day. "You get anything from her?"

"You're not going to believe what I got from her." Jet's smile was sly. "Seems like that goofy Professor Andersen doesn't have as good a memory as he thinks."

"What do you mean?" Sonia's attention was piqued.

It was Jet's turn to sit up and become more fully engaged. "So, I talk to this girl, Allie something. She says she has no idea where Mariana might have gone."

Sonia's eyes went to the ceiling. "As usual."

Jet leaned in. "But here's the thing. She says, she's sorry she can't help, but if anyone would know where Mariana might go, it would be these other two girls." Jet looked down at her pad to find the new names. "Let's see. Penny Rey Nelson and LaKiesha Washington."

Sonia sat forward in her chair as if she were trying to read the names on Jet's list upside-down. "And those names. They weren't on your list before?"

"Nope." Jet shook her head broadly. "Seems like Professor Smarty-Pants missed a few. This Allie said that Penny Rey and LaKiesha were real tight with Mariana. Real tight."

Sonia smiled. "Excellent. Good work, Kimosabe."

Jet simply leaned back nodding her head in self-congratulation.

"So, have you contacted either one of them yet?"

Jet held up her hands as if to cool Sonia's excitement. "I'm still trying to track down phone numbers for them." She dropped her hands. "Based on what this Allie said, I'm pretty sure they're both working in the horse industry. Probably right here in Lexington."

Sonia continued to lean forward, her fatigue gone. "Wouldn't that be great? If one of them knew where she was."

"I'm on it, Tonto. Me and my big white horse . . . . "

"Silver."

"Huh?"

"Silver." her voice rose. "The horse's name was Silver. Didn't you see that horrible Johnny Depp movie?"

"Oh, yeah, yeah." Jet waved her hand in front of her face. "Anyway. I'm on it. I'll get to them as soon as I can."

There was a pause in the conversation while each of the girls pondered the new possibilities. Eventually, Jet said, "So, when the heck is Brad getting back?"

Sonia shifted in her chair. "Don't get me started."

"About what?"

Sonia ran her fingers through her hair. "About when he's coming home."

Jet's face softened. "Problems?"

"No. Not really." She looked past Jet to the blue sky outside Jet's window over East Main. "It's just that he got a phone call from a certain DEA agent who needed his help with something."

The surprise in Jet's voice was completely obvious. "Robbie Alvarez? He got a call from Robbie Alvarez?" Jet's gaze drifted away for just the briefest moment.

"The one and only. And this time it was Robbie who needed Brad's help, so off he goes running to help his buddy."

Jet looked at Sonia over the glasses that weren't on her nose. "You okay with that?"

Sonia twisted her lips. "Sure, why wouldn't I be."

Jet simply shrugged.

"Look, Jet." Sonia's voice had an edge to it. "He's a big boy, and he's helping a friend. You know how it works in this business. A guy calls asking for help, you go. You go right away and you go fast."

Jet's face softened. "Are you sure you're okay with this. I mean, couldn't he have come home for a day or two first?"

"I guess you're—"

Jet's phone rang. She turned and put her hand up to silence Sonia. "Bluegrass Confidential Investigations. This is Jet speaking. How can I help you?"

The conversation lasted only a few moments. Jet hung up then looked down at the phone in her hand. "Well. That's unusual."

"What? Who was that?"

"That, my dear colleague," Jet looked at Sonia, "was one hot mamacita."

Sonia was silent for a moment, while names and faces ran through her brain. "Oh. You mean Gabriela?"

"In the flesh." Jet looked down at her phone again as if there was more information to be gleaned from the already-ended conversation.

"What did she want?"

Jet stood and turned to the window, looking down at the street below as she spoke. "What she wants is for us to come down to Papi's tonight. It seems she's working the dinner shift and there's something she wants to tell us."

"And she couldn't do it over the phone?" Sonia's voice reflected her confusion.

"Apparently not." Jet sat back down at her desk. "Maybe it's something she doesn't want anyone else to know."

Sonia drew herself back almost imperceptibly. "Or maybe she's afraid of something."

Jet paused before she spoke. "Could be." Then she lightened up. "Anyway, here's the good news. Brad's not back in town so I guess you and I are on our way to Papi's for dinner."

Sonia stood up. "Looks like we've got ourselves a dinner date. Let's go early though, we've got a big day at the races in front of us tomorrow. And trust me, I need some sleep."

"Not too early." Jet moved some papers around on her desk. "She said not to come before nine when the dinner crowd starts to slow down. But don't you worry now, dear; we'll catch a light dinner and listen to what she has to say. I'll have you home and in bed by ten. Okay?" The sound of her voice was as demeaning as her words.

Sonia walked out of the office shaking her head. "Oh brother. How do I put up with you?"

Jet stood up again as well and spoke to Sonia's back. "I'll pick you up around eight-thirty. I'm driving. You know how you get when you start slamming down those margaritas."

Sonia kept walking down the steps. "Yeah, yeah, yeah. See you at eight-thirty."

25

J et picked Sonia up around eight-forty that evening. They were both dressed casually, but with a little color and flair, just right for dinner at a Mexican restaurant.

When they walked in, the hostess greeted them and asked, "Two?"

Jet was quick to respond. "*Sí. Dos por favor.*"

Sonia leaned around Jet to get the attention of the hostess. "Any chance we could be seated with Gabriela?"

The hostess looked around. "*Sí.* Yes. She has a table open. *Por aquí.*"

It was clear to Sonia that Jet had not the slightest idea what the woman had said, but since the hostess took off quickly across the room, it was obvious they were meant to follow her.

Sonia and Jet were seated and ordered drinks. While they waited, Sonia looked around for Paco Castillo. She didn't see him anywhere. She closed her eyes. Thank God he's not working tonight. I just don't know what I would say to him.

Gabriela finally showed up to take their order. "*Buenas noches,* ladies. What can I get you this evening?"

Sonia was wondering if Gabriela would lean right in and

share the information she had. She didn't. She treated them like any other customers. "Tonight, our special is our shrimp fajitas with a citrus-based sauce. It comes with soft flour tortillas."

Jet fell right in line. "That sounds great. Why don't you bring that for each of us? Okay with you, Sonia?"

Sonia was distracted, still looking around the room, but she responded, "Oh, yeah. That'll be fine. Thank you. Uh, *gracias.*"

Gabriella walked quickly away, leaving Sonia wondering how the night was going to play out. As it turned out, Sonia and Jet had a fine meal and two margaritas each. They were enjoying the opportunity to be with each other socially. As they were finishing the last sips of their second margaritas, Gabriela showed up with the check. "Anything else I can get you, ladies? Something else to drink?"

Jet shook her head gently, *"No mas, gracias.* Just the check, please."

Gabriela reached into her apron and pulled out the check. When she laid it on the table and walked away, however, Sonia noticed that there was a second piece of paper lying under the check itself. As Jet picked up the check, Sonia nonchalantly slipped the paper into her own hand and tucked it away. She then picked up her purse and asked, "How much do I owe?"

Sonia felt like the note Gabriela had left them was burning in her hand, while Jet did some quick calculating about the tip and splitting the cost of the meal. They stood and headed for the front door, stopping to pay the bill.

Walking down the steps, Sonia pulled Jet aside and asked, "Did you see this?"

"Sure, I saw it. What's it say?"

Sonia read the note out loud. "Short break in ten minutes. Meet me next door, outside Charlie Brown's."

The partners looked at each other. Neither said a word. They continued down the steps and out onto the street. Charlie

Brown's was right next door and they stepped into its wooden lean-to type entrance and waited.

Six or seven minutes later, Gabriela joined them. As striking as she was in the soft light of Papi's, she was even more so in the semi-darkness of the evening. Tall and shapely in her tight, black shirt and pants, her long black hair lying in front of her shoulder in a sexy ponytail, her lips were colored the same bright red as the belt and high-heeled shoes she wore. She huddled close to the girls in the tiny space. She didn't wait for them to ask anything.

"Santiago is missing. I have looked and looked for him all over the barrio. No one seems to know where he is. Or at least no one is willing to say. I don't know how I'm going to find him, but I wanted you to know."

Jet didn't mince words. "Know what, Gabriela?"

Gabriela gave Jet a "Don't you get this," look. "Know that the boy my cousin was dating is missing. Gone at the very same time she is gone. Gone and no one will say where."

Sonia took a step closer to her and spoke furtively. "Maybe we can help you find him."

The look on Gabriela's face remained less than inviting. "I will find him. She is my cousin. He is one of us. I will find him. And if I find out he has hurt her . . . ."

Sonia and Jet were silent, at a loss for words. This was not the way they usually operated, nor was this a situation with which they were familiar.

Gabriela looked at her watch. "I've got to go. I wanted you to know. But remember, you will not find him. I will find him. And I will do what I have to do." She turned and was gone in an instant.

Sonia turned to Jet but said nothing.

Jet reached out and put her hand on Sonia's forearm. "Don't you worry. We've got this. This will all work out. We've got this. C'mon. Let's go home."

"I sure hope she doesn't do anything stupid." Sonia had come to know that she could handle difficult and dangerous situations, situations that could actually mean the difference between life and death. But this was different. Gabriela seemed like she could be a loose cannon, like she might do something that could make the situation worse—much worse.

Jet turned and put her arm around Sonia. "That's not going to happen. Just a lot of worry and anger going around. C'mon. Big day tomorrow. Let's get home and get some sleep. This will work itself out. I promise."

The girls walked back to Jet's car in silence. Sonia's mind was reeling. *What is she going to do if she finds him? What if he is the one who's done something to Mariana? What if Gabriela hurts him? What if she kills him? What if that means we never find Mariana?*

S onia was glad that Saturday was going to be a relaxed, fun day. She had awoken to a beautiful spring morning, with a forecast of temperatures in the high seventies along with plenty of sunshine. It would be a great day to be at Keeneland to watch the horses run.

Around twelve o'clock, Sonia heard a car horn she didn't recognize. Nonetheless, she was pretty sure it was Burnett coming to pick her up. She walked down the stairs that serviced her apartment and out to the street. She wasn't at all surprised to see that Burnett had already picked up Jet. What did surprise her was the car that Burnett was driving. As best as she could tell, it was a four-door Mercedes sedan, probably from the 1970s. Dark red, with a light tan leather interior, the exterior shone in the sunlight. As Sonia approached the car, Burnett popped out, ran around the back of the car to meet her, then opened the passenger-side rear door for her.

As Sonia stepped toward the car door, she couldn't help but notice Burnett's attire. It was entirely different from his regular uniform, yet somehow the same. Usually, he wore a dark-colored, slightly oversized suit, with a white oxford shirt and a dark bowtie. Today, he wore a crisp off-white linen suit, a light blue oxford shirt, and a bowtie that had a somewhat festive red and blue pattern. The only real change in his approach to dressing was his hat. Sonia couldn't believe it. It was an honest-to-goodness straw boater hat, a skimmer, right out of the 1920s. Its red and blue ribbon perfectly matched Burnett's bowtie.

Sonia was also surprised when she slipped into the car and found Jet dressed in a manner Sonia would never have expected. Instead of wearing some nice, but casual attire, Jet was dressed in an outfit reminiscent of Audrey Hepburn in *Breakfast at Tiffany's*. She wore a sleeveless, navy polka dot pencil dress with a skinny, red belt. Four-inch red-and-straw wedges displayed her freshly pedicured toenails, and she carried a tiny clutch with a chain strap for over-the-shoulder wear. What really finished off the look was something Sonia had never seen on Jet, bright red lipstick. The only piece missing was the foot-long cigarette holder.

Sonia smiled. Well, you really outdid me today, partner. Here I am in a simple yellow top, with white slacks and my best flat sandals, and you're trying to entice Burnett into your web of seduction by appealing to his mistaken belief that we're still living in the 1960s. The way Burnett looked at Jet, as he slid behind the wheel, made it obvious to Sonia that Jet's plan was working—perfectly. When Sonia's eyes met Jet's in the side-view mirror, she could tell that Jet was having the time of her life. Sonia hoped that it wasn't going to be at Burnett's expense.

It was a short trip to the track and the three of them were soon getting out of Burnett's car. They were in the parking lot directly across the street from the Blue Grass Airport. Sonia gazed across the street. "I've never seen so many private jets parked out there at the airport before, big ones. Is something special going on?"

Burnett gave her a funny look. "Keeneland, my dear. Keeneland is going on. Those jets belong to the people who own some of the horses that are running today. You can be assured that at least one or two of them are sheiks or something from the Middle East."

Sonia turned and followed Burnett and Jet as they walked toward the entrance. "Wow, who knew?" Her words drifted unheard into the breeze.

As they continued to walk, Sonia noticed something else. The long walk to the entrance pavilion included some sections of loose stone, creating a lovely natural look. As Sonia watched Jet struggle to keep her balance on her four-inch wedges, she was glad to be walking in her more reasonable flat sandals. On the other hand, Jet was making the most of the difficult situation by leaning heavily, and closely, on Burnett for support. At one point, she even turned around and gave Sonia a sly wink and a smile.

Sonia returned the smile, though hers was much less enthusiastic. Oh, brother. You're milking this for all it's worth, aren't you dear partner?

As they approached the building, Sonia assumed they would head for the General Admission entrance. Instead, Burnett lead them to the reserved seating windows.

"You wouldn't want to be standing out in the sun all day," he said to them over his shoulder, his wide-brimmed skimmer shading the big smile on his face.

After walking through the entrance area, Sonia, who had never been to Keeneland before, was surprised again. She immediately found herself near a small grassy area, the paddock. It was relatively close to post time for the first race, and several horses were being walked around and around on paths specifically designated with numbers, each one circling a shade tree.

Sonia touched Jet's arm gently. "What a beautiful place. It's just gorgeous. The gray stone walls, the dark-green trim, so classy, so traditional. It feels like we're on an English manor."

Jet snickered. "Except for the beer and hot dogs on the other side of that walk-through path."

Sonia's eyes widened. "And those are the racehorses, right here by us?"

Jet smiled. "Yes, honey. Those are the horses that will be in the first race. The stable-hands lead them around the paddock so you can get a close look at them before you bet on the race. The number on each path corresponds to the number the horse will be wearing during the race. They're beautiful, aren't they?"

Sonia was truly in awe. "They're magnificent. I've seen them up close on the farm several times now but watching them walk around. It's just . . . . it's just exciting."

Burnett turned to Sonia and winked. "And you're standing here at a race track that's soaked in tradition. In fact, most of the racing scenes for the movie, *Seabiscuit*, were shot here because the track looks almost the same now as when he was running in the 1930s."

Burnett turned to Jet and smiled. "Now, can I get you ladies some refreshment?"

Jet and Sonia spoke almost simultaneously. Jet said, "Wouldn't that be nice." Whereas Sonia was saying, "Well, we don't want to miss the race, do we?"

Burnett chuckled and smiled at Sonia. "Don't worry about that. There will be plenty of time before the first race, and plenty of other races today, as well. In fact, the Bluegrass Stakes will be the tenth race. The one before it, the Ashland Stakes, is for fillies. Those are the big races on the card today."

Sonia was enjoying herself but felt a little bewildered by it all. "Tell me again, what's special about those races, other than the fact that Frailing is running in one of them?"

Burnett took a second to make sure that Jet wasn't about to answer, then he started. His voice had the same authority it had when he spoke about forensic accounting. "First, you have to know how the three races in the Triple Crown are put together. You see, for each of those races, the Kentucky Derby, the Preakness Stakes, and the Belmont Stakes, horses have to be nominated in order to participate. Now, the term, 'nominated,' may imply to you that someone just says that they think the horse is good enough to compete. That's the furthest thing from the truth.

"In fact, there are twenty horses that wind up in the Derby. Those horses must first participate in what's known as the 'Road to the Kentucky Derby.' It's a series of around thirty-five or so races that take place at tracks across the country, in fact, around the world. The number actually changes from year to year. The top four horses that finish in each of those thirty-five or so races get points, and the twenty horses with the most points are eligible to run in the Derby." He gave Sonia a wink, "Now there are exceptions. But for the most part, that's how it's done. The race we'll see today, the Bluegrass Stakes, is one of the last races in that process. For Frailing, this is sort of a do-or-die race, in that he is right around the cut-off point for having enough points to make the Derby.

"Actually, the same is true for the fillies, the female horses. The biggest race of all for them is the Kentucky Oaks, run the day before the Derby, at Churchill Downs in Louisville. At least, that's how Churchill Downs likes to bill it. Actually, it's just another Grade I race for fillies. The ninth race today, the Ashland Stakes, is a qualifying race for the Kentucky Oaks. So, for the horses, and trainers, and owners, both of these races, The Bluegrass Stakes and The Ashland Stakes, are very much a big deal."

Jet sidled up to Burnett. "Now, how about those refreshments you promised? I'm sure there's something with bourbon available, don't you think?"

Sonia chimed in. "Mint juleps? I've never had one of those."

Jet smiled at her. "I'm sorry, honey. No mint juleps today, those are only for Derby Day, unless you want one of those frozen ones. And that's not the real deal for those things. But I'm sure there are other ways to get you some bourbon, aren't there, Burnett?"

Burnett was looking around, Sonia assumed, for a place to get a beverage. "Most certainly ladies. Although, you do have a choice. He pointed. There's the Moët and Chandon Champagne booth to our left, the Gray Goose Bloody Mary and Martini booth right over there, and to our right, of course, we could get you Maker's Mark bourbon. What's your pleasure?" He gave them a sly smile, "Trust me, we'll not be going upstairs to the Brats and Brew area."

Sonia smiled and took a moment to run the choices through her mind. Jet had no problem what-so-ever. "It sure feels like a champagne day to me, doesn't it Sonia?"

Sonia gave a silent nod of approval.

Burnett led the way. "Let us go procure some of France's finest libations."

As they followed Burnett, Sonia leaned in toward Jet and whispered. "You've got him eating out of the palm of your hand, don't you?"

"Oh, missy. You know ol' Jet. When she sets her mind to hookin' a fish, it don't take long for her to reel it in." Her accent was controlled, but definitely present.

"Yes." Sonia smiled. "But now that you've got him, what are you going to do with him?"

Jet's accent became stronger. "Honestly, I'm not sure I have the slightest idea where this fishin' excursion is going to wind up. But I can tell you one thing. Mercy, I *am* certainly enjoying the trip."

27

B y late in the afternoon, Sonia, Jet, and Burnett had enjoyed a wonderful day. The weather was beautiful. The horses were beautiful. Even the libations were beautiful—if you purchased them in one of the finer dining rooms like the Equestrian Room.

Sonia could feel the excitement rising as the day wore on and the two big races approached. She turned to Burnett. "So, the Ashland Stakes is for fillies, and it's an important race because of the Kentucky Oaks. Is that right?"

Burnett gave her a fatherly smile. "Yes. It's a stakes race for three-year-old fillies, and it's a prep race for the Kentucky Oaks. There have been some attempts to create a sort of triple crown for fillies, but that whole effort never really caught on."

Jet took out her racing program. "So, what are we looking for this time Burnie?"

Sonia watched Burnett's head whip around. Apparently, he'd never been called anything but Burnett, or for that matter, Mr. Saunders.

Eventually, Burnett answered. "You remember, don't you, that I told you about three different horses that were doing better than their breeding might imply? Well, one of those three is Frailing. You know about him. Another is a filly named Summer Wheat." He pointed to the horse's name in his program. "She's a lovely chestnut color and is having a heck of a year. She's running today in the Ashland Stakes." Burnett half-smiled. "If she has a good outing it will portend well for her appearance in the Oaks."

Sonia eyes widened. "Right here? The next race?" She turned to Jet. "Oh, let's put some money on her to win."

Burnett gave her another fatherly smile. "I'm not sure that's a wise bet. Even with her somewhat weaker bloodlines, her recent past performance has her going off at only two to one. If she wins, you won't make much money. Still, if you're excited about her, goodness me, it would be fun to watch her run and actually root for her."

Sonia started pulling Jet toward the betting windows, a place she'd never seen until a few hours ago, and with which she was now quite familiar. "C'mon. We're putting money on Summer Wheat. Big money. Five bucks."

"Oh, you're a big hitter, aren't you Ms. Sonia." Jet chuckled. "Five whole bucks on a horse going off at two to one. If you win you'll be able to buy a cup of coffee in a place like this—maybe." Sonia couldn't seem to wipe the smile from her face.

After placing their bets, the trio worked their way back to the reserved seats Burnett had gotten them. Sitting on the edge of her seat, Sonia watched as the horses were loaded into the gate. She was happy to see that Summer Wheat was, "in the two hole," as she had learned to call it that day, and she knew that was a good thing. Earlier in the day, Sonia had believed that all horse races were the same distance. She now knew that wasn't the case. She tugged on Burnett's sleeve. "How long is the race?"

Burnett was watching the loading gate through his binoculars. "A mile and a sixteenth."

"Wow." Sonia wasn't really sure if that was short or long for a race.

Jet rolled her eyes at Sonia's attempt to appear knowledgeable, then she smiled. "You're right, lady. Let's hope she can rock and roll right on down that track."

It took another few minutes to load all the horses into the gate. Sonia heard the track announcer's, *"They're at the post,"* and the moment the last one was secured, the bell rang and those classic words rang out over the PA. *"And they're off!"*

Summer Wheat got an excellent jump out of the starting gate and was quickly running third behind two other horses, a bay filly named Strictly Speed, and a gray named Kathy Q. As they passed the first pole, it was Strictly Speed in the lead, Kathy Q second, and Summer Wheat third.

Although she'd seen the same thing happen several times that day, Sonia was still surprised to see how far away the horses seemed as they ran on the far side of the infield. By then, the three horses had maintained their relative positions but had run away from the rest of the pack.

The trio hit the quarter pole and turned into the home stretch. Having run as close to the rail as possible to save inches all the way around the track, the three fanned out and started to run abreast as they headed for home. The crowd around Sonia was screaming, some of them banging their fists or programs against anything they could as they urged their favorite steed toward the finish line.

With less than an eighth of a mile to go, Summer Wheat found another gear. Though she was driving hard, she seemed to glide effortlessly past Kathy Q. Then Sonia watched as the stunning animal stretched and pushed every ounce of her magnificent body toward the finish line, her jockey tucked low on her back, urging her on.

With the finish line just a few strides away, Summer Wheat had closed the gap between her and Strictly Speed to less than a length. Stride for stride they ran, Summer Wheat's nose inching closer and closer to that of her rival. In a flash, they ran past the finish line, the crowd noise deafening. But as they slowly pulled up, the jockeys standing in their stirrups, it was obvious that Summer Wheat had fallen just short of completing her comeback.

Sonia, like many folks there, had been standing on her tippy-toes. She rocked back onto her heels. "Oh no. So close. So close."

Jet tore her mutuel betting ticket in half and stuffed it in her purse, making a big display. "Ain't that how it always goes. Just when you think you've got it made, you miss it by a couple of nose hairs. Isn't that so Burnett?"

Burnett turned and looked calmly at the two frustrated novice handicappers. He unconsciously ran a bent finger past his own nose. "Actually, I thought the race was quite a success."

They both looked at him curiously. It was Jet who spoke first. "And in what way is us losing a success?"

"Oh my, given her bloodlines, the chances of Summer Wheat running such a close second in a race of this caliber were quite slim." He looked up at the large screen that sat in the infield and faced the grandstand. "That's especially true, given the time in which they ran the race, 1:41.62. I think the fastest ever was 1:41.60, just two-tenths of a second faster. Come on, let's go down to the stable area. I'm curious as to the reaction of the owners."

Sonia used her program as a fan to cool herself, the day having become quite warm even in the shade. "Okay. But remember, we want to be back in time to see Frailing run. That's why we came here today."

Jet took her by the arm and they started to follow Burnett, who had simply walked off. "We'll be back in time, and with some winning tickets in our hands this time. Count on it."

Sonia smiled. "Oh, it really doesn't matter. I can't remember when I've had so much fun." After a moment, she went on. "I just wish Brad was here with us to enjoy it. You know, he used to work on a horse farm up near Paris when he was a kid."

"Yeah. You told me." Jet was pulling Sonia along. "Now let's hurry up. I don't want to lose Burnett in the crowd. I have no idea where we're going."

Within a few minutes, Burnett had led them back to the edges of the stable area. Sonia tugged on Burnett's sleeve. "Is it okay if we go back there?"

Burnett answered without looking back at her. "Not normally, but if we look like we really belong we might get a little closer than usual." He turned and gave her a big smile.

Stretching to see as much as she could, Sonia watched the stable hands and other attendants deal with the horses that had just run a demanding race. In her mind, they were all winners. The looks on some of the faces she saw, however, didn't seem to agree. Those looks ranged from acceptance to downright frustration. A few uncomplimentary words drifted in the air.

A man dressed in expensive-looking pants and a nice jacket emerged from what appeared to be Summer Wheat's stall area. Jet nudged Burnett. "Who's that?"

Burnett leaned close to her and covered his mouth with the back of his hand. "I'm not certain, but I believe that's Robert Edwards, he's one of Summer Wheat's owners."

Jet whispered back, "He doesn't look too disappointed, does he?"

"Why should he?" He spoke without looking at her. "His horse just won the second-place share of a $500,000 purse. And, it seems pretty clear that she'll be able to run in the Oaks next month."

Sonia swatted at a fly. "Wow, not bad." A few moments later she took hold of Jet's elbow and pulled her a step away. "Look."

"Look at what?" Jet arched her body, looking around.

"Look who that is. Don't you remember him?"

Jet strained to see better. "Oh yeah, that's Ron Harris. What's he doing here?"

Sonia shook her head. "I don't know. Any idea who he's talking to?"

Jet frowned. "Not a clue." She turned, walked over to Burnett and spun him around surreptitiously. "Look over my shoulder."

Burnett stretched his neck and opened his eyes wide, his head on a swivel.

"Subtly, subtly," Jet whispered intently as she tugged on the arm of his linen suit. "See those two guys? Any idea who they are?"

Burnett continued to stare, unaffected by Jet's urging. Clueless. "No idea, I'm afraid. They do seem fully engaged in conversation, now don't they."

Jet nodded. "I would say they do. But you don't recognize either one of them?" She looked up at Burnett. "Because we do. The smaller guy, that's Ron Harris. He's a broker."

Burnett looked at her, "A bloodstock agent? Is that what you mean?"

Jet sighed. "Yes, Professor. A bloodstock agent. But the other guy. You don't know him?"

Burnett pursed his lips. "Wait. Let me check something." He looked through his program for a moment. "You know, that could be Stefan Ashkenasi. He's the owner of Willowbay Farm down in Florida. That's where Summer Wheat was bred."

Sonia moved closer to Jet and Burnett. "Hmm. That's interesting. So Ashkenasi bred Summer Wheat, and then sold him to Edwards?"

"Could be. Farm owners don't usually act as breeders. Sometimes, however, they function in that capacity. Ashkenasi might well be Summer Wheat's breeder."

There was a moment of silence between them all. Finally, Sonia spoke. "C'mon. Let's get back. It's almost time for the Bluegrass Stakes and we haven't even bought our tickets yet."

28

It wasn't long before Sonia, Jet, and Burnett were back in their seats, waiting for the day's biggest race, The Bluegrass Stakes. By the time the horses were being loaded into the gate, Sonia was literally bouncing in her seat.

Jet looked at her and shook her head. "Now don't go getting crazy, at least not until they're heading for the finish line."

Sonia's smile was radiant. "Oh, but isn't this great? The sun, the grass, the bright green leaves on the trees over there in the distance. And now we're going to watch Frailing run. How could it be any better?"

Jet snorted, "It could be better if we'd already turned these ten-dollar tickets into a whole lot more money. Given his bloodline, lots of folks don't think Frailing can really keep up with these other nags. The odds are in our favor. Hell, he's going off at five to one."

Sonia's smile didn't fade. "Well, I'm sticking with Burnett. If he says that Frailing is outrunning his bloodlines, then I'm all in. Right, Burnett?" Her foot was tapping a mile a minute.

"Oh, please, Sonia." Burnett was dispassionate. "Just remember that true accountants never watch the horses in order to make money. We get our thrills from watching the outcome of certain mathematical propositions being either proven or disproven."

Jet looked at Sonia but tossed her head toward Burnett. "And it doesn't hurt if they wind up making a bunch of money along the way." Then she turned to Burnett. "Now does it, Burnie?"

Once again, Sonia watched Burnett's head whip around as the name "Burnie" sunk into his consciousness. She could hardly keep from laughing right in his face.

A few moments later, the bell rang and, once again, the crowd noise rose as the public address announcer gave them what they wanted to hear, *"And they're off!"*

Sonia watched Frailing, the beautiful bay Thoroughbred, with its gleaming, dark brown coat and black mane and tail, explode out of the starting gate. She feared his starting position, fifth from the rail, might stand in the way of his getting a jump on the other horses, but that wasn't the case. The massive animal quickly maneuvered past four other horses and was hugging the fence by the time the pack had reached the first turn.

Sonia was literally jumping up and down. "He's in the lead. He's in the lead. Go, Frailing! Go! Go!"

By the time the horses reached the half-mile pole, Jet was holding onto to Sonia's arm and jumping with her. "Go on you nag! Show 'em what you've got!" She turned to Sonia and shouted over the crowd noise. "He's gonna do it! Look at him! He's gonna do it!"

Sonia's experience was dreamlike, watching that beautiful creature coming out of the backstretch in front of the pack. It was almost as if he was floating across the hard ground while the others were lost in a cloud of dust. "He's got it! He's got it!" she shouted.

As they turned toward the quarter pole, it became obvious that a black colt and another bay were closing on Frailing, though Sonia was certain it didn't matter. He was so far ahead he couldn't possibly lose. But as they turned into the stretch, Sonia couldn't believe her eyes. It was like her spatial orientation had gotten all messed up. There was Frailing, running just barely ahead of the other two. In fact, from her angle, she couldn't be sure he was ahead at all.

Jet started smacking her program on Sonia's arm. "C'mon damn it! Get goin'! Get goin'!" She was shouting. Sonia was shouting. Everyone was shouting. It was like the grandstand itself was roaring. And shout as they might, Sonia watched as first the black colt and then the bay passed Frailing. In fact, in the time it took for the horses to turn into the home stretch and then cross the finish line, Frailing had fallen from first place to sixth. He finished totally defeated and out of the money.

Jet leaned back, raised her arms, and looked to the sky as if appealing to the gods of racing. "Why, why?"

Sonia looked at Jet with dismay on her face. "How could he do that? How could he have been so far ahead and then just totally collapsed like that? How could he?"

Burnett turned to them with no particular emotion on his face. "Interesting. Fascinating really. Not at all what I would have expected based on his earlier performances."

The crowd noise had subsided so instantly it was almost surreal. Sonia turned to Burnett. "What do you mean?"

"Well," Burnett sounded a bit professorial, "in all his prior races, Frailing has been able to run in front almost wire to wire. Of course, usually by the end of the race, the horses that come from behind, the closers, are gaining on him. But in almost every case he's had enough speed to hold them off at the end and come in first—in most cases."

Jet squinted her eyes. "So, why not this time? Was it the jockey's fault? Did he take Frailing out so fast that he had nothing left?"

Burnett maintained his equanimity. "One could proposition that was the case. Of course, we'll never know. The trainer might have instructed him to do so. All kinds of different things come into play."

Jet was shaking her head. "I know one thing that's not going to play. It's these ten-dollar win tickets." She dipped gently into her southern accent. "They're not gonna play no how."

Sonia put her hand on Jet's arm. "Hey. Don't worry. We got our ten bucks worth of entertainment, didn't we?"

Jet smiled at her, then turned directly to Burnett, her eyes looking deeply into his. "I guess you're right. We're out here in the beautiful weather, with great people. Couldn't be any better, could it, Burnie?"

Burnett seemed unable to come up with an appropriate response to such a direct question. He gave his lapels and bowtie a quick non-adjustment. "Well, then. If you don't mind. I really would like to go back to the stable area one last time. Given Frailing's disappointing performance, it seems like we might be able to hear some fascinating discussions going on back there, but only if we remain very discreet."

Walking back to the stable area, looking as much as possible like owners, the three of them slipped silently past security guards who were primarily focused on protecting the winner of the race. Sonia wondered if they would actually get to hear anything interesting. It seemed to her that any conversations that were less than positive would be held in private. However, as they approached the barn which held Frailing, it was quite clear that someone was very upset.

Jet reached out her hands, stopping both Sonia and Burnett from going any farther. She stepped forward and turned her back toward the barn, looking only at her friends. "Do you all see Jackson Paine over there, talking to Limey?"

Sonia nodded, but Burnett said, "I don't know the man."

Jet leaned over and spoke softly. "He's Frailing's owner."

Sonia squinted at the tall man. "Yeah, but he seems fine, like that's just how things go with racehorses. So, who do you think is doing all the yelling?"

Jet turned, stretching and looking in several directions. "I don't know, but there's no question they're pissed, really pissed. And look. Limey sure looks like he's pretty uncomfortable about something, doesn't he?"

The trio stood there in silence for several minutes. Sonia was trying to sift out any words she could from the heated discussion going on inside the barn. The few words she could understand seemed to imply that promises had been made. There was something about a "new way of doing things," or something like that. Clearly, though, she felt that someone believed they had been lied to or assured of something that didn't work out.

Finally, the heated discussion was over, and for a moment, Sonia, Jet, and Burnett didn't quite know what to do. Just as Sonia was about to suggest that they move on and start for home, she watched a trim, gray-haired man walk out of the barn, his face still red. She turned to Jet and spoke softly. "Do you recognize who that is?"

"That's George Masson," Jet said, almost silently.

Sonia nodded, "So it is."

Burnett leaned in and whispered. "George who?"

Jet covered her mouth with the back of her hand. "George Masson. He's the owner of Downstream Farm, and I'm pretty sure he's Frailing's breeder."

The three of them stood in silence, staying still, hoping not to draw any attention to themselves. A few moments later, a smallish blonde-haired man walked out of the barn, looking to Sonia like he had just gotten quite a tongue lashing. It was Ron Harris.

As Harris walked away, Sonia watched the few people who were left in the area. The one man who caught her attention, the one who looked off-stride, at a loss, nervous, was the Englishman with the giant hands, Limey.

29

S onia had slept in on Sunday morning. She'd had a wonderful time at the races the day before, the disappointment of Frailing's performance notwithstanding. After the races on Saturday, Jet, Burnett, and she had all gone to a hip lounge in the local Hilton Hotel, right in the middle of downtown. When Burnett had offered to take both Sonia and Jet out to dinner, the silent message Jet had sent to Sonia made it clear that she was ready to be alone with her forensic accountant. Sonia had begged off and Burnett had dropped her at her apartment.

The pace of the past week had been pretty intense. Several sessions with Burnett, sneaking into Oakley's office to download the keystroke software, meeting Gabriela, a second trip to Downstream Farm, a big day at the races; it was no wonder she'd felt whipped and had been glad to relax all morning. By the afternoon, however, Sonia was getting antsy. It had been just over a week since Brad had gone off to work for an old client and then on to help his buddy Robbie Alvarez. Simply put, she missed him.

What was worse, there were moments when she actually felt lonely. Before Brad had come into her life, Sonia had been very content to work hard during the week and then enjoy her week-ends, primarily by herself. She would read, explore a shop or two downtown, maybe take a trip out into the countryside. But things were different now. Now, any day in which she didn't see Brad was a day with a hole in it. She loved his smile, his jokes, his bright blue eyes. She loved the way he always seemed to be touching her, not in a sexual way, just in a loving, "staying in contact," sort of way. Of course, the romantic stuff wasn't bad either. When her phone rang, it took only a moment before it was in her hand and she was answering it. "Hello."

"Hey, sweet thing."

"Hey." A smile of relief crossed her face. "How are you?"

"Just missing you, wishing I could be back in Lexington, holding you, or, well . . . ."

She fell into one of Jet's accents. "Captain Dunham, please. Behave yourself, sir."

"Oh really?" came the reply. *"That's what you want? For me to behave myself?"*

There was a slight pause before Sonia answered. "Wellll . . . maybe not too much."

"There's my girl." Brad's voice was light and airy. *"So, what have you been up to?"*

Sonia spent the next few minutes briefly relating all that had gone on since he'd left. *"Sounds like a busy, busy week. Are you making any progress on the missing girl? What's her name again?"*

"Mariana. Mariana Castillo. And actually, not much. The only break we've gotten is that Jet managed to come up with the names of two more of her friends, girls we can talk to. Other than that, we're still kind of stuck."

"And your other cases?"

"We've got something in place to catch the young guy who's stealing from Steven Brownlee." Sonia kept her voice calm, making things sound sort of run of the mill. "And Jet says she's working on a plan to catch Nick Petropoulos, the cheating husband who runs the skating rink."

"Uh oh." Brad's voice pitched upward.

"Uh oh, what?"

Brad chuckled. *"Uh oh, I hope it's more solid than the plan she came up with to catch that guy you all called Bob Dylan."*

"Yeah, yeah," Sonia scolded him. "Just remember, she's the one who fleshed out your crazy plan to stop that truck on its way to Memphis. She did pretty well on that one, didn't she?"

Sonia could feel Brad's smile come through the phone. *"That she did, sweetheart."* Sonia had been walking around and around her apartment, as she often did when she was on the phone. She finally sat down on the couch in her tiny living room. "And what about you. How are things going for you? When are you coming home?"

There was a moment of silence before Brad answered. *"Things are, well, things are moving along. Robbie's got me working with him on this deal he's involved with, but I'm afraid I can't tell you anything about it. DEA stuff you know."*

Sonia tried to hide the worry in her voice. "Is it dangerous?"

"Nothing we can't handle, babe." His voice was reassuring. *"Don't you start worrying."*

"And when *are* you coming home?"

"Well, it looks like this thing should wrap up sometime late this week."

"Another week?" Sonia had wanted to hide her disappointment, but it just slipped past her and colored her words.

"Yeah. I'm sorry about that, but we've got to wait for some guys to make another move on something. Still, I'm pretty sure it'll go down later this week. Then I've got one other thing to take care of and I should be home by Friday night, Saturday the latest."

Sonia wasn't thrilled to know that Brad would be gone another whole week, but at least she now had a relatively specific time to look forward to. She was already beginning to plan a nice home-cooked dinner in her apartment next Saturday night. Shrimp scampi over freshly cooked linguine, a nice salad, warm bread, wine, and for dessert, maybe something a little spicier.

"Are you there. Sonia?"

"Oh, I'm sorry. I was just thinking. So, you're home Friday night?"

"That, or early Saturday. It depends on getting a few things done and then on what flights are available."

"Well, mister, don't you go making any plans for Saturday night. That time's for us." There was teasing in her voice and perhaps just a touch of severity.

"Yes, ma'am. Certainly, ma'am," he teased. *"Orders received loud and clear, ma'am. Listen, babe, I've got to run. Great to talk to you. Can't wait to see you."*

"Yeah, great to talk to you too. You have a great week. I miss you." She hung up.

Sonia looked at the clock. One ten. It's going to be a long afternoon and evening. Maybe I need to go to a movie or something.

30

Jet walked into the BCI offices promptly at ten o'clock on Monday morning. She found Sonia sitting at her desk. "Good morning, early bird."

Sonia looked up from her work. "Good morning to you, sunshine. Welcome to a new week." Her words were brighter than the tone of her voice.

Jet continued walking toward Sonia, stopping in the doorway of Sonia's office. "Yes, it is a new week isn't it? In fact, lots of things feel new." In contrast, her voice seemed dreamy.

Sonia raised an eyebrow. "I'm not sure I get what you mean."

"You know, spring is here, flowers are blooming, the ponies are running. Everything feels," she grinned and shrugged, "I don't know, fresh and new."

Sonia leaned back in her desk chair. She gently waved her pen in the air. "You know. I can't say that I've ever seen spring have such a profound effect on you before. This wouldn't have anything to do with what happened after I left you and Burnett on Saturday evening, would it?" The pen found its way to Sonia's lips.

Suddenly, Jet was the demure southern belle. "Whatever are you implying?"

"Oh, I don't know. Could it be that the birds and the bees weren't the only things buzzing around ol' Burnett later that evening?"

"I haven't the slightest idea what you're talking about." Now the accent was in full bloom. "The colonel and I spent an entirely proper evening together speaking of the weather, politics, and such. And I must say, I'm beginning to be just the slightest bit insulted by your veiled insinuations that other things, things of an unsavory nature, might have occurred."

With that, Jet turned, stepped out of the doorway, and headed for her own office. A few steps into her journey, however, she stopped, looked through the glass wall, and gave Sonia the most Cheshire Cat-grin she had ever seen.

Sonia shook her head and went back to work. "The colonel, oh, my goodness."

SONIA AND JET spent Monday afternoon splitting their time between working other cases and trying to track down the two new girls they had heard were friends of Mariana's. Sonia spent a few more hours getting time-stamped shots of Mr. Afternoon Delight heading over to visit his happy home-making hussy, while Jet hung around the drug store waiting for the shoplifting girls with the penchant for using women's high-end makeup—for free. When they did show up, Jet was frustrated that she could never quite catch the girls "in the act," but there was something else that caught her eye, something that had her questioning her assumptions.

Just after four o'clock in the afternoon, Sonia walked back into the BCI offices. She could see that Jet was clearly wrapping up her day. "You out of here already?"

Jet stood and slung her purse strap over her shoulder. "You got that right. I've had enough of dead-end phone calls and shoplifters for one day. Want to join me for a drink?"

"Not tonight." Sonia stepped into her own office. "I missed my run yesterday, and after I file this one report, I think I'm going to go home and give that a shot." She put her purse on her desk and turned back to Jet. "So, no luck with finding those two girls?"

Jet let out a quick breath. "Making some progress, but not much. I even called that smarty-pants professor and told him we'd found those other two names. But when I asked him if he knew how we could reach either of them, he had no clue."

"Did he seem bothered by the fact that he had forgotten to mention those girls to us in the first place?"

"Nah. Just went on and on about how busy they always were." She waved her hand in the air. "Blah, blah, blah. Personally, I think he's kind of a dolt."

Sonia stepped back out of her office. "One question."

"Yes?"

"You've got a plan for how we're going to wrap up Mandy Petropoulos' case?"

Jet dropped her chin and gave Sonia her librarian look. "Sweetheart, I've got a plan to catch ol' Nick-the-Dick bumpin' skate guards with his roller-derby queen and it's a killer if I do say so myself. But I think you'll enjoy it better if you wait to hear about it until just before we put it into action." She gave Sonia a big smile, turned, and left.

Sonia sighed. Somehow, I'm not sure I even want to know what you've got planned. She finished up some things and left the office a few minutes later. She walked the short block up East Main, turned onto Ashland and headed for her apartment. It was a beautiful spring evening, so she made certain to absorb the beauty of the old neighborhood as she walked. When she turned onto Central Avenue, a strange sensation came over her. Turning around, she saw a black BMW convertible with darkened windows slowly making the same turn she had made. Sonia wondered if the driver was lost or something, but as soon as she stopped and looked at the car, the driver seemed to find what he or she was looking for and took off. Sonia shook off a tiny shudder. Sometimes I think I should never walk around here alone. A woman never knows.

She walked past the house that stood in front of her garage apartment, strode up the stairs, and within a few minutes was dressed and ready for a run through some of the most attractive old neighborhoods in the city. As she came down the stairs and started her run, her heart was light. Even though she missed Brad, she felt at peace with the world. Except for one thing, the same question that always seemed to be chewing on her brain. What the hell happened to Mariana Castillo?

31

Stepping into the BCI offices at eight o'clock on Tuesday evening, Sonia was surprised at what she saw. Sitting on the couch in the waiting area was a young woman with blue eyes and a long, blonde ponytail. Clearly, it was Jet. Clearly, it wasn't.

Sonia knew that Jet was attractive and was never shy about showing off her feminine attributes, but she was a slender, athletic type of attractive, and her wardrobe choices were young and stylish but always tasteful. It appeared that this young woman had most likely had her clothing sprayed onto her body, particularly in critical areas. In addition, whereas Jet was in no way flat-chested, this young woman's cups seemed to runneth over, thanks to the powers of a super push-up bra, Sonia assumed.

"Jet, what are you doing in that getup? I mean," Sonia ran her fingers through her hair, "those pants are something, and I love the top, but really, how are you even breathing?"

Jet stood and wiggled as she ran her thumbs inside the waist-band of her pants. "Only when I'm standing" She stood as tall as she could. "I can only breathe when I'm standing."

"Well, I've got to say that you could really grab people's attention in that outfit—in a hooker kind of way. But whose clothes are those anyway?"

"Oh, they're mine, lady. They're mine. I bought them specifically for tonight's adventure and charged them to the business." She brushed invisible dust off her pants. "Yup, you'd better believe that." She kept rolling her shoulders and wiggling, trying to get comfortable.

"Uh, huh," said Sonia softly. She wasn't going to argue about the expenditure. She knew that Jet would never normally wear clothing that suggestive. "And how is that getup going to be part of the adventure?"

"Look. One of us has to get past Burly Bouncer Boy to get the shots we need. And the only way we're going to be able to do that is to have the other one out there roller-skating, grabbing his attention." She walked into her office, Sonia following. Checking the mirror on the old armoire, Jet ran her ponytail through her hands. "So, let me ask you, which of those parts do you want to play in our charade?" She slipped into her southern accent. "You gonna be the taker of pictures or the roller-skating *di*version?" Given Sonia's roller-skating skills, both women knew it was a rhetorical question.

Sonia let out a deep breath. "Okay, but are you sure wearing those clothes will be enough to get Burly Bouncer Boy's attention?"

"Just you wait and see." Jet checked the mirror one last time. "Just you wait and see."

Around thirty minutes later, Sonia and Jet walked into The Wildcat and right under the EVERYONE MUST WEAR SKATES sign. Sonia wished she could avoid strapping on those wheeled implements of torture, but she knew that in order to be close enough to slip quickly into Nick's office, she would have to get at least far enough around the oval to position herself against the wall at that end of the room. Jet, on the other hand, seemed to relish the upcoming opportunity.

Moments after Jet had gotten her skates laced up, she was on the floor taking big, athletic strides as she flew around the rink. A few heads turned as she passed by, taken by her energy. Those eyes belonged to the younger skaters. The other heads that turned did so because of the effect created by Jet's outfit. Tight, skimpy, white shorts with shiny studs around the waist were the only thing between her red, high-top roller-skates and the beautiful, though extremely daring, floral bustier she was wearing. The bright, blue pendant that hung from her neck drew the eyes of most skaters to the bounty her push-up bra was putting on display.

Burly Bouncer Boy stood guard at his normal station, just outside of Nick's office. Surrounded, as he often was, by a small gaggle of college girls, even Jet's breath-defying outfit didn't get his attention on her first few passes. Undeterred, she increased the display of her athleticism, finding ways to spin and twirl each time she was at his end of the rink. It didn't take long before the tall, muscular, man-child was looking over the heads of the co-eds each time she passed.

It took a few minutes for Sonia to clomp and stumble her way down to the proper end of the rink and take her position near Nick's door. As soon as she did, Jet gave her a wink as she passed by and headed for one last loop around the floor. Sonia wondered what would come next. It didn't take long for her to find out.

Approaching her target's domain, Jet picked up speed and attempted a switch from forward to backward motion. In the process, she seemed to catch one skate on another and tumbled to the ground with a thud. Her arms and legs sprawled, she lay on her back, motionless.

It took only moments for other skaters to stop and ask if she was alright. More importantly, it was less than a minute before a certain burly young man was on his knees next to her, offering his assistance, though he struggled to focus his attention above Jet's shoulders.

Sonia was a little torn as she moved quickly through the empty space created by the bouncer's absence. Is she okay? Did she do that on purpose? Sonia wondered if she should give up the plan and run to her partner's aid. But imagining the dressing-down she would get if Jet had risked life and limb in order to create this opportunity and then she failed to do her part, Sonia put her thoughts of Jet's peril aside and slipped through the door into Nick's office.

Skates still on her feet and her trusty phone in her hand, Sonia saw that the office space was partitioned into two sections. No one was in the section she first encountered. She could, however, hear sounds coming from around the partitioning wall. They were not quite the sounds she expected.

Although the music coming from the huge sound system outside the office thumped incessantly, Sonia's ears focused on the sounds of slapping and moaning. Along with that came mumbling, words she couldn't quite make out.

He's hitting her. *Figlio de puta*. That son-of-a-bitch is hitting her. Her Italian blood boiled.

Steeling herself, Sonia moved carefully to the edge of the partition, grateful that the area's carpet was muting the sound of the skates on her feet. She wanted to go right around the partition and attack the bastard, but she knew getting video of him hitting the young woman would have a much greater effect on him. She checked her phone one last time before stepping to the edge of the partition. She stopped.

The words just barely came to her, whispered intently on the other side of the partition. "Do what I want. Do what I tell you. Do it now, damn it, do it." The other sound was becoming clear as well.

Smack! Smack!

"Again, do it again. More. Do it."

Smack! Smack! Smack!

Sonia couldn't trust her ears. She had no choice. She had to know what was going on. Not wanting to get caught, she hit RECORD and carefully stuck the phone around the partition. Slowly panning back and forth, she hoped she was getting what she needed.

After a long minute, Sonia brought the phone back around the wall and began quickly looking at the images. Her heart leaped into her throat. Nothing could have prepared her for what she saw.

Smack! The sounds continued. The heavy breathing. The passionate utterances.

Sonia looked at the images again. She saw the riding crop. Closing her eyes, she rubbed her forehead. It was all too bizarre.

Smack!

Sonia slipped out of the office area, skating carefully after she left the office area's carpet. She found a wall and pressed herself against it. Taking a deep breath and looking around, Sonia realized Jet was nowhere in sight.

As she hustled over to the skate room, Sonia passed the first-aid station. Sitting on a bench in the brightly lit room, being attended to by the over-anxious, burly young man, sat Jet. As Sonia walked by, Jet gave her a surreptitious wink.

Finally back in her own shoes, Sonia waited outside the building, leaning on her car. Her eyes locked on the front door, it was only a few minutes before she saw Jet emerging from The Wildcat, limping and leaning suggestively on Burly Prince Charming. Thanking him for his heroics, Jet left him at the curb. Miraculously, by the time she made it to Sonia's car, Jet's limp had disappeared. She sent Sonia a sly grin and another wink. "Well, how did it go, partner? You get the shots we needed?"

Sonia twisted her lips. "Really? You couldn't tell me you were planning on doing that?"

Jet smiled, a twinkle in her eye. "Listen. I've been skating all my life, survived plenty of those spills that weren't on purpose. I knew what I was doing. Now, did we get what we needed?"

"We got it," she ran her fingers through her hair, "but you're never going to believe it."

32

Sonia had gotten to the office by nine o'clock on Wednesday and had called Mandy Petropoulos. Mandy had agreed to meet with Sonia and Jet at eleven. She arrived dressed in springtime colors—pink shirt, white pants, light-green shoes. They didn't do much to brighten her countenance. Sonia greeted her in the waiting area. "How are you?"

"Okay, I guess. Honestly, I'm not sure how eager I am to hear what you've got to say."

Sonia took her by the hand. "Don't you worry. This is not going to be pleasant, but it may not be as painful as you think. C'mon. Let's join Jet in her office."

Jet rose to greet Mandy. "Good morning." She pulled up the wooden extra chair in the office so Mandy could take a seat next to her behind Jet's desk.

Sonia took a seat in the red chair across from them. "Before we show you these images, can I ask you a question?"

Mandy looked wary. "I guess." There was real apprehension in her voice.

Sonia spoke calmly, reassuringly. "You've hired Jet and me to find out what's going on with your husband, right?"

Mandy nodded her head silently.

"You've already told us what he demands of you every night. And now, because he's changed his routine on Tuesdays, you think he's cheating, correct?"

Mandy's voice was soft and tentative. "That's right."

Sonia looked over at Jet before she continued. She turned back to Mandy. "Can I ask what it is you're hoping for here?" Her voice was gentle. "Are you hoping that he's not? Are you hoping that he is and that our investigation will give you the strength to ask for a divorce? Mandy hesitated, her eyes looking up then drifting downward. "You know, I really hadn't thought about it. I guess I just needed to know if I was right. Am I right?"

Sonia spoke, her voice more forceful. "Before we answer that, let me ask you again. If you are right, are you going to ask for a divorce?"

Mandy's eyes opened wide. "Oh gosh, I don't know." Her face turned to Jet. "How could I do that? I don't make enough money to survive on my own." Mandy's back stiffened. "Don't you remember? I work for Nick. If I ask for a divorce, he'll fire me. I won't have any money. Then I'll probably lose the kids. I won't have a place to live, I won't have a job." She seemed to collapse down into the chair. "I won't even have my kids."

All three women were silent for a minute. Jet turned around and grabbed a thermos and an old ceramic cup with the faded word, "Magee's" on it. "Can I pour you some coffee?"

Mandy nodded. There was no discussion of cream and sugar.

Finally, as she poured, Jet asked, "Tell me about Nick's relationship with his dad."

Mandy took a tiny sip of the black coffee. "What do you mean?"

Jet pressed. "I mean, what is Nick's relationship with his dad like? Can Nick do no wrong in the old man's eyes? Is he always under the old man's thumb? What gives there?" She sounded somewhat accusatory.

"Oh, I told you," Mandy spoke softly, almost sadly, "Nick's dad was a man's man, a womanizer really, but he always kept Nick on a real tight leash." A sad smile crossed her face. "It was one of those, what do you call them, paradoxes? The old man could do anything he wanted, but Nick was supposed to play it straight, at least in public."

Mandy stopped, but neither Sonia nor Jet spoke. She found a spot on the old desk to put the cup down. "Honestly, I think the old man really hoped that Nick was doing the same things he was, but behind his back."

Jet nodded. "Yeah, I think I know what you mean." Her eyes shifted to Sonia.

Sonia tried her best to be upbeat. "Let me pose a scenario to you."

"Okay."

Sonia looked directly at Mandy, hoping to judge her reaction to what was coming. "What if Nick did something that might embarrass the old man?"

Mandy screwed up her face. "Like what?"

Sonia continued. "Listen, I'm sorry to be circumspect, but please, just answer the question." She kept watching Mandy's reaction carefully. "What if Nick did something, I don't know, something the old man wouldn't be so proud of?"

Mandy pushed her hair out of her face. "Oh, no question about it. All hell would break loose. You've got to understand, these are Greeks. The most important thing for a Greek man is his honor. Of course, conquering as many women as possible counts too." The tiniest chuckle rose out of her throat. "If Nick did anything that embarrassed Vasilios, he'd cut Nick's balls off."

Sonia and Jet shot looks at each other but didn't say a word.

Mandy's hand had trembled when she'd first taken her coffee. It was steadier now as she reached out again for the cup. "Not physically, of course, though he might smack him around a bit. But he'd certainly punish Nick big time. Why?" She looked to Jet, who was next to her, then back across the desk to Sonia, her eyes full of questions. "Why are you asking about all of this?"

Jet looked at Sonia, and Sonia nodded. Jet hit PLAY on the video file that was loaded on the open laptop that sat in front of Mandy. From across the desk, Sonia watched Mandy's face for her reaction while Mandy and Jet watched the screen. Up popped a full-screen view of the video Sonia had shot the night before. Although the view kept changing, there was no question about what was going on.

There was Nick, his pants down, on his hands and knees. There was the tall, athletic redhead. The sounds of the voices were clear, along with the smack, smack, smack of the riding crop. Sonia watched as Mandy's eyes widened, stunned that the demanding voice was Nick's and that the hand that was swinging the riding crop belonged to the redhead.

Mandy sat in silence, the look on her face a combination of shock and disgust. Finally, her eyes still locked on the frozen final image, she said, "What is that? How'd you get that video?"

Jet leaned toward Mandy. "Don't you worry about how we got it. You do recognize your husband, right?" There was nothing gentle in the way she spoke.

Mandy turned to Jet. There was nothing gentle in the way she spoke either. "Of course I recognize him, but who's that girl." Then she turned to Sonia, softer. "Is she one of the college girls? She doesn't really look like a college girl."

Jet looked up at Sonia then turned to Mandy. "Honestly, we're not sure if she's a college girl or not, but as far as we can tell, she shows up every Tuesday with the rest of them. And several of them clearly know her." She sat up straighter. "More importantly, what do you think about what's going on in that video?"

Mandy's hand shook noticeably as she put the coffee cup back on Jet's desk. "My god it's disgusting. That girl, that woman, she's ... she's a ..."

Jet finished the sentence. "Dominatrix." She waited a moment for a response, but it didn't come. Eventually, she gently squeezed Mandy's arm. "And?"

Mandy hung her head and whispered. "And he likes it." Silence hung in the room, the sound of the ancient heating system suddenly taking center stage.

Finally, the energy in her voice beginning to rise, Mandy sat taller again, her hands moving to her thighs. "I don't get it. He likes it. He likes that girl," she scrunched her face in disgust, "doing that." Then she turned to look directly at Jet, her voice demanding. "How long does it go on? How long does she do that to him?"

It appeared to Sonia that Jet was going to answer. She decided to take over instead. "We're not really sure. Long enough for us to make that video. Long enough, don't you think?"

33

Sonia watched as Mandy sank back into the chair, the wind knocked out of her. How can she deal with this? My god, she must hate the fact that he's cheating on her, but like this? It's so creepy.

Sonia looked across the desk, wishing she could take Mandy's hands in hers. "Listen, Mandy. Now that you've seen that video, you have a decision to make. There are several paths you can take. You can confront him and beg him to stop, maybe get professional help. Or, I guess, you could just let it go. Live and let live. At least you're getting one night of peace each week. Or . . ." Sonia paused for a long moment. "Or you can use it as leverage."

Mandy knit her eyebrows. "What do you mean? How do I use this as leverage?"

Sonia deferred to Jet, revenge being much more Jet's cup of tea. "Listen." Mandy turned to Jet and Jet continued. "Right now, Nick's got everything he could possibly want. He's got a beautiful wife and kids, a nice home, he gets his sexual needs fulfilled whenever he wants, and he's got this other thing on the side. Oh, and one other thing. He gets to be the Grand PooPah of his own business, a business he didn't build, making everyone there do his bidding."

Mandy shrugged her shoulders. "I guess. Yeah."

Sonia watched as Jet's energy rose, her voice getting stronger. "So, let me ask you one question, Mandy Petropoulos. Of all those things, which is the one he would least want to lose?"

Mandy remained slumped in her chair, her answer almost inaudible. "The business. There's no question, it's the business."

Jet leaned in, demanding Mandy's attention, her face only inches from Mandy's. "That's right. Everything he has, all the power, what little money he has, even his bimbo, they all come from the business. And guess who just took over control of the whole thing?"

Mandy looked up to Sonia for help answering, "I don't know. Vasilios?"

Jet shook her head, her voice strengthening even more, grabbing Mandy's attention back to her. "No. Not Vasilios, you. You just got everything you need to take control of the whole damn mess. Don't you understand? You've totally got Nick-The-Dick by the short hairs."

Sonia wondered if Jet realized that the term, "Nick-The-Dick," had, up until that moment, been used only in their private conversations. Too late now.

Trying to let a little steam out of the moment, Sonia ran her fingers through her hair then rose. She walked around the desk, stood behind Jet, and spoke softly. "What Jet is saying, is now that you know that Nick has been involved in something less than, what? Less than manly? Something he would never want his father to know about. You have power. You can make demands. And, though it'll be messy, I'm sure you'll find that in the end, Nick will do whatever you want."

Jet jumped in, turning Mandy's attention back to her yet again. "So, here's the question, Mandy. What is it that you want?"

Mandy sat, looking first to Sonia, then to Jet, then back to Sonia again. "Well, I just don't know. What should I want?"

Jet was about to speak, but Sonia cut her off. "That's for you to decide." Her voice was a calm counterpoint to Jet's emphatic urgings. "Really, you need to go home and use whatever time it takes to think this through. Do you love him, really love him? Do you want things to continue the way they are? If not, what do you want to change?"

It was Jet's turn again. "Or do you want to stick it to the bastard for all the terrible ways he's treated you over the last few years. Remember this, girl, you can get whatever you want from this guy, and if I were you, I would want out. Not only would I want out, I'd want out with everything I'd need to start a new life—money, the kids, a new place to live."

Mandy looked to Sonia, her eyes clearly asking if that were all true.

Sonia, spoke even more softly, leaning downward. "These are tough calls, Mandy. Maybe my partner, here, has a predisposition for socking it to a cheating husband, but I don't necessarily think she's wrong. All you have to do is show this video to Nick and you get one big 'do-over' with your life, a fresh start . . . if you want it."

Mandy's head moved slowly back and forth. "No. No, I could never do that. I could never sit there and show him that video."

Jet's words came quickly. "Don't you worry about that. Sonia didn't mean that *you* would have to show him the video. We would never let you do that. No, we'll show him the video, and we'll be certain to have a little muscle with us to ensure that nothing goes wrong when we do. In fact, we'll set it up so that you're out of town with the kids when we confront him, and you won't be coming back until all of this is settled."

Sonia stood taller, her voice becoming more conversational. "Do you have someplace where you can go, someplace safe? Preferably, someplace he wouldn't think to look for you?"

"I don't know. I do have a couple of college friends he's kind of forced me to lose contact with. He'd never know who they are or where they lived."

It was Jet again. "Good. That'll work. You start today. You contact one of them and you make arrangements to go to their home as soon as we've got all the pieces in place."

It was becoming obvious to Sonia that Mandy was clearly getting on board with the plan, though she did have her concerns. "But what happens when you've shown him the video and he leaves here? What keeps him from coming after me and doing something horrible?"

Jet gave Mandy a wink. "Sweetheart, do you think this is our first rodeo? We know exactly how to handle this. When Nick is in our office, we'll not only show him the video, we'll show him the e-mail that's ready to go to his dad, video attached. Also, it won't be just Sonia and me. Not only will we have one of our larger male acquaintances with us, we'll have your lawyer with us as well."

Sonia took over from there. "You see, before you leave town, you'll have gotten together with your lawyer and come up with the exact terms of your divorce settlement, however you want it to be. Then, while he's still reeling from being caught and fearing that he's about to lose the business, we'll have a document ready for him to sign. 'Sign it now, or it only gets worse,' we'll say. Chances are it'll take him a minute or two to figure out that he doesn't have any other choices, then he'll sign it. We're pretty sure he'll sign it."

Sonia could hear herself breathing as the room became suddenly silent again. Eventually, Mandy rose very slowly. "I guess this really is the best thing, isn't it?"

Sonia gave Jet a, "let me handle this part," look. "Yes, sweetheart. This really is the best thing. But don't worry, nothing is going to happen until you let us know for sure that you're ready. If you change your mind, you can look at other options. It's just that we really don't think you have any *better* options."

Jet and Sonia both stood. Jet helped Mandy steady herself then walked with her to the door, softening her tone of voice. "It's all up to you, honey. Just know that we're here for you, and we'll be helping you achieve whatever it is that you want." Sonia walked ahead of them.

As they reached the door, Sonia opened it and guided Mandy out onto the landing at the top of the steps. Everything looked bright and clean to her, almost as if the whole world was getting a fresh start. "It's all in your hands now. You go think about it. Just let us know what you decide."

Sonia and Jet stood together on the landing. They watched Mandy walk slowly down the two flights of steps and through the parking lot to her car.

Sonia turned to Jet. "That woman has some tough choices to make."

Jet almost chuckled. "Not the way I see it. In my book, the only things she has to decide on are the terms of the divorce. Now, what say we go downstairs and get ourselves some lunch?"

Sonia sighed. "Sounds good. One question, however."

Jet, who had started down the steps in front of her, stopped and looked up at her. "And what would that be?"

"Exactly who is this manly man who is going to be with us when we show Nick the video?"

Jet threw her arms out in a grand gesture and headed down the steps. Over her shoulder, she tossed, "It's a good thing one of us is in a relationship with a former marine."

34

After lunch that day, Sonia had gone out to get a few more shots of Mr. Afternoon Delight. Since her case against him was going to be entirely circumstantial, she wanted to have plenty of different images from plenty of different days.

Meanwhile, Jet had decided to spend one last afternoon trying to catch whoever it was that was purloining the high-end makeup from her client's establishment. She had a thought she wanted to check out.

Hanging out in the drugstore at about the same time she usually did, Jet saw the small group of girls she had been certain were the guilty culprits. This afternoon, however, she shifted her attention to a person who had, on many of the days that something disappeared, popped in around the same time the girls did—a young boy, maybe fourteen or fifteen years old, not particularly large or small. He was wearing loose jeans, untied sneakers, and a dark blue T-shirt. The hood of his plain, gray sweatshirt was up.

As he usually did, the boy walked over to the counter that held the large variety of candies that were available at the store. No surprise. What other reason brings a teenaged boy into a drug store? After the boy paid for several *Payday* bars, he started for the door. A moment later, however, he slipped down one of the aisles.

Jet felt certain she knew what was coming next. Instead of following the boy, she went directly to the front door. In just over a minute, she looked up to see the boy heading right toward her. She simply held her ground waiting until her gaze caught his eye.

The moment the boy sensed Jet looking at him, he stopped, his face flushing a dark red. The look of panic that came over him caught Jet off guard. She realized almost immediately that this wasn't some slick, devious boy stealing makeup for his girlfriend. This was something else.

The boy stood frozen as Jet approached him, walking slowly down the narrow aisle. She was certain he was surprised when she simply walked right past him, quietly saying, "Follow me." He remained frozen until she stopped, looked over her shoulder, repeated herself, and then walked on—risking the fact that he might just bolt.

Instead, the boy turned and followed Jet to the back of the store. She stopped and waited for him; he looked up at her sheepishly, embarrassed. "Just answer me one question, son. But you answer it honestly now, you hear?" She was looking directly into his eyes.

He silently nodded.

Her voice was quiet, calm. "That makeup you've got stashed in your hoodie. Who is that for?"

There was no answer. The boy was silent.

Jet took a deep breath, then tried again. "Son?"

The boy looked up at her, his eyes pleading, but it seemed his answer was stuck in his throat.

Jet pursed her lips. "It's for you, isn't it?"

Still no answer, at least not from his lips. His eyes, however, told her enough.

As a high school athlete, Jet had spent her share of hours in locker rooms. She'd had enough experience with other girls that age to know that each young person experienced their own bodies, their own sexuality, differently. Though she'd never had any desire to experiment, she had felt curious eyes discreetly checking her out. She knew that adolescence could be a confusing time for girls—and now that she thought about it, probably for boys as well. Whatever was going on with this young man, Jet was not inclined to turn his life inside out. She simply walked over to him and held out her hand.

The boy reached into his hoodie and pulled out two tubes of lipstick, bright red, and one mascara. His hands shook noticeably as he placed them into Jet's outstretched palms. His eyes, his face, his mouth indicated he was on the verge of speaking—nothing came out.

"So, listen." Jet's voice was soft but strong. "If I tell the owner his problem with someone shoplifting makeup is over, am I going to be putting my butt in a sling?"

No answer.

"Am I?

The boy nodded, indicating his accession. After a moment of silence, his shoulders turned just slightly, as if he were asking permission to leave. He froze, waiting for Jet's response.

With the tiniest of smiles on her face, Jet waved the back of her hand forward. "Go on. Get out of here. But don't you dare make me regret this."

The boy turned and headed for the door. Before he got there, Jet called out gently. "Son."

He stopped, turned around, apprehension on his face.

"I want you to wait for me outside."

The boy's eyes opened wide, but Jet believed he would obey her instructions. She walked to the counter at the front of the store and, without any words of explanation, paid for the makeup. She took the flimsy plastic bag the clerk put them in, stepped outside, and silently handed the bag to the boy.

Without looking back, she walked past him and headed for her car.

Less than twenty minutes later, Jet was back in her office. The sense of satisfaction she normally experienced after having wrapped up a case was definitely eluding her. Instead, she opened her armoire, took out a semi-clean glass, and poured herself a short drink. It wasn't enough to numb her feelings, but somehow the activity helped her put the afternoon behind her. She sat at her desk and crafted an email to the drugstore owner. It indicated that the shoplifting had been taken care of and that he should send them a check. If the problem arose again in the near future, BCI would take care of it with no charge. After re-reading the message, she sent it, took a deep breath, and started making phone calls.

～

WHEN SONIA RETURNED to the BCI offices several hours later, she saw Jet sitting at her desk. The look on her face was not encouraging. "What is it Jet? What's happened?"

"Something, and it ain't good."

Sonia stepped into the office and took the seat across from Jet's desk. "Well? What?"

Jet rummaged through the mess on her desk, pulling out a yellow pad. "Remember, last week, when I got the name of two more friends we should track down?"

"Uh huh."

"Well, this morning I found out that LaKeisha Washington wasn't working here in Lexington." She put the pad, the first pages rolled back over the top, in front of her. "She was working on a horse farm in Florida. You know, there's a big horse industry down there too."

Sonia leaned in, resting her elbows on Jet's desk and her chin on her folded hands. "And you haven't been able to reach her?"

"No. Worse than that." Jet let out a big sigh. "I wasn't able to reach her at the phone number I'd found, so I called her employer." She simply stopped speaking.

Sonia leaned farther forward. "And?"

"And it looks like we're never going to get to ask LaKeisha Washington where she thinks Mariana might be." Jet's voice was almost a whisper.

Sonia dreaded the answer she was sure she was going to receive. "Why?"

"Because on Thursday, March tenth, at five-thirty in the morning, LaKeisha Washington was killed by a hit-and-run driver. She's dead."

There was a stunned silence in the room. Slowly, things started to come together in Sonia's mind. "She was run down at five-thirty in the morning?"

"Uh huh."

"Then she must have been on her way to work." Sonia scratched her head. "Where'd it happen?"

"You're not going to believe this, right in the parking lot of her apartment complex."

"In the parking lot?" Sonia leaned back in the chair, her hands dropping into her lap.

"Yup."

"Who drives fast enough to kill a pedestrian in a parking lot?"

"Good question." Jet looked down at the yellow pad, her finger tracing a path to the information she sought. "When I spoke to the folks at her farm, Willowbay Farm, they said that the police thought it was someone who was up early and just taking off for work themselves. They thought that maybe, it being so early, the driver just didn't expect to see anyone else in the parking lot and allowed themselves to become distracted. They've checked the other resident's cars, but they haven't come up with anything. I guess it could have been someone who was picking up a friend early in the morning. Who knows?"

Sonia brushed a wisp of hair out of her face and leaned back in. "Yeah, but the speed. You'd have to be going pretty fast to hit someone and kill them. Wouldn't you?"

"I guess." Jet lifted her shoulders, opening her hands. "Sometimes things just go south."

It was a long moment before Sonia spoke again. "Or maybe sometimes things go just as you plan them."

Jet sat up tall in her seat, leaning in, matching Sonia's posture. "So, I'm getting the feeling that you're thinking what I'm thinking."

"That this was no accident?" Sonia's voice had a quiet edge to it. "That somehow, right around the time that Mariana Castillo went missing, one of her closest friends just happened to die at the hands of a hit-and-run driver, someone who managed to kill her right in her own parking lot?"

Jet nodded. "Yes, that's exactly what I think." Her next question came quickly. "So, what do we do now?"

Sonia stood up. "Well, I'll tell you the first thing we're going to do. We're going to find Penny Rae Nelson as fast as we possibly can." She ran her fingers through her hair. "You've already got several calls in to her, right?"

Jet looked up at her. "Right. And where are you going now?"

Sonia started for the door. "You and I, dear friend, are going to go downstairs to get a cup of coffee. Then we're going to walk around this neighborhood and try to think our way through this mess together. You know, two brains and all that. So, c'mon. Get up and let's get going. We've got to try to find this other girl before something happens to her."

By then, Sonia was on her way to the offices' outer door and Jet was reaching for her purse. Sonia spoke while she walked. "Don't worry about that. I'm buying. Let's just get going. Somebody's daughter is out there and we need to find her before it's too late."

35

Around ten-thirty on Thursday morning, Sonia looked up from her desk and saw Jet enter the waiting area. She called out, "Hey," then waved Jet into her office, her eyes returning immediately to the papers on her desk.

Jet was carrying her battered, freshly-filled thermos of coffee and a cinnamon roll. "You calling me in here in order to levy a tax on my breakfast?"

"What?" Sonia hadn't looked up.

"You looking for twenty-percent of my cinnamon roll?"

Sonia raised her eyes and smiled. "Well, whatever gave you that idea?" She reached to the far side of her desk, grabbed a paper plate that hadn't been overly used and held it out."

Jet rolled her eyes. "I'm going have to sneak in here through the back door if I don't want to lose half my breakfast every day."

Sonia pointed to the only door into their offices, "It seems to me you just did. How'd that work out for ya?"

Jet tore off a piece of the pastry and put the ragged portion on Sonia's plate. "There."

Sonia took her first bite and quickly swallowed. "I've got

news. I just sent Michael Oakley a bogus invoice from the Bluegrass Sump Pump Company."

Jet took a seat. "Do tell. Difficult to do?"

"Absolutely not." Sonia's eyes twinkled. "With Burnett's ability to fabricate the invoice and help from Brownlee on some particulars, it was no harder than sending a real invoice."

Jet unscrewed her plaid-patterned thermos and poured a small portion of coffee into its lid. She motioned to Sonia as if to ask if she wanted any, but Sonia shook her off. "So, does that do it for Oakley? Have we got him?"

Sonia licked sugar off her fingertips. "No. We'll have to wait to see what he does with it. He's either going to ignore it, which tells us he knows we're on to him, or pay it. I'm hoping he does the latter and we find out a lot more about his operation. For now, we're just going to sit still and watch."

Jet pointed to Sonia's laptop. "And we've still got the keystroke thingy tracking what he does on his computer, right?"

"Absolutely." There was a lilt in her voice. "He can't do anything on that computer without us knowing about it. If we're lucky, he'll complete the last phase of his scheme on the same computer, not his personal one. There, we have no idea what he's up to."

Jet took a sip from the red, plastic cup. "Well then, we'll know soon enough if Burnett's plan is going to work or not, won't we?"

"Yup." Sonia popped another piece of cinnamon roll into her mouth, a small smile crinkling the skin around her eyes.

~

AT THREE IN THE AFTERNOON, Sonia looked up to see Jet walking in circles within the confines of her office. She stood, knocked on the glass wall between their spaces and mouthed, "What's up?"

Jet walked out of her office and over to Sonia's. She stood in the doorway.

Sonia was still standing by the glass wall. "So?"

"So, this is the part of the job I hate, waiting." Jet moved to Sonia's desk and half-sat on its edge. "I mean, Mandy's got all the information she needs on that cheating, perverted husband of hers, and all we can do is wait until she makes up her mind to move in one direction or the other." She casually pointed at Sonia's iPhone sitting on her desk. "You've got almost all the shots you need of Mr. Afternoon Delight, right? One or two more and that's wrapped up. And with today's rain, you're not likely to get anything good this afternoon."

Sonia looked out their large windows overlooking East Main. The world really did look gray and dreary. Lost in her own thoughts, she didn't respond.

Jet nodded toward Sonia's laptop. "And Michael Oakley. You've sent him the bogus invoice, so all we can do is wait to see what he does with that." She paused, seemingly done with her complaint. Eventually, she continued. "Then there's Penny Rae Nelson. I've tried everything I can to find her. I'm sure she's not working on any farm here in Lexington, pretty sure she's not even in Kentucky. Until I hear back from my last set of inquiries, nothing much I can do there either. It's like there's absolutely nothing for us to do right now but wait." She shrugged her shoulders and twisted her lips. "I'm telling you. I'm just not well suited for this part of the job."

Sonia walked over and lifted her light-blue spring coat off her simple coat rack. "I know exactly what you mean. Want to go downstairs and get some coffee?"

Jet shook her head quickly. "No, I emptied that whole thermos. I don't need any more today."

Sonia slipped on the coat, picked up her purse, and walked right past Jet and out into the waiting area. "Then I suggest you do exactly what I plan to do."

"And what's that?"

"Go home. We're not accomplishing anything here this afternoon and it's been a long week already. I'm headed home to just sit and relax a bit and wait for a call from Brad. Why don't you do the same? In fact, don't you have some financial issues you need help with?"

"No. Not that I know of."

"Nothing a forensic accountant could help you with?" A smile emerged on Sonia's face.

The smile was suddenly reflected in Jet's as well. "You know, come to think of it, I'm not really sure that I'm doing everything I can to ensure my long-term financial security. I really should have somebody come and look over all of my assets."

Sonia stopped, looked back at her friend, and smiled. That's my girl. "Don't let any of those assets slip by him unexamined, sweetheart. See you in the morning."

Sonia stepped out into the rainy afternoon. There was no question that the rain and the unexpectedly brisk air sent a chill through her body. It was either that or the fact that in the parking lot across the street sat a black BMW convertible that reminded her of the car she had seen on Central Avenue the other evening. In the rain and gray, it didn't seem like there was anyone in it.

36

Sonia arrived at the office just before ten on Friday. She found Jet at her desk. There were chairs set up in the waiting area. "What's going on? Somebody joining us this morning?"

Jet gave her a coy smile. "Absolutely. And who do you think it might be?"

"Well, if it were eight in the morning, I would say it was Burnett, but at ten . . . ?"

"Oh, it's Burnett alright." She winked. "He's got news for us."

Sonia returned the coy smile. "And how is it that you didn't have to call me at seven thirty and tell me to be here at eight?"

Jet walked out into the waiting area and began laying out some of Magee's famous pecan Danishes. "I don't know. Maybe Burnett has developed a slightly different world-view lately."

Sonia continued into her own office but said loudly enough for Jet to hear, "Or maybe someone kept him up late last night, you know, going over personal assets and such."

The southern belle's honor was besmirched. "Heaven knows, I have not the slightest idea of what you're talkin' about."

At that moment, the outer door to the BCI offices opened. The rain from last night had been replaced by clean, clear sunshine.

Some of it poured into the windowless area. It filled the space with golden light.

Sonia looked at her watch. Precisely ten o'clock on the dot. *That's our Burnett.*

Jet walked over to Burnett and extended her hand, not as in a handshake, but rather as if she expected him to bend and kiss it.

Burnett took her hand gently but eschewed the kiss. "Ah, good morning, uh, Ms. Jet. And how are you this morning?"

Before she could answer, Sonia interrupted from across the room. "Somehow, Burnett, I have a feeling you have a pretty good idea how she's feeling. So, how are *you* feeling today?"

It appeared to Sonia that Burnett couldn't help himself. He tugged on the lapels of his jacket and straightened his already straight bowtie. "In fact, Ms. Sonia, I am downright chipper. I have news to share regarding our joint enterprise."

Jet took a seat at the table, smiling up at Burnett. "Okay, then. Come and sit down. I won't bother to offer you one of these Danishes, unless, of course, you're hungry." Her eyes posed the obvious question, but Burnett simply waved his hand. "Okay, then, why don't you go ahead and share this news with us. It sounds like it's something we'll enjoy hearing." She patted the chair next to her with her fingers as she spoke.

Sonia sat as well. "Yes, Burnett. Come over here and share. We could all use a little good news on this bright sunny morning."

Burnett sat, stiffly, in the chair next to Jet; his body was erect, but there was a new softness, a new gentleness, to his countenance.

Sonia smiled inwardly. *Looks like you're doing some nice work there, lady.*

Burnett began. "So, as you well know, yesterday morning we sent Mr. Oakley a bogus invoice from The Bluegrass Sump Pump Company, in the exact amount of the last invoice he so surreptitiously slipped past Steven Brownlee." He stopped.

Jet obliged. "Yes, Burnett. We know that. What else?" She took a bite of her pastry.

"And last evening, Ms. Sonia sent me new files from his computer." He smiled. "It appears that yesterday Mr. Oakley obliged us by paying that invoice directly to The Bluegrass Sump Pump Company account to which he has personal access under the fictitious name of James Beam."

Jet banged her fist on the long, white, plastic table. "Ol' Jim Beam? Son-of-a-bitch has no business sullying the name of a purveyor of fine bourbon, now does he?" She huffed. "Anyway, we've got him, right?"

Burnett raised his hands in front of him, extending his two index fingers. "Well, now, we certainly have gotten him to commit himself, haven't we? Yet, there are two issues that are clearly incomplete."

Sonia glanced quickly to Jet, then asked, "And they are?"

"First, as we said before, in order to have true leverage over Oakley, we have to catch him maneuvering that money out of the false Bluegrass Sump Pump Company account into his own personal account."

Jet looked at Sonia. "We've got that covered, don't we?"

"We hope." Sonia took a short breath and continued, her voice hopeful but not overly confident. "We know that he has always waited three days and then transferred the funds into his personal account. Assuming he does it on the company computer, we'll be able to follow that trail. We'll have caught him with his hand in the cookie jar."

Jet seemed totally satisfied with the answer. She turned back to Burnett. "So, what's the second thing?"

Before Burnett spoke, his eyes brightened and his eyebrows arched. "Apparently, Mr. Oakey is involved in a scheme more nefarious than we had imagined." Once again, Burnett stopped, almost begging for someone to ask him to continue.

This time it was Sonia who obliged. "And . . . ."

"And, in my careful examination of the Bronson/Brownlee financial records since the date of Mr. Oakley's hire, I found that more money has passed through the Bluegrass Sump Pump Company account than has been misappropriated from Bronson/Brownlee."

Again, there was a stilted silence. This time Jet had no patience. "Well damn it, Burnett, go on with your story."

Burnett was a little taken aback by her outburst, but after a beat, he continued. "Okay then. So, what do you think could be the reason for more money going into Mr. Oakley's fallacious account than has come out of Bronson/Brownlee?" He looked back and forth between their faces, clearly enjoying the tension he was creating.

Finally, Sonia tentatively shared her thought. "He's taking money from somewhere else as well?"

Burnett lit up. "Exactly." He unconsciously rubbed his hands together. "He's not only taking money from somewhere else, he's taking money from several *somewheres* else."

Jet looked at him, her head cocked. "How is he doing that?"

Sonia interjected. "Phishing. Is he phishing?"

This time Burnett did run through his lapels and bowtie routine. "Well, I'm not sure what that means, but it appears that Mr. Oakley has gotten several other companies to direct money into that account."

Sonia leaned forward addressing both Jet and Burnett. "My guess is that he's phishing, sort of. I'll bet he's just sending invoices to companies hoping some of them would go ahead and pay them."

"Even if they hadn't done business with the company?" Jet asked.

Burnett sighed, "Oh ladies, I can't tell you how it burdens my accountant's soul to tell you that some companies' accounts payable departments are in such disarray that when an invoice comes across their desk they just assume that eventually, the proper paperwork will find its way to their department. They go ahead and pay it. Without question, those who do so are not following any of the procedures recommended by the—"

"Yeah, yeah, we know, Burnett." Jet turned. "Don't we, Sonia?"

Sonia smiled. "Yes, we do." She turned back to Burnett. "So, we think he's sending invoices to all kinds of companies, hoping some will pay? And if they contest the invoice he just apologizes and politely drops it as if it was an honest mistake?"

Burnett's voice was tinged with resignation. "I believe you are correct, sad as I am to admit it."

Jet reached out and grabbed her coffee, then leaned back in her chair. "Ain't that just a kick in the ass? So, what do we do if we find out we're right about all this?"

Taking her cue from Jet, Sonia leaned back as well. "Let's not worry about that. Our two main goals here are to prove that Oakley is stealing from Steven Brownlee and to get his money back. I think all we can do for now is sit and watch what happens on Tuesday or Wednesday. That's when he's likely to be transferring money out of the sump pump account, and, we hope, using the company computer to do it."

Burnett stood up rather abruptly. "Well, ladies, it has been my pleasure to inform you of the latest developments in our joint undertaking. And now I will take my leave."

Sonia watched as Burnett stood still, not moving, but looking directly at Jet.

A moment later, Jet popped up. "Oh, professor. Let me walk you to the door."

Sonia smiled. Wow. He was waiting for that, wasn't he? Yikes. She's got him hooked like a catfish on the end of some little girl's line. She watched as Jet and Burnett walked to the door speaking in hushed tones.

As they reached the door, Jet turned toward Sonia. "Listen, honey. We're going downstairs to get some coffee. I'll be back . . . . I'll let you know when I'm back."

Sonia looked down at the half-eaten Danishes and the half-full coffee cups on the table. She smiled.

JUST BEFORE NOON, Sonia looked up from her desk and saw Jet enter the BCI offices. "Well, look who has returned. Everything go okay downstairs?"

Jet gave her a blatantly content smile. "Lovely, thank you. We just enjoyed a little coffee and shared something sweet."

"And the coffee and pecan Danish we had up here weren't good enough?"

Sonia watched as Jet unconsciously turned and looked back at the leftover treats on the table in the waiting area. "Oh. I guess we could've stayed up here, couldn't we?"

The smile that crossed Sonia's face was rather smug. "I would have thought so. So, were you going to stay down there all day, or what?"

"Actually, we were having a lovely time talking about all the interesting facets of forensic accounting and I would have enjoyed staying longer." Jet held her phone up to Sonia as if Sonia could read it from across the room. "It's just that I saw I missed a phone call from that woman who was helping me track down Penny Rae Nelson. I thought I should return her call from up here, where all my notes are."

As if by reflex, Sonia glanced through the glass wall into Jet's office. Like she could ever find anything on that desk. She turned back to Jet. "Absolutely. Get right to it. We've got to find that girl before something happens to her."

Jet turned and started toward her office. "On it."

A few minutes later, Jet walked back over to Sonia's office, a sense of relief in her voice. "We've found her. She's working on a farm just outside of Saratoga Springs, New York."

Sonia breathed a sigh of relief. "You know the name of the farm?"

"In fact, I do. It's Holdenbrook Farm. Apparently, it's owned by some couple named Bonnie and Giles Daneck. The farm manager is a guy named Franklin Hayes. I've got a call in to him right now. The woman who answered said Hayes would be back later this afternoon. I'm going to hang here while I wait for his return call. What are you up to?"

Sonia's face broke into a big smile. "I, dear friend and partner, am leaving early. As you might recall, my paramour," she said with a glint in her eye, "may be home tonight, or at least by tomorrow. I am spending this afternoon cleaning my humble abode and getting in whatever provisions I will need to create a fine dinner for my love. It'll probably be tomorrow night before we eat. Know what I mean?"

Jet's smile was now as broad as Sonia's. "Do I ever. You go and enjoy yourself. I won't bother you unless something important comes up." She made a shooing motion with her hands. "Go on, go. Go enjoy the pleasures of your wanton love, while I sit here slaving away trying to keep this business afloat."

Sonia was not bothered in the least by the taunt. "Well, thank you very much." She stood and gathered her things. "And with that, I bid you adieu."

L ooking around her apartment, Sonia could actually feel the lightness in her own spirit. She wasn't sure if Brad would be home Friday evening, or early on Saturday, but she knew one thing. She hadn't seen Brad, or touched him, or kissed him, in precisely fourteen days, and sometime in the next twenty-four hours, she would be in his arms again. She cranked up the volume of the music on her phone, The Beatles, as she moved through her cozy home smiling, re-cleaning the little kitchen, the living room—the bedroom. The music stopped abruptly. She was receiving a phone call. It must be Brad.

Sonia didn't even look at the phone's screen. She just picked it up and said, "Hello?"

"Sonia?"

"Oh, Jet. I thought it would be Brad. What's up?"

"Listen, Sonia, I got some bad news. I got a call back from Franklin Hayes, the farm manager at Holdenbrook Farm, you know, where Penny Rae was working?"

"Uh, huh."

"You're not going to believe this, but Penny Rae Nelson went missing on March eighth."

Sonia swallowed hard, unable to say anything.

"Are you there? Did you hear what I said?"

"I heard, I heard." Sonia's voice faded away, "I just . . . ."

"I know. It's crazy, isn't it? Just crazy."

Sonia remained stunned, silent.

"Are you okay, honey? Sonia?"

"Yeah. Yeah. I'm okay." Sonia started pacing around her tiny apartment. "Actually, I'm afraid we both kind of saw this coming, didn't we?"

"I guess. Still. One girl dead. Two missing. This is a real bitch."

Sonia's voice tightened. "Listen, Jet. We've got to figure this out. We've got to do something before we find out Mariana's dead too." She absently pushed back the white window curtain and stared outside as she spoke. "What else do we know about Penny Rae? Do they have any information at all?"

"Well, when I finally got to talk to this Hayes guy, I asked him why nobody told me she was missing when I first called. He said that the police had told them to be careful who they spoke to and what they said because this was a full-on police investigation."

"Did he tell you anything else?" As she spoke, something caught Sonia's eye.

"When I told him I was a PI looking for one of Penny Rae's friends, he started talking. He said that Penny Rae just simply failed to show up for work on March eighth. It was two days later before the police were finally called in. They went to her apartment, but they didn't find anything disturbed or missing. Two days after that, her car was found in Bennington, Vermont."

"Vermont?"

"Yeah, Bennington, Vermont. It isn't terribly far away from Saratoga Springs, where the race track and the horse farms are."

"What else?" Sonia leaned to her left and strained to see more clearly beyond the pin oak tree that stood guard in front of the garage over which she lived.

"It seems that her car was found in the parking lot of the Grey-hound Bus station there."

"So, she might have been running away, and took a bus somewhere?"

"Could be. On the other hand, Bennington is right on the edge of the Green Mountain National Forest. I guess some folks suggested she had gone to the park to go hiking with some kind of group, but that doesn't wash. From what I've learned, she was no flake." Sonia's eye was focused on the front bumper of a black BMW that was parked near the corner of Ashland and Central Avenues, across the street from her home. *"She wasn't the kind of person who just didn't show up for work without telling anyone, especially being responsible for animals. No, our best hope is that she was running away for some reason. Maybe, just maybe, in the same way Mariana is running."*

Sonia could hear the hope in Jet's voice, but Sonia's fear was that both Penny Rae and Mariana were not just missing, they were . . . . She closed her eyes, trying to avoid the inevitable conclusion to that thought.

After a moment's silence, Jet asked, *"So what do we do now?"*

Sonia barely hesitated. Looking absently around her apartment, she began, earnestly. "We start over. We go back over every inch of ground we've already covered. We talk to all of Mariana's friends again, everyone she works with, everyone in her family, asking about her and LaKeisha and Penny Rae. We go back to Downstream Farm. We talk to that flakey professor, to see if he can shed any more light on things. We check in with Gabriela to see if she's found Santiago yet. We do it all over and over again until we unearth something, some little thing, that helps us find Mariana and, I hope, Penny Rae as well."

This time there was a long pause as Sonia's mind was racing through possibilities. When she looked out the window again, the black BMW was gone. After a moment, she became aware of the silence and assumed Jet's mind was going a mile a minute as well. "Listen, pal. I've got to get ready for tonight. I still haven't heard if Brad is coming in tonight or tomorrow. But you go home and start to think about a plan we can use to effectively retrace our steps. Call me Sunday evening and we'll talk about how we'll start next week."

Jet chuckled softly. "So, you're going to be busy doing something else this weekend?"

Sonia knew that Jet was trying to lighten the mood, teasing Sonia about her long-awaited reunion with Brad. She appreciated the effort, but it fell flat. For the moment, at least, even the thought of being in Brad's arms wasn't enough to relieve the dread she felt. Two, no, three young girls missing or dead? What the hell is this all about? She had to figure it out—and she was stumped.

38

Sonia had been walking around the room in a daze, unable to let go of her thoughts about Mariana, Penny Rae, LaKeisha, and, at the back of her mind, that black BMW. She was grateful when the phone rang and broke the grip of those thoughts. "Hello?"

"Hey, babe. How are you?"

"Brad." She sighed and absently touched her cheek with her fingertips. "It is so good to hear your voice."

"Are you okay? Everything okay?"

"Yeah, yeah. It's just so good to hear your voice, to talk to you." She was trying to sound as upbeat as possible. She wasn't succeeding.

"Come on, Sonia. Tell me the truth. Something up?"

"Oh, it's just this case. I just found out that another girl is missing. That's one girl dead for sure, two others missing. God, I wish you were here to help with this."

"Have no fear, babe. You know what they say about us Marines, 'From the halls of Montezuma to the shores of Tripoli.' Hell, I'm sure Lexington fits in there somewhere between those two places." In contrast, his voice was full of hope, even joy.

Tears filled the rims of Sonia's eyes. She let out another sigh, then a tiny laugh. "You'd damn well better be on your way, Marine, and be sure to bring that whole darn NCIS gang with you."

"I don't know about that ma'am. If you recall, the Marines are always looking for a few good men, and I'm guessing one good marine is all you'll need. But heck, if I need to call in a few favors from my NCIS buddies, not a problem. I'll do it in a heartbeat."

"So, will I see you tonight?" There was hope in her voice, along with a remnant of pain.

"No, I'm sorry, babe. It's already too late for me to make any kind of decent connections. I'm booked on an eight o'clock flight out tomorrow. I'll be home at eleven thirty-two AM. Can I count on you to pick me up at the airport?"

Sonia was still struggling, but her smile radiated through the phone. "You can count on me for a lot more than that, Marine. I'll be picking you up at eleven thirty-two," her eyes roamed her apartment, "and you won't be rid of me until ten o'clock on Monday morning. Maybe later."

"Sounds great, babe. You have a great night, and I'll see you before lunch."

"Can't wait. Have a safe trip." She hung up the phone, a quiet smile on her face.

The minutes went by. Sonia kept puttering around her apartment, starting to think more about the meal she would make on Saturday. Something Italian, for sure, it was her specialty. A thought crossed her mind. She realized that she had never asked Brad what airline he was coming in on. In fact, she didn't even know what city he was coming from. What if the plane was late or something? She couldn't ask the counter folks anything if she didn't know the flight number, the airline, even the city of departure. She picked up her phone.

Sonia dialed Brad's phone but got a recording. *"The number you have reached is unavailable. If you would like to leave a message—"* She hung up. She was sure she had his number right; it was programmed into her phone. But, sometimes . . . . She dialed again. *"The number you have—"* Click.

That's weird. He just called me.

Sonia decided to check the logs on her phone. She looked at the screen. Weird. That's my last call, but it's not his number. He must have called me from some other phone. Hmm. Area code 410. I wonder where that is. She dialed the number.

A man answered. *"Hello?"*

Sonia was perplexed but pressed on. "Hi. I wonder if I could speak to Brad Dunham."

"Oh, Dunny? He's not here. He just left."

"That's strange. I just received a call from him a few minutes ago. It was from this phone number."

"Yeah. He said his phone crapped out and he asked if he could use mine."

"So, his phone's not working?"

"Not right now. Not until he gets it charged. Can I help you with something?"

"Not really." She was feeling uncomfortable, not knowing how much to share. She decided to go just a bit further. "I just needed to ask him something about his flight tomorrow."

"Don't know much about that."

"Do you have any idea when he might be back?"

"Actually, no. He just said he had to go and wrap up something with his wife and that he'd be leaving for Kentucky tomorrow."

The air suddenly disappeared from Sonia's lungs. She hung up the phone.

～

AT ELEVEN TWENTY-FIVE SATURDAY MORNING, Jet pulled into the parking structure at Blue Grass Airport. She parked, walked across the roadway, and entered the terminal. Turning left, she was almost immediately in front of the escalator down which arriving passengers flowed. The weather was clear, so she was relatively certain the flight that was supposed to arrive at eleven thirty-two would be on time.

A few minutes later, arriving passengers began making their way down the moving staircase. One of the first ones to appear was Brad. Jet watched as he looked around, searching, she assumed, for Sonia. When his eyes found Jet instead, he cocked his head.

Brad cleared the escalator with his carry-on baggage in his hand. He walked directly over to Jet. There was confusion on his face and in his voice. "Where's Sonia?"

Jet's lips were tight, her answer terse. "She couldn't make it. She's out of town. C'mon. I'll give you a lift back to your place." She turned and began walking toward the exit.

"Wait. What do you mean she's out of town?" He reached out and grabbed her elbow. "Where'd she go? Is she okay?"

Jet pulled away and continued toward the sliding doors. All Brad could do was to follow. He caught up with her, grabbed her elbow again and jerked her around. "What's going on?"

Jet's blue eyes were ice cold. "Tell you the truth, Brad. I really don't know." She spun and ripped her arm free again. "Wait 'til we get into the car. I'll try to explain then."

Neither one spoke until they had reached the car and Jet had pulled the Camry out of the parking structure and through the exit gate. She turned right onto Man-O-War Boulevard. Her knuckles were white on the steering wheel, Brad's breathing slow and tightly controlled.

As soon as they were clear, Brad spoke. "Now will you tell me what's going on?" His voice was far from gentle.

Jet didn't respond at first. Waiting at a stop light, she reached into her purse and pulled out her phone. She found her voice messages and called up the one she had received earlier that morning. She hit PLAY and SPEAKER, and, without looking at him, handed the phone to Brad.

Sonia's voice came through the phone, loudly enough for them both to hear. It was obvious that Sonia had been crying. *"Jet. Hey, something's come up. I'm on my way up to Cincinnati. Don't worry. Everyone's okay. It's just that . . . well, I've just got to be away for a while. Also, somebody needs to pick Brad up from the airport at eleven thirty-two. I don't know what airline. I don't even know what city he's coming from. Could you be a doll and pick him up for me? And please don't tell him where I'm going. Just say that I had to go do something and that I'll be in touch as soon as I'm able. Love you, lady."*

The recording ended. Jet shot Brad a look that seemed to fill the car with frost. The message on her face was crystal clear. *What've you done to her, you bastard?* She never said a word.

It did seem to Jet that Brad was honestly confused. When he finally spoke, his voice was noticeably shaky. "You don't know what this is about? You don't know what's happened?"

Jet just shook her head.

"And when did you get this call?"

Jet's eyes remained on the road as she maneuvered through traffic. "My phone was on SILENT all night. I heard the message around eight-thirty this morning. Apparently, she called at six fifty-four. Sounded like she was already on the road."

"Well, as soon as you get me home, I'm on my way to Cincinnati." The tone of Brad's voice was clearly that of a professional investigator, hot on the trail of a victim or a perpetrator. "I'll bet she's at her folks' place."

Jet gave him a sideways glance. "Oh, no you don't, cowboy." Her voice became accusatory. "You didn't hear her ask me to not tell you where she was?"

Brad just looked at her, stunned.

Jet's voice was steel. "Now, you listen." She turned left onto Harrodsburg Road. "The only reason I told you where she went was so that you wouldn't go off the deep end and do something stupid." She gave him another quick, nasty look. "I know all about you, and your guns and crap like that; and I don't want anybody getting hurt. So, what you're going to do when I drop your ass off at your place is just sit the hell still and wait for her to call you."

He rose up in his seat. "But—"

"But nothing." Jet was just barely holding herself in check. The vein that ran down her forehead was popping up. "She said she'd call when she was ready, and that's exactly what you're going to wait for. You understand?"

Jet could tell that Brad was fuming, but he didn't respond. Neither one of them said another word until Jet had gotten Brad back to his place, a nice house on a street off Tates Creek Road. He reached into the back to grab his bag and then closed the door softly, clearly working hard to control his frustration. Jet rolled down the window. "Now you just sit there and wait for her to call one of us. Don't you dare go up to Cincinnati. She doesn't want to see you right now, and she's not going to. You'll see her when she's ready . . . if that time ever comes." Jet stomped on the Camry's gas pedal and it took off as fast as it's little four-cylinder engine could carry it. A small chirp from her tires put an exclamation point on their conversation.

39

Sonia spent the weekend in Cincinnati. However, fearing that Brad would come looking for her, she chose to crash with her sister Tee and Tee's roommates rather than stay with her parents. It was a little weird for her to be back in a tiny apartment near the university, but she had to admit that it felt good to be surrounded by lots of activity.

Sonia and her sister drank lots of coffee and Tee listened patiently while Sonia tried to work out in her mind how Brad could have seemed so in love with her while he was married to another woman. Tee was kind enough to not bring up the fact that John Eckel had left Sonia standing at the altar several years earlier, but eventually, however, Sonia brought it up herself. It was a weekend full of tears and tissues and something Sonia hadn't been very familiar with before moving to Lexington, bourbon.

~

AT TEN O'CLOCK on Monday morning, Sonia looked up from her desk and watched Jet walk into their offices. Jet stopped for a moment then continued walking directly into Sonia's workspace. "I was hoping I would hear from you over the weekend."

Sonia took a sip of coffee that had already turned cold. "I'm sorry. I just couldn't handle it. I needed time to think. Thanks for just giving me space."

Jet sat down tentatively on the edge of the chair across from Sonia's desk. "Wasn't easy. And now? Can we talk now?" Her voice was soft, gentle.

Sonia picked up some notes she had been working on, tapped them into a tidy rectangle, then moved them to the corner of her always-neat desk. "I'm here and I'm ready to work."

Jet paused, then looked at Sonia with caring in her eyes. "Look, sweets. If you're not able to tell me what's going on yet I'll wait. But you're going to have to do it sometime and the sooner you do, the sooner you and I are going to be able to start making things better for you. So, what do you say? Can we do it now?"

Before she could say a word, tears began to roll down Sonia's face. Her voice vacillated between broken and angry. She explained to Jet how she had found out that Brad was still married to someone else and that she didn't even know where that person was. Jet filled in the blank for her, saying that Brad had flown in from Baltimore. When Jet asked Sonia what she planned to do, Sonia stopped and thought for a moment. She used a scrunched tissue to wipe a tear off her face, being careful not to smudge her mascara. "At this point, I have to put our work ahead of everything else." She reached deep and bore down. "I want nothing else to do with Brad Dunham. Let's go find those girls. Their lives are a lot more important than my crummy love life."

Jet didn't respond and Sonia sat silently as well. After a long moment, Sonia sat tall and took a deep breath. "And there's something else I need to tell you." She took another, shorter breath. "I think I'm being followed."

Jet stood up straight, her eyes open wide. "What?" Her voice bounced off the wood and glass walls of the tiny office. "When? Where? For how long?"

Sonia started slowly. "I'm not sure when it started, but this weekend, when I was with Tee, my mind just kept cranking and cranking over things, so many things I could hardly keep anything straight." She started speaking more quickly. "But one thing that kept pushing itself to the forefront of my mind was this black BMW convertible. It was parked outside my apartment the night I found out about Brad, but I've seen it before, several times." She went on to tell Jet about seeing the car on the street, seemingly following her, and in the parking lot across from Magee's. "In fact, wasn't it a black car that splashed me outside of Papi's?" She stopped.

"Son-of-a-bitch." Jet's anger flowed through her words.

Sonia's voice turned darker, even more serious. "There was even one night I thought I saw a man standing at the back of the parking lot when we left the office, but when I took a second look, he was gone."

"And did you get a good look at him?" Jet began pacing around the tiny office. "Can you describe him?"

"No, other than he's tall." Sonia felt caught between anger and exhaustion. "But the more I think about it, the more I know I'm right. Somehow, for some reason, someone is following me." She looked directly up at Jet. "Maybe following both of us."

Jet's fists were tight, her voice even tighter. "Somehow, for some reason? You know the reason, Sonia. Someone has done something terrible to Mariana and they don't want us to find out who it is." Jet leaned down and banged her fist on the desk. "And we're not going to let that happen. Damnit, we're going to find him." She paused and stood straight. "Look. We're licensed PIs and we can run license plates. We're going to check the registrations and owners on every black BMW convertible in Lexington, in all of central Kentucky. We'll catch that son-of-a-bitch, and when we do, we'll find Mariana, too."

Sadly, the first thought that crossed Sonia's mind was that part of her wanted desperately to turn to Brad for help, but she knew in her heart she would never turn to him again—ever. The second thought that crossed her mind was that it was less likely than ever that when they found Mariana she would be alive.

THINGS SEEMED like they were stuck on PAUSE for Sonia over the next two days. Brad kept calling, leaving messages all but begging for a chance to meet with Sonia. She simply refused to respond. The same felt true for their investigations. Try as they may, call after call seemed to lead them nowhere in their efforts to find Mariana and Penny Rae. An exhaustive search of license plate numbers connected with black BMW convertibles turned up not a single name or other piece of information that could help them discover who was following Sonia.

On Tuesday afternoon, Jet walked into Sonia's office. Sonia could tell by the gray pallor of Jet's face that the news was not good. She asked tentatively. "What?"

"I just got off the phone with Franklin Hayes, the farm manager at Holdenbrook Farm. It seems that over the weekend some hikers in the Green Mountain National Forest found a shallow grave. They've just identified the body as Penny Rae Nelson's."

Sonia sat silent, her eyes drifting absently to the waiting area, the weight of yet another loss crushing downward on her. Her fingers drummed a tiny pattern on her desk.

Jet dropped her purse on Sonia's desk. "I guess that's it then. We're down to hoping to find Mariana alive."

Sonia's eyes regained focus as she turned to Jet. "Well . . . wait." Even with the painful news, there was a tiny bit of hope in her voice. "Has any new information come out of the investigation, now that they know what happened to Penny Rae?"

Jet took her normal seat across from Sonia, her head shaking solemnly. "I guess not. The only thing we know for sure, other than that she's dead, is that whoever abducted her drove her car to Vermont. Apparently, he buried her in the forest then drove her car into town and left it in the parking lot of the bus station. Of course, the car was wiped clean of prints, and Penny was strangled, so there was no blood."

Sonia stood up and walked over to the whiteboard she had just installed on the exterior brick wall in her office, just to the left of the armoire she used as a closet. "So," she spoke slowly as she wrote on the whiteboard, "why does the guy drive the car all the way to Vermont?"

"I don't know." Jet shrugged. "Maybe just to get far enough away from the scene of the crime? Maybe he already knew about the national forest."

"And what about the bus station? Why leave the car at the bus station?" Sonia was still staring at the whiteboard as if there was some answer there she just couldn't see.

Jet's level of engagement was increasing. "Maybe it means nothing. Maybe he figured no one would notice it for a long time, like if someone took a one- or two-day trip."

Sonia could feel herself coming alive. She turned to Jet. "Think about it. Somebody finds Penny Rae somewhere, at work, outside her apartment, somewhere. He kills her, then puts her in her own car and drives her somewhere, making it look like she's simply gone away."

"Yeah, I get that."

"So, how does he get back?" Though she was standing, Sonia's toe began tapping. "He killed her near Saratoga Springs, maybe right outside her apartment. He drives her to Vermont. How does he get back to New York?"

Jet's face lit up. "He takes the damn Greyhound Bus."

Sonia walked from the whiteboard over to Jet and leaned over her, wagging her finger. "That's right. The son-of-a-gun rode the

Greyhound back to New York. Somehow, he took the bus from
Bennington, Vermont to Saratoga Springs, New York, if," her
voice faded downward, "that's where he killed her."

"Wow, and there were times you thought maybe you weren't
cut out for this kind of work. Of course that's where it happened.
That's where she lived. Nice job, partner. Nice job."

Sonia started pacing around her office. "Well, let's not get
ahead of ourselves. But at least now we have something to go on."
The pace of her speech quickened. "We need to talk to the police
in Bennington and see if there's surveillance footage from the bus
station there and then do the same thing in Saratoga Springs. It's
not much, but at least we've got some questions to ask, and we
know the right people to pose them to. You start making some
calls to the police in Bennington and Saratoga Springs, and I'll
talk to Brad about . . . ."

Jet looked sharply up at Sonia. At the very same moment,
Sonia realized that her head was leading her somewhere her
heart didn't want to go. There was complete silence in the room.
Sonia sat down in her chair, sighing. Much more quietly, she said,
"You make those calls. I'll try to figure out what else we can do
from this end."

40

Two-thirty on Wednesday afternoon found Sonia sitting at her desk, waiting for Burnett Saunders to appear. She and Jet had spent the last two days in intense conversations with the police departments from Bennington and Saratoga Springs. Searches of bus station surveillance videos were being done in Vermont and New York. Sonia and Jet were waiting for the results.

At precisely three o'clock, Burnett Saunders opened the door to the offices of Bluegrass Confidential Investigations, a large box in hand. "Greetings, ladies. I bring you treats."

Sonia remained at her desk, but Jet stood and walked out of her office toward Burnett. "Well, what do we have here?"

With all the grandeur he could muster, Burnett bowed at the waist. "I realize how partial you ladies are to Magee's and its wonderful assortment of splendid fare. But I'm sure you do realize that there are other treats in this town worth savoring as well. And so, today, I have brought you a box of donuts from one of the most esteemed establishments in all of Lexington, Spalding's Bakery. No doubt you've heard of it. But I wondered if you have ever indulged."

Jet leaned forward and planted a tiny kiss on Burnett's fore-head. She had just a touch of her southern twang as she spoke. "Honey, I grew up in this neck of the woods. Of course I've enjoyed a Spalding's donut or two in my time."

Sonia, on the other hand, walked out of her office saying, "Honestly, Burnett, you're correct. I have heard of Spalding's many times, but I have never enjoyed their bounty."

They all moved to the table Jet had set up in preparation for Burnett's visit. Sonia took her first bite of a glazed donut. "Whoa, this is delicious."

Jet did the same, swallowing quickly. "So, what is the occa-sion, Professor. Is this strictly an instructional culinary seminar or are we celebrating something?" There was a pleasant smile on her face.

Burnett began his classic lapel and bowtie routine. Somehow, however, it seemed to Sonia that he decided it felt unnecessary. He stopped midway. "Ladies, we are here to celebrate hubris."

Questions in their eyes, both women looked at him, then at each other, then back again.

"That's right. We are here to celebrate the unmitigated conceit of one Michael Oakley, a person so full of himself that he used the same computer with which he has been stealing from several firms to move those ill-gotten funds into his own personal account."

Jet smiled and looked at Sonia. "Can I say it now?"

Sonia smiled broadly, perhaps for the first time in days, bits of sugar on her lips. "Yes, my dear. You can say it now."

With a great big smile, Jet bent her fisted arm and pulled it dramatically downward. "KA-CHING!"

Sonia chuckled. "We've got him now." She turned to the forensic accountant. "Don't we Burnett?"

"Absolutely." His voice actually sounded more masculine than usual. "We have a trail of him moving money, not only from

Bronson/Brownlee, but from other firms, into the Bluegrass Sump Pump Company account that he accessed as Mr. James Beam." He flicked the tip of his nose with his index finger. "And we now have a trail of Mr. James Beam authorizing transfers of said funds from the Bluegrass Sump Pump Company account into the personal account of one Michael Oakley. Done and done."

Jet rocked back in her chair and both she and Sonia literally applauded Burnett's accomplishments. His response was to bow his head and acknowledge their applause with a queenly wave of his hand. After the laughter subsided, Sonia asked, "So, we've got him dead to rights, but will any of this hold up in court?"

Burnett became more serious. "Actually, it's a little fuzzy, if you don't mind an accountant using lay terminology." He placed one arm across his chest and brought the opposite fist to his chin. "You see, placing that keystroke-recording software on his computer would have been entirely illegal if Mr. Oakley himself owned the computer. Since, however, Mr. Brownlee owns the computer, and since he gave you permission to download the software onto the computer, that was not, in and of itself, illegal."

Jet licked a little sugar off her fingertips. "Cool."

"However," he responded, now pointing a finger in Sonia's direction, "since we then used that software to track Mr. Oakley's access to his personal accounts, things become a little less black and white. In my opinion, as I strive to follow all of the admonitions of the Financial Accounting Standards Board, the organiz—"

"Burnett." Jet interjected.

He stopped short. "Anyway, I think we should be extremely cautious about opening ourselves to any potential litigation that might be the result of our tracking Mr. Oakley's use of his personal account."

Jet leaned forward in her chair, lips pursed, squinting her

eyes. "So even though we've got him, we can't do anything to him?"

Burnett sat up even straighter in his chair and made no attempt to squelch the complete fulfillment of his lapels and bowtie regimen. "Ladies, if you will allow me, I will spend the next few moments explaining to you how even the honorable art and science of forensic accounting can have a dark side—a side of which we might now choose to avail ourselves."

THURSDAY MORNING, Sonia stood at the door of Magee's, keeping her eye out for Steven Brownlee. Just before seven o'clock, she gestured to Hildy, mouthing, "Bring 'em out." Scooting over to one of the large tables, she took a seat across from Burnett.

Brownlee walked in, looked around, and locked eyes with Sonia. She motioned him over to their table. "Good morning, Mr. Brownlee. Thank you for joining us."

"My pleasure." He looked carefully around the room. "Gosh, it's been forever since I've been in here. What a great place."

Jet reached out, put her hand on his arm, and pulled him gently down into a seat between her and Sonia. "We thought you'd enjoy it." She extended her hand toward Burnett. "Mr. Brownlee, this is Burnett Saunders. He's the forensic accountant." She turned back to Burnett. "Burnett, this is Mr. Brownlee."

Burnett stood and extended a hand to the older gentleman. "Mr. Brownlee, sir."

Jet looked over her shoulder. "Oh, and here comes our food."

Sonia looked back toward the kitchen as well and saw three of the guys and girls who worked back there bringing out four veggie omelets, two almond croissants, and two pecan Danish. There were already four cups of coffee on the table.

Brownlee watched, surprised. "Wow, what a feast."

As the staff members placed the food on the table, Jet

squeezed Brownlee's arm again. "Yes, it is, and we want to thank you for it."

Brownlee dipped his head down, adjusting the glasses that often slid down his nose. He didn't say a word.

"You see," Jet waved her arm over the bountiful spread, "we charged all of this to Bronson/Brownlee." She gave Sonia a sly smile.

The look on Brownlee's face became even more confused and a little defensive.

"Now, Mr. Brownlee," Sonia leaned in, smiling, touching him on the arm as well, "we thought you wouldn't mind. Not after what Mr. Saunders has done for you." She turned to Burnett. "Tell him about it, Burnett."

Burnett sat up taller in his chair and put his hands on his lapels. Without saying a word, Jet reached over and gently stopped the process.

Burnett looked at her quizzically and then smiled. "Okay then, Mr. Brownlee." His voice became professorial. "As the ladies have already told you, we've tracked Mr. Oakley's transactions and have a complete record of how he has been embezzling money not only from your firm but from others. In addition, we can prove that he has eventually moved those funds to his own personal account." He paused, but then continued on his own. "They've also told you that, given how we came by some of this information," he glanced briefly at Sonia then back to Brownlee, "they've decided it might not behoove you to take this information directly to the police."

Brownlee nodded, his face still uncertain. "Right," he said softly.

"Therefore," Burnett's pride in his work expressed itself in his smile and the sparkle in his eyes, "we made a bit of an executive decision. Last evening, after business hours, Ms. Vitale and I gained access to Mr. Oakley's personal account. We made a transfer of $28,474.97 directly back into the Bronson/Brownlee general account." He went on without pausing. "These figures represent all of the funds Mr. Oakley has diverted to his own account, plus interest for the period during which those funds were not at your disposal."

Brownlee's eyes opened wide. "You stole the money back?"

"Certainly not, Mr. Brownlee." Burnett had a look of righteous indignation on his face. "As an accountant in good standing with the Financial Accounting Standards Board, I would never steal anything. This is simply an accounting procedure in which unauthorized debits have been redirected as credits into the originating account. It's simply a matter of bookkeeping."

Brownlee took a deep breath. "And all of this is legal?"

Jet stepped into the conversation. "Well, Mr. Brownlee," She gave him a coy smile, "it's all in how you look at it, isn't it? If you look at the money Oakley stole as an unauthorized loan, all you've done is take your money back with a reasonable amount of interest."

Brownlee rubbed his neck. "Yes, but without his permission."

Jet's voice became almost motherly. "Now, think about it this way. Is Oakley going to go to the police and say that, without his permission, you took back the money he stole from you?"

Brownlee looked around the table and smiled. "I guess not." A moment later, however, he grimaced. "But still, even being made whole, it bothers me that Michael has done this and is going to get away with it. Especially since he took money from other firms."

It was Sonia's turn to speak. "You needn't worry about that either." She squeezed Brownlee's arm and smiled as she spoke. "It seems that whoever got into Oakley's accounts and returned the money to you, also sent notifications to the other firms involved. They were advised that they might have paid unauthorized invoices to a company that doesn't exist anymore and that they might have been the victims of fraud." She winked. "And, of course, they now have the bank names and account numbers that will lead them directly back to Oakley."

Sonia leaned back in her chair. "In fact, we anonymously sent the police some information on Oakley's fraudulent behavior and a message that said we thought he had a plane ticket out of the country for later this morning."

Brownlee's eyes opened wide and his voice rose. "He's leaving the country?"

Sonia smiled mischievously. "Noooo. We just said we *thought* he had a ticket to leave the country. They're most likely picking him up as we speak and almost certainly before he has any idea what has happened." She continued, "Still, Mr. Brownlee, I think we would all be a little more comfortable if you took the morning off, maybe went up to Cincinnati or Louisville or somewhere else for the day. You know, just don't come back until you hear that Oakley's been arrested." She put her hand back on Brownlee's arm. "We certainly wouldn't want anything to happen to you before Oakley is behind bars."

Brownlee released his arm and adjusted his glasses. "I guess. Still, can't those other companies get in trouble for getting information from Oakley's computer?"

Jet leaned back almost gleeful. "You see, since they weren't involved in any surreptitious activities, they're standing on much more solid ground when they bring cases against Oakley. And the fun part is that he has no idea that they've been contacted. He'll be caught entirely off guard when the police show up at his door and drag his butt off to jail." Her eyes went coyly to the ceiling. "And of course, you'll have no choice but to fire any employee who has been arrested for fraud." She smiled at Brownlee and her hand went to his arm. "Trust me, Mr. Brownlee, you've gotten your money back, and all is well in the heavens and on earth."

Steven Brownlee looked around the table and down at the women's hands on each of his arms. He smiled. "Then thank you all for the services rendered." It was his turn to wave his arm over the feast that was spread on the table. "Breakfast is on me."

Sonia joined the others in the smiles and laughter that followed. Deep down, however, her heart ached. She was a grown-up. She could deal with disappointment, at least as she faced others. But in her private world, almost nothing could relieve the pain or take away the reality of Brad's betrayal.

41

Sonia was home alone on Friday evening. She tried watching television, but there was nothing on TV worth watching. Or maybe it was just her mood. She alternated between pacing around the tiny apartment and plopping down on the couch to give television yet another try. She also gave reading a whirl, a Sue Grafton novel, but nothing could hold her attention, nothing but a growing sense of dread.

Friday had been another day of waiting, waiting for Mandy to make a move. More importantly, she was waiting for something to break in their efforts to find Mariana Castillo.

Finally, at about seven o'clock, Sonia's phone rang. "Hello."

"Ms. Vitale, it's Gabriela. Gabriela Castillo."

Sonia popped up. She started pacing around the room, faster than before. "Yes, Gabriela. Are you okay?"

"Sí. I am okay. I am driving to Miami. It's a hell of a drive, but I'm already at Daytona. I'll be there in a few hours."

"Why are you going to Miami?"

"Because I finally found la gusáno, the worm."

"Who? What?"

"Santiago. I finally found him. It took me almost two weeks to find

him, and then I had to wait until I could get a few days off from work to go after him. But I finally got one of his friends to tell me that he had run off in the middle of the night to Florida, and that there was a girl with him."

The pitch of Sonia's voice started to rise. "Is it Mariana? Have you found Mariana?"

Gabriela's voice rose as well but in a different way. *"No, not yet. But I will be in Miami late tonight. Tomorrow I find la gusáño. And if he has her . . ."*

Sonia was momentarily at a loss for words. She took a quick breath. I don't even know if I want him to have her or not. It would be great to find her, find her still alive. But what if he's hurt her, or worse, what if he had her but now she's gone? The only word that softly came out of Sonia's mouth was, "Right."

There were a few moments of relative silence, as neither woman spoke. Through the phone, Sonia could hear the whine of the tires and Hispanic pop music playing in the background. Finally, she spoke. "How did you get his friend to tell you he'd gone to Florida?"

Gabriela's voice rose even further. *"Escucha señorita, listen. You do your work your way. I do mine my way. I found him, didn't I? Or at least I know where he is. Soon I'll see him. He'll tell me what we need to know."*

Sonia stopped moving, stood silently still.

"Okay then. I just called to let you know what's going on. I'll talk to you." The phone went dead.

As soon as she had gotten off the phone with Gabriela, Sonia tried to call Jet. She wasn't able to get through, but she left a message saying she needed to speak to Jet as soon as possible. This might be getting out of hand.

At seven-thirty, Sonia heard a knock on her front door. Her need to share this new information with Jet drove her directly there. She opened the door quickly. She rocked back. "Brad? What are you doing here?"

Brad's bright blue eyes stared directly into hers. Behind the softness of his voice was an intensity she had never heard before. "Why do you think I'm here? I've been home a full week and you haven't been willing to see me." He was slowly leaning forward. "Don't I get to talk to you? Don't I deserve to know what's going on? You're killing me here. I've got to know. What is it? What've I done?"

Sonia stood still, stunned. What's he mean, 'What've I done?' He knows what he's done. What the hell does he think this is all about? Not a word came out.

"Sonia. Answer me." His voice was quivering, but not in anger. "What's going on? Why won't you talk to me? Why won't you tell me?" It was hurt she could hear in his voice. Real hurt.

Her voice was firm. "Brad. I don't think we should see each other anymore." Anger smoldered through her chocolate eyes.

"Not see each other? Why? What the hell is going on?" His anger was growing.

Unconsciously, Sonia began to back up. It wasn't that she really thought he would hurt her, but just seeing his pent-up frustration flashing across his face, his hands balling into fists, she couldn't help but become fearful. He stepped into the apartment after her.

"What's going on here?" It was a different voice, a female voice. It came from behind Brad. It was Jet. She had climbed up the stairs to Sonia's apartment shortly after Brad.

He stopped talking, but his eyes never released Sonia. Sonia stood silent, frozen, hoping to look strong.

Jet squeezed quickly past Brad and into the apartment. She conspicuously placed herself between him and Sonia. "Everything okay here? Are we having a problem?"

Brad didn't answer. Sonia did. "No. There's nothing wrong. Brad would never hurt me."

At the words, "hurt me," Jet spun around, appearing ready to attack.

Sonia grabbed her by the arm. "No. No. We're okay. It's all okay."

Brad still hadn't said a word, but his eyes finally released Sonia. He looked at Jet, then back to Sonia. "I was just leaving." The look in his eyes made it clear that he had something more to say. He never got to it. He turned and stepped out the door. In moments, he was down the steps and gone in his Corvette, its deep-throated engine roaring into the night.

Jet opened her arms and Sonia walked slowly into them. "You're alright. You're going to be alright."

Sonia spoke softly, almost whispering. There were tears on her face. "He's so angry. I've never seen him so angry."

Jet released her hug. She pushed a wisp of hair out of Sonia's face. "I know. I could see it."

They moved to Sonia's couch and sat side by side in silence, Sonia's mind racing. She had come to think of herself in new ways—strong, smart, courageous when she needed to be, a professional. But that didn't mean she wasn't still a woman. And when a woman had given her heart to a man and then found out that he had been lying to her, deceiving her, none of those qualities stood in the way of the pain she would feel, especially if she had been seriously deceived once before.

Sonia felt Jet take a deep breath and inch back just a bit on the couch. It was clear to her that Jet was about to say something difficult. She looked up at Jet's blue eyes—blue but much softer than Brad's.

Jet started. "Honey, why do think he's so mad?"

Sonia was taken aback. "Why's he so mad? Because."

"Because why?" The look on Jet's face was one of complete focus.

Conversely, Sonia's face reflected total surprise, almost disbelief. "Because of everything that's happened, what he's done."

Jet reached up and gently pushed that wisp of hair out of

Sonia's face again. "Do you really think that's why he's mad? Is he mad because of what he's done?"

Sonia shot out her answer, her anger flaring. "No, because he got caught. He's mad because he got caught."

Jet sat silently for a moment, her eyes turning downward toward her own hands. "And did you tell him he got caught?" She looked up. "Does he realize you know he's married?"

Sonia's eyes moved quickly back and forth as she ran things through her mind. "I guess, well, I guess not." She thought another moment. "No, I guess I just told him I didn't want to see him anymore."

"So, you've never told him that you heard that he was married? You've never actually confronted him with that?"

Sonia thought about it, her eyes roaming around the room. She looked directly at Jet. "No. I guess I haven't." There was little emotion in her voice.

"And you're absolutely sure that he is?"

Sonia was quick to answer, reflexive. "The guy said he was. He said he was trying to wrap something up with his wife before he came back to Kentucky."

Jet took a deep breath. "And you really don't know why Brad is angry?"

Sonia shrugged. "I guess it's because he doesn't know what I found out. He doesn't know why I won't see him anymore."

Sonia waited for Jet's response. It was a moment in coming. "Well then, maybe you owe him that much."

"Do you think so?" Sonia screwed up her face. "Do you really think so?"

"Listen. When you told me he was married, I couldn't believe it. I wanted to cut his balls off." Jet's hands reached out to cover Sonia's. "But this, watching you in pain." She shook her head. "This can't go on forever."

Sonia wiped her nose with the back of her hand as she listened.

Jet's voice became more matter-of-fact, more pragmatic. "Honey, you've got to tell him you know. You've got to talk to him about it, put it to bed. You need to be able to move on."

Sonia stood up slowly and walked toward her kitchen area. "I know. I know. But . . . it just doesn't seem right that I have to take responsibility. I didn't make this mess."

Jet watched as Sonia put on some tea water. She stood and followed Sonia into the tiny kitchen area, standing behind her. "I'm sorry, honey. But I think that what you can't face is the fact that he's married." She reached out and put her hands on Sonia's shoulders. "You've been angry, but you're also in some sort of denial. It's like if you don't talk to him about it, then maybe it isn't really true." Jet gently turned Sonia around to face her. "Sweetheart, you've got to do this. You've got to tell him you know. You've got to see what he says. And then, assuming it is true, you've got to tell him it's over and that you never want to see him again. You've got to get some closure about this, and part of that is accepting the fact that Brad is married."

Jet gently pushed Sonia out of the way. "Now, *I'm* going to make *you* some tea. And maybe with just a little splash of Jim Beam to make it go down better."

Sonia stepped back and let Jet put teabags in the green and red ceramic cups she had bought Sonia last Christmas and which should have been stored away until this year's holiday. She knew Jet was right. She would have to face Brad and get this all out in the open once and for all. And she would have to do it soon because she just couldn't live like this any longer. Still, for now, she just wanted to sit and drink tea and feel the comfort of her very best friend in the world sitting next to her in silence.

42

Jet had decided to spend the night at Sonia's place. After calling a friend to take care of her dog, Diogi, she curled up on the sofa, knowing that her mere presence in the tiny apartment was a comfort to Sonia. When Sonia woke up on Saturday morning, she could smell freshly brewed coffee. Slipping out of bed, she dragged herself to the kitchen table.

The person she found there had clearly grown up on a plantation in the deep south. "Well, butter my grits, look who the cat has done dragged in for breakfast. And look what I've cooked up for your most important meal of the day, little Sunshine. We've got eggs and bacon, sausage patties, grits and a whole stack of my famous buttermilk pancakes."

Sonia looked at the cherry pop-tart laying on her plate. "Is that what this is?"

Suddenly the accent was gone. "It's not my fault you don't have one single decent thing to cook for breakfast in this apartment."

Sonia's voice was soft. "Sorry."

Jet stood and walked to the coffee maker. "Hey, don't worry about it. I hear pop-tarts covered in butter have miraculous medicinal effects. Anyway, there's plenty of coffee." She poured the rich, brown liquid into the same cups they'd used the night before. "And if you can manage to get yourself dressed, I understand there's a bakery known for its almond croissants pretty much right around the corner."

Sonia raised her hand to her lips. "Yeah, I don't think so. Not today." She huffed. "I'm not sure I want to eat anything."

Jet stepped over to the table and handed Sonia a cup of coffee. "Watch it, it's hot."

"Thanks."

Jet took a seat at the table. "So, before all the ruckus with Mr. Hotstuff last night, you'd called me about something that was going down. Do you even remember what it was?"

It amazed Sonia that through all that had happened with Brad the night before, and then the conversation she'd had with Jet, she'd never told Jet about the phone call from Gabriela. She sat in the chair opposite Jet and spent the next few moments telling her that Gabriela had found out where Santiago had gone and was, at that very moment, in Florida, trying to track him down. She didn't fail to mention that she was worried Gabriela might hurt the boy.

Jet put her cup down. "It's interesting that you say that. I was going to tell you that I'd gotten a phone call from my friend at the Lexington Police Department, Malcom Weathers. It seems that LPD has finally gotten some information back from the police in Bennington and Saratoga Springs. Using the surveillance video from the bus stations, they were able to establish that the morning after Penny Rae disappeared, only four passengers got on the bus in Bennington and off in Saratoga Springs. Two of them were older women, and one was a teenaged boy. The other one was a tall guy, middle-aged or so."

Sonia's eyes widened. "Were they able to identify him?"

"No. But they were able to track him because he was wearing one of those floppy fisherman's hats. Unfortunately, he kept it down low the whole time. It's clear it's the same guy getting on and off the bus, but we don't get a facial image and there's no particular reason to believe he was involved in Penny's murder."

Sonia leaned forward. "What about his name. Can't they get his name from the manifest or something?"

"Honey," Jet's voice was motherly, "apparently, you haven't traveled by bus lately. Listen, you can go online and buy a ticket and that ticket would have your name on it. But you can also just wait 'til the bus pulls into its stop and get on board. The driver comes around and collects the right amount of money for your trip. No name. No ID. Apparently, that's exactly what this guy did."

Sonia slumped back in her chair. "Alright . . . . So, what *do* we know right now?"

Jet's response was a blank look, so Sonia continued. "First, we know that the three girls all went to the same school, and all worked on the same research with Professor Andersen."

Jet jumped in, but not enthusiastically. "Yeah. I spoke to him again yesterday, as well. He said he was sorry if he missed giving us Penny's name, and LaKeisha's too. Still, he hadn't heard from them since they'd graduated and he had no reason to believe they'd been in touch with each other; although that was something he wouldn't know about one way or the other, is it?"

Sonia gave Jet a crooked look. "What'd you think about all that?"

"Honestly, I couldn't help but wonder if the professor was dodging us." Jet held her coffee cup in both hands, close to her lips, speaking through the steam that rose from the cup. "I wondered, maybe, if he'd been a little too close to one or more of the girls, you know?"

"And?"

"And, I made a few follow-up phone calls to some of the girls I'd spoken to before. But none of them had ever heard any rumors of him messing around with his students that way. In fact, some of them kind of thought of him as a gelding, if you know what I mean."

Sonia gave Jet an inquisitive look.

Jet responded by making a scissors-type motion with her fingers, indicating the loss of a certain body part. "Kind of seemed like a dead end, you know?"

Sonia blew on her hot cup of coffee. "Okay. Nonetheless," she spoke evenly, slowly gaining a little momentum, "they went to the same school. They all did research on the virus that was making the mares spontaneously abort, whatever the hell its name was. We also know that Penny's body was buried in the national forest near Bennington, and there's a chance that the guy who brought her there rode a bus back from Bennington to where he abducted her, probably Saratoga Springs."

Jet took over, matching Sonia's steady pace. "And we know that Santiago, the boy who Mariana was dating disappeared at exactly the same time she did. So, what's the connection? Did Mariana tell Santiago something about the other girls? Did *he* run down LaKeisha? How is he related to the guy who we think took Penny Rae?"

"Come to think of it, what about Limey?" Sonia added. She was sitting taller. "We know his relationship with Mariana might be more involved than they were letting on."

Jet screwed up her face. "Yeah, but how could he have been involved in LaKeisha's death down in Florida and then Penny Rae's in New York?" She cocked her head. "Unless . . . ?"

Sonia's eyebrows rose. "Unless what?"

"Unless," Jet's eyes squinted, "someone sent him to do those things. He certainly knows his way around the world of horse farms, doesn't he?"

"I guess." Sonia relaxed back into her chair. "Still, we know all these things and yet, it seems like we really don't know anything. Most importantly, where the hell Mariana is . . . and," her voice trailed off, "if she's even alive."

Sonia and Jet sat in silence. Finally, Sonia put her cup down on the table with just the tiniest thud. She was in her pajamas, her hair a mess and she was wearing not a stitch of makeup, except what was still on from the day before and smudged. Eventually, a new light came into her eyes. "I've got it." She nodded. "I know what we're doing wrong."

Jet put her cup down, mimicking Sonia's action. "Well lay it on me, lady. I'm ready for something to change."

Sonia sat up taller. "We've been going at this sideways."

Jet moved to match Sonia's posture. "What do you mean?"

"Look." Sonia's index finger tapped the table as if there were some list of facts imprinted on it. You've done a great job tracking down every person we could find who knew the girls while they were in school. Right?"

"Right."

She tapped again. "And all three girls wound up working in their field, working with horses, right?"

"Right again."

She tapped a third time. "And you've called every one of the friends, some more than once, and yet no one seemed to have any idea what was going on in their lives. Correct?"

"Correct."

Sonia leaned back just a little. "How does that make sense? Absolutely no communication between these girls and any of their former colleagues at school? These were successful students, not pariahs. They couldn't just lose contact with every person they ever knew at school. Not one hundred percent."

Jet's face matched her word. "So?"

"So," Sonia rolled her lip between her teeth. "I think someone is lying to us. Maybe more than one person." She banged her hand on the table with just a little emphasis then pointed right at Jet. "Damn it, somebody knows something. They've got to."

Jet paused before she spoke, quietly. "So, what do we do? We've already spoken to everyone we can think of."

Sonia stood up and started pacing around the tiny apartment. "No. We've had conversations with them. We've communicated with them over the internet and by phone, but we haven't really spoken with most of them, have we?" She turned and looked right at Jet. "I mean, face to face. Looking them in the eye."

Jet sat still, but her eyes remained locked on Sonia's. "You know, you're right. There's only been a handful that I've met with personally."

Sonia stopped and turned directly to Jet. "And that's where we've been going wrong. We need to get out there and talk to these folks face to face, eye to eye. We need to watch their reactions when we ask about the girl's relationships, their work, their boyfriends, whatever."

Jet slumped back in her chair. "You realize, of course, that most of those friends from Mayweather have graduated and taken jobs all over the country. It's a special program and its graduates are highly sought after. We'd have to do a ton of traveling in order to speak to all of them personally."

Sonia was unfazed, her energy at its highest level in days. "Then we start locally and move out from there. First, we talk to the folks who are right here in Lexington. Then we go to the towns in the surrounding area. We just keep going farther and farther until we find something."

Jet let out a long sigh. "Or until something else turns up and we realize we're too late."

Jet's words stopped Sonia in her tracks. She moved back to her seat at the table, speaking softly. "I know. But until then, that's our plan. We start first thing Monday morning."

43

At ten o'clock on Saturday evening, Gabriela walked down a commercial street in the Allapattah section of Miami, a predominantly Hispanic area of town. She was looking for the type of nightclub that might attract her prey. She found exactly what she was looking for.

Gabriela walked into the club and past one of the huge air conditioning vents. The AC was turned on full blast, but it was no match for the heat and humidity of the subtropical night. The room's oppressiveness was dramatically increased by the sheer amount of humanity it held. Young men and women seemed squeezed together by the flamingo-colored walls and the low, black ceiling tiles. Any space left between those bodies was filled with music and smoke, some of which had an aroma that might well be described as sickeningly sweet.

Gabriela maneuvered her way across the crowded floor. It seemed to her the denizens of the dark netherworld-like venue had decided the only defense against the weight of the warm, wet air was nakedness. Everywhere she looked, skin of varying shades of darkness, some natural, some just tanned, glistened with sweat. Only the most private parts of the young bodies were covered. Even those were generally on display through skimpy pieces of cloth, some all but transparent, others wet and clinging. Either way, they highlighted, rather than disguised, the natural attributes of the bodies they were supposed to hide.

Pushing her way up one flight of steps, to a small balcony within the room, Gabriela was fully aware of the stares of almost every man in the club. Even those who were dancing with other women couldn't resist the impulse to follow her with curious eyes. Her thin, statuesque body and long dark hair, adorned with clothing and jewelry designed to draw attention, had given Gabriela lots of practice with just such an experience. Somehow, she knew exactly how to take in every look, every comment passed from male to male, without ever appearing to notice. Had she been on the prowl for any kind of carnal pleasure, her gratification would have been assured.

But that was not Gabriela's purpose. She was there because she knew it was Santiago's kind of place—cheap and sexy. She had never confessed to Sonia that she had physically threatened one of the young boys in the barrio in order to get him to tell her where Santiago had gone. When the boy had told her that Santiago had a female with him, she had pressed him to describe the woman. Unfortunately, after her most serious threats, she'd had to accept that the boy really didn't know much. He'd told her Santiago was on his way to Miami Beach, and Gabriela knew she would have to go there herself if she wanted to learn anything further.

Perched on her little balcony, Gabriela watched the room full of bodies sway, almost in unison, to the heavy thumping of the music. It took only a few minutes before a dark-haired, dark-eyed stud found his way next to her, a beer in each hand.

He gave her a broad, tooth-filled smile. *"Cerveza?"*

"Gracias." She took the beer, giving him a small smile, then turned away from him, still surveying the room.

"Busca a alguien?"

Though her Spanish was more than fluent, Gabriela didn't reply.

"I said, are you looking for someone?"

Gabriela nodded, "Yes," never taking her eyes off the dance floor.

His smile broadened, "Then maybe I can help you."

It was all for naught, as Gabriela never saw the smile, and didn't respond to the statement. She could, however, sense his frustration building and feel him moving closer to her. Normally, she would have enjoyed playing this guy for the fool he was, but she had more important business to attend to. She turned, gave him a big warm smile, and lifted her beer in a toast. *"Gracias, mi amigo."*

Before he could stop her, Gabriela slid past him and off the balcony. She glided into the room, floating deftly between dancers. Before she got to the front door, however, her female intuition paid off. Walking through that door, laughing and jostling with his friends, was Santiago Gomez.

Rather than walk directly up to him, Gabriela made a swift move to her left and stationed herself behind a pole, obscuring any view Santiago might have of her. The music thumped, the dancers bobbed, the heat and wetness pressed downward. Gabriela watched as Santiago made his way to the bar. The whole time, she searched the crowd for the face she really wanted to see.

Gabriela waited for the next half hour, as Santiago and his friends drank and generally made fools of themselves trying to pick up girls. Every few minutes some self-confident *caballero* would approach her, but years of dealing with her own attractiveness had given her a full repertoire of looks, many of which were easily understood to mean, "Don't bother."

Finally, when she was convinced that Mariana was not going to be joining him, Gabriela began making her way over to Santiago. The music flowed from one song to another. In moments, Gabriela was standing directly behind him.

She leaned in. *"Buenas noches, mi amigo,"* she whispered into his ear, the heat of her breath startling him.

He turned around, shock on his face. "Gabriela. *Que demonios.* What are you doing here?"

Her lip curled as she spoke. "I think you know *pendejo.* I'm looking for my cousin. Now, let's say we get out of here so we can talk and hear each other."

Santiago stepped back as much as he could on the cramped dance floor, waving his arms in front of his body. "No way. Get away from me, bitch. I'm not going anywhere with you."

Gabriela looked at him inquisitively, pure confidence. She reached up, put her left hand behind his neck, and pulled his head down as if to kiss his ear. At the same time, her right hand grabbed his left and pulled it suggestively toward her most private parts. Just before it reached exactly what he hoped it might, she pulled it just a little to the right. She whispered in his ear again. "Do you know what that is in my pocket?"

Santiago's eyes were open wide as he pulled his hand away from hers and tried to back away.

But Gabriela simultaneously kept her grip on his neck and slipped her right hand into her pocket. "Diamondback, nine-millimeter. Locked and loaded and ready to blow your balls from here to kingdom come." Letting go of him, she nodded at the door. "Let's go."

When Santiago started walking toward the exit, one of his friends began following. Gabriela turned around, pulled just enough of the gun out of her pocket for the friend to recognize what it was, then wagged her finger at him and gave him a rich, warm, threatening smile. It appeared he had gotten the message because he stopped and simply watched as Gabriela and Santiago left the club.

Out on the street, her eyes searching the surrounding area, Gabriela nudged Santiago, moving him to the left. Within a few moments, they were standing behind a bench at a municipal bus stop. She spoke softly into his ear from behind him. "Why don't we sit here and talk *mi amigo*?"

Santiago looked around, possibly hoping for some help. None appeared. Eventually, he walked around the bench and took a seat. Gabriela stood closely behind him. She leaned over him, assuming that if anyone were watching them, it would seem like they were lovers, involved in an intimate and playful conversation.

She ran her fingers through his black, almost-shoulder-length, hair. "Now, *hijo de puta*. What have you done with my cousin?"

Santiago tried to turn his head around so that he might answer her, but Gabriela used her hands and her body weight to keep his head facing forward. He spoke, as if to the street. "I don't know what you're talking about. Your cousin? You mean Mariana?"

Gabriela slipped the handgun out of her pocket and pressed it against the back of his head, her moves hidden from view by her body as she leaned over him. "Of course I mean Mariana. She's missing, and she went missing the very day you left Lexington." She rocked the gun back and forth against his head. "The very day you left Lexington with a woman."

"Effie? You mean when I left town with Effie?"

Gabriela pressed the barrel of the handgun harder into his head. Her voice strengthened. "No. Mariana. You left town with Mariana, and now no one knows where she is."

"*Dios mío.* I'm telling you it was Effie." His voice was almost panicked, pleading. He spoke quickly. "Effie came with me. She just wanted a ride to Florida. She has a cousin down here too. She just wanted a ride. I swear it."

Gabriela paused. "Take out your phone." Her voice was calm, controlled.

"What? Why?" His body squirmed. His voice was shaky.

"Just take it out." Santiago did what he was told. "Now, call Effie. Call her right now."

Santiago dialed the number, and within a few moments, Gabriela could hear a tiny voice coming from his phone. She stretched her hand out over his shoulder. "Give me the phone." His hand was shaking as he passed it to her.

"Effie?" Her voice sounded strangely upbeat. "*Buenas noches. Cómo estás?*" There was a pause as Effie answered. Gabriela continued. "*Sí,* this is Gabriela, Mariana's cousin. I'm here in Miami." She looked down at Santiago, squinting her eyes. "*Sí,* I'm having fun with Santiago. He said maybe we should get together tonight. *Dónde estás?*" There was another pause. "Where? Oh, I bet Santiago knows where that is. Listen, we'll call you back in a few minutes. We'll try to get together for some drinks. Okay?"

Gabriela hung up the phone. "Okay, so Effie is down here." There was a touch of disappointment in her voice. She gave the phone back to Santiago. "And you know nothing about where Mariana is?"

"No, no."

"When was the last time you saw her?" She was leaning down, almost whispering into the top of his head."

"I don't know." He tossed the answer. "Been weeks, easy."

Her voice tightened. "And when I get back to Lexington, I'm not going to find out you've done something to her?"

It seemed to Gabriela that Santiago was starting to feel more confident. It showed in his voice, in his answer. "No bitch. I don't know where she is and I don't care."

Gabriela paused again, looking up and down the street. It may have seemed to Santiago that she was becoming confused. Then the crack of the gun's butt, hard against his head, sent a lightning bolt of pain through his brain.

"*Gracias, amigo.* You've been very helpful. I hope you enjoy the rest of your *vacaciones.*"

Santiago bent over, grabbing the back of his head, the hot blood slipping through his fingers. "*Puta. Pérra.* You hurt me, you bitch." He jumped up off the bench and turned on her.

She was gone.

44

After learning from Gabriela that Santiago was no longer a viable suspect, Sonia and Jet had spent Monday through Thursday beginning the task of re-interviewing everyone they had spoken to about Mariana—this time face to face. It was slow going.

One of the few things they accomplished in those four days was wrapping up the case of Mr. Afternoon Delight. A brief meeting with his hard-working wife had ended with her indication that she would be heading directly to her lawyer. All of it brought little joy to Sonia.

Right after that meeting, Jet had dragged Sonia downstairs to Magee's. There, Jet had convinced Sonia that the time had come to quit stalling. She needed to talk to Brad, put things to bed, and she needed to do it as soon as possible. Jet had sat at the table, listening, as Sonia made a phone call setting up a meeting with Brad for that evening at eight o'clock.

Sonia made arrangements to meet Brad in the bar at the downtown Hilton, The Bigg Blue Martini. She knew it wouldn't be crammed with folks and noisy, yet she didn't want any setting too intimate. This was going to be her last conversation with Brad—period.

Sonia walked into the bar at precisely eight o'clock. She was wearing black pants that hugged her body and a white wrap-around blouse that showed off her feminine attributes. She had put in the time to make sure her hair and make-up were perfect. She checked a mirror as she passed it. This may be my last evening with him, but darn it, I'm certainly going to give him something to remember.

Brad was, of course, waiting for her when she got there. The room was dim and chilly. In fact, he was the only patron in the place.

Brad was seated at a table in the corner with two glasses of wine already on hand. Sonia came in and walked directly to him. He stood as she took her seat. "I hope you don't mind. I ordered you some red wine. I know you enjoy it."

"I'd rather bourbon on the rocks, please. Basil Hayden."

She could see that Brad was a little taken aback, just as she had hoped he would be. He called the server over and asked her to bring Sonia the bourbon she had requested.

"You're looking lovely this evening." The bright blue of his eyes seemed somehow diminished.

"Thank you." Her answer was more curt than pleasant.

He made a feeble attempt at an upbeat sound to his voice. "Everything okay with you?"

"Fine. Everything's just fine." Still curt.

Brad fiddled with his wine, a drink Sonia knew was not his preference. "So, thank you for agreeing to meet with me tonight."

Just then, the server appeared with Sonia's bourbon. "Thank you, Miss." Then nothing.

Brad tried again. "I know this is difficult for you, for both of us, but I think—"

She stepped right in, her voice level, but with no indication of a willingness to negotiate. "Listen, Brad. Let's not play around like this is some sort of date or cordial meeting. I'm here for one reason and one reason only." She stopped, making him ask.

"And that is?"

Her words were strong, clear, to the point. "To tell you why we're over, why I never want to see you again."

Brad took a deep breath. "Would you mind if I tell you?"

Sonia rocked back. "Tell me what?"

"Tell you why you don't want to see me anymore." There was an urgency in his voice.

Sonia brushed that wisp of hair out of her face. What the hell is this all about? This bastard is not going to turn this around on me. No, he is not.

Before she could answer, Brad spoke. "It's because I'm still married."

Sonia was stopped cold. She had rehearsed and rehearsed every possible way she could say those words. She'd kept changing her mind, but she was determined to say the words, "You're married," in such a way that he would wither right in front of her. *Figlio de puta*. Now he'd gone and stolen that moment. She was livid, but she was silent.

"I know. I know you heard and I'm sorry. I am so, so sorry." His voice, his whole demeanor, was contrite.

Sonia exploded, shouting at him in just barely audible tones. "You son-of-a-bitch. Yeah, I found out. I found out the man I loved, the man who let me think he loved me, was married. And how do you think that made me feel. *Come uno scemo*. Like a fool! I thought I could never trust a man again. But no, no, you had to come along and sweep me off my feet. You had to save my life, twice, then look at me with what I thought was love in your eyes. And the whole time, the whole damn time, you had your little wifey stashed away somewhere near Baltimore, or some damn place like that."

Sonia leaned forward, venom in her eyes and her voice. "And I'm done with you, you bastard, done with you." With that, she waved her arm in a grand gesture. Unfortunately, the sweep of her arm managed to catch both glasses of wine, knocking them over onto the table, red liquid pouring down into their laps and onto the floor.

The server was quick to hop to their rescue, showing up with a couple of bar towels, but the damage was done. Sonia looked down at her pants and white shirt, now soaked with large swirls of red wine. "Damn it. Damn it." She stood up.

Her eyes burned at Brad. She could tell he was stunned. Sitting there in a pool of red wine, he was still speechless. It wasn't until she turned and started to walk away that he jumped up.

"Sonia. Sonia, wait. Let me explain. At least let me explain."

Sonia's eyes shot over to the server, who was mortified. Caught in the middle of this scene, it was obvious all she wanted to do was wipe up the wine while at the same time remaining totally invisible. It wasn't working.

Brad looked at the server as well. "I'm sorry. So sorry. I'll pay for anything I need to. Just . . . I'm sorry."

Sonia stood still, seething.

"Please, babe. Come over here." He pointed at a table a few feet away, farther from the door. "Let's sit here at this table. Please, just give me one minute to explain, to tell you what happened."

Sonia looked at the server, lost. She was shocked when the server, eyes downward, wiping and wiping the table, whispered, "Give him a chance honey. He's too darn good-looking to throw back until you see if he can get the hook out of his mouth."

Emotionally off balance, Sonia followed Brad to the other table, not saying a word.

When they were settled, Brad reached for Sonia's hand, but

she pulled it back. He started. "Sonia. I know this is difficult to hear, but please, please let me tell you the story, the whole story. Then, if you want us to be done, so shall it be. I promise you, just let me say what I want to say and then it will all be up to you."

Sonia sat, motionless.

45

Sonia listened as Brad began. "Sonia, you know the story of my folks, and of the woman I was in love with when I was with NCIS."

She just stared at him, expressionless. *Here it comes. The same old sob story. I've heard this all before, damn it. It's not going to fly again.*

"And I know you've accepted how all that changed me, especially when the woman I loved was killed right before my eyes."

One simple blink of her eyes. Her toe tapping. Yeah, yeah.

"What you don't know was how broken I was afterward. I can't even describe to you how lost I was, how empty I felt."

Her face screwed tighter, her eyebrows pulling together. Just like me right now, you creep.

"You see, when I was lost like that, and alone . . . well . . . this other woman I worked with, she came alongside me. She comforted me."

Sonia twisted her lips. *Oh, and I bet you took advantage of every move she made, poor thing. I bet you sucked her dry, didn't you?*

Brad was clearly waiting for responses, but he was getting

none. He went on. "So, after a while, it just started feeling comfortable, you know, spending time with her, neither of us talking much. And I wasn't . . . well . . . I wasn't really fully in control of how I was feeling. It was just like I was bobbing along on some ocean, just going where the tide was taking me."

Under the table, her hands were clenching and unclenching, while above the table she was motionless. She stared at him. Yeah, and taking her along for the ride, I bet. Dragging her right in, weren't you?

"Then, after a while, I guess you could say we were dating, or more like just being together. Next thing you know, I was asking her to marry me."

She took a tight, small breath. Oh, I don't doubt it. Poor, poor me, I was so lonely I can't be held accountable for my actions.

"And she said, 'Yes.' So, we ran off to a Justice of the Peace and got married. No fanfare, no big deal, just a quiet city hall wedding. And then there we were, married, living together, looking like everything was alright . . . . But it wasn't."

Sonia sat up taller, the heat of anger growing inside her—anger at what he had done to that woman—anger at what he had done to *her*. What? She wasn't able to give you everything you wanted, including the freedom to be with other women? Is that it? Did she want you to actually be loyal to her, you bastard? Sonia knew Brad was waiting for a response, but she hadn't said a single word since he'd begun. She didn't see any reason to start.

Brad ran his hand over his short brown hair. "In fact, it didn't take long for her to know it. She knew it before me. Later, she said that she'd been in love with me, but she knew I'd never really been in love with her."

Sonia realized she was so angry she was barely breathing. Oh, poor baby. The woman's love for you wasn't enough?

His eyes fell to the table. "You see, she realized that I just wasn't whole yet. I simply hadn't put myself back together. And though it felt great to be loved by her, I just wasn't able to love anyone, not her, not anyone."

Sonia's toe stopped tapping. Her hands remained still. Try as she might, she wasn't able to silence the little voice in the back of her mind. Remember when John left you at the altar? Remember how you felt? Could you have loved anyone then? No, you couldn't. You weren't whole enough, were you? You were too broken. No matter how much someone had loved you, you wouldn't have been able to love them back. Would you?

"You know." He looked up at Sonia. "I tried. I told her that I would try, try to get whole again, get healthy. And I did try. I just couldn't do it." He shrugged. "Then one day she came to me and said she was done." He tented his fingers, his elbows on the arms of his chair. "She wasn't mad, she didn't raise her voice. Hell, she didn't even ask for a divorce. She just said it was over and she'd found a new place to live. She even asked me if I would help her move her stuff, which I did." He leaned back in his chair, away from the table. "It was all so surreal, helping this woman who was supposed to be my wife move out of our apartment, all 'let's get this one next; no, you keep that, I don't need it.' Next thing I knew, I was alone again, and honestly, although I missed the comfort of her being around, I really didn't miss *her*. I never had really loved *her*."

Try as she may to stay rigid, defensive, Sonia felt some of her energy wane. She sighed. I get that. I know what it is to hurt. Still, she uttered not a sound.

Brad sat up, his voice stronger. "So, here's the deal. Last week, when I finished with that client up in Boston and then helped Robbie Alvarez with his case, I took a side trip to Baltimore. I looked her up. I told her it was time, that we needed to get officially divorced."

Sonia spoke for the first time, softly, tentatively, not sure she wanted to respond. "And what did she say? Was she shocked, or mad, or what?"

He shook his head. "No. She wasn't any of those things. She knew it was coming."

Sonia got fired up again. Her eyes blazed. Her voice flamed. "Oh, so she knew it was coming?" She leaned in toward him, venom in every part of her body. "She knew because you stay in touch with her? She knows *allll* about us. Is that it? Have you been telling your wife all about us?"

Brad raised his hands as if to protect himself from physical onslaught. "No. No. It's not like that. She knew because . . . well for two reasons." He took a big breath. "First, she knew because this had to come sometime. We hadn't seen each other in several years. We almost never talked. The—"

"*Almost* never talked? So, you *do* still talk to her, *don't* you?" Even through her olive complexion, Sonia's face was bright red. "You're still connected to her, *aren't* you?"

Brad was silent for a long moment. When he spoke, it was softly, calmly. "Sonia, she knew because she knows you, knows how I feel about you."

"What do you mean she knows me?" Sonia screwed up her face—anger mixed with confusion. "How could she know me?"

His voice remained calm. His eyes rose to meet hers. "She knows you because she's the one who helped you learn how to hack into the computer system at Dahlia Farm. She's the one who told you about the woman who was killed by the deranged sailor."

Sonia swallowed hard. I knew it. I knew there was something weird when that woman knew so much about him and what he felt. It just didn't pass the smell test.

Though not bold, Brad's voice was stronger. "Listen, I know this is all hard to digest. I know it's hard for you to believe. But trust me. She and I were never really in love and were never really married . . . not really." He rubbed his hands together, clearly at a loss for what to do with them. "Sure, the law says we're still married, but we never really were. And now, this past week, I was in Baltimore setting up our divorce, trying to make everything legal so I could move forward with you. So we could get married."

Sonia shuddered. Married? He's never even said "I love you," and he wants to get married. No. No way. Not after . . . she shook her head, no. Brushing her pants as if she could wipe away the wine that had already soaked into them, she popped out of her seat, threw her purse over her shoulder, and walked directly out of the bar and into the lobby.

Brad stood at the table. "Sonia. Sonia. Wait come back. Can't we talk?"

SONIA MOVED QUICKLY through the lobby, directly to the elevators. Working desperately to hide the tears that insisted on trying to spill out of her eyes, she pushed "P" and rode down to the parking garage. Stepping out of the elevator, Sonia was shocked when her forward motion was suddenly stopped as if someone had grabbed her foot. Confused, she looked down to see the red, three-inch high heel on her right foot had gotten stuck in the crack between the elevator itself and its framework. Struggling to free the spindly shank of the shoe, she was even more stunned when it snapped off, leaving her standing three inches taller on her left side than on her right.

Frustrated beyond belief, there was no holding back the stream of tears that gushed down her face. "Son-of-a . . . ." Trying to right the ship, Sonia leaned one hand against the cold, concrete wall that housed the elevator shaft and awkwardly lifted her left foot, slipping off the undamaged shoe. Staring in disbelief at the peep-toed beauty she held in her shaking hand, she was instantly convinced that its partner would never be functional again. She reared back and threw the shoe as far down the aisle of parked cars as she could, just barely swallowing an expletive.

Fully aware that she was now both soaked in wine and shoeless, she took a deep breath, bracing herself. She kicked off the broken shoe and left it lying where it fell as she walked barefoot toward her car.

Completely immersed in the pain and embarrassment the evening's rendezvous had heaped on her, Sonia was barely aware of the sound of a car starting and pulling out of its parking space at the far end of the garage. Moments later, however, she instinctively turned around in response to the sheer volume of the engine's noise. Stunned much more deeply than she had been moments ago, Sonia saw a car speeding right at her. Caught in a small passage in which there were no parking spaces, she had no choice but to turn and run.

Still barefooted, Sonia ran as hard and as fast as she could. Run! Run! Just feet before the car overtook her, she reached the end of the passage. Diving headlong between two parked cars, she landed face down on the concrete floor, the roar of the car passing while she was still in mid-air. As the squeal of tires disappeared around the end of the aisle, Sonia lay stunned, listening as the car flew out of the parking structure.

A long moment went by before Sonia crawled to her hands and knees and tried to pull herself together. Standing slowly, she surveyed the damage to her body before heading for her car. Her knees, elbows, and chin were all scraped and bleeding, but what rattled her most was the image of the black convertible she was almost certain was a BMW.

46

S onia walked into her office around ten on Monday morning, coffee in hand, but with no croissant. She sat quietly, not working, just gently rubbing her fingertips over the scrape on her chin. Thoughts of Thursday night's debacle twisted up her insides, as did the thoughts that came to her every time her eyes landed on the photograph of Mariana that sat on her desk.

Jet walked in around ten-thirty. "Morning sunshine." She strolled right into Sonia's office, put her purse down on Sonia's desk, and sat in the red chair. "How're you doing this morning?" The concern in her voice was obvious.

On Thursday night, they had spoken at length about the parking lot incident, with Jet hot to go to the police. Sonia had pointed out that they had already checked the registration of every black BMW convertible in the area and come up empty. "I don't have a bit more information to share with them than what we already had." When they had finally gotten to the topic of Sonia's conversation with Brad, Sonia had said, "What he never did was apologize for not telling me what was going on. He never did that, did he?" There had been little forgiveness in her voice or her eyes.

Jet had replied, "Well, honey, sounds to me like you never gave him the chance. Not that he deserved it."

Sonia had not responded, apparently unwilling to acknowledge the possibility that perhaps she should have given Brad that opportunity. Jet had let it slide.

The Monday morning conversation was more business-centered. Jet started. "You realize, don't you, that tomorrow's the day that we meet with Nick Petropoulos and let him know we've got him by the balls."

"Yup." Sonia took the lid off her coffee. "You know, we were hoping that Brad would be there just to make sure nothing got out of hand."

Jet looked at Sonia, wide-eyed. "I would *never* ask you to let Brad be a part of anything we do."

Sonia screwed up her face. "Don't you think the very idea of it turns my stomach? I never want to work with him again. It's just that I still think we need muscle at that meeting. We need to protect Mandy, even though she's not going to be in the room with her creepy husband."

Jet spoke tentatively. "And you want me to ask Brad if he'd do that for us?"

Sonia looked away, hiding the hurt in her eyes. "Do what you have to do."

Jet stood and moved to her own office. She put in a call to Brad Dunham. At first, things were a bit tense between them, but Jet got down to business. She asked Brad if he would be present with her at the offices of Hoskins and Hoskins, Attorneys at Law, the folks who would be representing Mandy. She told him about the video they were going to show Nick Petropoulos.

"Look," Brad suggested, "you need me to do this for you alone. You girls never want him to know that you're the ones who've hung him up by his own petard. And make sure it's Bill Hoskins and not Samantha Hoskins that's in the office with him. This should be intimidating, a scene right out of the *Sopranos*."

Jet was a little unsure about not being present at the meeting, but she decided Brad was probably right. "Yeah, okay." Her voice was muted.

"What about copies of the video?" Brad asked.

Starting to feel more comfortable, Jet leaned back in her chair, tapping her pen against her desk as she spoke. "We told Hoskins to indicate in the divorce agreement that copies of the video would be kept in a sealed file in Hoskins' office safe. That way, Petropoulos would know it was always available to haunt him, and he'd have no reason to ambush Mandy and try to get the video from her."

"Good thinking." Brad was all business, professional. "Also, you and Sonia should keep a copy as well. He might be able to track me down. After all, we'll be meeting face to face. But if he never hears your names or has any reason to believe you were involved in making the video, he'll never think to try to get it from you."

Jet thought she sensed just a tiny hitch in Brad's voice when he spoke Sonia's name. Damn, he's still got it so bad for her.

AT ELEVEN FORTY-FIVE ON TUESDAY, Jet's phone rang. Looking at the phone, she knew who it was. "Hello, Brad."

"*Hey. Good news. Everything went down pretty smoothly with Hoskins and Petropoulos. Looks like Mandy's going to get everything she wants, including Nick leaving her alone as much as possible.*"

"And the kids?"

"*She got full custody. Of course, he'll get his visitation rights, has to. And don't forget, the real power in that family is Vasilios Petropoulos, the grandfather. If this agreement had cut him out of seeing his own grandkids, I'm afraid it might have made it pretty tough to get everyone to play ball, agreement or not.*"

"Yeah, Brad, you're right." She took a quick breath. "And Nick. Did he get crazy?"

"You know, I could see him getting a little hot under the collar, but I just used an old trick I learned in NCIS."

Curiosity crept across Jet's face and voice. "Do tell."

"Well, Hoskins brings him into the room. I lay back, actually sitting way at the end of the long conference table. I don't say a word."

Jet sat just a bit taller in her chair. "Until when?"

"Until never. I never said a word the whole time. I just sat there staring at him."

Her eyebrows furrowed. "And how did that accomplish anything?"

"Let me ask you a question. You're in a lawyer's office and he's laying some really heavy stuff on you. At the end of the table is a guy who doesn't get introduced, doesn't say a word. What do you think he's there for?"

Jet smiled. "If he looks like you? Muscle. No question, he's muscle."

"And exactly how bad a badass is this muscle?"

"You know," she chuckled, "I guess I don't know. But then again, I'm pretty sure I don't want to find out."

Jet could hear Brad's smile over the phone. *"Bingo. Intimidation 101. Just sit there and don't say a word."*

Jet spun her swivel chair around and gazed out the window over East Main. "Yeah, Brad. I'll bet you learned a lot of cool tricks over the years."

Jet had expected a snappy comeback, but all she got was silence. Finally, Brad spoke. *"I'll tell you one trick I never learned; I never learned how to get through to that stubborn Italian partner of yours."*

Jet's voice softened. "Time, pal, time. Look, I know you're hurting. I know she's hurting. It's just going to take some time. But you know what?"

"What?"

"I think it would help if you would tell her you know what you did was wrong. Tell her that holding back the fact that you were married, even though you thought you were taking care of it, was still lying to her."

There was a pause before Brad spoke. *"She won't even talk to me."*

Jet looked out her window as she spoke. "Someday she will, and when she does, you'd darn well better tell her you were sorry for lying to her and that you'll never do it again." She paused. "You wouldn't do that again, would you?" He didn't need to answer.

47

Sonia had spent the better part of Wednesday out in Bowling Green, Kentucky. She was still certain that her plan to talk to all of Mariana's old classmates, co-workers, friends, and family face to face was the right way to go, but it was turning out to be tremendously time-consuming. When she walked into the BCI offices late that afternoon, she was surprised to see a certain forensic accountant sitting with Jet at her desk, her partner's long blonde hair pulled in front of her shoulders. "Well, well, well. I can see that while the cat's away, the mice will play."

Sonia could see Burnett starting to blush, but it was Jet who spoke. "Cat's away, schmat's away. These little miceys gonna play whenever they want."

Burnett spoke up. "What she means to say, Sonia, is—"

"Burnett, just you hush now." Jet tapped him on his forearm, her accent all *Gone With the Wind*. "Don't you go lettin' her get you all flustered. It's none of her business if my accountant feels he has to do an audit of my personal assets every few days."

Sonia watched as Burnett seemed to become even smaller in his oversized suit.

Jet looked back to Sonia. "So, missy, how'd the trip go?" The accent was gone.

Sonia moved into Jet's office and took a seat on the wooden chair against the wall. "I'm guessing you can tell from the look on my face, I got nothing. The girl hadn't heard from Mariana since graduation and had no idea where she would go if something was wrong. What about you?"

"Two more trips into the hinterland and the same result you got. I know you're right about this face to face thing, but geez, this is wearing me out."

Burnett came alive, looking at Sonia. "Well, I've just been telling Jet that I have some news that might brighten up your day."

Sonia reached over and picked up Jet's coffee cup. She took a sip and winced. "Cold."

Jet raised her eyebrows as if to imply that beggars couldn't be choosers.

Sonia reached down to her side and drew a large imaginary handgun. She pointed her finger directly at the accountant. "Okay, Burnett. Go ahead. Make my day." All three of them chuckled.

Burnett went on. "You know how those three horses have been doing exceptionally well, until, of course, Frailing just faded at the Bluegrass Stakes?"

Sonia nodded, "Uh, huh."

"Well, it looks like Summer Wheat is running in the Oaks this Friday, as we'd expected, and the other one, Run Lucky, is going off at eight to six in the Derby on Saturday."

"Nice." Sonia didn't really know what eight to six meant.

From the look on his face, Sonia could tell that Burnett had expected a much greater response. "No, really Burnett. That's nice. I'm excited for you."

"I don't think you understand, Sonia. The Kentucky Oaks is this Friday, and the Derby is Saturday."

Jet smiled at Burnett. "And . . ."

"And my firm has reserved seating in a grandstand box for both events."

"So?"

Burnett straightened in his seat and his hands began moving toward his lapels. A look from Jet changed his mind. "It just so happens that it's my year to take advantage of those tickets. We're going to the Oaks and the Derby. The three of us, we're going the whole weekend, and a historic weekend it might be."

Sonia smiled at both Burnett and Jet, Burnett because he was enjoying himself so, and Jet because she seemed genuinely pleased to see Burnett letting go a bit. "Well then, looks like we're all on for Derby weekend in Louisville." A little chill of excitement ran through her body.

Jet pushed some papers around on her desk, appearing to look busy. "By the way. How many seats are there in that box?"

"Oh, it's very comfortable for four, why?"

"Just asking."

Sonia sensed a strange vibe in the close quarters of Jet's office but couldn't put her finger on it.

A few moments later, Burnett stood, reached out both his hands, and took Jet's between them. He bent a little at the waist. "Having delivered my excellent news, good lady, it is now time for me to depart. I have work to do, and—"

"Yeah, we know, honey. You do your best work in your own space." Suddenly the white gravy in her voice bubbled up. "Go on. Run along now and leave us women folk to the scrubbin' and cookin'." A minute later, Burnett was gone.

Sonia watched the door close behind him. "What a lovely man he is, isn't he Jet?"

The gravy was gone. "Lovely for sure. Still and all, he's a strange bird."

"What's that mean? I thought you liked him."

"Oh, I do." Jet bent her arms and interlocked her fingers,

pulling them back over her head in a dramatic stretch. "It's just that sometimes things like, 'I do my best work in my own space,' well, it can kind of get to you."

Sonia sat in silence.

"I guess that's the difference." Jet looked across the floor around her desk, apparently searching for something.

"What's the difference?" Sonia asked.

Jet spoke while bending down. "The difference between men and women."

Sonia scooted into the more comfortable red chair in front of Jet's desk. "What the heck are you talking about?"

Jet came up, hair-tie in hand. She deftly slipped her silky ponytail through the elastic band. "You know, how men are always focused on the task, getting things done and all? But women, we care about the process, *how* things get done?"

"I'm not sure what you mean."

"Let me give you an example." Jet finished her task by pulling the ponytail through her fingers several times. "A woman says to her husband, 'Honey, would you go to the store and get some bread, so I can make some sandwiches for lunch?' " She rocked back in her chair, opening her arms. "He says, 'Sure. What kind of bread do you want?' Then she says, 'Some sort of roll or bun. Whatever.' "

Jet made a walking motion with two of her fingers. "Off he goes to the store." She reached out her empty hands and smiled. "He comes back and hands her a package with some Kaiser rolls in it." Jet went back to her ponytail. "She says, 'What other kinds of rolls did they have?' Then he says, 'You told me to go get you some sort of roll for our sandwiches, and I brought you Kaiser rolls. Why are you asking me about anything else they might have had?' "

Sonia looked blankly at Jet. Why is she telling me this story?

"Don't you see." Jet's eyebrows went up. "All the guy wanted to do was make his wife happy by completing the task. He got rolls. Task completed. End of story."

"What's your point?" Sonia brushed that wisp of hair out of her face.

Jet bore down. "Don't you see, Sonia? When a man needs something, he's a hunter. He finds it, he bags it, he takes it home. Task done. Now a woman, she's a gatherer. She has to look at every possible option. She not only wants the things, she wants the process to be right, too."

Sonia leaned back in the chair, crossing her arms over her chest. "Okay. I'll give you all that. Now, why are we having this conversation?"

"Sweetheart." Jet's head leaned heavily to one side, her voice almost pouty. "Don't you see. That's what's going on with you and Brad."

Sonia sat straight up. "Now wait a minute."

"No, you wait a minute Sonia." Jet leaned in swiftly and put her hands squarely on her desk. She spoke quickly and with conviction. "Look, Brad was married. It wasn't real and he wasn't with the woman anymore. Then he falls in love with you. He knows he should tell you, but what he thinks is important is that he gets the divorce. So, off he goes. He starts the process. He accomplishes the task. He thinks you should be happy."

Sonia leaned in as well. "But I'm *not* happy. He *lied* to me."

Jet let the energy subside. "Yes, lady, he lied to you, lied by omission, and that was total crap, real caveman stuff. But that's where his little lizard brain was, bless his heart."

Sonia sat in silence for a long time. She spoke quietly. "So, you think I should let it go?"

Jet shrugged her shoulders gently. "I certainly think you could give him a chance to explain, to apologize. I'm pretty sure that he knows that what he did was wrong. But here's the thing. Do you love this guy or not? Can you forgive him?"

There was another long silence before Sonia could answer.

When she did, her voice was low, still conflicted. "Yes. I love him. I never stopped loving him, but—"

"Well, sweets. If you love him, truly love him, you can forgive his caveman stuff because that's just who he is, how God made him. If you don't love him enough to do that . . . then you don't really love him. That, my dear, is the question. Can you love him for what he is, what he does, even if he does it in a way that's," she shrugged, "not the way you wish he had?"

48

Sonia had thought long and hard about what Jet had said on Wednesday afternoon. It did all come down to trust, and when she'd searched her heart deeply, she'd found there was no question that she believed Brad loved her. They had met that evening. She had gotten her apology and he had gotten his forgiveness. By the time they left the cozy little bar on Euclid Avenue, Charlie Brown's, they were officially engaged. The only thing missing was the ring.

After their moment of reconciliation, while most couples would have started discussing wedding plans, Sonia had taken a deep breath and then told Brad about being attacked by the BMW. His reaction was what she had feared—almost over the top. Holding his shaking hand, speaking softly and calmly, she had assured him that she was alright and that she and Jet had done everything possible to track down the owner of the car. Nonetheless, she was quite certain that after he had taken her home, Brad would be on the phone with his NCIS buddies.

Just after ten on Friday morning, Sonia slid into Brad's Corvette and they took off for Louisville. It was a trip that would take about an hour and a half. Around eleven-thirty, they met Jet and Burnett in the lobby of the double-towered Galt House, the historic hotel right on the Ohio River. It was there they would stay the night. After lunch, they all hopped into Burnett's classic Mercedes sedan and drove over to the even-more-historic race-track, Churchill Downs, with its iconic twin spires and manicured lawns. Races had started at ten-thirty that morning, but the Kentucky Oaks wouldn't run until five forty-nine, so they had plenty of time to soak in all the sights and sounds of the beautiful racing venue.

Although Brad had worked on horse farms as a young man, it was Burnett who was, by far, the most knowledgeable about the coming race. Sonia smiled as she watched him go on and on, telling Brad about how Summer Wheat was one of the three horses running beyond their breeding, and how the chestnut filly had a real chance of winning the race.

Sonia, Jet, and Burnett felt they had a special connection with the horse, having seen her run at Keeneland just a few weeks earlier. They each placed a bet on her, just for fun. Soon they were all back in their grandstand box, surrounded by more best-dressed men and women than Sonia had ever seen in her life. She was wearing a classic, dark blue, fitted dress, and dark blue wedges. Jet was more flamboyant, wearing yellow pants; long yellow earrings; a broad-brimmed, light yellow, straw hat; and a flowing white top—a top with a daring plunge in the front. The blouse had Burnett off balance most of the day.

"Just wait 'til tomorrow at the Derby," Burnett said, a big, knowledgeable smile on his face. "Then you'll see some real sartorial splendor."

Right around five-thirty-five, Sonia saw Burnett, the smile gone from his face, move to the edge of his seat. Clearly, he was focusing intently on the information board across the track.

"Oh, my goodness. My, my goodness." Burnett was shaking his head.

Sonia gently grabbed his arm. "What is it Burnett? What's going on?"

Burnett pointed to the large, electronic board across from the grandstand. "Look for yourself. See there, on the board. Summer Wheat has been scratched."

Sonia craned to read the board herself. "She's not running in the race?"

"Exactly. She'll not be in the race." It was clear that he was perplexed. "I wonder why."

Brad asked, "I guess there's no way to know the reason, is there?"

Sonia reached into her purse. "Unless, gentlemen, we look it up on our phones. I'll bet someone is broadcasting the race, and they've made some announcement as to why she's been scratched." Within a few moments, she was able to report to the group. "It seems that Summer Wheat has been scratched because of a hairline fracture in her foreleg. Oh, wait, here's a clip of his jockey talking to a reporter."

"We was jus' out on the track doin' our regular routine and then suddenly she came up lame, real lame. I jus' walk her back to the barn and call the trainer. They use the x-ray and they see a thin, long crack in the bone. But, no, we didn't have no accident or anything. The bone, she just broke on her own."

Sonia stood up, looking around in frustration, then she plopped back into her seat, her face and shoulders drooping. Finally, she looked up at Burnett. "Why did they wait so long to scratch her from the race?"

Burnett shrugged, unable to keep his hands from his lapels. "I imagine it was just hard for them to face the reality that this exceptional horse wasn't going to run today—maybe ever again."

"What a shame." Sonia's lips protruded in a pout. "Well, there goes another part of our historic weekend of horse racing, right Burnett?"

"I'm afraid you're correct, Ms. Sonia." Burnett eschewed

touching his lapels but apparently couldn't resist a quick tug on his bowtie. "First Frailing failed to make the Derby because of his dismal showing at the Bluegrass Stakes, and now this. I'll bet the owners and trainer are just crushed."

Brad asked, almost nonchalantly, "Who's the owner?"

Burnett checked the program. "The owners are Robert and Jean Edwards. The trainer is Jack Devlin. Bred in Florida."

For some reason, something tingled in Sonia's mind. "Where in Florida?"

Burnett rechecked the program. "Bred by Stefan Ashkenazi at Willowbay Farm. I believe that's somewhere near Ocala."

Burnett's reply didn't mean anything special to Sonia, but that wasn't the case for Jet. She turned to Sonia, her eyes wide open. "Hey, remember I told you that I tracked down LaKeisha Washington on a horse farm in Florida?"

"Yeah. They told us that she'd been killed in a hit and run accident? If you want to call it that."

"So, what farm do you think she was working on?" Jet was clearly making some important point.

"The farm that bred Summer Wheat? Willowbay?"

"Willowbay Farm." Jet's voice was strong, clear. "That's where she was. I talked to the farm manager, John somebody. He's the one who told me all about LaKeisha."

Sonia's head was spinning so much that she couldn't help but stand up and gesture to the other three. "So, there are three horses doing exceptionally well this year. One of them, Frailing, is bred right here in Lexington, on Downstream Farm, where Mariana Castillo worked. Another one is bred in Florida, on Willowbay Farm, right where LaKeisha Washington worked." She turned to the man in the bowtie. "And the third one, what's his name, Burnett?"

Burnett was already looking up at her. "Run Lucky?"

"Right. Where was he bred?"

Burnett glanced back down at his program. "Honestly, I don't know. They don't list the Derby horses' information in today's program."

Sonia checked her phone again. "Give me one sec. What I'm guessing, though, is that I don't even have to look it up. Jet, what was the name of the farm that Penny Rae worked on?"

Jet's hands were sliding over her ponytail, clearly in response to the sudden tension in the air. "I'm pretty sure it was Holbrook, or something like that."

Sonia looked at her phone, waiting for her inquiry to be answered. "I got it. Not Holbrook, Hol-*den*-brook." She read right from the Google entry. "Holdenbrook Farm, owned by Bonnie and Giles Daneck." She looked back to Jet, then to Brad. "Run Lucky was bred on Holdenbrook Farm, the same farm that Penny Rae Nelson worked on.

49

The Kentucky Oaks went off at five-forty-nine, exactly as scheduled. Surrounded by thousands of screaming horse racing fans, Sonia hardly noticed. She held her tongue for the one minute and fifty seconds it took to actually run the race, primarily because no one could have heard her ask or say anything anyway. As soon as it was over, however, she pulled Brad's head down toward her. "We've got to do something. We've got to go to the police right now."

Brad looked at her and smiled. "Honey, remember, you're in Kentucky."

"What does that mean?"

"Sweetheart." Brad's voice was just short of condescending. "It's Derby weekend. Every cop in this state is either working on crowd control somewhere or preparing for tomorrow's Derby party. Now you want to give them a call and tell them what?"

Sonia stood tall, her voice firm. "We're going to tell them that we've found the connection between the three missing girls. We know that each of them worked on one of the farms that produced these, well, winning horses." Even as she said it, Sonia could hear that the connection was not nearly so clear in her words as it was in her mind.

Brad pulled Sonia close and looked down into her face. "Listen, babe, I know that you're right. There's no question that there's some sort of connection there. It's just that we don't know what it is, and we're not going to get the police to do their best work until we bring them something more substantial." He turned, looking off into the distance. "I'm thinking that what we do now, is go down to the barns and see if we can pick up something, anything, about who is thinking and saying what."

Burnett had been able to overhear the last part of their conversation. "Given what's just happened to Summer Wheat, I'm thinking it's going to be pretty difficult to get near that barn." He had fallen back into his professorial tone. "What with the caliber of the race and then the sudden scratching of Summer Wheat, I think the press will mob the place, and the security folks will be doing everything in their power to keep anyone who doesn't belong there from getting close."

Brad just smiled. "Well then, it looks like I'm going to have to deputize this young lady and make both of us members of that security detail."

The blank look on Burnett's face said it all.

Jet, however, jumped right in. She lightly punched Brad's arm. "Go get 'em, cowboy. We'll wait right here and keep the wagons circled."

Brad grabbed Sonia's hand and pulled her after him as he left the box and headed for the barns. "C'mon."

Sonia stumbled a bit, trying to keep up. "How are we going to get back there, Brad?"

"Listen, over the years I've learned a trick or two." He was speaking while he looked forward, away from Sonia. She struggled to hear him. "The important thing is that you look as comfortable and official as I do." He turned back toward her. "Try to tell yourself that you wish you were home with your kids, and you're just here asking questions and protecting folks because that's your job."

As they approached the line of security guards, Sonia was glad that she hadn't worn anything too flashy, something that would have made her security personae harder to believe. Within moments, she was also wishing that she and Brad had press credentials hanging around their necks. Burnett had been right. The press folks were swarming the place. So was security. She knew that in lieu of press credentials, she and Brad were going to have to rely on sheer bravado to get past the security line. That was until she saw Brad reach into his pocket and pull out a small leather wallet.

As they approached a line of security personnel, Brad flashed the wallet, mumbled something and just kept on walking. Sonia put on the most serious face she could muster and walked right behind him. Son-of-a-gun, he just pulled off the phony credential thing you see on TV all the time. Wow, well done Captain Dunham.

As soon as they were past the security line and around the corner of one of the barns, Brad turned to her. "Now what?"

"Well . . . I'm working on that." Her eyes were scanning the whole area. "I haven't the slightest idea where Summer Wheat is," she turned to Brad and winked, "but you know what they say. When in Rome . . . ." She looked around for a few moments, then saw several reporters walking toward one of the barns. She pointed. "Here we go. It's either Summer Wheat or the winner they're headed for. We'll find her soon enough."

It wasn't long before Sonia and Brad were standing twenty-five feet away from a tiny group of reporters asking questions about Summer Wheat's condition. The press was much more interested in the race's winner. Brad leaned in toward Sonia, speaking furtively. "Do you recognize anyone?"

"Actually, I do." Sonia nodded in the direction of a trio of people. "That's Stefan Ashkenazi on the left. He's the one who bred Summer Wheat on his farm down in Florida. The man and the woman, that's Robert Edwards, one of Summer Wheat's owners. I saw Ashkenazi and Robert Edwards at Keeneland. The woman must be Edwards' wife, Jean."

Brad held the back of his hand up to his mouth. "They don't look very pleased, do they."

"Well, I guess that's understandable." Sonia shrugged gently. "Who knows if Summer Wheat will ever race again?"

Brad scanned the rest of the crowd. "Recognize anyone else?"

Not being as tall as Brad, Sonia was on tip-toes, scanning the crowd. "No. I guess the rest are all stable hands or . . . . Wait a minute. Oh, my gosh, there *are* two more guys I recognize."

"Who?"

"See the two guys who just walked out of the barn," Sonia was pointing, her hand held close to her chest, "one tall one and the other a short guy?"

"Yeah?"

"Wow." Sonia turned away from the men. "The little guy. That's Ron Harris. He's a broker, a bloodstock agent. The last time I saw him he was getting reamed by the guy who owns Frailing. No," she tipped her head, "wait a minute, not Frailing's owner, his breeder."

Brad kept his eyes directed straight ahead as if looking past the crowd. "And who's the other guy?"

"Oh, that's Limey. He works . . . Wait a minute. He works on Downstream Farm. Frailing's not even here today." She looked up at Brad. "What's he doing here, and with Ron Harris?"

Brad glanced down at Sonia then looked up again. "Could just be friends? Maybe he's up here just for the race. He's in the industry, right?"

"Yeah. I guess." Her voice reflected her doubts. She turned and faced the men again. "But, take a look at him. How would you describe him?"

Brad focused on the two men. "The little guy?"

"No," she shook her head, "the big guy."

"Tall. Muscular. Big hands."

"You're right. Tall, big hands. And what did the police tell us about the guy they had on video riding the bus from Bennington to Saratoga Springs after dumping LaKeisha's body?"

Brad gave her a quick look. "Dumping her body, you think."

"Yeah." She rolled her eyes. "Anyway. How did they describe him? Tall, right? I wonder if we asked them to look at the video again, would they say he had big hands?"

Brad smiled gently. "Bit of a stretch for surveillance video but might just be worth asking."

Sonia tugged on Brad's sleeve, energized. "Did you see that?"

"See what?"

She moved her mouth closer to his ear, almost whispering. "The look Ashkenazi just gave Harris as he left the barn. I'll be damned if that didn't look like he wanted to ream Harris the same kind of new one that the other breeder did."

"What other breeder?" He looked confused.

Sonia's frustration showed in her voice. "*Frailing's* breeder. Didn't I tell you that we overheard him saying something about being promised a whole new something or other? I can't remember his name. But he was as pissed as Ashkenazi looks right now. More so, really."

Suddenly Sonia sensed two security guards walking up behind her and Brad. She spun, pulling Brad with her. "Looking pretty good here, guys."

Brad tipped his imaginary hat and smiled. "Everything seems secure." They walked past the guards and back toward the grandstand.

50

Sonia took her seat at the breakfast table in the Galt House restaurant. She was sitting across from Burnett and Jet, next to Brad. She was also sitting in Louisville, Kentucky, home of the Kentucky Derby. The night before, they had eaten "Hot Browns" for dinner at the place of the meals' origin, the historic Brown Hotel on West Broadway.

Sonia had been to the races two other days in the past few weeks, but this was different. She was coming to realize that to be in *Lou-a-vul,* Kentucky, on the first Saturday in May, was to be in a very, very special place.

The Kentucky Derby festival had been in full gear for over a week. There had been full and half marathons. That same weekend there had been four lift-off times for huge hot-air balloon events that filled the sky with orbs of every color imaginable, all of them lit either by the bright sun of morning or the soft glow of sunset. On the previous weekend, one of the largest fireworks displays in the country had taken place. Battling displays from two bridges had filled not only the sky with light, but the Ohio River with bursting flashes that reflected the energy and excitement of the season. The Pegasus Parade had filled downtown with marching bands, equine units, and huge inflatable characters. The Derby Festival was pure Americana at its best.

The afternoon wore on. Sonia watched as the grandstands at Churchill Downs filled with celebrities of every kind, as well as ordinary commoners bedecked in their Derby finest. Colorful women's hats and fingers holding mint juleps filled the entire venue with a sense of excitement and celebration. Jet was resplendent in another flowing outfit, a sleeveless dress with bright red and yellow flowers. She also wore a yellow, wide-brimmed hat that covered her from shoulder to shoulder. Sonia, on the other hand, had worn another simple dress, white, and red pumps. In honor of the occasion, she had added a large necklace of blue and white stones that draped down almost to her bust line. On her head, she was wearing a dark red fascinator with a long white feather flowing out of it. It made her feel a little silly, but after all, it *was* the derby.

The feeling didn't become electric, however, until the University of Louisville Band stepped in place and started playing *the* song. At that very moment, it was the song that was reverberating throughout the entire Commonwealth of Kentucky. *My Old Kentucky Home*. The thousands of voices in the stands sang along, if only on the well-known chorus.

For all that was going on around her, however, Sonia was not fully present. She was distracted. Her mind kept chewing on the connection between the three girls and either Ron Harris or Limey. Or maybe it was both. She pursed her lips. Am I just fooling myself? It's not two dead girls and one missing girl, it's three dead girls, isn't it?

Sonia wasn't sure if it was the large field of horses that were running in the Derby that day or the fact that they moved extra slowly in order to let the TV coverage eek out every bit of airtime they could before the race, but it seemed to take forever before all twenty horses were in the gate. Then, in an explosion of one bell and thousands of voices, they were off.

Run Lucky, the third horse that had become of so much interest to them, came charging out of the three hole, relatively close to the rail. Within the first eighth of a mile, the pack was thinning, each rider trying to keep his mount close to the rail, covering as little ground as possible. As they came out of the first turn, Run Lucky was running fifth, well off the pace of the same black colt, Coal Minor, and bay, Carmel Delight, that had dominated the Bluegrass Stakes. All the way around the backstretch, Run Lucky stayed in that position. Sonia watched, hoping he would win, though she wasn't sure why.

The crowd went wild, and Sonia was almost lifted off the ground as the horses passed the quarter pole and turned into the final stretch. Unlike Frailing, Run Lucky was known as a closer, a horse with a great burst of energy at the end of a race. And, true to form, Sonia watched as he drifted to the middle of the track and seemed to kick into another gear. Moving steadily closer and closer to the leaders, it seemed to Sonia that he could win this race if only he didn't run out of track. Into the stretch he was running fourth, then third, then sliding past Coal Minor. Run Lucky was charging, only inches behind Carmel Delight. Flying down the track, he was suddenly a nose ahead of Carmel Delight, then more. In the final eighth, the last furlong, Run Lucky started to pull away, on his way to winning the most prestigious horse race in the world. A length ahead, then a length and a half, the crowd noise crescendoed into a deafening roar.

Sonia's eyes were glued to the magnificent animal as he seemed to float away from the others, but what she couldn't understand was why he began drifting to his right. He began veering harder, faster, then . . .

A hush crashed down over Churchill Downs. The roar of the crowd still ringing through the rafters. Run Lucky's leg had crumbled under him. Tossing his jockey, he had stumbled to the ground. Sonia knew that hers were not the only eyes that never saw which horse won the race. So many in the crowd had no choice but to stare at the suffering, the abject horror, of such a beautiful animal, broken, his future, his life, slipping away. Sonia buried her face in Brad's chest.

51

The Kentucky Derby is known as "The Fastest Two Minutes in Sports." That day, however, those last few moments lingered in the minds of every human present for a very, very long time. Eventually, as the medical crew was dealing with the severely injured horse, Sonia and those around her started to regain their focus. She pulled Brad close to her. "We've got to learn everything we can about this."

"Babe, you watched it happen." He looked gently into her eyes. "You saw the horse break down right in front of you. There was no foul play."

She continued to speak softly, but the urgency in her voice rose. "I'm not talking about that. It's this whole thing. The three missing girls, the three winning horses, something happening to each of the horses. Something bigger is going on here, Brad, and somehow, some way, it's right under our noses. I just can't tell what it is."

Brad looked at her and shrugged. "What? What do you want to do right now?"

"What I want to do right now is get back there to the barns and learn anything we possibly can." The urgency in her voice matched the look on her face. "There must be something we can find out just by hanging around there."

Brad looked over the massive sea of people. "Babe, every single person in this whole place would like to get back there. It's just not happening. First, security is going to be tighter than a bull's butt in fly season. Second, this is such a major event, you wouldn't be able to get past the media, even if security let everyone in."

She ran her fingers through her hair. "Maybe you could use one of your NCIS tricks again."

"Things like that only work when nobody's really paying attention." His eyes were scanning the entire scene. "That's not going to be the case today." He turned to her. "Look, we can give it a try. But don't be surprised if we don't make it very far."

Sonia turned to Jet and Burnett. "There's always one more race after the derby. Why don't you all watch that then meet us at the car? We're not likely to make much progress. I just feel like we've got to give it our best shot."

Burnett reacted strongly. "No. We'd like to come with you." He turned to Jet. "Right?"

"You ain't just whistlin' Dixie, Professor."

Burnett's reaction seemed strange to Sonia, but there was no time to argue. "Okay."

The foursome took off. Even with one race left, the crush of the crowd leaving the racetrack was hard to believe. While they were still a long walk away from their goal, the army of media being held back by security made it clear that they would get nowhere near Run Lucky's team.

Brad turned to Sonia, tugging on a few strands of her hair. "Look, it's only right. This is a devastating time for anyone involved with that horse. They don't need a bunch of rubber-neckers coming by just for the chance to be part of the tragedy. C'mon. Let's just go."

"Okay," Sonia let out a sigh of resignation. "Let's all get back to the car."

As they turned and headed for the parking lot, Sonia simply couldn't keep from turning around and looking in the direction she wished they were moving. She stopped and grabbed Brad's arm. "Look. Look who that is over there."

Brad's eyes scanned the sea of people. It took a moment before he recognized two men, one very large, one small. "Son of a gun, it's the broker and that guy from the farm."

"Right." Her voice was full of life. "It's Ron Harris and Limey. Can it possibly be that they're connected to Run Lucky as well? Do they have something to do with all three horses?"

Brad continued to survey the crowd. "Listen. I'm not much for coincidences. If I were a betting man, I'd say that if we look up the bloodstock agent involved in the sale of Run Lucky it's going turn out to be the little guy who's standing right over there."

Sonia was standing on her tiptoes trying to keep track of Harris and Limey as they worked their way through the crowd. "And Limey?"

"Well, I'm not thinking his name will show up anywhere, but he is the one who most fits the description of the guy who rode the bus out of Bennington."

Jet stretched her body trying to see the two men. "What do we do now?"

Brad put his hands on Sonia's shoulders and turned her around. "You three go to Burnett's car and wait for me. I'll be—"

"No," Sonia's voice tightened, "We're not going back to the car. It's not easy keeping track of two guys in this huge crowd. You and Burnett go off and follow from the right. Jet and I are going to follow from the left. That way, if one slips away, maybe the other won't. And if they separate," she turned and began walking, "we'll all meet back at the car, whenever . . . ."

Brad reached out, grabbed her arm, and spun her around. "Is

this how it's going to be from now on?" Only the smile on his face told her that he wasn't really challenging her.

She smiled and brushed that wisp of hair out of her face. "Get used to it mister. This *is* the way it's going to be." Then she stretched up and planted a kiss on his cheek. A moment later she and Jet disappeared into the crowd.

Less than thirty minutes later, Sonia and Jet looked up and saw the men approaching Burnett's car. She could tell that they were less than pleased. "What happened?"

"We lost them. You too?"

"Same here." She shrugged. "It's okay. We weren't likely to learn anything important from them anyway. I think what's important is that in all likelihood, we've just learned that Harris and Limey are somehow connected to all three horses, or farms, and we already know that all three of those farms are connected to our missing girls."

Brad pulled her close. "And we move on." He opened the car door. "Let's go. And when we get back to Lexington, I'd like us to meet with Jet back in your offices."

She raised her eyebrows. "It'll be late."

Brad reached up and touched Sonia's face lightly with his fingertips. "I know, but what I've got to say, I want to say to both of you; I don't think we should wait any longer to have this conversation."

52

Sonia and Brad had gotten to the BCI offices just about twelve minutes before ten that evening, the time at which they were to meet Jet. Sonia wasn't surprised when Jet walked in promptly at ten, but she was surprised to see who was with her. "Burnett, are you here to join us?"

Jet grinned and didn't give Burnett time to answer. "It seems that Burnett, here, is starting to feel like he's really one of us. Isn't that true, Burnett?"

"Actually, yes." He cut short his normal pre-statement routine after the tugs on his lapels. "But more importantly, how could I become aware of all that I've learned about this poor missing girl and not do everything I can to help find her?"

Sonia looked up at him and smiled. "Well said, Burnett. We're glad to have you aboard."

Everyone took a seat around the white, plastic table Sonia and Brad had set up in the waiting area. The room fell silent. All eyes turned toward Sonia. "Brad has asked if he could say something to all of us. I'd like to give him that opportunity."

Brad spoke evenly. "Okay, thank you." His eyes passed slowly over the other faces at the table. "I want you to know that what

I'm about to say is not easy for me. In fact, I can't think of anything I'm less eager to say than this." He paused.

Jet jumped in. "Well, spit it out. It's been a long, long day and not a pleasant one. Whatever it is, spit it out."

Brad continued. "Listen, from the perspective of someone who has been involved in every kind of investigation from theft, to kidnapping, to murder, there comes a time when the team has to step back and re-evaluate the situation."

No one else at the table made a sound.

Brad looked directly at Sonia. "Now, based on statistics, I have to tell you that the longer anyone is missing, the greater the chance that they will never be found, particularly alive. Of course, the statistics are skewed by whether it's a child or not, but one way or the other, unless someone has run off on their own, time is absolutely your enemy in a case like this."

He let his gaze travel across the table to Jet, then to Burnett. "And here's the deal. Mariana Castillo disappeared on March twelfth or thirteenth. That's a full eight weeks ago. Those are bad numbers, really bad numbers. Then there's her two former colleagues. They're dead, we know that for a fact; one was murdered, one most likely murdered. Add in the reality that these three girls were all former colleagues and that there is some sort of connection between horses from the three farms, and it becomes pretty clear."

Sonia couldn't say the words. Apparently, neither could Jet or Burnett, so Brad went on. "The chances that Mariana is alive are, well, very, very small." Brad reached out and squeezed Sonia's hand. "I'm sorry, babe. I think you need to shift your resources. No more running all over the place trying to find where Mariana is hiding. She's not hiding, not in my opinion, and you're wasting resources following that line of thinking. I think you have to assume she's dead and shift all your resources to finding out who killed her. And I'd like to be a part of that effort."

After a long pause, Jet leaned forward, her hand clasped

demurely in front of her on the table and speaking more softly than usual. "So, what is it that we actually do?"

Sonia let go of Brad's hand. "Well, first of all, I don't think we're going to be able to get much help from the Lexington Police or the offices in Bennington or Saratoga Springs unless we kind of get in their faces. Someone's going to have to make a trip up to Saratoga Springs and then on to Bennington. I assume they'll be willing to send a copy of the surveillance video to LPD, but we need to be there in person, get the lay of the land, talk to folks, get the most out of that footage."

"I'll go." Every face turned toward Burnett. It was he who had spoken.

Sonia reached out and touched Burnett's arm. "Really, Burnett? You'd go?"

Without thinking, Burnett's hands went to his lapels. Jet didn't try to stop him. "Listen, I'm sort of a detail kind of guy. I guess it goes with being an accountant. I'll go, and I'll try to look as carefully as I can at every place and person that makes sense."

Jet was quick to speak. "Are you sure, Burnett? Really sure?" Her concern for him showed through to everyone else at the table. Sonia knew that, given how uncomfortable Burnett often was with other people, what he was offering was almost heroic.

Sonia picked up the thread in a totally businesslike fashion. "Excellent. Tomorrow morning we'll get you some sort of letter of credential from LPD and send you up north as soon as possible."

Jet spoke up. "What else can we do?"

Brad was about to speak, but Sonia beat him to it. "Well, we've got to know more about this Ron Harris. I'll go online and sniff out everything I can learn from his electronic footprint. You know, where he went to school, who he's worked for." She looked at Brad. "What his finances look like."

Brad turned to Jet. "With Burnett looking into that farm up in New York and Sonia already having made contact with Downstream farm right here in town, we still need someone to go poke around in Florida. Do you think you could get on a plane and get down there, just to talk to folks?"

"I guess. Sure." Jet looked at Sonia, then back to Brad.

Brad ran his hand over his short brown hair. "Now, Summer Wheat came up with a broken shin just yesterday. Everybody's going to be minding their Ps and Qs for a bit. Maybe you should wait a day or two before you go, then start by asking questions around town first, working your way toward the farm itself."

Sonia turned to Brad. "And what about you? What are you going to be doing?"

"Babe, sometimes there's just no substitute for good, old-fashioned surveillance. I'm guessing that Ron Harris' office is here in Lexington, home of the industry. I'm going to find him and stick to him like glue. I might even let him figure out that I'm tailing him. Sometimes, a guy who's got something to hide can't stand it if he thinks he's being watched. Trying to be extra careful, he runs out and does something stupid. If he does. I'll be there to catch him at it."

When the meeting wrapped up, Brad insisted he walk Sonia to her car. After what had happened the other night, she was more than willing to have his protection. In addition, she loved that he had come to care so much about the case. She loved that he had come to care for Jet, even for Burnett, to a degree. There was only one thing that she hated . . . the reason the investigation had shifted focus.

53

On Monday, Sonia walked into the BCI offices at ten o'clock. She'd already been downstairs at Magee's, so she had coffee and two pastries in hand—and a dull ache in her heart. She was surprised to see that Jet was not standing in her own office, but rather, in Sonia's. "Hey."

"Just standing here thinking." She looked at the pastries in Sonia's hand. "One of those pastries for me?"

"Sure, take whichever one you want." Sonia held out the two cinnamon rolls and let Jet choose. "What are you thinking about?"

Jet turned and looked at Sonia's whiteboard. On it were the names of all the different people they had spoken to in an attempt to locate Mariana. "I don't know. It's so hard accepting that we're no longer trying to find Mariana alive. And look at this list." She pointed. "Every single name has been crossed off except for one."

Sonia took a seat at her own desk but swiveled the chair sideways in order to continue her conversation with Jet. "And where does she live? Timbuktu, I imagine."

Jet's eyes were still on the whiteboard. She pointed. "No, look.

She lives right down in Danville." She turned to Sonia. "From what I understand, she's a server in one of the small restaurants there. I spoke to her on the phone, but she was kind of squirrely."

"She wasn't completely honest with you?"

"I don't know. Maybe." Jet turned back to the whiteboard.

Both girls were silent for a minute. Just as Sonia was about to speak, Jet turned to her. "Listen, I know we have to accept what's happened to Mariana. But still . . . . And this girl, she's right down in Danville. When I spoke to her on the phone," she shrugged, "I don't know, it's hard to put my finger on it."

Sonia looked at her watch. "You know, we could be in Danville by eleven thirty."

Jet looked at Sonia. "You mean try to find her right now?"

"Why not?" Sonia popped another bite into her mouth then went on. "If she *is* trying to avoid you, we may just be able to find her and surprise her. After all, Danville's a pretty small city, almost just a great big town. How many places are there where she could work?"

Jet thought about it for a moment then nodded. "Sounds like a plan."

Sonia got up, wiping her hands together without benefit of a napkin. "Okay, then. Get your stuff. Looks like we're going to Danville." She glanced down at Jet's uneaten pastry sitting on her desk.

Sonia and Jet got their purses and moved toward the outer door of the BCI offices. Sonia reached for the doorknob but was surprised when it opened away from her, as if on its own. A moment later, an attractive Hispanic woman stepped past the swinging door, into the room.

Sonia stepped back. "Gabriela. What are you doing here?"

Gabriela half-squinted her dark eyes. "Is that any way to greet the woman who went all the way to Florida just to help you?"

Jet stepped in front of Sonia, defensive. "Now, as I recall, you decided to go to Florida all on your own, without even talking to us about it."

Gabriela slipped past both Sonia and Jet and into the BCI waiting area. She looked around as she spoke, the sound of her high heels clicking off the wooden floor and brick walls. "At least I took the time to call you and tell you I was going." She walked over to the glass walls that separated the girls' offices from the rest of the room and looked into each office. She turned to face them. "Anyway, it was worth it. At least I found out that *pendejo*, Santiago, wasn't behind all this."

Sonia and Jet stood silent, just slightly apprehensive.

Gabriela walked around the waiting area and back toward the girls, checking out every inch of the space, her fingers running along the top of the leather couch. "So, have you learned anything else? Do you have any idea what has happened to my cousin?"

Sonia looked briefly at Jet, then her eyes fell downward for a moment. She took a deep breath and looked directly at Gabriela. "I'm sorry. Things are not looking good. One of the members of our team, someone with a lot of experience in these things, has advised us that we should probably be focusing on who hurt Mariana rather than where she might be."

Gabriela's face was totally still, but little flushes of red appeared at her neck. Her eyes darted back and forth between the girls.

Jet picked up the conversation. "We've looked everywhere we can think of—spoken to everyone we can find. It's just that she's been gone eight weeks now, and, well, you know . . . ."

Sonia reached out her hand to comfort Gabriela, but Gabriela stepped back just enough to be out of reach. "So, where are you going now, out on some other case—something more important?" Her voice had a real edge to it.

Sonia stepped forward, again reaching out toward Gabriela. "No, no. It's not like that. We're sending our colleague Burnett up to New York." She nodded toward Jet. "Jet's going to Florida, to check on a horse farm down there. We're still trying—trying as hard as we can." Her voice was emphatic.

"What do you mean going to Florida?" Gabriela shifted her gaze to Jet. Her question had come quickly. "I just got back from there."

Jet stepped forward, again getting her shoulder slightly in front of Sonia. "We're not sure, but something happened to another young girl down there and we're just trying to see if there might be a connection."

Gabriela was silent, though Sonia could see from her furrowed brows that she was mulling something over.

Eventually, Jet put her hand on Sonia's shoulder and turned her toward the door. "Now, if you don't mind, we have an appointment down in Danville—someone we need to talk to about another case." Jet tried to move the group toward the door.

Sonia obliged. "Really, we're so grateful for what you did in Florida, Gabriela. And we can't even imagine how difficult this must be for you."

Gabriella hadn't moved. Finally, she relented. She followed Sonia and Jet out onto the landing at the top of the stairs.

Jet raised her hand to reach out to Gabriella but stopped in mid-motion. "And I promise, as soon as we hear anything, we'll let you and your whole family know."

"Yes, we promise." A sad look crossed Sonia's face.

Gabriela looked at the other two women standing at the top of the stairs with her. "You understand how important this is to me?"

Sonia nodded. Jet said, "Absolutely."

Gabriela started down the stairs. "*Gracias, señoritas.* Thank you." Her high heels clicked down the wooden steps.

Sonia and Jet stood at the top of the stairs and watched as Gabriela descended, never looking back. Sonia half-whispered, "I assume I know why you didn't tell her what we hope to find in Danville."

Jet kept her eyes on Gabriela. "And why is that?"

"Because you're not sure we can trust her."

Jet put her hand on Sonia's shoulder, indicating it was time for them to start down the stairs as well. "You got that right, girl. I don't know why, but I just don't trust her."

54

It was a pleasant drive from Lexington to Danville. The weather was nice and driving through the rolling hills of central Kentucky always seemed to quiet Sonia's spirits.

Pulling into town, Sonia was struck by the fact that they were looking for someone they didn't know, working at a place they couldn't name, in a city with which they weren't very familiar. Danville seemed much larger than she had imagined.

They were in Jet's Camry. Her eyes roamed the scene in front of her. "Okay, now what? I guess we tool around town once or twice just to get the lay of the land?"

"Uh huh." Sonia looked at Google Maps on her phone, trying to get a sense of things. "Then we just park somewhere downtown and play the part of tourists."

Jet looked sideways at her friend. "Tourists?"

"Yeah," Sonia spoke while looking sideways out the passenger window, "we can stop almost anyone on the street and tell them we're looking for someplace to eat lunch. Nothing fancy, just clean and decent." She turned back to Jet. "These are nice folks here. I'll bet they'll go out of their way to tell us about a number of places we could go."

Jet pulled to a full stop at a traffic light. "Alright, but then how will we know which one to choose?"

"What did you say that girl's name was?"

Jet gave Sonia a wry smile. "Catch this. Jennipher Alston, with a ph."

"What?"

"Jennipher Alston, and she spells it J-e-n-n-i-p-h-e-r."

Sonia turned her eyes forward again. "Huh. Anyway, we could say something about having an old college friend who lives in town and works in one of the restaurants. Heck, in a town this small, someone might even know exactly where she works."

"Wouldn't that be nice." Jet looked at different storefronts as she drove carefully down the main street. "And before we left, I found her picture on Facebook."

"Really? Well, I guess there's not that many Jennipher's with a ph in Kentucky."

"You'd be surprised. There were several Jennipher's with a ph, but mostly they were all in showbiz or modeling careers. When I added Danville, I'm pretty sure I got the right one."

"Let me see."

Jet kept her eyes on the road but grabbed her phone off the dashboard and handed it to Sonia. Sonia quickly opened it to the picture of Jennipher Alston that Jet had saved. Red-haired and freckled in her thirties, Jennipher was attractive but used little makeup to enhance her natural beauty.

After driving through town twice, Jet chose a parking spot on 3rd Street. It was right outside a quaint little place called the Hub Coffee House and Café. "No rule says we can't get lucky and find her in the first place we look."

Sonia slipped out of the car. "Or not. Only one way to find out."

Together, the girls stepped inside. One quick look around the rather small shop and Sonia felt certain that unless Jennipher was in the back, cooking, she was not working at The Hub at that moment. A quick conversation with the college-aged boy behind the counter confirmed that she didn't work there at all. Sonia turned to leave.

Jet moved with her, but then stopped and turned around. "Do you have any idea where our friend might be working?" She showed him the picture of Jennipher. His answer sent them out the door, wondering where they should try next.

The girls walked a short distance and turned left onto West Main Street. Within a block, they were standing in front of a place called Cue on Main. Jet put her hand on Sonia's back and nudged her through the door, into the restaurant. They stood still, taken by the exposed brick, golden oak-tinted tin ceiling and brass rails. As they stared, an older man who appeared to be the owner, or perhaps just a significant employee, walked up to them. Within moments he was telling them about the history of the place, a former billiards hall with a three-lane bowling alley in the basement. It was all very fascinating. However, there was no Jennipher to be found there.

Out on the street again, Sonia sighed and turned to Jet. "Any idea where we try next?"

"Damned if I know," Jet rubbed her stomach, "but I hope the next place is decent. I need to eat something."

Sonia thought about the cinnamon roll still sitting on her desk back in her office. Then, before they could take off in search of a "decent" place, she noticed two young men, again, college-aged, walking up the street toward them. She assumed they attended the very fine liberal arts college in town.

Just as the young men were abreast of the girls, Jet stepped out and stopped them. "Excuse me, guys." She gave them her best smile, gently pulling her blonde ponytail down in front of her shoulder and stroking it. "We're looking for an old friend of ours from Mayweather College, outside of Midway. Either of you guys know Jennifer Alston?"

The taller of the two boys was quick to shrug his shoulders.

But the shorter, rounder boy raised his eyebrows. "Jennipher Alston? Went to Boyle County High School?"

Sonia jumped in, reaching out to innocently touch his arm. "Actually, we don't know where she went to high school, we know her from college. But we're pretty sure she lives around here."

The shorter boy gave his friend a quick look, a smile spreading across his face. "Yeah, well, kind of around here. I'm pretty sure her folks own a farm, five or ten miles outside of town. But I know Jenn. We went to high school together; she was a year or two ahead of me."

Jet picked up the conversation. "We think she's working at one of the restaurants here in town." Her voice was just a bit syrupy. "You wouldn't happen to know which one, would you? We'd love to walk in and surprise her."

"Yeah, sure. She's down at The Homestead, just down the block here. I don't know if she works lunch or not, but I've seen her down there once or twice working the dinner shift."

Sonia gave the boy one of her best smiles and a sincere thank you. As they walked away, she saw the tall one punch the shorter one in the arm; it was one of those "Way to go," punches. Apparently, the young men had thoroughly enjoyed their passing conversation with two very attractive "older" women.

A few minutes later, Sonia and Jet walked into The Homestead, a restaurant whose ambiance recalled the pioneer days of Danville. A large mural representing the first settlers in the area filled the main wall on the side of the room. Artifacts from those early days were artfully displayed on small shelves and in cupboards around the room. All the dining furniture had a rustic look.

Most of the ambiance of the room went quickly past Sonia's senses. What she zeroed in on was the freckle-faced female server who was helping customers at the corner table make their selections. Sonia turned to Jet, but Jet's smile indicated that nothing need be said. Fearful of being seated in the wrong section of the room, Sonia moved directly to a table she believed would clearly be in Jennipher's section. She and Jet took seats as Jennipher turned toward them and smiled an, "I'll be with you in a moment," smile.

It took a few minutes, but eventually, Jennipher came to their table. "Sorry. We're running a little behind today. What can I get you ladies to drink?"

Sonia was taken a little off guard. She'd been so focused on finding Jennipher, then on sitting at one of her tables, that she hadn't even thought about whether or not they were going to actually eat lunch. She looked over at Jet.

"Just bring us two white wines and your menus." Jet let out a small sigh. "We'll take it from there."

Jennipher was gone in a moment, and Sonia looked back to Jet. "We're eating?"

"Honey, it's been a rough couple of days." Jet unrolled her cloth napkin, taking out a heavy knife and fork, each with an engraved *H* at the end of its handle. "Now, what say we drink a glass or two of wine and eat some lunch while we watch and get a sense of who Ms. Jennipher with a ph is."

Sonia looked around, truly absorbing the room's motif for the first time. Before she could speak, however, Jennipher was there with the two glasses of wine and the menus. "Here you go, ladies. Would you like to hear our specials?" Without conferring, both women shook their heads in the negative. "Okay then, I'll be back in a minute to take your orders."

Sonia looked at the menu, then across the table at Jet. "Let's just get salads and keep it light." Her voice was soft, conspiratorial. "If Jennipher gets off before we're done, I want to be able to get up and follow her. We need to ask this girl some questions."

"Face to face, as you've said." Jet's voice was soft as well, her eyes following Jennipher as she walked away.

It wasn't long before Jennipher was back and took the order for two small salads. Sonia was surprised and pleased at how quickly their lunch showed up, lessening the chance that they might be trapped in their seats while their quarry left work. Just the opposite occurred. After having quickly eaten their salads, the girls had to linger over their wines for almost an hour before Jennipher came to the table, apparently hoping to nudge them into paying their tab so that she might clock out.

After paying, the girls left The Homestead. They positioned themselves outside the front of the building, waiting for Jennipher but trying to look inconspicuous—just a couple of tourists wondering what to do next. A few minutes later, Sonia watched through a window as Jennipher took off her apron and clocked out. She turned her face away. "She'll be out soon."

Sonia could tell from the look on Jennipher's face that she was surprised to see the two women still standing outside the restaurant as she left. She gave them a quick smile, then turned left and started walking away.

Sonia called out. "Jennipher?"

The server stopped and turned around, a quizzical look on her face.

Sonia continued. "Jennipher. Could we ask you a question?"

Sonia could sense the young woman withdrawing into herself, apparently unsure of what was happening—and clearly more apprehensive than one might have expected.

Jet stepped in. "No need to worry, honey. We just want to ask you a question about someone we're looking for, someone you went to college with."

Sonia would have expected Jennipher's obvious anxiety to lessen, a least a bit, but she got no physical sign of that. "Really, we're trying to find a friend of yours who might be in trouble, and we thought maybe you could help. Do you remember Mariana Castillo?"

Jennipher nodded, her short red hair glowing a little in the afternoon sunlight. No words came out of her mouth. Eventually, however, she said, "Mariana. Sure, I remember her. She was in the Equine Research program like me."

Jet adjusted the sunglasses she had put on. "And . . . ?"

"And what? That's it." Jennipher raised her shoulders. "She was in the same program as me. We had classes together. She was a nice girl. What's this all about?" She was clinging tightly to the purse and folded apron that she held close to her chest.

Sonia walked closer to Jennipher—slowly, cautiously. She spoke even more gently. "Listen, Mariana has gone missing. It's been almost two months now. We're private investigators and her father has hired us to try to find her. You don't happen to know where she is, do you?"

Jennipher's answer came quickly, edgy. "No. I haven't seen her since we graduated. How would I know where she is?"

"Sweetheart," Jet reached out to the girl but she withdrew. "We're not saying you know where she is. We're just wondering if you've heard anything at all about her recently. Heard about her or her classmates. Anything?"

"No, no." Jennipher's eyes were having a difficult time finding a place to settle. "Look, I graduated from Mayweather and then came home to work on my family's farm." She shook her head. "I don't stay in touch with anyone from the program."

Jet looked quickly at Sonia, then turned back to Jennipher. "You don't talk to anyone from the program?"

Jennipher's eyes shot up to the left for the briefest moment. "No." She paused. "Look y'all, I've got to go. I've got to get home. Good luck with everything, but I've really got to go." She turned and started walking away again, quickly.

Jet called out. "One last thing."

Jennipher stopped, frozen for a moment before she turned around to face the girls.

Jet took just one step toward her. "If you hear anything about

Mariana. Would you give us a call? You can Google us. Bluegrass Confidential Investigations."

Jennipher hesitated just half of a beat. "Sure." She turned and walked away. It was clear she was absolutely done with the conversation.

55

B rad had been right. Lexington being the nominal capital of the horse breeding world, Ron Harris' bloodstock agency was located in a nondescript office building on South Broadway, near the center of town. By eight o'clock on Monday morning, Brad was sitting in his second car, an unobtrusive 2005 Toyota Corolla—a better choice for surveillance than his brand-new Corvette. He was hoping that Harris would show up for work sometime that morning. He did, but not until ten o'clock.

Brad was glad when he saw Harris arrive, it meant that he had made contact with his target. He realized as well, however, that Harris was going into his place of business. He might not come out for several hours. Since the whole notion of following Ron Harris had come about over the weekend, Brad hadn't had an opportunity to check out Harris' office—to find out if he had any employees. That meant that he would just have to sit in his car and wait, possibly for several hours, until he had a chance to make the intervention he was planning. It was frustrating, but it was something his experience had prepared him for well.

As Brad sat in the car waiting, he had time to ruminate on the changes that had occurred in his life over the last year or so.

Not too long ago he had still been a United States Marine attached to NCIS. Then he had come back home to the Bluegrass, started Semper Fi Investigations, and spotted a beautiful dark-haired woman who worked at another PI firm right across the street. The next thing he knew, he was helping her solve a murder and falling in love with her along the way. Then there was the trip to see the wife he'd never divorced, a big blow-up with Sonia about not telling her beforehand what he was dealing with, and finally, a reconciliation. And now he was sitting in his car, engaged to be married, and about to have a friendly conversation with a guy he was pretty sure had just murdered three young women. He popped a piece of gum into his mouth. "Ain't life somethin'."

Just after twelve o'clock, Brad saw Ron Harris leave the building and head for his shiny black Lexus. Harris slipped into the driver's seat, fired up the car, and spent a moment settling in, putting on his sunglasses and adjusting his radio. Those activities only took a few moments, but they were moments he came to regret.

Just as Harris moved to put the Lexus in gear, the passenger door opened and a large, rugged man with bright blue eyes slipped into the passenger seat. "Good afternoon, Ron."

"What the . . . ?"

"Calm down, Ron." Brad's voice was quiet, velvet over steel. "We're just going to have a pleasant little conversation here, and if you don't do anything stupid you might just be able to leave this car without the worry of how to get blood stains out of that beautiful teal shirt you're wearing. It is teal, right? I mean, that's what they call that color?"

Brad could tell that Ron Harris' brain was spinning a mile a minute. "Who the hell—"

Brad raised the index finger of his left hand and held it up in Harris' face. "Now Ron, be careful not to make me angry. I come in peace. I just want to ask you some questions. But, should you become unruly . . . ." Brad put his right hand inside his jacket and pulled his Glock 17 out of its shoulder holster.

Brad watched as Harris' head pivoted back and forth, clearly looking in vain for someone to help him. Brad smiled and let his eyes leave Harris and drift around the parking lot. "Don't bother, Ron. There's no one around to help you. I've been sitting here for hours, and you're the only one who's shown up the whole time. Really, it's just the two of us." He gave his shoulders a quick shrug. "Now, can we get started?"

Harris' face twisted into the most menacing look he could muster. "Listen, you son-of-a-bitch. I don't know what the hell you want from me, but if you don't get out of my car—"

Although Brad had chambered a round before holstering his weapon, for effect, he grasped the Glock's slide with his left hand and slid it backward, ejecting one round and chambering another. It made the familiar sound that Harris had heard a million times in movies and on TV but had probably never heard in real life. Brad could tell by the way the flustered man was looking at the gun that it now scared the hell out of him. "So, Ron, tell me about your business. What is it that you actually do for a living?"

Harris' eyes were glued to Brad's gun. His voice was shaky. "What do you mean? I broker horse sales. I help people buy and sell racehorses." It was clear that panic was rising in his whole body. The pitch of his voice certainly was. "Why the hell are you asking me this?"

Brad remained as calm as an early summer morning on a Kentucky horse farm. "So, you help people find the horse they want to buy and then you make the deal for them. Is that it?"

Harris took a short, difficult breath. "Yes. Yes, sometimes. Or I help people sell a horse. I don't know." His eyes were wide, his voice fractured. "What the hell do you want me to tell you?"

Brad looked right into Harris' eyes. "I want you to tell me about Frailing. You brokered the deal for him, didn't you?"

Harris paused. Brad could see him trying to get control of himself. "Yeah. Yeah. I helped that banjo guy buy him. So what? That was just . . . just another deal."

Brad turned his eyes forward, feeling no need to fear anything Harris could do. "And who was it that bred Frailing?"

The look on Harris' face became more confused as he gave a straight, simple answer. "He was bred on Downstream Farm, that's Masson's farm, George Masson."

Brad lifted his eyebrows. "Nothing unusual there?"

"No, no. Masson bred the horse, Paine bought it. No big deal."

"And Frailing? He came from great bloodlines?" Brad sounded like a father who was asking his son about the ownership of a small stash of marijuana he had found in his son's closet.

Although the air conditioner was running in the car, Brad could see the sweat pouring down Harris' face. "Well, good, but not great. No, he came from good stock, but—"

Brad half squinted. "But he really did exceptionally well this year, didn't he?"

Harris had been staring at Brad and his gun the whole time, trying to understand what this was all about. He finally released his gaze and looked out the windshield. "Yeah, yeah. He did okay." He turned back to Brad. "He turned out to be a good horse, a good buy for Paine."

Brad paused for a minute, giving Harris time to start to put some things together in his mind. "So, tell me about Summer Wheat."

Brad watched as Ron Harris' eyes bugged open. He could tell that alarm bells were going off for Harris—that he was starting to get it. "Ron? Summer Wheat?" Brad could see that Harris' tongue was getting thick, a tell-tale sign of panic.

"Um, uh." Harris swallowed hard, his Adam's apple bobbing up and down. "What do you want to know?"

Brad stayed cool and gave Harris a friendly smile. "C'mon

Ron. You must be getting this by now. Frailing comes out of Downstream Farm and does really well for a horse with his bloodlines. Then, Summer Wheat, it's kind of the same thing. You want to guess what other horse I'd like to talk about?"

Ron Harris just shook his head. His teal shirt now the color of dark ocean water.

Brad's smile tightened. "Would it make sense to throw Run Lucky into the conversation? Would it, Ron?"

Ron Harris stared wide-eyed at Brad, frozen.

"Okay, Ron." Brad rubbed his slightly scruffy chin, his voice becoming just the slightest bit impatient. "This is taking longer than I'd like; and honestly, I haven't had a thing to eat since early this morning. So, let me help you out."

Somehow, Ron Harris' eyes managed to get even bigger.

Using his Glock in place of his pointing finger, Brad reviewed. "Three horses come from three different farms, Downstream, Willowbay, and Holdenbrook. They each have racing success way beyond expectations. Oh, and then there's this one other thing that happens. Three young women all get murdered, and it turns out that each one worked on one of those three farms. That's something, isn't it Ron? Oh, there's one other thing. It seems that one person was involved with all three horses. Do you know who that one person is, Ron?"

Harris didn't make a sound—move a muscle.

Brad's head wagged slowly. "I'm sorry Ron, but it was you." He let out a big sigh. "You're the only person who was connected to all three horses, all three farms, and therefore . . . all three murdered women."

Ron Harris' eyes flared. He lunged forward, trying to grab Brad. Unfortunately, having seen all those public service announcements over the past twenty years, the first thing Ron had done when he'd gotten into his car was put on his seatbelt. Simultaneously, two different things went poorly for Ron Harris. First, his seatbelt tightened, keeping him from reaching Brad.

Second, Brad smacked him in the face with the butt of his Glock, right between his eyes. It sent pain blazing through his brain and blood running instantly down his face.

After Ron's low moan subsided, both men sat in silence. Finally, Brad said, "You know, Ron. I'm pretty sure you can clear this all up for me. Don't you think this would be a good time to start doing that?"

Harris sat in the car, blood, sweat, and perhaps even a tiny tear pouring down his face, the panic in his eyes being replaced by a look of resignation.

A few moments later, Brad reached into his jacket pocket and took out his phone. "Okay, Ron. I've given you your chance." He started scrolling on his screen. "I guess we'll just call the police and have them come and join us. I'm sure that when I tell them about this whole crazy set of coincidences, they'll probably want to ask you some more in-depth questions themselves." He chuckled. "They're like that, you know, always wanting to get to the bottom of things."

Ron Harris came to life. "No wait, wait. I'll tell you. I'll tell you all about it. But you've got to believe me, I didn't kill those girls. I don't even know what you're talking about. I never hurt anyone."

"Ron?" The look on Brad's face was the same one that father would have had when his son told him the marijuana was a friend's—he was just holding it for him.

"Seriously," Harris' voice was full of desperation, "I don't even know what girls you're talking about. It was just business. We were just doing business."

His Glock in his right hand, Brad reached out and put his big, powerful left hand on Harris' thigh, close to his most prized possessions. He enjoyed watching Harris' whole body stiffen in panic when he did. "Okay, Ron. Last chance. C'mon now. Get a hold of yourself and start telling me everything you can about the horses, the farms, the girls."

Brad sat and listened as Ron Harris spilled his guts. Ten

minutes later, Brad holstered his weapon, opened the door, and slid out of the car. "Okay, Ron. Go clean yourself up. And then go get yourself a lawyer. But listen, pal. I wouldn't plan on leaving town anytime soon. I'm thinking that would be the last thing you'd want to do right now."

Brad closed the door softly and walked away from the car, his calm bravado on full display for the benefit of Ron Harris. As he got to his own car, however, his insides were doing flips.

56

As soon as Jennipher had gotten a few steps away from them, Jet smacked Sonia's arm with the back of her hand. "Quick. Let's go." It was an intense whisper.

Sonia's first step matched Jet's. So did her voice. "Yeah."

They quickly made it to the Camry. Jet hit the button on her key to unlock the doors. "You didn't buy all that crap from Jennipher, did you?"

Sonia slipped quickly into the passenger seat, a look of determination on her face. "Absolutely not. She's hiding something. No doubt about it."

"Are you kidding?" Jet gave Sonia a quick glance. "She looked like Diogi did the day I came home and found six jelly donuts missing and his face covered in powdered sugar. And another thing. There's this girl up in New York, Sarah something. Sarah Hastings, I think. I spoke to her the other day. She said she stays in contact with Jennipher. Clearly, Ms. Jennipher has been lying to us." Jet started the car, watching the rearview mirror as the redhead continued walking away.

Sonia stared at the side view mirror. "We're going to follow her, right?"

"You bet." Jet's eyes remained locked on her rearview mirror. "I don't know what that gets us, but this is the first time we have even the slightest reason to think we may be able to find out what happened to Mariana, and it's all because of you, Sonia."

Sonia looked over at Jet. "What do you mean?"

"Face to face, girl. You're the one who said we had to talk to these folks face to face. I'm telling you. I'm not sure I would have gotten the same sense of things talking to this girl on the phone, or by email. But face to face, I'm sure something here smells rotten."

Sonia was about to speak, but she was cut off by Jet. "Wait. She's getting into her car. Can you see it? That little puke-green Chevy something?" Jet squinted at the mirror. "Alright Miss Jennipher with the ph, let's see where you go now."

Sonia was frustrated that she couldn't pick up the car in the little side view mirror, but she watched Jet's face as Jet kept track of the car. "You got her?"

"I got her" Jet nodded. "And here she comes, she's going to come right past us."

"Be careful she doesn't see us following her."

Jet looked to her right and gave Sonia the biggest "Ya think?" look she could muster.

Sonia shrugged her shoulders. "Sorry."

Jet pulled out into traffic and followed the little, puke-green car through town. It only took a few minutes for both cars to work their way out into the countryside. "Damn, it ain't easy following someone on this kind of road and them not seeing you."

Sonia responded, "Uh-huh." As she did, thoughts of the day she and Brad had followed a drug dealer down the interstate from Lexington all the way to a little town in Tennessee ran through her mind. She was acutely aware of the fact that they had used two cars in order to avoid detection, alternating behind the target every few minutes and at each stop. Now, Jet was trying to keep up with the puke-green car and yet stay far enough behind as to not arouse suspicion. Sonia knew it was a tough task.

After a few minutes of silence on the open road, Jet finally spoke. "So, what got you about Jennipher's story?"

Sonia took a quick breath and let it out. "Mostly the fact that she never asked about what had happened to Mariana. I mean, wouldn't that be the first question you would ask if someone told you I was missing?"

Jet smiled. "Honey, if you were to go missing, all I would think was that you and that blue-eyed devil were hunkerin' down in some little love nest somewhere, trying to figure out what it would take to repopulate the world with blue-eyed *Eye-talian* beauties."

Sonia rolled her eyes. "Seriously, anything else grab you?"

"Well, I've got to say," Jet was serious again, "as soon as we get back to Lexington, I'll be contacting Burnett. He's up there in New York, and I want him to try to track down this Sarah Hastings." She checked her side view mirror. "Clearly, she was one of the horsey girls at that school too. Now if something's happened to her," she turned momentarily to Sonia, "we're not only onto somebody who knows who hurt Mariana, we can be pretty sure that Miss Jennipher with the ph might have had something to do with it."

Sonia was surprised. Her own line of thinking hadn't taken the Sarah Hastings discrepancy that far, but she had to admit that if Jennipher was saying she never communicated with Sarah Hastings at all, and then it turned out that Sarah was missing too, something was definitely up with this red-haired woman.

Jet had been hanging back as far as she could from Jennipher's car while still keeping it in view. Fortunately, the road they were on was relatively straight for a country road. Eventually, things changed. "Okay. She's pulling off. That must be her folks' farm."

Sonia sat up straighter. "Keep going past the entrance." It was a trick she had learned from Brad.

"Yes, sir."

As they approached the Alston farm, Sonia watched the puke-green car rumble up toward the main house, kicking up a small tail of dust. "No, wait." She reached out and put her hand on Jet's arm. "We've got to see where she goes. Maybe she never even noticed us. Just pull over here. Let's watch what she does."

"If you say so, captain." Jet pulled the car onto a grassy spot by the side of the road. She got as close to the classic Kentucky horse farm fence as she could.

Sonia rolled down the passenger door window, hoping to get the best view possible. "She's not going into the house. She's going up the stairs to the top of that garage. She must have an apartment like mine. You know, over the garage?"

Jet was leaning forward, her head almost over the steering wheel, straining to see as well. "Yeah, I can see her. She's inside. Now what?"

Sonia turned back to Jet and lifted her shoulders. "Honestly, I don't know. I guess we just find a better place to park, and then we wait."

Jet kept her eyes locked on the apartment door. "Wait for what?"

Sonia's eyes drifted back to the apartment as well. "I haven't the slightest idea."

57

After Brad had left Ron Harris, he'd headed directly back to his office. Surrounded by old wood flooring, nine-foot ceilings, old-fashioned woodwork and the latest in high-tech equipment, he sat at his well-worn desk feeling off balance. He believed Harris about not killing those three women, but he found it hard to believe that Harris was right about who had. What Brad needed most at that point was to lay his eyes on Sonia—Sonia and Jet. If Harris was right, and if Brad couldn't find that person quickly enough, then they might both be in danger.

Brad tried calling the girls—tried them both. Neither one answered. He let out an exasperated sigh, "Pick up your damn phone." He couldn't let it go at that. He had to try to find them. He banged his fist quietly on his desk. Maybe, just maybe, there's something in their offices that will help me find them.

Brad ran across East Main, dodging traffic rather than waiting for the light. He scooted up the steps to the BCI offices only to find the door locked. No surprise. On the other hand, given his experience, it was also no surprise that Brad knew how to jimmy a lock, especially one that was over sixty years old. It didn't take much effort before he was walking through the waiting area headed for Sonia's office.

Poking around on Sonia's desk, Brad found nothing that would help. He let the words come softly out of his mouth. "Damn, she keeps a neat desk. How the hell does she ever find anything?" He turned and started to leave Sonia's office, heading for Jet's. As he passed through the doorway, however, something caught his attention. Stepping back, he looked at the whiteboard that he had never noticed hanging on the wall before. She must have just put that up. Looking more closely at it, he saw a list of names. All but one was crossed out. The one that appeared to still be in play was that of a woman identified as Jennipher Alston. Next to it was the word, "Danville".

It was just a hunch, but Brad had to follow it. Walking out of the BCI offices, and down those wooden steps, he scurried across the street, climbed into his 'Vette, and took off for Danville. In his mind, the balance between his concern for Sonia and Jet and the observation of posted speed limits leaned heavily on the former.

JET HAD BACKED up a short way along the mostly empty country road and found a place where no one from the Alston farm could see her Camry. Sonia slipped out of the car, walking a few steps through the grass to yet another section of horse farm fencing. She leaned her elbows on the top of the fence, looking through a pair of small but high-powered binoculars.

Jet joined her. "Where the hell did you get those?"

"Oh, they were a gift from Brad," Sonia said while she used the binoculars to scan the farm. "He gave them to me when we'd worked out the business arrangements between the two firms, remember?"

"Of course I remember the business arrangements." Jet furrowed her brow. "But why did he give you the binoculars?"

"He said that if we were going to be partners, even just occasionally, I should have professional equipment." Sonia lowered the binoculars and gave Jet a sweet smile. "I think he did it just to be nice."

Jet stood close to Sonia, straining to see the garage apartment into which Jennipher had disappeared. "Can you see anything?"

Sonia lifted the binoculars again. "Well, yes and no. With these things, I can see if there are any fingerprints on the doorknob. On the other hand, as long as that door stays shut, there's nothing worth seeing."

They stood quietly for the next few minutes, Jet taking a turn with the binoculars. "Hey, wait a minute." Her voice climbed. "Looks like Jennipher is leaving again, either that or going to her folk's house." She kept the binoculars to her eyes. A moment later she spoke again. "Oh, and here come her parents." She waited, watching silently as things transpired on the farm. "Yeah, they're all getting into the parent's pick-up. They must be leaving." She lowered the binoculars and nodded toward the farm. "What do we do now?"

Sonia turned and walked quickly back to the car. "First, we get the hell out of here." She spoke fast, full of energy. "Get in and get us past the entrance to that farm before they get there. We can't let them see us."

Jet jumped into the Camry, fired it up, and took off, the sound of small stones pinging off its fenders. Before the parent's bright red Ford F-150 made it back to the main road, Jet had pushed the Camry past the entrance. Just beyond a bend, she pulled the car to the side of the road again. "As long as they head back to town, looks like we're in the clear."

Sonia watched in the side view mirror. "And there they go." She let out a big sigh. "Whew, that was close." Neither of them spoke for a moment, then Sonia tapped the dashboard twice. "Okay, let's get this thing turned around and get back to the farm." She checked the time on her phone. "I'm guessing there's no one left there, at least for a little while, and I'd love to get into that apartment to see what we can find."

Jet made the difficult U-turn on the small country road, then headed back toward the farm. Pulling off to her right, she parked, tucked up close to a tall water maple tree that was surrounded by high brush. "Okay, genius, exactly how are we going to get into that apartment?"

Sonia reached down between her feet and picked up her purse. She rustled through it for a moment, retrieving a small, black, leather pouch. "First, being a farm, there's a good chance that the apartment is not even locked. Second, if it is, I believe these will help." She lifted the soft leather flap on the pouch, revealing a set of lock picks.

Jet stared at the pouch and its contents. "And I guess those come from Brad as well?"

Sonia had a smug look on her face. "You don't think Brad and I spend all those evenings just sitting around gazing into each other's eyes, do you? The same night he gave me those binoculars he also gave me these lock picks." She gently touched the tip of each of the different tools, one of which was very sharp. "He's been teaching me how to use them." She turned to Jet and grinned. "And I've gotten pretty darn good at it if I don't say so myself. Let's go."

Knowing that they would have to move through trees and some low brush in order to avoid being seen by anyone who might still be in the house, the women left their purses in the car and locked it. Swinging wide around the driveway and traveling along the tree line, Sonia and Jet were able to make it to the garage apartment pretty much hidden from view. The stairs that led up to the apartment ran diagonally along the side of the garage that faced the road, touching the ground right at the corner of the building. When they got to those steps, Sonia stopped.

Jet leaned close to her from behind. "Now what?"

Sonia stood frozen. She didn't reply.

"Seriously, now what?" Jet put her hand on Sonia's shoulder. "Are we going up those stairs or not?"

"Shhh. Listen. Is that music? You think somebody's up there?"

Jet leaned closer to the steps, her ear cupped with her hand. "I don't know, but that's definitely music. Either she left the music on or there's someone up there listening to it."

There was another moment of silence as Sonia wondered about their best strategy. Then her hand shot out and touched Jet's arm. "Listen. The music. It stopped, right?"

Again, Jet leaned over Sonia's shoulder, straining to hear. "Yeah," she whispered, "I don't hear it anymore. I guess somebody's up there, but who?"

"Well, there's only one—"

Both their heads popped upward as the sound of a door opening floated down to them. Ducking backward, around the corner of the building, they stood frozen, their backs pressed against the short side of the building. Soon, it became obvious that whoever had stepped out of the apartment was hurrying down the steps. Sonia's eyes scanned the surrounding trees, her mind scrambling. Should we run? Before she even had time to make up her mind, she heard the sound of footsteps on gravel.

Sonia's head turned toward the sound. Her heart skipped a beat.

58

In a flash, Sonia had seen a face and then it was gone—scrambling back up the steps, a blur of blue jeans and a white shirt. It was the face that had been sitting in a frame on her desk for the last few weeks.

Sonia started running up the stairs, following. "Wait! Wait! It's okay. We're here to help!"

Jet, being the more athletic of the girls, scooted past Sonia on the steps and was standing next to the woman before she could use her keys to open the door. The woman spun on Jet, the look of a trapped and panicked animal on her face—one of her keys protruding from between her fisted fingers like a weapon.

A second later, Sonia was on the large landing outside the door as well, talking fast. "Mariana. We're here to help you. My name is Sonia. This is Jet. Your father sent us. Your father, Paco? He's so worried about you. He asked us to find you. Are you okay, Mariana?" Mariana continued to back away until her body was trapped by the wooden railing that surrounded the landing. The look on her face made it obvious to Sonia that she was still processing everything. She was still frightened.

Sonia consciously kept her hands at her side. She spoke

slowly, carefully, her brown eyes sending messages of reassurance. "It's okay. You're safe. You're going to be okay."

Mariana stood frozen, dark eyes staring out of a pretty but anxious face, her trim, well-conditioned body taut and ready for battle.

Jet spoke softly as well. "Sweetheart. We've all been looking for you. Me, Sonia, your cousin Gabriela. Everyone just wanted to know where you were, that you were okay."

Sonia tried again, reaching out to Mariana tentatively. "Really. We're here to help." Her voice rose a tick. "Ask us anything you want. We're just so happy to have found you, to know that you're . . . . She paused, nothing but the warm sun and the gentle sounds of a few birds filling the space between them.

Finally, Sonia stepped forward slowly, very slowly, eventually able to close the distance between them. She cautiously wrapped her arms around the young woman. Mariana stood motionless, a statue. After a few moments, her fear began to crumble, to fall away. She buried her face into Sonia's shoulder. Sonia could feel the wetness of Mariana's tears as they slid out of her eyes and down Sonia's neck. Finally, dissolving into a sobbing, shaking pool of pent-up emotion, Mariana began rocking back and forth in Sonia's arms.

Jet inched forward and put her arms around both of them. A moment later she whispered into Mariana's dark, wavy hair. "C'mon, let's get you back inside. Give me those keys and I'll open the door."

It took a moment for Mariana to respond, to let go of Sonia. Eventually, she released herself enough to be able to hand Jet the keys. Jet unlocked the door and they all stepped inside.

Sonia looked around, seeing a pleasant but small apartment, not at all unlike her own. With lots of wood and light-yellow curtains, this apartment had dark brown walls and an area rug that spilled reds, oranges, tans, and yellows on the floor. There were two major differences, however, between this place and

Sonia's. First, unlike Sonia's, this one looked out on the beauty of a Kentucky farm; the green freshness of spring filled the entire view from a window that overlooked the small gravel parking area next to the garage. Second, the folded-up bedding at the end of the couch made it obvious that this tiny apartment was designed for one person but had been housing two.

Sonia led Mariana to the couch. "C'mon, Mariana." Her voice was almost a whisper. "Sit. Sit here. Can I get you some water?" Sonia waited for a reply, but all she got were eyes that seemed to be pleading for something. She nodded. "Yeah, let's get you some water."

Jet stepped toward the little kitchen area. She waved her hand. "I've got it."

Sonia kneeled down next to Mariana and tossed a, "Thank you," to Jet.

In less than a minute Jet was back with the water, handing it to Sonia, who then handed it to Mariana. Jet took a seat in the only other chair in the "living room."

After Mariana had taken a long drink, Sonia took hold of one of her hands. "Are you okay?" Her eyes searched the girl's. "Do you believe that we're here to help you?"

A long moment passed. Then, in the thinnest voice, with almost no hint of Hispanic heritage, Mariana answered. "Yes. Yes. Thank you for coming."

Sonia got up from the floor and sat sideways on the couch next to Mariana, her leg tucked under her body. She and Jet sat quietly, patiently, waiting a solid minute before Mariana could get enough control of herself to speak.

Finally, Mariana broke the silence, her voice wavering. "So, it was my dad who sent you?"

Sonia was quick to answer. "Yes." She reached out her hand, placing it reassuringly on Mariana's knee. "I don't know if you really heard me before. My name is Sonia," she turned and looked at her partner, a quick smile on her face, "and this is Jet."

Her eyes returned to Mariana. "We're private investigators. The police had kind of run out of options in their search for you, so your father came to us. He's been so worried. Your whole family has."

The nearly empty glass in Mariana's hand was shaking. "They're okay? My mom and dad." Her eyebrows rose. "They're okay?"

"Yes, sweetheart. They're fine. And they're going to be so relieved when they know we've found you."

Mariana took another sip. She gazed down into her lap. "Good."

Sonia let the silence hang in the air for a long time.

Finally, Jet's impatience got the best of her. "So, you going tell us why you're hiding out here? Can you tell us what's going on?"

Mariana looked first at Jet, then back to Sonia. She started softly. "It wasn't supposed to be like this. It wasn't supposed to be bad." The pitch of her voice started to rise. "It was supposed to be a good thing, a *great* thing." Her eyes filled with light. "We were going to change things forever. The horses, they were going to be stronger, better, healthier than ever before."

Mariana looked back and forth between Sonia and Jet. "It was our dream. All of us. We worked together on it. But not for our sakes. It was for the horses."

Sonia glanced over at Jet, who returned the look. Neither one spoke.

"It was our dream, but it got all twisted. It's so stupid." Her voice trailed away as her eyes fell again. "We let it become all about the money."

Mariana paused for a long time. "Listen, sweetheart," Sonia reached up and pushed a strand of tear-soaked hair out of Mariana's face, "you can trust us. We're here to help you. But we can't help if we don't know why you ran away, why you're hiding." She needed more information, critical information—who would kill the other two girls, and why. She knew she would just have to be patient and let the story come out of Mariana at its own pace. She hated it.

As Sonia continued to sit on the couch, turned sideways so she could face Mariana, Jet got up and moved around, finally leaning against the wall near a window that looked out over the farm.

Sonia reached out and gently squeezed Mariana's hand. "C'mon, sweetheart. Help us understand."

59

Mariana put the water glass down on the coffee table in front of her. "Okay. I'll explain. But you've got to believe me." Her eyes darted quickly between Sonia and Jet. "When this all started, we never thought anything bad would happen. We never thought we were doing anything wrong, not really. This was all for the horses. We were using the latest scientific breakthroughs to create a new, better life for the horses."

She shrugged. "Oh, we knew we were breaking some rules, not following the normal scientific protocols for experimentation." The pace of her speech quickened. "But damn, those things slow everything down so much. It might have been years and years before we would have been allowed to even begin trying the things we knew would work. He just wasn't willing to wait."

Sonia interrupted, her eyebrows raised. "He?"

"Professor Andersen," Mariana leaned toward Sonia, "he's the genius."

Sonia's eyes whipped over to Jet, whose mouth was open.

Mariana seemed not to notice. "He's the one who knew that we could do so many wonderful things for these beautiful animals if we were allowed to make a few tiny changes in their genetic structure." Her eyes rose momentarily to the ceiling. "It's so simple, so small. Just a few changes and all those problems with nocardioform placentities would be gone, and cerebella abiotrophy, and a whole lot of other diseases." She shook her head quickly. "But no, the scientific community wouldn't hear of it. They said we had to follow all the rules of scientific experimentation.

"And the breeders, most of them, they said we would be messing with nature, and that it wasn't right, or even legal." She was animated, almost angry. She picked up her glass and took a quick sip of her water. "Hell, I think they just didn't want to give up their special place in the world as the grand wizards of horse breeding." She nearly spit the words out. "They wanted it to stay all mysterious as if their intelligent breeding of the animals was the only thing that could improve things. But it's not. There are better ways—scientific ways." She put her glass down with a tiny thump.

Sonia stood up and began walking around the room, sensing the need to put a little personal space between Mariana's energy and herself. "Okay, I'm starting to get a little bit of a picture, but I still don't understand. What is it that you all were doing?"

Mariana had settled down a bit. "Listen, I know this is going to sound crazy to you. But it's true; every bit of it is true."

Sonia glanced quickly at Jet, giving her a "here we go" look.

Mariana took a deep breath and began. "So, here's the deal. While we were at Mayweather—"

Sonia put her hand up. "We? Who we?"

Mariana rolled her eyes as if Sonia and Jet should have already known. "Me, LaKeisha, Penny Rae. That's who."

Sonia swallowed hard. "And . . . and do you know—"

Mariana's eyebrows lifted. "And do I know what happened to them?" Her anger flashed. "Of course, I know what happened to them. They're dead." She took a long, slow breath. "First, I heard about Keisha, about her being killed in a hit and run." She looked up at the girls, pleadingly. "I mean, who gets killed by a hit and run driver in their own parking lot?"

She took another deep breath. "Then, when I tried to call Penny Rae, I couldn't get in touch with her. All I could get from the folks she worked with was that she had disappeared. They had all kinds of ideas about what had happened, where she might have gone, but I knew in my heart something bad had happened." Mariana's eyes settled on Sonia. "That's when I knew I had to run, I had to get away before something happened to me."

She reached out and picked up her water glass again, taking a long, final, drink. "Since I've been hiding out, I've kept checking the local news up in Saratoga Springs. At first, they didn't know much. But since they found Penny's body in Vermont, they've figured out a lot. They're pretty sure she was strangled to death right in her barn, first thing in the morning, right on the farm where she worked. They know the guy who did it drove her car to the national forest there, and they even have an idea about how he got back to New York—on a damn bus."

Sonia and Jet exchanged quick glances.

"He killed them. He wants to kill me. I *had* to run. I *had* to get away from him."

"Who? Who killed them?" Still standing, Sonia leaned down toward the girl.

Mariana looked into Sonia's eyes as if wondering why Sonia was so slow to understand. The words exploded out of her. "Andersen. Professor Andersen. *He* killed them. I'm sure he did it. It must have been him." Anger seethed in her eyes; her body was literally shaking.

Sonia's mind reeled as she stood taller. Gentle, almost goofy, Andersen. According to Mariana, he was some kind of a genius and willing to bend the rules of scientific discovery. But a murderer?

The women remained silent. Jet walked aimlessly around the

room, expending her pent-up energy, occasionally looking out the window. Sonia took a seat on the couch. She reached over and took the empty water glass from Mariana, placing it on the coffee table. "So, you and LaKeisha and Penny Rae, you were working with Professor Andersen?"

"Yeah," she spoke softly, calmly this time. Her eyes drifted away from Sonia. "He had gotten all that money to do research on nocardioform placentities, but he didn't use it all for that. He bought some equipment and material that he could use for the research he really wanted to do, research on improving the actual genetic structure of the horses. He was going to make their lives better."

Sonia asked gently, "Okay. Then what?"

Mariana's gaze returned to Sonia. "Well, he'd developed the protocols he wanted to use, but he wasn't allowed to try them."

"And?"

She shrugged. "We decided to do some embryo transfers."

"With horses?"

"Look," Mariana lifted her eyes and her shoulders, her voice a little impatient, "embryo transfer has been done in horses for years, just not with Thoroughbreds. If a mare with good bloodlines is too old or not in good health, we can still impregnate her, then transfer her embryo to a healthier mare, one more likely to carry the foal to term. The biggest problem is trying to get a recipient mare to be in the perfect part of her cycle right at the moment you're taking the embryo from the donor mare. That has to be done seven or eight days after impregnation."

Sonia looked at her, squinting her eyes a bit. "Is this for real?"

"Yeah." Mariana smiled almost condescendingly. "It's done all the time. We just follow all the sterile procedures necessary, use a special wand to flush the donor mare, then collect the fluid from the procedure. We use ultrasound equipment to make sure we're getting exactly what we need. After several filtering steps to reduce contamination, we put the embryo in a pipette so that we can insert it into the recipient mare."

Still leaning against the wall, arms crossed, Jet shook her head. "Sounds crazy to me." She lifted her shoulders. "But if it's so normal, what's the big deal?"

Mariana smiled gently, condescendingly. "You don't get it, do you. It's not that we were doing embryo transfer, hell that's done more and more, and with newer and newer treatments like intra-cytoplasmic sperm injection. It's that we did it with Thorough-breds, which is not allowed, *and* after we genetically manipulated the embryo."

Sonia and Jet exchanged a glance.

Mariana cleared her throat and continued. "It's how we inter-rupted the process." Sonia could tell that pride was starting to accompany Mariana's description of what they had done. "You see, before we started dealing with real horses, on real farms, Professor Andersen had figured out ways to manipulate equine genes in order to improve a horse's performance on three indices: strength, speed, and endurance."

Jet walked to the middle of the room. "Now wait a minute. You guys were messing with the genes of horses? You can't do that. That's wrong." Her voice rose. "It must be wrong."

Mariana gave her a knowing smile. "Oh yeah? Talk to the folks at the Horse Genome Project. It's a big international effort to define the DNA sequence of the domestic horse. In fact, the University of Kentucky is a part of the whole thing. They're just doing the most fundamental research, but still . . . ."

Jet's head rocked back. "Damn."

Mariana's voice reflected her growing impatience. "Look you guys. Can't you put this together? The Horse Genome Project is a good thing, good for all horses. What Andersen did was figure out how to mess with the DNA of an equine embryo in order to produce a horse that would be faster, stronger, and have more endurance. Doing that for Thoroughbreds is totally forbidden, but it's a dream come true for anyone who wants to create winning racehorses."

Sonia's eyes widened. "And that's what you guys wanted?"

"No." Mariana's voice was strong, her face defiant. "Not me or the other girls. We just wanted to be able to make it possible for all horses to have better lives, to find therapies and treatments for diseases like Cushing's disease, respiratory diseases, all kinds of problems. But the professor, he said we could work around the whole scientific community roadblock if we just focused on the characteristics that Thoroughbred breeders were interested in."

Jet had drifted back to leaning on the wall. "Why would that be?"

Mariana looked up at Jet. "Because some of those breeders might be willing to bend the rules if we helped them produce winning horses."

Sonia sat up straighter, all the pieces were starting to come together. "Horses like Frailing, and Summer Wheat, and Run Lucky. Horses that were racing beyond their breeding, right?"

Now it was Mariana who slumped back in her seat. "Right."

New clarity was coming to Sonia's mind, along with new questions. "So, how'd you guys pull that off without anyone knowing? How were you three involved with the professor after you left school?"

Mariana looked tired. This lengthy explanation was clearly taking something out of her. "Listen. All three of us worked with Andersen when he had that grant to solve the nocardioform placentities problem. He took us into his confidence and let us work with him on learning how to manipulate certain genes in equine embryos. After we graduated, he helped us get jobs at three really important horse farms, horse farms where he already had a special kind of relationship, if you know what I mean."

She took a deep breath and continued. "Then, three years ago, we all worked together to put Andersen's theories to work in a clinical trial, so to speak. But we had to do it without anyone knowing about it. So just when a certain mare was bred on one of the farms, we'd put a plan in place. Seven or eight days after the mare was impregnated, the other two girls would meet the one who worked on that farm. In the middle of the night, we would do a sterile flush and collect the embryo using portable ultrasound equipment. Andersen would be waiting for us in a nearby motel. He'd have the proper equipment to keep the embryo viable while he worked on it."

Jet looked directly at Mariana. "You all did this in the dead of night?"

"Uh, huh." Mariana's voice had become almost nonchalant. "And twenty-four hours later we came back and reintroduced the embryo into the same mare after Andersen had done his magic."

Sonia ran her fingers through her hair. "And no one ever knew?"

"Well," she slipped into the role of the professional that she was, "the mares would all be a bit sluggish for a day or two, but that often happens early in pregnancy, so no one really made a big deal of it."

Jet's tone of voice became more accusatory. "You didn't answer her question. She asked if anyone else ever knew."

"Well, I'm not saying we couldn't have gotten away with it without anyone knowing, but there was a significant cost involved, and the money came from the breeders who were willing to let us do our clinical trial. It helped that they owned their own farms, too. That way they could keep anyone who might get suspicious away from us."

Sonia raised up. "Breeders like Ashkenasi and Masson and the Danecks?"

Mariana seemed totally surprised by Sonia's ability to connect those names to the plot. She squinted her eyes as she spoke. "That's right. They gave the professor a bunch of money so he could afford to do all this."

Jet jumped in, not supportively. "And of course, they would

not only get a horse that would outperform, they'd have the inside track on how to produce other horses that could do the same thing. Right?"

Mariana was silent. Her face dropped again.

Jet persisted. "Right, Mariana?"

Her soft answer was sent to the floor. "Right."

60

The room was silent for a few minutes while Sonia and Jet absorbed Mariana's incredible story. Sonia took a slow breath. "Okay. So, that's what you three girls and Professor Andersen were doing with those horses, but what went wrong? Why did he hurt those girls?"

Mariana's eyes remained glued to her lap. "Like I said. It became all about the money."

Sonia looked to Jet to share another "here it comes" look. Instead, she saw Jet looking absently out the window as she listened.

"You see," Mariana's voice became stronger as she started, "all three of us were top notch students, but Mayweather is a really expensive school. We all knew we would be graduating with student loans to pay off and how tough it would be to get by." She shrugged. "Then the professor met with each of us individually. He said that if we'd be part of his plan to create genetically modified Thoroughbreds, he would get us good jobs—and give us twenty thousand dollars a year each." She shook her head apologetically. "That's a lot of money."

She looked at her water glass sitting on the table, clearly

hoping there was still some liquid in it. There wasn't. "Then, after three years, when the horses started running in races, each of us would get a bonus of fifty thousand dollars. That meant a huge amount of money *and* an incredible opportunity to see all the work we'd been a small part of come to fruition."

"Whoa." Jet scratched her head doing some quick ciphering. "That's three hundred and thirty thousand dollars all together. That's beaucoup bucks."

Mariana's energy was rising. "Yeah. That's where the breeders got involved. They were putting up the money that Andersen gave us and paying for equipment and stuff."

Sonia shared a sardonic smile with Jet. "Yeah, and I'll bet there was a little in there for the professor's personal use as well."

"Yeah. He even started his own company he never told anyone but us about, Equine Futures Ltd."

Shock filled Sonia's eyes; she saw it reflected in Jet's as well— shock and recognition. They both remembered the company's name from the list of registrations for BMW convertibles in the area—black BMW convertibles.

After a moment, Jet kept pushing. "So why did everything suddenly go sideways?"

Mariana's voice got smaller. "It was Penny Rae at first. She called me, and then Keisha. She said that she had seen that guy Ron Harris talking to Mr. Daneck."

Sonia sat up taller, focused. "Ron Harris, the broker?"

"Yeah."

Now it was Sonia's energy that was rising fast. "So, he's involved too?"

Mariana shrugged her shoulders. "I guess. He certainly knew what was going on."

Sonia ran her fingers through her hair. "Okay. Go on." Her foot was tapping impatiently.

"Penny Rae didn't mean to eavesdrop." Mariana turned her palms upward, apologetically. "She was just close enough to hear some things. What she heard was that Daneck was paying a fortune to the professor, big, big bucks, like a million dollars or something. Penny assumed that the same was probably true of the other breeders. And if she was right, then the professor was getting like three million dollars or something and we were getting just a tiny portion of that." She gave her head a quick shake. "It didn't seem right." She stopped speaking.

Jet stood taller, no longer leaning on the wall. Her voice had an edge to it. "Go on, girl. We need to hear the rest."

Mariana took another deep breath. "So, Penny Rae asks us to get together on a three-way call. We talk about it and she says we should go to the professor and demand more. I was kind of unsure about it, but Keisha jumped right on board. Next thing you know, Penny's telling us that she's going to call the professor and tell him that he'd better give us more money than he'd promised—a lot more." Mariana sat back, holding up three fingers as her tone intensified. "Look, those three horses? We helped him with those genetically modified embryos and now they were three-year-olds and winning like crazy." She raised her eyebrows and her shoulders. "He couldn't have done any of that without us. You've got to be specially trained to do that embryo transfer stuff and we were. We even figured that the professor might be getting extra money because the horses were doing so well."

Sonia spoke softly. "And Penny Rae made that call?"

Mariana looked directly at Sonia. "She made it and she said he didn't seem too upset. He just said he'd have to think about everything." Tears began trickling down her face again.

Sonia spoke even more softly. "And then?"

Mariana choked her words through silent tears. "I spoke to Keisha the next day. She said to just be cool and let things play out. Then, the morning after that, I tried to call Keisha again. No answer. I'm going out of my mind, so I Google her name and I find there's some news story about her being killed in a hit and run accident."

Sonia kept her voice soft, soothing. She needed to hear everything she could from Mariana and now was the time. "So, you knew something was happening?"

"Oh," anger flared through the tears on her face, "I knew it. Then I try calling Penny Rae and find out she's been missing for a few days. There was no question. I knew he'd gotten to Keisha, and a couple of days before that to Penny Rae." She paused, wiping tears from her face with the back of her hand. "I tried to be really careful while I finished my work week. Then, Friday night, I stopped by to see my dad and tell him I loved him, and my mom too." Mariana looked toward Jet as if to answer the unasked question. "I was afraid to go see them at their home just in case he tried to kill me and they got hurt as well." She turned to Sonia. "It was better to see my dad at work where there were lots of people around."

Sonia realized she was gently stroking Mariana's leg, comforting her. "So that's it. You ran the next morning. Did you come right here? Have you been here the whole time?"

"Yes." She reached for a tissue from the box on the coffee table. "Jenn and I weren't really close at school, but I knew about this place, and that she was a nice person. I thought it would be best to hide with someone the professor would never think of as one of my close friends. My car is hidden in the garage downstairs."

Sonia nodded slowly. "That's quite—"

"Hang on." Jet pushed a light-yellow curtain away from the window, glancing out at the entrance to the farm. "Looks like we've got company."

Sonia and Mariana both sat up straight. They responded almost simultaneously. "What?"

Jet peered out the window more intently. "Someone's coming

up the driveway." Her voice filled with disgust. "Black BMW." Her lip curled as she quietly said, "Equine Futures."

Sonia popped up and joined Jet; Mariana stood right behind them. "Oh, God. That's him. That's his car."

Sonia looked at her quickly. "The professor, right?"

"Yes." Mariana was frantic. "That's his car. Got to be. He always drives that kind of car. Says something about it making him look like a secret agent or some bull like that."

Jet pushed the others away from the window. "We've got to get out of here." She turned. "Mariana, is there any other way out of here? A window we could climb out of?"

Mariana just stood there wide-eyed and silent.

Jet grabbed her by the shoulders, shook her. "Mariana! Another way out of here?"

Mariana nodded. "Yes. But here he comes, and if we go out the window in the bedroom, we'll be on the fire escape on that side of the building. He'll see us for sure."

It only took a moment for Sonia to realize they were trapped.

61

The three girls instinctively drifted to the back of the room, knowing they had no real options. Sonia's mind ran immediately to her Glock, which was, unfortunately, safely tucked away in her purse—back in Jet's car. Damnit. No more big guns. I've got to get a little one I can have on me—always!

They waited for a knock on the door. Instead, the door crashed open, kicked down by the large man standing on the opposite side. No frumpy lab coat and blue-checked shirt, he was dressed in stylish brown corduroy pants, with a tan vest sweater over a yellow button-down.

Instinctively, Sonia put her five-foot-four body between the man and Mariana, an ineffective yet authentic effort at protecting the young woman. Wide-eyed, she stared at him. He hadn't seemed so big to her sitting behind the desk in his office. Now, though, he seemed huge. There was a black gun in his hand and it was no small weapon.

"Good afternoon ladies. Do you mind if I come in?" The smile on Andersen's face turned Sonia's stomach. No one answered.

"I'll take that as a no." He stepped into the room, pushing

aside the broken door, and waved his gun at the little couch. "Why don't you all have a seat."

Jet stuck her chin out. "All three of us?"

"Oh, I'm sure you'll fit." His crooked smile and surprisingly preppy attire seemed a strange counterpoint to the snide tone of his voice. "Anyway, it's time you three start to become very well acquainted. I'm pretty certain you'll soon be sharing some very close quarters."

The three women remained motionless, Sonia racking her brain for some snappy comment to throw at Professor Spencer Andersen. She came up blank.

His tone became strangely cordial. "And Mariana. How nice to see you again. I take it you're aware that I've had some encounters with your colleagues recently?"

Mariana started to charge Andersen. "You son-of-a-bitch."

The professor's black handgun came up quickly, pointing directly at Mariana's head. It stopped her in her tracks.

"Sweet lady," his voice was syrupy, "please don't make me shoot you right here in your friend's apartment. Just think of the additional pain she'll suffer when she has to wipe your blood off her floor—and her walls—off everything in here, really." His dark brown eyes, eyes Sonia had thought were attractive when they had first met, scanned the whole of the tiny apartment. She didn't see anything attractive at all about the man now.

Mariana backed off, but her face showed nothing but contempt. "How the hell did you find me." She raised her chin in defiance. "How'd you know I was here?"

The professor waggled his gun in the direction of Sonia and Jet. "Oh, you can thank these two industrious ladies for that." He smiled. "You see, they came to me hoping I could help them find you." He shrugged, almost imperceptibly. "But sadly, you'd already slipped away, and I had no idea where you were." A broader smile crossed his face. "On the other hand, I could tell how conscientious they were, and how committed they were to finding you. It struck me that all I had to do was to stay in touch with them and they would lead me right to you. Oh, I became a little impatient for a while, but everything has worked out in the end, hasn't it?"

Sonia and Jet shared a frustrated glance.

The professor smiled at her. "By the way, Ms. Vitale. Isn't it interesting that Mariana was holed up in an apartment so like your own?" His eyes lit up. "And all three places, your office, your apartment, and this place, all at the top of some steep stairs."

Sonia spit out the words. "Figlio di puttana." It sent chills down her spine, knowing that it had been Andersen tracking her in his car, following her home, watching her at her office.

He continued. "I never realized how fortuitous it might be to discover someone hiding in just such a spot. Certainly limits escape routes, now doesn't it?" He smiled. "And I do want to thank you for leading me to my prized student."

Sonia's fist clenched. They had been so careful about being followed. She couldn't understand how he'd managed it.

The professor smiled a fatherly smile and glanced at Mariana then Sonia. "She was the smartest of them all you know. Very bright, very diligent. Actually, I cared for all three of them. They were helping me with my most important work. You could almost say I came to love them."

Sonia couldn't help but take a half-step forward. "And yet you used all three of those sweet girls for what, your own aggrandizement? What a big, impor—"

The black handgun spun in Sonia's direction and pointed right at her face. "That's enough you little wop bitch. You damn Italians. You all think you're so special when you get educated, but you're nothing but a bunch of ignorant immigrants. You should've all stayed back where you came from."

Sonia's mind was reeling so fast she barely sensed Jet moving forward, her voice drawing the professor's attention away from Sonia. "Oh, and you're so smart, huh? You're the one who diddled with those embryos? You're the one who created those winning horses?"

The professor smiled graciously. "Yes, I am, thank you."

Jet walked even closer to him, "Well it looks like you screwed the pooch there, Professor Smartass. What happened to those horses in the end? They all won the big races, did they? Oh, wait a minute. It seems I recall they all broke down, every one of them." She gave him her over-the-glasses look. "Now, whose fault was that? Did somebody miss something when he was messing around with—"

The professor took one quick step forward. His huge left hand swung around like a baseball bat in the hands of an all-star player. It struck Jet on the side of her face and knocked her to the ground. The professor's eyes glared down at Jet, but he didn't say a word. Then he calmly turned back to Sonia and Mariana.

"Well now, ladies. Perhaps we've had enough discussion of my successes and temporary set-backs. Right now, my problem is what to do with the three of you." He paused. "You see, Ms. Vitale, had you all just led me to Mariana, I wouldn't have had to involve you in this, what should we call it, final solution? But since you've spoken to her, and since I'm sure she's been more than forthright in explaining our whole arrangement, I'm afraid that you and your colleague on the floor, there, are going to have to be a part of that final process." He waved his gun again. "So, up you go, Ms. Jet, or whatever your real name is. It's time for us to vacate these premises and find a more suitable location for your demise."

Sonia reached down and helped Jet up. Her throat tightened when she saw the huge red mark on Jet's face, knowing full well the swelling and bruising that would follow. Sonia looked directly into Jet's eyes, hoping to receive some message, some indication of how they were going to get out of this horrendous situation. She found nothing there.

"Ladies, ladies." His voice was patronizing. "Time is not on our side. I certainly wouldn't want Mariana's sweet hostess to come home right now and step into the middle of this. That would put an extra burden on me. After all, disposing of all three of you at the same time will be challenging enough." His eyes drifted upward and to the left for the briefest moment. "I'll just have to come back and deal with the other young lady at some later time."

Andersen looked out the doorway, surveying the surrounding landscape. "Looks like we're clear for now, ladies." Waving his gun, he motioned them toward the door. "Alrighty, then. Let's go. Mariana, why don't you lead the way. We'll let Ms. Vitale's colleague follow. You, Ms. Vitale, seem the most volatile to me at the moment, so let's keep you closest to me."

Mariana walked out of the apartment and started down the steps, followed by Jet, Sonia, and then the professor. The beautiful afternoon sunlight and the lush green of spring created an odd counterpoint to the panic and fear Sonia was feeling.

When they reached the ground, the professor directed them to his car. Sonia could hear the gravel crunching under her feet as he spoke. "Okay, then. Ms. Vitale, I believe you'll find the trunk unlocked. Why don't you open it and crawl right in?"

A memory shot through Sonia's mind. It was some young African-American woman on TV talking about how women should try to survive an attack or abduction. She'd said that once a woman got into a car with an assailant, the chances of her ever being found alive diminished significantly—almost to zero. With that image still raging in her brain, Sonia knew what she had to do, she spun away from the car and started to—

The black gun appeared in Sonia's peripheral vision for just an instant. Blackness came a millisecond later.

62

S onia awoke in black darkness, an incredible ringing in her ears. Discovering her hands were tied behind her back, she tried to do an assessment of her body's condition. Her feet were bound as well. Her mouth was taped shut. It didn't take long, however, for her to realize there was wetness on her face and a strange metallic taste in her mouth. I must be bleeding.

Trying to get a sense of where she was, Sonia stretched every one of her senses to its limit. As her eyes adjusted to the darkness, she realized there was the tiniest bit of light in her world. Though her hands were taped painfully together, she was able, just barely, to feel with her fingertips. She touched something rough but soft. She was lying on it. Then there was the smell. After a moment of searching her memory bank, it became unmistakable. Rubber, carpet, a faint hint of gasoline. I'm in his trunk. Shit! I'm in his trunk. Sonia wanted to scream, but she knew it probably wouldn't do her any good; and, she decided, she was probably better off with Andersen thinking she was still out cold.

Sonia struggled to calm her breathing. The moments ticked by. She had trouble giving them context. She became aware of muffled sounds outside her blackened cell. Is that Andersen talking? To whom? Are Mariana and Jet out there? Are they still alive?

Sonia strained to hear every sound, sounds beyond the voices. Where are we? Are we at some deserted site? Is he about to kill us all right now, together? Will I be the last one to go? Has he already killed one of them? Oh, Jet, Jet. I'm sorry I got you into this. You never wanted to handle this case. It was me. I wanted it. You just came along because of me. Sorry. I'm so sorry.

Sonia didn't know if it was anger or fear or guilt that suddenly brought clarity to her besieged brain. Another memory crossed her mind, that same TV newswoman and her story on female abductions. The reporter had gone out of her way to make certain that her audience was aware that every car built since 2002 had an emergency release lever in the trunk for just such situations. She'd also said the release was supposed to be an iridescent color. Her heart pounding in her chest, Sonia squirmed, stretched her neck, and looked as far to the left and right as she could. She finally located the lever in the far corner of the trunk. Frustrated, she quickly realized that, being bound hand and foot, she wasn't likely to be able to take advantage of it.

Already weary from pulling and straining against the strong, sticky binding that held her captive, Sonia paused, closing her eyes. Think. Think. An image passed through her mind. There was warmth in it. It was Brad's bright blue eyes and warm smile close to her, beaming. More importantly, in the same image were Brad's hands, each one bearing a gift. In his right hand was a pair of small, but powerful binoculars. In his left was a leather pouch, the pouch that held the small set of lockpicks she had planned to use to gain entrance into Jennipher's apartment. They were picks of the highest quality, made of surgical steel—one of which had a very sharp edge. She remembered that leather pouch was now tucked neatly into her back pocket, just inches away from the duct tape that bound her hands.

Beads of sweat mingled with the drops of blood on her face,

the taste of both in her mouth. Uncertain about the number of minutes that had passed—or how many were left in her life and the lives of two others—she wrenched her body back and forth, trying desperately to get her hands on that leather pouch. Twisting and turning to the point that she was certain her shoulder was about to pop out of its socket, she was finally able to pull the pouch out of her jeans.

Her hands were wet with sweat. It was only a moment before the pouch that was, at first, under her control, had slipped to the floor of the trunk. Daaaaamn!

She stopped, trying to calm herself, struggling to take a deep breath through a nose that was clogged with the remnants of her tears and terror. As the sound of Andersen's voice continued to infiltrate Sonia's hellish prison, she twisted and strained. Finally, she was able to roll over and squirm until the pouch was, once again, in her hand. Open the pouch. Open the pouch. The last one on the left—no, no, the right. Pull it out. Don't drop it. *Don't* drop it. That's it. Carefully. Slowly. Carefully. Turn it. Turn it. That's it. Twist. Stretch. Careful! Don't lose it. That's it. Cut. Saw. Saw. Faster. Faster. Tired. So tired. Breathe. Go. Go. Cut. Saw. That's it. Almost there. Almost there. Go. Go.

The tape that held Sonia's wrists gave way. Her aching hands were finally free. Relief flooded her mind, but only for a moment. Bending, twisting, within the confines of the tiny trunk, she managed to reach down and free her ankles as well. She pulled the now-wet and slimy tape from across her mouth.

As she tried to prepare herself for whatever came next, angry words penetrated into Sonia's dungeon. Angry words, then three fast, loud blasts. She froze. Gunfire. The sounds were followed by screaming. It was frantic, totally-out-of-control screaming. It chilled Sonia to the bones of her already freaked-out body. Screaming, screaming. It dissolved into weeping.

Sonia's mind exploded into full panic. What happened? Who

was that? Who's out there? Did he just kill one of them? Was it Jet? Jet, I'm so sorry, I'm so sorry.

Her mind, her whole body, was exploding with fear, loathing, regret. She squirmed. She suffered. But she also made plans. Changing the manner in which she held the lockpick in her hand, Sonia slid around in the trunk, assuming a position from which she could attack. Her cracked and bleeding lips whispered. "Come on you bastard. Come on. I'm ready for you."

And then it came. There was the sound of something metallic touching the trunk, then someone trying to open it. Her whole being snapped in response. Her mind, her body, her soul, wanted to erupt out of the trunk, to devour the evil that was doing this to her, to Jet, to Mariana. She wanted to swallow it and force it down into the acids that racked her insides. Her body had become a roiling mass of retribution.

She heard the lock click. The rage inside her reached a fevered pitch. Light slammed in as the lid was suddenly lifted. Her tortured legs uncoiled and she sprang head-first out of the trunk. Blinded by the sudden flash of daylight, she missed her target. As her body flew through the air, it was snatched up and pulled into the arms of the powerful man. She squirmed, she struggled, swinging the lock pic wildly until her face was pulled close to his, revealing . . . revealing bright blue eyes.

63

Sonia was squinting, her body wracked and aching, totally spent. But it was Brad's arms that were holding her. It was Brad's face pressed against the side of her head.

Stunned into silence at first, Sonia's voice exploded. "Where's Jet? Where's Jet?" she screamed, squirming and struggling in Brad's arms.

Controlling her frantic motions, Brad placed her on the ground. He kneeled down next to her, brushing blood away from the side of his face. "Babe, babe. It's over. You're okay."

Sonia looked up at him, still squinting. "Jet. Is she alright? Is she?"

It was only a moment later that Jet came running frantically over to the car. "Sonia, Sonia, are you okay?" She knelt down as well, pushing Brad out of the way, wrapping both her arms around Sonia. Her voice was mumbly in Sonia's ear, coming through her hair. It was almost as if Sonia heard her more through the shared vibrations of their heads than from Jet's voice. "It's over, girl. I thought . . . but it's over." Jet rested her forehead on Sonia's shoulder, tears escaping from her eyes.

Brad slid his shoulder past Jet and looked into Sonia's beautiful eyes. His voice was comforting but energized as well. "You hurt? I'm here, babe. Don't worry, I'm here. Are you sure you're not hurt?" He pulled her close to him. "She's right, babe. It's over. It's totally over, for you, for Jet, for the girl. It's done, babe, done, and you're alright. You're all alright."

Sonia was still just coming to her senses. She realized she was on the ground, her back leaning against the black BMW. She saw that she was on the Alston farm. She felt the gravel of the small parking lot under her hand, her bottom. She sensed the sun warming her skin. She blinked. *I must have only been out for a few minutes.*

Suddenly, Sonia's heart leaped in her body. She had to see Mariana as well—see her—know for real that she was okay. But when she looked along the ground to her left, it wasn't Mariana she saw. It was the crumpled body of Professor Spencer Andersen. His eyes open wide but lifeless. Blood pooled out of the wounds in his chest. It was clear to Sonia that Andersen's reign of terror was over.

Sonia's voice was thin and wobbly. "What happened? Who shot him?"

Brad ran his fingers through Sonia's hair, down the side of her head, caressing her face with his fingertips. As he did, Sonia noticed something leaning against the car, in the same way she was. It was Brad's M16, the one she had seen down in Tennessee and then again out in western Kentucky. Somewhere in the back of her mind, she could hear Brad saying, "The M16 can fire in three-round bursts or function as a fully automatic weapon." It took only a second for her to realize that it was Brad who had killed Andersen.

Sonia leaned her head back and looked into Brad's eyes. "You did it, you killed Andersen."

Brad shook his head.

She persisted. "You did, right? You shot him. You saved us."

Brad let out a small sigh and smiled. "No, babe. I would've, but I didn't."

Sonia furrowed her brows. "You didn't shoot him?"

"No," Brad nodded to his right, "she did."

Sonia whipped her head around, past Andersen, to two women who were sitting on the ground, hugging. She turned back to Brad. "Who is that? There, with Mariana?" Before Brad could speak, Sonia knew the answer to her own question.

Jet reached out, clearly needing to touch Sonia, feel the life force in her. She spoke. "That's Gabriela."

Sonia turned back to Brad as he spoke. "She got here just before me. She challenged the guy, and when he pointed his gun at her she shot him—shot him dead."

"And you?" Sonia asked, confusion on her face. "How did you get here?"

"Well, after Ron Harris told me what was going down, I knew I had to find you."

Sonia reached out and gently touched the cut on Brad's face. "You spoke to Ron Harris? He told you something?"

Brad looked downward, a little sheepishly. "Well, you see. Mr. Harris and I got together in his car this morning and had a little tête-á-tête."

Sonia reached her hand out and lifted his chin. "Aaand?"

Brad smiled again. "You'd be surprised how much a man will tell you when you use a little persuasion. So, I went to your office and saw on that whiteboard of yours that you might have come to Danville." Brad let his eyes release from Sonia and roam across the idyllic farmland upon which she was sitting. "I got my butt down here as fast as I could. On the way, I called my buddies at NCIS. They pinged your phones for me and I followed the signal out to the farm." He turned his face back to her. "Just as I got out of my car, I saw the guy forcing the three of you down the steps. So, I got my M16 and took a kneeling position, to make sure I could make the shot at that distance. He was pretty far away." He snorted just a bit. "I was going to stop him, but just before I take the shot, here comes this woman, right out of a little stand of trees. She walks right up to Andersen. A moment later he's pointing his gun at her, and she's shooting. I never fired a shot."

Sonia's eyes went back to the other women. "And everyone else? They're okay?"

"Alive and well, babe."

Sonia continued gently touching Brad's face. "And you, who cut you?"

Brad chuckled. "I don't know. Maybe it was some wild woman come flying out the trunk of a car." He put his finger on her lips. "But don't you worry. It'll heal . . . given a little TLC."

Sonia turned her eyes toward the other two women. Mariana's head was on Gabriela's shoulder. She was quietly weeping. Sonia could tell it was the kind of weeping a woman does when she can finally release all the pain, the suffering, the worry, that she has carried through an excruciating trial. She also knew that Mariana would be weeping that way for quite a while. When Sonia turned back, she saw that Jet had tears of joy in her eyes. She reached out to her very best friend, closing her own eyes tight. Their embrace was sweet beyond imagining.

Eventually, Brad stood and pulled Sonia up into his arms. "C'mon babe. Let's get all four of you back inside. You don't need to be sitting here next to a dead body while we wait for the police." They moved toward the garage. Jet followed.

As Sonia and Brad walked to the stairs, Gabriela and Mariana got up and joined them. "Cómo estás, chica?"

Sonia nodded, figuring she'd gotten the gist of Gabriela's question. "I'm fine. And thank you. Thank you so much."

Gabriela winked at her. "Not a problem." She looked down at Andersen's body. "Seriously, it was my pleasure."

Brad started to move Sonia up the stairs, but she stopped and turned back to Gabriela. "But why were you here? How did you know to come?"

Gabriela smiled. "Because the two of you are terrible liars. I could tell, when I talked to you this morning, that you were not telling me the whole truth. You were hiding something."

Sonia raised her eyebrows. "And?"

"And so, I followed you." She shrugged. "I could tell you were coming to Danville for some reason, something that had to do with Mariana. I just followed you and sat in the car the whole time you ate in that Homestead place. When you followed that girl, then I followed you. It was simple."

"But," Sonia squinted her eyes, "we were watching carefully to make sure we weren't followed because of the black BMW."

Gabriela gave her a wry smile. "True, but that's not what I was following you in."

Brad chuckled. "Still, that's a lot of following."

The squint in Gabriela's eyes let Sonia know that Gabriela couldn't tell if Brad was laughing with her or at her.

Sonia tipped her head. "But when he came into the apartment, Andersen, why didn't you come to help us?"

"Listen, chica," she wagged a finger in Sonia's face, "I was coming, but I know what a gun looks like—and I could see his. I thought Mariana might be in there and I was afraid to just jump in. What if he shot her, first thing? So, I just tried to get closer to the garage, and by the time I did he was bringing you three out."

Sonia stood silently listening, leaning into the arms that wrapped around her, Brad's arms.

Gabriela looked down at Andersen. "And then he pointed that gun at me. *Con eso bastó.* That was enough. It was easy to shoot him then."

Sonia felt a shiver go through her body, so strong she sensed that Brad could feel it. "Well, thank you. Thank you again."

Brad got all four women moving up the stairs, back into Jennipher's apartment. Mariana went through the broken door first, followed by Gabriela, then Jet. Sonia was walking as well, but Brad had her pulled so close to his side that he was providing much of the energy that was moving her body up the steps. When they reached the top, Sonia stopped and turned around. Looking down, she saw the body of Professor Spencer Andersen lying next to the black BMW convertible, its trunk still open. She turned just enough to look Brad in the eyes. "Gabriela? Is she going to be okay?"

Brad brushed some hair out of Sonia's face. "Yeah. We're in Kentucky, babe. Three hundred thousand people have concealed carry permits here. The law says a person can use deadly physical force to protect a third person against imminent death, kidnapping and a few other things. Given that the guy had a kidnapped prisoner in his trunk and was pointing his gun at Gabriela, I'm thinking her use of force will be considered justified."

"Oh." Sonia's voice was small, but not weak. She stood still for another long moment and looked over the strangely idyllic scene. "Listen." She turned directly toward Brad's blue eyes. "Thank you for trying to save my life again, but," her voice softened as she slid into her rarely used Italian dialect, *"non rendiamola un'abitudine."*

Brad stepped back, his blue eyes searching her face. "What does that mean?"

Sonia gave him a sly smile. "Let's not make this a habit."

64

On Tuesday morning, Sonia walked into Magee's holding Brad's hand. It had been almost twenty-four hours since things had come to a conclusion in Danville, but Sonia's nerves still jangled from time to time. She looked around the room, not seeing any of the people she was expecting. She moved to one of the larger tables, sending Brad to get them each a coffee and a treat. Of course, for Sonia, that meant an almond croissant.

Sonia sat at the large table by herself, waiting for Brad. She ran her fingertips absently across the worn, smooth surface of the table at which so many folks had sat—eating, and drinking, and sharing their stories. She was reminded of the time she, Brad, and Jet had met with Brad's friend Robbie Alvarez after wrapping up a different difficult situation. That time had felt happier, more celebratory. This was different.

Just as Brad got to the table with their coffee and pastry, Sonia watched Jet and Burnett walk through the door. Seeing the large, dark bruise on Jet's face shocked Sonia. Unconsciously, her hand reacted by moving quickly to the cut over her own eye. She gently rubbed her fingertip back and forth over her swollen eyebrow. Her eyes also led her to the cut on Brad's face.

As Burnett went to get coffee for Jet and himself, Sonia noticed something else. Jet, she of the perpetual ponytail, had recently begun wearing her hair down in front of her shoulders. This morning it was back to its perennial style. Sonia knew that Brad or Burnett, or any other man for that matter, wouldn't have noticed or paid any attention to the change. But for Sonia, the message was clear, even if it might not have been to Jet herself. Relationships have a tendency to run their course, and whether it was because of his conservative nature, or any number of other reasons, Sonia could tell that the relationship had cooled.

Burnett sat down at the table, handing Jet her coffee. "Well, it's certainly nice to be back in town and sitting with some of my favorite new friends. Here's to a task well-completed and to the safe return of Ms. Mariana Castillo." His coffee cup went into the air.

Everyone responded. Smiles went around the table. Burnett continued, starting with his lapels and bowtie routine. Jet made no attempt to stop him. "Now, in my absence, I missed the final accounting of several elements in our endeavor. Would someone like to fill me in?"

All eyes turned toward Sonia, but Brad seemed to sense she was not in the mood to speak. He reached out and put his hand reassuringly on her forearm. "Well, we managed to get Ron Harris picked up by LPD. He may or may not have done anything illegal, but there are plenty of folks in the breeding and racing industries who are going to want to find out some things about his business dealings." He took a quick sip of his coffee. "As far as we can tell, he knew about Andersen's manipulation of the equine embryos, and he was the one who made promises to the breeders. He told them they would be able to reap huge profits when people came to believe that they were able to do such an incredible job breeding winners." He gave Sonia a quick glance. "It didn't appear, though, that he had any knowledge of the girls' involvement, and I feel certain he had nothing to do with their deaths."

Burnett spoke over the coffee in his hand. "And the breeders?"

Sonia mustered the strength to pick up the explanation. "It's kind of murky. They certainly knew what they were involved in, and there's no question the Thoroughbred industry has made it clear that using genetic manipulation to create more successful racehorses is unacceptable. My guess is that they will be stripped of the right to race any of the horses they breed, and they certainly could be looking at some sort of charges of fraud." She shrugged. "At least none of them had anything at all to do with what Andersen did to those poor girls. And as for the owners. I think they were totally clueless about the whole thing. They just bought the horses Harris recommended and were thrilled when those horses did so well." She gently picked up her coffee. "Of course, I doubt that they'll be able to keep all the winnings from races won by disqualified horses."

Burnett asked, "And what about the gentleman, Limey?"

Jet spoke, her hand unconsciously covering the bruise on her face. "Just a friend of Harris' and, of course, of Mariana."

Sitting up taller, taking charge, Sonia spoke. "Well, I'm certainly glad about one other thing. That the police decided not to arrest Gabriela."

"Right," Jet ran her ponytail through her fingers, "and I'm still wondering about something. How the hell did Andersen follow us to Danville? Ever since the other night, we've been so careful about watching for that BMW."

Brad smiled. "I was curious about that myself. Remember the GPS Sonia and I put on that truck we followed to Memphis? Well, before we left the farm yesterday, I took a good look at the professor's car. Inside, I found a small computerized receiving device. Looks like the professor put one on each of your cars."

The southern belle appeared. "Well, I'll be."

A small breath of warm air crept into Magee's as the front

door opened. With it, came Mariana, her father, her mother, and her cousin Gabriela. The smiles on their faces shone a little light into the darkness that had been lingering in Sonia's heart.

Paco spoke first, the patriarch. "We called Ms. Jet this morning. She told us that you would all be here at ten. We just wanted to come here as a family and thank you for all that you've done." He looked around briefly at the women who surrounded him. "We were so brokenhearted when we heard about those other girls, and so very grateful when our Mariana came home to us safely. We know it's not much, but we wanted to show our appreciation as a family." He turned to his wife and smiled. "So, Lily has baked you a *pastel de tres leches*. It's a traditional cake we eat at celebrations in Mexico. It's not much, but it is filled with gratitude."

As she put the gift on the table, Lily's smile lit her face as if it were reflecting a cake covered with birthday candles.

Sonia stood up, walked over to Paco, and hugged him. Jet stood as well. "It was our great pleasure to help you, *mi amigo*." She swung her arm wide in an inclusive motion. "You and your whole *familia*." Brad and Burnett stood, and everyone shook hands and smiled.

As a quiet conversation enveloped the group, Sonia slid over to Gabriela's side and spoke softly. "Thank you for making the trip to Florida. Thank you for finding out that Santiago wasn't involved in Mariana's disappearance. And thank you so very much for rescuing us."

Gabriela looked directly into Sonia's eyes. "Well, I'm certain Santiago did not enjoy my being there, but it was worth learning he wasn't the one who took Mariana." She gave Sonia a sly smile. "Also, I learned something else. I think I could enjoy your kind of work. I think I could enjoy it very much."

65

After coffee and treats and celebration with the members of BCI and the Castillo family, Burnett drove back to work. Stepping into the offices of Halston and Glass, Certified Public Accountants, he greeted some of his colleagues as he worked his way back to his own, well-appointed, personal space. Closing the door, as was customary in a profession which often handled private and sensitive information, he took a seat at his expansive desk.

Opening his computer, he pulled up the files for a client who had created a business several years ago and needed the services of an accountant who could not only handle day to day business but knew how people might go back into an account to look for irregularities. Since the client was interested in keeping an extremely low profile for the business and was extremely busy, he had agreed to give Burnett power of attorney and discretionary powers in the account.

As Burnett pondered the extremely large amount of resources in the account, over two million dollars, he was faced with a challenge. The owner, who had never identified a line of successive ownership, had suddenly passed away. The only person who had access to that money, and in fact, de-facto ownership of it, was Burnett himself.

Deciding to forego any changes in the account at the moment, and in order to lessen the chance of being asked any uncomfortable questions, Burnett hid the file from Equine Futures Ltd in a folder marked Bluegrass Confidential Investigations.

AUTHOR'S NOTE:

As I'm sure you can imagine, I was not in the barn with Penny Rae on the fateful day she lost her life, Tuesday, March 8, 2016. In fact, as I'm sure you've assumed, THE STORY YOU HAVE JUST READ IS NOT TRUE. NONE OF THE EVENTS OR CHARACTERS PORTRAYED HAVE ANY RELATION TO ACTUAL EVENTS, OR TO ANY PERSONS LIVING OR DECEASED.

That having been said, I would like to share with you the fact that in mid-April of that year, I wrote the description of Run Lucky, one of the fictitious horses in this story, breaking down during the Kentucky Derby and having been euthanized. Sadly, just six weeks later, on the day the 2016 Preakness was run, two beautiful horses perished at Pimlico Raceway, one of heart failure, the other with a broken leg. My condolences go out to everyone connected with those magnificent animals.

I would also like to make one other point to my readers. Having enjoyed the story at least enough to make it to this *Author's Note*, some may still find the major premise behind the story, the genetic manipulation of racehorses, to be based on the liberties authors often take. I would direct you to two websites that I believe will bring to light for you the fact that this is not at all a fantastic notion. The first, www.uky.edu/Ag/Horsemap/ abthp.html, describes briefly the *Horse Genome Project* that is currently underway at sites in over twenty countries, including at the University of Kentucky in Lexington. It is also true that the outbreak of nocardioform placentities described here did, in fact, occur in 2011, with a minor uptick again in 2017.

The second site I would direct you to is www.thehorse.com/ articles/35467/embryo-transfer-from-one-mare-to-another. The article you will find there describes precisely how and why embryos are transferred from one mare to another. This is something that Mariana, LaKeisha, and Penny Rae, students trained in this field, would have been able to accomplish, albeit with some difficulty outside the confines of a sterile clinical setting.

Finally, I would like to thank all of the readers who have made it all the way to this final note. I hope you've enjoyed the journey. And should you ever make a trip to the Bluegrass Region, and Lexington in particular, please stop by Magee's for a warm greeting, a fine cup of coffee and a wonderful almond croissant. You'll find it right on East Main, directly across from the white house that sits adjacent to the school district's Central Office. Also, I would really appreciate it if you would visit my dear friend, Marcos Valdez, at his fine establishment, Papi's Mexican Restaurant. Without his help, all the Hispanic flavors that wind their way through this book, in fact through this series, would probably turn out to be more like Spanglish than authentic Mexican dialogue. While you're there, go ahead and order a "Sonia's Special." I think you'll enjoy it.

fjm

ABOUT THE AUTHOR

After a long career as a professional musician and educator, having written several instructional texts along the way, Frank Messina turned his attention to writing fiction in 2016. He holds a Doctor of Education degree from the University of Massachusetts at Amherst.

A native of Long Island, New York, Frank moved to Lexington, Kentucky in 1978. Having lived there for almost forty years, he now considers Lexington his home and is excited about sharing the beauty and culture of this wonderful little city as he leads readers through the exciting, albeit fictional, world of Sonia Vitale and the ladies of Bluegrass Confidential Investigations. *The Bluegrass Files: Twisted Dreams*, is the second in a multi-volume series.

Follow f j messina at:
@fjmessina on facebook; @fjmessina on Instagram
@fjmesina on Twitter; on fjmessina.com
Or contact him at:
fjmessina.author@gmail.com

Be the first to know about new releases!

Sign up for our email list at fjmessina.com and receive a special video gift,
"A tour of f j messina's Lexington."

BOOKS BY F J MESSINA:

The Bluegrass Files: Down the Rabbit Hole

The Bluegrass Files: Twisted Dreams

The Bluegrass Files: The Bourbon Brotherhood

The Bluegrass Files: Mirror Image

The Bluegrass Files: Revenge

and coming Spring 2021 -

The Bluegrass Files: Broken Glass

And a personal request . . .

In this world so full of wonderful books to read, nothing is as important to an author as recommendations from the folks who have read their work.

I would greatly appreciate it if you would take a moment to write just the briefest review of any or all the the books of mine you have read. A simple post on Amazon, or even on the f j messina facebook page or fjmessina.com would mean the world to me.

Thanks - f j

Made in the USA
Columbia, SC
27 July 2021